WHOM MY SOUL LOVETH
A Christian Novel

By
Nada Jabbour Hatem

**Delight thyself also in the LORD and
HE shall give you the desires of your heart.
Psalm 37:4**

WHOM MY SOUL LOVETH
by Nada Jabbour Hatem

Printed in the United States of America

ISBN 9781622306862

Unless otherwise indicated, Bible quotations are taken from The King James Version.

www.xulonpress.com

I pray
this book
blesses you.

Best wishes

Ruth Halen

CONTENTS

INTRODUCTION

"Whom My Soul Loveth" is a romantic novel where the author wishes to take us on a long journey of the life of a beautiful young woman—Dalal—born in wealth and power, in the Middle Eastern country of Lebanon, who would later fall in love with the Christ that shone in the lives of her neighbors.

Her story tells us how much she suffered in her walk with Christ for the sake of His name, as she indeed passed through 'the shadow of the valley of death' for her newly found faith.

The story begins in Lebanon, then moves to England, and finally ends in America only to experience more suffering and pain in her quest to stand firm in her faith and overcome persecution. Yet, along the way, she finds the love of her life, 'whom her soul loveth', that brings along suffering of the heart, lots of happiness, ecstasy, and fulfillment.

Can this brave young woman win the battle and attain victory over the immense problems she encounters, then come out of the fiery furnace as pure as gold?

Will this young woman be able to end her years of misery and desolation to reunite with her only love after the continents separate them?

Will the willow tree dance again? Only time will tell!

Chapter 1
DALAL

Two stories are etched in my mind ever since I began to retain memories and form ideas: The story of my parents' marriage and my extraordinary birth. I am a descendant of a long line of prominence, wealth, and power, including the title of "Pasha" that began with my early ancestors for five generations until today. In the old country, this lineage is a type of Feudalism where we owned entire villages and everything in them. My grandfather had five daughters and an only son—my father—the heir apparent to the family's wealth and position. The family pinned its hopes that one day he will carry on the family tradition. That naturally meant that my father must fulfill his biological duty and, in turn, produce a male heir to carry the family name and make certain the tradition continues.

After my father completed his studies and returned from England with a PhD in economics, it was truly a day to remember. Eligible, beautiful young ladies of our village, dressed up in their fanciest garments, clamored around this dashing and handsome young bachelor hoping that he would catch a glimpse of her as sure candidate for future wife. Following the tradition of searching for a bride, he would start from the immediate kinship and choose a beautiful young maiden of a similar social standing. His future wife's role was to bear him children as first priority, and at the same time, "keep it all in the family." Many a maiden from our clan were available, but one incomparably stood out.

My mother's beauty surpassed that of her peers, her intelligence and charm matched that of my father's. She descended from the same family and same religious confession. The family saw that this would be the perfect marriage for both. As arranged marriages go, this was arranged with a pre-approval stamp from both of them. The wedding took place in much pomp and circumstance where nothing was spared. My ancestral village in Mount Lebanon was adorned with the best of ornaments, in a sea of flowers such as lilies, roses, snapdragons, carnation, accompanied with much frolic, and mirth. Women put on their imported designer clothes, and quaffed to a hilt, with men not that much far behind.

Needless to say, most of the villagers attended this memorable wedding, with all age groups; very old men and women on their canes made special efforts to be there to witness this big event, among hundreds of boys and girls filling the streets of the village with their joyful sounds. The celebrations lasted for several days.

The newlyweds honeymooned in various destinations in Europe and the United States, on a trip that lasted for two whole months. Upon their return, my father was given a very prominent position in the government as a Director in the Ministry of Finance, and my mother became the talk and curiosity of our town. Naturally, the talk and curiosity were mostly limited around one subject—whether or not a pregnancy was eminent. The older women always thought that three months into the marriage were more than enough.

My mother was only nineteen then and my father was eight years older, the perfect child-bearing age. However, as months passed by with no news of a pregnancy, the family was in an almost silent, funeral-like mood. More months passed, and things moved from bad to worse. Serious concern changed to worry as the first year of marriage passed by without the big news. "Perhaps because she's still a teenager," older women would rationalize; "Perhaps when she reaches twenty, she'll become pregnant." However, this theory proved false the first month of her twentieth year. As worry enveloped the whole village, and the family became more stressed at the lack of good news, fear set in that the bride might perhaps be barren. The family did not spare a dime in taking her to the best doctors; even tried some non-conventional village-type 'remedies' such as boiling special kinds of herbs, found in the mountains around us, to be added to my mother's diet, in addition to certain prayers written on a piece of cloth to be put in my mother's bed.

Three years into the marriage, and after numerous consultations with physicians both local and foreign, the family was now wishing and willing to settle for a baby girl first, even if it meant the male heir would be delayed! For the family, especially for my grandfather who wanted to make sure that he saw a male to carry the name and fortune before his death, this was a major concession. Ten years lapsed, and no heir was apparent. One day, my grandfather—who was also my mother's uncle—summoned my mother for a quick, important meeting.

Mother said, "As the chauffeur arrived at our village house carrying a letter from my uncle and father-in-law, I immediately had a severe headache upon finishing reading the letter which he wrote in his shaky hand. My heart beat so fast that it was skipping beats. What does he want? Why does he want to see me so soon without anyone's knowledge, including my husband's? Why does he want to see me at his farm instead of his house? What? Why, What—? Many questions raced, with no answers, as the automobile raced up the mountain road to my uncle's farm. The farm was not a strange place for me; from time to time, we used to go there, and I loved it. The farm had an equestrian center, and I excelled in riding horses and jumping, when I was still quite young. As I grew older, my visits to the farm became more infrequent, and I seldom rode thereafter—but for some strange reason, now I was not thrilled at all to be going there.

When the car stopped, I immediately jumped out and ran directly to meet my father-in-law. He was sitting on the porch, with a pipe dangling from his thin lips. I always thought my uncle loved me; he often told me so. He always thought I would be the perfect wife to his only son and heir. For I was his niece long before I became his daughter-in-law; he rarely saw me without giving me a big hug and a kiss on my forehead. As I got closer to where he sat, he did not even extend his hand to greet me. His eyes narrowed with anger, avoided eye contact, and did not attempt to hide his evasiveness. Thoughts were racing through my mind. "What has happened to him; what wrong have I done; and what's going on?" I tried to inquire about his calling me to this place; but instead of voicing an answer, he gestured strangely with his hand at me, making me forget what I was going to say.

I began to tremble all over, as all the problems of disappointments and the intense desire for giving my family the much-awaited heir, weighed heavily upon me.

Before letting my imagination take over and what this 'dictator' wanted to tell me—at least that's what I thought of him at the moment—he asked, "Do you love your husband, Huda?" The tone with which that question came through felt as though someone had doused me with a bucket of icy water. Anyone would have scoffed at such a question, and perhaps I should have answered it as such, "you ask your niece, who has been happily married to your son for ten years, such a question?" But the tone with which my uncle uttered those words made me ponder and weigh my words carefully.

"Of course, Uncle, I love my husband."

"How much do you love him, Huda?" He coldly pressed on, unwaveringly; my calculated reply came equally cold yet emphatic, "Of course, I love him very much, and you know that, Uncle."

"Do you care about his happiness and his family future, as well as political future?"

"What kind of a question is that, what do you mean his political future?" My irritation manifested itself by raising my voice in a sharp tone, "You know I am his right arm in this respect, and I spare no effort to please him and make him happy. But with all due respect, Uncle, I do not like your questioning, nor am I amused by it."

"Then I don't think you'll like and be amused by my request either, which requires a lot of sacrifice on your part," he said.

My uncle is a strong, tough man; his word is always final; and for him to ask me to sacrifice in this serious manner must underlie a dangerous plot, but I composed myself and sternly asked, "What do you mean *sacrifice*?" I am willing to sacrifice if I can, but cannot make any promises."

"I did not ask you if you can, I am demanding you do!" he retorted, but I quickly asked, "of course, Uncle, what do you want from me, what kind of sacrifice are you talking about?"

He took a deep breath, pinched his thick eyebrows and pressed his cold lips, put his hands together, now swollen with blood-filled veins as though readying himself for a major fight, and pointing his finger, almost poking me in the eye. He said, "Hear me well, Huda, I want you to convince your husband by telling him to find himself another wife. You should tell him that he must do this for the sake of his political future. Let me finish first," he interjected, as I was about to reply, "and please do not interrupt until I finish talking because I know what's going through your mind right now; I want you to hear me till the end, and then I'll let you reply."

I could not figure out what kind of magic power possessed me at that moment, which left me tongue-tied and completely helpless. There I was listening to what my uncle was telling me, in such calmness, as if I were sedated. I could not remember how I managed to keep a smile on my face, not knowing whether it was a smile of pain, derision, or both. At the same time, I did not know what possessed me and made me able to look my uncle straight in the eye and listen to all his ranting.

"Huda, I am not asking you to divorce your husband—far from it—but that you would allow him to marry another woman for the sake of bearing him and the family an heir loom. You, of course, realize the problem that you have, and it's the only way that your poor husband can have an heir to carry his name, and for me not to remain without a male grandchild."

"To remain without a male grandchild! To remain without a male grandchild?" I asked, repeatedly, in my disbelief. After having asked this, I did not know what caused my uncle to get up from his chair, walk away, and stand farther away from me. Might this be the calm before the storm?

"Since you are the great lord of the land, Marwan Pasha, and since you think this is such a simple matter, planned in such an orderly way, why not close the deal and point me to this bride or rather the 'container' that you've chosen for your son, Salah?"

What I just said did not amuse my father-in-law; I was able to detect a certain fear and caution in him. Had he anticipated my reaction? He must have calculated and accounted for my response while planning all this. Did he expect me to become furious and shed a tear or two? It, however, seemed that my reaction caught him off guard, I saw him retreat with fear and visible astonishment. No reply came from him, which prompted me to repeat my question with a sharp tone, "Who is this woman you're buying for your son? Is she from some rich blue-blooded family, or a poor woman from the common folk of this village?" I then burst out laughing hysterically. I wanted to rise from my chair, but I felt my knees buckle under me. I then pushed the chair towards a small table on which a tray and a lemonade pitcher sat. I poured some in a glass and took a big sip; the traditional rose water in the lemonade brought back some balance to my body, and I felt refreshed and returned from a semi-conscious state back to reality. I kept rewinding and playing my uncle's words in my mind. I returned to my old self—a woman of strength and intelligence. After all, I was Salah Pasha's wife—the other leader in the village—who loves me and worships the ground upon which I tread, regardless whether or not I bore him a son.

My memory took me back to the years of love and companionship that my husband and I had together, in an effort to regain my strength and courage to face this 'old man' standing before me, who is intent on destroying my happiness and my family to satisfy his vanity and selfishness. I was able to stand and move a couple of steps towards him. I reached for his golden cane, in which he takes so much pride, symbol of his authority and power, and I threw it so hard to the marble floor, it shattered to pieces. Then I charged toward my uncle and hurled at him a hail of insults the likes of ruthless, tyrant, obnoxious, and accusing him of covering his Machiavellian scheme under the guise of sacrifice. "Even if I was certain of my pregnancy, today, after many years of trying, and even if it were a boy I carried, I would not spare an abortion if only to keep him from a grandfather such as you!"

I could not remember what happened next, but I vaguely recall sirens followed by a commotion of women crying, until darkness enveloped me. I do not recall how long I was in that state, but when I woke up, I found myself in a hospital bed, in a strange room full of strange faces. Before I attempted to talk, I saw my husband Salah entering the room hurriedly and moving closer to my bed extending his hand to hold mine. "Thank God you're OK, not to worry," he said, as he tenderly held me. His voice and touch brought me a lot of comfort. I asked him, "Where am I, is this a hospital?"

"Yes, my love—you are in a hospital."

"What happened, and why am I here?"

"Nothing to worry about, love; it was a simple incident, I'll explain later."

"What are you talking about? What incident?" I asked nervously.

"Just relax now and get some rest, the important thing is, you're all right now; just a bit shaky though."

I sat in my bed trying to recall what had exactly happened just before I blacked out. My memory was now slowly coming back, and I remembered the disgusting conversation that took place between my uncle and me. Then I wondered if my husband knew about it by now.

"Where's your father?" I asked Salah, "We were together at the farm. He was the cause of all this." Salah looked at me tenderly, but with sadness and worry, as if I had lost my mind, and said, "What are you saying, Huda? What does my father have to do with this? Relax sweetheart, don't exhaust yourself any further." I reacted angrily and screamed, "I am not losing my mind; I am asking you, where is your father? Did he not tell you about the bride he is about to choose for you, who would carry your son and his grandchild?"

My husband's face paled, he stood, marched out of the room and returned with a physician. They were both whispering; I could not make out their conversation. It was summertime, and like most people, we lived in our mountain village house. I was not very familiar with this hospital, but I recognized the physician who was an old friend of the family, Dr. Jamil. He and my husband continued their whispering as they looked strangely at me from time to time, then both walked out. Suddenly, I realized that Salah might not have known what had taken place between me and his father and may have concluded that I had experienced some sort of a mental breakdown, especially since I went through some severe infirmities in the last few months, thinking I was pregnant; I'd missed my period for two or three months. As a result, I gained weight, and all pregnancy signs would appear, only to realize, later, they were false pregnancies. Those past occurrences, as well as what happened to me during my ill-fated visit, made my husband certain that my condition evoked worry. I wanted to avoid such difficult situations, so I decided not to talk about it anymore until I was well enough to talk calmly and wisely.

In the meantime, I kept wondering what happened to me after I confronted my uncle and passed out. I wondered how my uncle managed to bring me to the hospital without any indication that he had anything to do with it, and whether Salah knew anything about it.

The doctor came in and gave me an injection, I soon became drowsy and went back to sleep. I slept for two hours or so; when I woke up, I saw my husband still there, sitting near me. Time passed, and we both were silent awhile. It was now 10 p.m. my husband got up, smiled at me and stroked my head, bent down to kiss me saying, "Good night, Huda." I waited for him to leave, and then called the nurse who was taking care of me to ask her about what had really happened—or at least why I was here.

At my incessant questioning, she told me that I had been at the farm riding, when I fell off the horse's back and passed out. A farmhand contacted my family and my husband, and an ambulance was sent to the farm to bring me to the hospital. "So—It was simply an accident that I fell off the horse. What an intelligent fabrication," I thought. I guess my husband was right when he told me it was an accident; for he truly believed the story his father made up, and really thought that I had lost it. I became very angry, ringing the bedside bell several times. The nurse came running in with several other hospital staff; I then requested the doctor come, immediately.

"He's at his home, Mrs. Huda, shall I call another doctor?" she said.

"No, you must call Dr. Jamil, immediately." I billowed louder.

The nurse left the room, confused and afraid. Within minutes, Dr. Jamil entered my room, looking perplexed. I rose from my bed, shut the door, and asked him to listen to me very carefully. He sat beside me and held my hand as gently as a father would, and was very attentive to what I was about to say. I felt comfortable with him. I was able to tell him everything that took place at the farm. Then I asked his help in conveying all I had just told him, to my husband.

Dr. Jamil looked concerned; I could sense he would rather upset me than upset my uncle. The tears of despair streaming down my cheeks may have caused him to put his interests aside, temporarily, and focus on my condition. He promised to investigate my story, secretly, by questioning the farmhands, especially the women who worked there. Consequently, Dr. Jamil felt comfortable relating to my husband how his father summoned me secretly to his farm, how he asked me to divorce my husband, and encourage him to find another wife to bear him children. The shock from hearing caused me great distress, and consequently, to pass out. My husband was convinced. He was very apologetic but tried to defend his father by ascribing the whole incident to a father's undiminished love for his son, and his desire to see him happy. Furthermore, my husband assured me that he would stand by me regardless, and would not allow anybody to hurt me.

Dr. Jamil, on the other hand, recommended we both take a trip, abroad, to get away from this charged atmosphere. Actually, this suggestion was mainly directed at me so I could forget about pregnancy and children. He also suggested I take a job somewhere or volunteer in charity causes, and do more useful things in my life besides counting days of the month awaiting pregnancy. Then he added, "If meanwhile you get pregnant, that's fine, otherwise enjoy your life, your youth, and the company of your husband."

The doctor's words fell on my heart like rain falling on dry land. They gave me courage and hope. Consequently, Salah and I seriously discussed opening a high-end fashion clothes boutique that I would personally manage. Since I always loved to wear fashionable, designer garments, I undoubtedly would make this boutique the best boutique in Lebanon. Material gains would not be my objective; rather I would use this store as an outlet that would free me from the prison of my thoughts and my misery, to propel me into a life of hope.

***

I traveled between Rome, Paris, and London, visiting the primary fashion houses, in preparation for my boutique. Construction was taking place at home. Money was no object, the extravagant preparations made it the talk of town, and fashionable ladies were impatiently awaiting a big opening in downtown Beirut. Meanwhile, I had forgotten what transpired between my uncle and me; I had not seen him in a long time. I had not spent much time with my husband either, as my frequent travels took me away from him. He sometimes would catch a plane to meet me somewhere in Europe on weekends. I also stopped going to doctors and lived to fulfill my plans, completely ignoring what others were saying or advising. As for the store progress, I sent invitations to a select group of people as opening day celebrations were approaching. The whole atmosphere was abuzz with anticipation, just as it was for our wedding, ten years ago.

One day, as I took my husband to show him the store and all the preparations that I had made in anticipation for opening day, he stood in awe. He congratulated me on what I had accomplished and told me how proud he was. On the way back to the house, he asked, "What are you planning to name this elegant store?" But before I replied, he began suggesting a few European and Arabic names. I was listening, without uttering a single word. Then I said, "There is still a little time left. I will surprise everyone on the eve of the opening." My husband thought this was part of trade secrets, but in fact, I was a little worried because I had not thought of a name yet.

We arrived home, exhausted. I fell into a deep sleep. The next morning, I woke up with a stomach-ache and nausea; I rushed to the bathroom to relieve myself, but was unable to lift my head without suffering a dizzy spell. Salah had left the house earlier that morning. I had an important social gathering that evening, which meant I *had* to get better. Not being able to lift my head, my only recourse was to call my personal physician, Dr. Mounir, who was also a good friend. Upon listening to my complaints, he came rushing to see me. He frowned, then smiled, and asked me to go with him to his clinic for some routine tests. He assured me it would not take longer than one hour; and promised to get me back in time to get ready for my evening social. The tests indeed did not last longer than one hour, and the remaining hours I spent crying, uncontrollably. I tried, in vain, to control myself, as I kept asking the same question repeatedly, "Are you sure? Is it true? I am pregnant? Is it true I am pregnant?" The answer was always, "Yes, Huda, you are pregnant."

Two hours passed in tears and laughter, with the same thought ringing through my being, "I am pregnant. I am finally going to be a mother and give my husband a child." I was in a state of sweet delirium and exuberance beyond description; most of all, I was in shock. Yes, my pain and suffering would eventually come to an end; and yes, my dream would finally become reality. No one would refer to me as 'barren' behind my back. I looked intently at my doctor and said, "I will have a beautiful baby-girl, and I will call her 'Dalal' because I will raise her with all the glory and pampering I can possibly provide, as her name suggests."

"How do you know you're carrying a girl?" He asked.

"Because my heart yearns for a girl" I simply said.

"Don't you prefer to have a son who will carry his grandfather's name and the family name?" He asked.

"No." I impetuously shouted. "I do not want a boy; I want Dalal."

On the way home, I asked my doctor, "Can you keep a secret?" He replied jokingly, "It depends."

"I am asking you do not tell my husband about my pregnancy until after the opening of my boutique; and, at least, not until two months have passed. I do not wish a repeat of past false pregnancies only to lead to disappointments." He looked at me with gentleness in his eyes and said, "Huda, perhaps because of the sudden joy at the news of your pregnancy, I forgot to tell you that already almost eight weeks have lapsed."

"Two months?" I exclaimed, shaking him with both hands. "How could that be? It is impossible." I obviously was caught up with my work, travel and all the preparations, that I forgot myself; and because of my experiences with past false pregnancies, I did not pay as much attention to the pregnancy. Was I in denial?

"Perhaps your lack of anxiety about getting pregnant helped in your becoming pregnant," my doctor said. Still, I urged him not to mention this to anyone until at least after the awaited boutique opening night.

"If the word gets around, everybody will be concerned about if I walked, sat, or stood, you know how villagers think. So, please don't mention it. I will bring the good news to my husband and family the day after the opening."

In the morning, as I was sitting in a chair sipping a glass of milk and passing my hand over my stomach, caressing the little child inside, I heard myself uttering whispers of love, "My lovely Dalal—Dalal." I felt a beam of light shining before my eyes and imagined that beautiful name 'Dalal' written in neon lights above the new boutique. "Yes. Oh, yes. That's it; 'DALAL' is going to be the name of my boutique." I smiled with pride and satisfaction.

I was now experiencing morning sickness, not the imaginary symptoms I felt in the past, but ironically doing my best to conceal it until after the grand opening. That same evening of the event, as my husband and I were driving towards the boutique, he turned to me and said, "You are really a very successful business woman; you made everyone—including me—wait anxiously and impatiently for the grand opening to reveal the name of this boutique, won't you tell me? I am your husband. I am the one who is financing this project after all—remember?"

I then drew closer to him, planted a gentle kiss on his cheek, and teasingly whispered in his ear, "It will only be a short time till the opening, you waited for a whole year, and can't you wait now another hour? Of course you can, sweetheart."

All what was planned to celebrate this event, from food to music to famous singers and dancers, made the grand opening a huge success. When the time came for me to make my speech and present the anticipated name of the store, I said to all the people waiting outside with eyes fixated on the slightly-moving curtain hiding the name, "Congratulations to all on the birth of 'Dalal'."

The applause exploded, everybody cheered. Hundreds of colorful balloons were released as fireworks lit up the sky. Music played on, people turned their heads to get a glimpse of the unveiled boutique name, shimmering in neon. With tears welling up in my eyes, I held on to my husband's hand tightly. The look on his face said it all, he was impressed with all the glitter and pizzazz; but still, unbeknownst to him, now my eyes were fixed on the name with a tender beating sensation of the heart, thinking what a wonderful delight the daughter growing inside me will bring to our lives.

We returned home late that evening, after a long and exhausting day. I could barely stand on my two feet, so I threw myself on our bed; my husband did the same while muttering something I could barely hear. He said, "Dalal is a beautiful girl's name, but not for a store; why did you choose that name anyway?"

I turned to him, gave him a hug, and whispered, "Because first this boutique is a woman's boutique, and a woman is to be pampered; that's why I called it Dalal; second, and most important, it is because I plan to name our daughter Dalal!" Salah turned over and gently pushed me away yawning and said, "Good night sweetheart." He pulled the covers over his head and went to sleep. "Good night, *Abu Dalal* (Dalal's father)," I said.

Salah missed the signals and paid no attention to what I was trying to tell him, for obvious reasons. He was not taking this issue seriously, but I told myself I would tell him the same story come morning when he has had a good night's rest. I thought that perhaps I would ask Dr. Mounir over for an early cup of coffee at our house, and have him be the bearer of the good news. "Yes, that's what I'll do," I thought. I was fast asleep before I could think of anything else. Next morning, I was up before Salah, to call the doctor. I invited Dr. Mounir and his wife to have breakfast with us and conspired with him to break the news about Dalal to my skeptical husband. Salah was not surprised to see the doctor so early in the morning, besides being my doctor, we were friends; his wife, Nawal, was one of my best friends. They both were present at the grand opening, and it was easy to talk about 'Dalal'. While sipping coffee, Dr. Mounir addressed my husband and said,

"Congratulations on Dalal."

"Oh, thank you Doctor, glad it's all over. By the way — did you like the name?"

"Sure, it's a beautiful name, perhaps it will be a good omen for both of you."

Salah laughed loudly and said, "We've not seen the good or the bad yet, it is only a few hours old; wait a year or so, then we'll let you know whether it's a good or bad omen."

"Huda happens to be a little pregnant!"

"What! Who? Huda, my wife is pregnant?" He asked with total confusion and disbelief.

"You heard me right, Huda, yes your wife, is pregnant."

Dr. Mounir uttered these words very calmly and in a matter of fact manner, just as a physician would. I was now laughing uncontrollably just looking at Salah's reaction as he was still asking and wondering what was going on. Then, and finally, he grasped the news, looked at me with tears filling his eyes and said, "I'm going to be a father Huda, a father? We are going to have a child?"

I believe that no words or expressions written anywhere could describe that moment in our lives; my desire to be a mother would soon become a reality, and Salah and I would be overjoyed with our newborn, be it a boy or Dalal."

***

I heard the news of my own birth and childhood so often from various sources: My mother, grandmother, aunt, and even our housekeepers. I have seen it documented in photos, movie reels, and read about it in articles in the society pages of magazines. Perhaps my grandmother's description of the event was the one I loved the most.

Grandmother told me that after the second trimester, every day that passed, felt like a month of anticipation for a little boy! Everybody in the family was counting the remaining time, day-by-day, and hour-by-hour.

Since my birth was to occur in early summer, there was an extra effort to prepare a nursery befitting the expected addition, in our summerhouse, in the mountains of Lebanon, where the air is always fresh and cool. Baby packages were arriving weekly from the United States and Europe, as nothing was spared to make mother and baby comfortable.

June 25, 1956 was the date for my arrival into this world; my mother was admitted into the best hospital in Beirut, only a stone's throw from the beautiful, blue Mediterranean. It was 12 noon when the clock struck, as if to announce the birth of the newborn child, and in unison, a baby's cry drowned out the clock! According to my grandmother, she heard the most beautiful voice in the world. She went out of the room with tears of joy to let everyone know that a newborn baby girl was born to the Abu Suleiman family; it wasn't what they expected, but a child of any sex was welcome. Afterwards, Dr. Mounir emerged from the delivery room with the baby in his arms to make it official. He said that the newborn was the most beautiful baby he had ever seen, among the thousands of babies he delivered. Of course, he probably says this to all parents!

Ever since I could remember, everybody was taking pictures and film clips of me since day one—sleeping or awake, sitting or walking, the first tooth, the first pair of shoes, the first day of school—and the list of '*firsts*' goes on. There's even a special room in our house called Dalal's Museum; it contains tens and hundreds of albums, film clips, magazines, and newspaper clips where my name or picture appears, not to forget old toys of all kinds.

Despite my mother's undying love for me and her knowledge that she is unable to have any more children, she made certain that she would bring me up in the best way fitting our family's reputation, traditions, and social standing. My mother planned, long-term, the way she would bring me up, and that I would become her little, princess. I took piano lessons at an early age, ballet, and other classical dance lessons. I excelled in every field; not only that, but I was able to fluently speak three languages by the time I was ten—Arabic, French, and English—an enviable feat.

To my father, I was everything; he seemed to live just to see and hear me. He was always so proud of me. He would often take me with him wherever he went, as was feasible, just 'to show me off,' as he would put it. As a result, early on, I developed high confidence and love for people; I was able to converse freely with high-ranking officials, celebrities like the famous Lebanese singers Feyrouz and Sabah, and prominent personalities such as the first lady and wives of ministers. The downside was, I did not get to play or spend much time with people my age, nor was I able to confide in other girls, as girls usually do. My social life was mostly spent with grown-ups, as I was overprotected, and mature, beyond my tender age, quite precocious.

I watched my mother making plans, organize, and make her own decisions, always standing by my father to lend support when needed. I was able to see how she was able to divide her time between being a wife, a mother, and a successful businesswoman. At the same time, she always found time to take care of her appearance, making certain she always maintained a well-kept figure. I also observed her personality and the way she planned and schemed to push my grandfather into stepping down from his leadership role so that my father would fill that role. Despite her claim to have forgiven my grandfather for what he had done to her many years ago and let bygones be bygones, I could sense that all was not as she would have us believe. Down deep in her heart, she never forgave him.

***

As always, mother would never forget my birthday on June 25; year after year, she would have a feast instead of just throwing a big birthday party. Everybody anticipated this date; preparations began weeks earlier. Every year, she would surprise us with outdoing what she did the previous year. So on my Sweet Sixteenth birthday, she decided to have something out of the ordinary, for this age was very special to girls; she encouraged me to participate in Miss Teen-Age Lebanon. "A beauty queen? And why not?" I thought. Nature endowed me with my father's stature, and my mother's nimble movements, wide green eyes, and creamy fair skin. That evening, mother allowed me to use make-up for the first time — other than the smearing I used in mimicking her when I was younger. I wore a beautiful dress that dropped to the shoulders, baring my skin and showed a little, acceptable cleavage. The shoes were of moderate height, so as not to look too tall. To this day, I still remember my father having an argument with my mother when he saw me slowly coming down the stairs from my bedroom, adorned with every kind of what he called 'paint.' He promptly called mother, went into his office, and closed the door behind them. My parents avoided having arguments in front of me, his voice was barely audible as I was trying to listen in, "You let Dalal put all this 'paint' over her face and wear such a dress?" he asked.

Mother replied in her usual quiet tone to calm him down and said, "Just for tonight, sweetheart; it's her sweet Sixteenth birthday and the beauty pageant. This is a once-in-a-life-time occasion, Salah, and you know what it would mean to her."

"But she looks like a woman of twenty five, poor girl."

My mother tried to calm him down, "What do you want me to do if God shaped her like that, put her in a bottle and seal it?"

In a tone full of anxiety and worry, my father replied, "But by presenting her like that to people, we will get into a situation we could live without right now; we could spare ourselves some obvious headaches."

My mother laughed, but I could get the gist of her laughter, as I was still eaves dropping on their conversation; soon they emerged hand-in-hand, both laughing. My father was obviously convinced; I do not know how she always managed to convince him! What a charmer she must have been, and how weak my father seemed to be when she was around. She could cast a spell on him at will and whim, although he had a strong personality when he was around others.

I was prepared for any surprise my mother would pull, expecting anything; but frankly, the Miss Teen-Age Lebanon contest never crossed my mind. I always thought our family was above those people who would push their daughters into exhibiting themselves before hungry eyes; but who was I to question my mother at the time? My mother was the first socialite lady in our community; as long as she was content with what she was doing, I did not question it, but instead, I stood with confidence and pride as I took my place among other contestants.

Needless to say, I was crowned Miss Teen-Age Lebanon, and then proceeded to cut the immense-sized cake while the whole throng was singing "Happy Birthday".

Chapter 2
THE NEIGHBOR'S DAUGHTER

$\mathscr{I}$ love the fall season in our village; perhaps it is my favorite season. I love the smell of the first rain after nearly five months of none; I love the yellows and reds the leaves begin to turn, I also love our beautiful garden, and the small-walled-pond around which we spend our little summer evenings. My favorite tree, however, is the large willow with its drooping, weepy branches that provide the needed shade in sunny Lebanon. It, somewhat, also gives that special solitude and romantic, magical setting to our house in Beirut. Even when summer is over and we head back to the city for the winter and school, we can still enjoy the outdoors and the fresh air for nearly two more months, before the cold weather sets in.

We have a gardener who takes care of the garden year-round. He transforms its rich soil into beautiful landscapes, boasting multi-colored flowers in the spring and throughout summer and fall. I used to love chatting with our gardener Abu Wafiq, or to me, 'Uncle Wafiq'. I also used to enjoy talking to all the workers and the live-in help in the house, asking their thoughts and opinions on different subjects, as well as listen to any grievances they may have. Many seemed to offer plenty of good advice and wisdom. My mother used to observe my movements and behavior with them and tell me, "You are so extro-verted, just like your dad, but you must always remember that you are of a different mold from those people. Do not stoop down to their level nor try to bring them up to yours."

I used to listen to my mother and obey her in everything except for this mentality; I loved every person who worked for us, as they also reciprocated their love to me. So every chance I got, I used to seek them, talk to them, joke with them—and sometimes even pull pranks on them, particularly our poor gardener who was the recipient of many a trick. He was very special to me. Though he was in his early fifties, the worries of life and exposure to the sun made him look a lot older.

One day, following a long vacation, I wanted to surprise him with a special visit to his favorite spot in the garden, and take my usual red rose from him. As I walked in the garden looking for him, I approached the gate that separates our house from the neighbor's; something new drew my attention to that house. It was a much smaller house than ours was, and vacant for many years; but just on that day, I saw life come back to the house. I heard people talk and children scream. I stood on a bench to peek at the house to see what was going on behind the gates. There were two small children playing in the garden with a woman. All I could see was her back, I was not able to make out her face, no matter how much I tried; but I was able to notice her long blonde hair. I stood longer just to get a good glimpse of her, but to no avail, as she headed back into the house without turning her face in my direction. I finally gave up, stepped down off the bench, and continued to fetch 'Uncle' Abu Wafiq. I saw him carrying a beautiful red rose, hurrying towards me with open arms and the largest smile I ever saw on his face.

"Miss Dalal, welcome back Miss Dalal, welcome back Miss Dalal—The house and the threshold missed your presence Miss Dalal," he said, repeating it over ten times, it seemed.

"Uncle Abu Wafiq." I shouted, "It's good to see you again; seems we have new neighbors?" He wiped his brows after handing me my red rose, and sighed, "What can I tell you Miss Dalal; yes we have new neighbors, and what neighbors they are" he continued with a tone of admiration. That increased my curiosity, so I continued my interrogation, "When did they arrive?"

"Two months ago."

"Who are they? What's their family name? Where did they come from?"

"America." He said it with a sense of admiration. "But I forgot the family name."

"Are they Lebanese or Americans?" I inquired, as I still remembered the very blonde hair of the woman in the garden.

"Mrs. Nancy, the mother and wife is American, but she seems to be fluent in Arabic, you'd be surprised to hear her."

"The father must be Lebanese then?" I inquired further.

"Yes, he's a big doctor."

"But what's the name of this *'big'* doctor?" I asked while laughing at the way he was describing him.

Abu Wafiq shrugged his shoulders up and said, "I don't know; I heard them calling him '*Daddy*', but did not inquire any further. The important thing is that's he's a 'big' doctor and not just anybody."

How strange Abu Wafiq could be sometimes, as well as some of his remarks; he made me laugh and amused me by his theories and understanding of things. It was funny how impressed he was by these titles; my questioning went on.

"Does this couple have more than these two small children?"

"I heard they were twins—boy and girl—Miss Dalal."

"Twins?" I exclaimed.

"Yes, they're the cutest twins I ever saw, and they also speak Arabic," he said proudly, "but not as fluent as their older sister Amal."

"Their sister Amal? I thought you said there were the only children," as my curiosity was now peaking.

"No—no Miss Dalal, Amal is the older sister, and she looks to be your age—sixteen or seventeen."

"Did you have a chance to talk to her to know that she speaks fluent Arabic?"

"Yes, yes—as the matter of fact I saw them all and introduced myself the day they arrived, because they knew no one. You know how this neighborhood becomes deserted in the summer. I took a couple of workers with me and helped them carry some heavy stuff. They were quite grateful to the extent that after they settled down, they invited us for dinner. They're very nice people, never saw anyone like them."

"And Amal? Tell me more about her, since you said she must be my age."

"Amal? She's a very kind girl, intelligent and well-bred; on top of that, she is a lady."

"And how did you know she is a lady?"

"If you had seen her, Miss Dalal, how she was helping with the housework, washing dishes, helping her mother, and taking care of her younger siblings—"

Cutting him off, I asked with astonishment, "Don't they have maids?"

Slapping his hands together in despair, he said, "No, no maids, no chauffeur, no gardener, no cook, no nothing."

Here I truly wondered, because most people in this neighborhood have hired help; no one lives here unless they are from the upper crust and has at least one live-in maid. From Uncle Abu Wafiq's description, and the old automobile parked behind the house, I was sure they were not wealthy—they could not be poor, but certainly not wealthy. I began to think more about them; I concluded that whoever they might be, at least the house is now inhabited and no longer ghostly; there is life in it. I spent some more time with 'Uncle' Abu Wafiq in the garden, and then went back into our house.

I had no idea why I felt good to have neighbors despite knowing that neither of my parents—especially my mother—would bother to introduce herself—unless they belonged to the society to which we belonged, even though it is customary in Lebanon to do so—at least in small villages—but not in Beirut. According to our gardener's description, these poor people had no chance. I walked toward my parents who were drinking coffee on the balcony. I sat with them, told them a little about the new neighbors, but none commented; all I could hear were grunts, acknowledging that they were listening. I then went into my bedroom to read some literature that I had received from my school, since it was only two days away from the new school year.

***

On the first day of school, I was always chauffeured, and as usual, the chauffeur would step down, open the car door for me, and keep on waiting until he made sure I was safe inside the gate. This was no strange scene; most girls here were chauffeured to school. As I walked a little bit further, I noticed an unfamiliar face—long blonde hair, medium height, a bit on the slender side, standing alone, looking somewhat lost. I felt sorry for her and decided to approach to see if I could help. She looked 'foreign' to me, so I asked her, in English, if she needed any help. I could tell she was relieved, as she had a wide grin spread over her beautiful face. She thanked me for my kindness, and to my surprise, she introduced herself in fluent Arabic! "I am Amal Shaheen; my family and I came from the United States a couple of months ago."

I always thought of myself as being smart, but today it took me a while to figure out this girl standing before me was the neighbor's girl that our gardener told me about. Only after I introduced myself to her, was she able to put me on the spot by saying, "Oh, you're Dalal who lives in the house where Abu Wafiq works?"

28

I was stunned for a few seconds. Strange, for the first time, I was being known for my association with the Gardner Abu Wafiq and not by my prominent father, 'Bey' Salah Abu Suleiman, or the granddaughter of Marwan Pasha, or the daughter of the lady who owns boutique Dalal; but I never heard anyone connecting my name to Abu Wafiq's.

"So you're Amal, our neighbor? 'Uncle' Abu Wafiq told me about you, but it just did not occur to me that you would be in this school." I did not mean to hurt her feelings, but my words came out as if I was telling her, "What are you doing here in this expensive private school?"

She only gave me a sweet smile and said, "And, I too, did not expect to be here, but glad to meet you anyway, Dalal."

"Dalal," she called me by my first name, as if she had known me for a long time. I then asked her if she would like me to show her around; she handed me a piece of paper. After having read the paper, carefully, I was surprised and said, "I cannot believe it—We are going to be in the same classes?"

I continued looking at her, examining her innocent face and simple clothes. Yes, I guess she would also be with me in the advanced classes that might qualify us to skip the first year of college. There were ten of us in this advanced group—the cream of the crop—but it was hard for me to accept that such a girl, who mops the floor, helps her mother clean house, washes the dishes, and what not, be eligible for advanced classes, just like me. However, the way she nonchalantly replied was like a slap in my face—or so I took it.

"Great! Thank God, I am happy for you."

Amal was certainly genuine in her manners, but I was confused. How could a family having no housekeepers afford this school, or perhaps she had a scholarship? The bell rang, announcing the beginning of the first class; it saved me from wasting my time thinking about such trivia, then we walked together to class. When the bell rang again to announce lunchtime, everybody let out a big sigh. We had a full hour to eat and relax; my classmates began going toward the cafeteria, most with other classmates. Again, I saw Amal walking alone, so I promptly invited her to have lunch together. Amal seemed to be appreciative of such a gesture. I could not help but notice her bowing down her head and closing her eyes for a short while, before beginning to eat. As we ate, we talked mostly about our classes and teachers. I became more interested in knowing more about Amal, so I asked, "Tell me Amal, you look more like a foreigner than Lebanese—you know, with your blonde hair and all; but you seem to speak Arabic very well, how so?"

"Oh, my mother is American. It's true that I was born and raised in the United States, but my parents insisted that I learn Arabic, so they provided me with Arabic teachers who would only speak Arabic with me and my mother."

"What a great idea. Tell me more about your father, what does he do?"

"My father is a doctor of chemistry—a PhD."

"And what brought you here to our area and our neighborhood in particular?"

"The Lebanese government offered my father a lucrative five-year contract to head a team of scientists to research certain infectious diseases. In addition, to lure him here, they offered him free housing and free education for one of his children, hence my presence in this wonderful school. I cannot thank God enough for the way He opened doors for us to be in my father's country of origin—for the next five years."

"Your answers are quite intelligent, Amal, but forgive me if I ask you your age—not that I don't have an idea, since we're in the same class, you could be one year older, younger, or the same age as me; I'm just curious."

Her answer stunned me; in two months, she will be only sixteen. This means that she was three months younger than I was, and here I thought I was a 'genius,' being so advanced in my school at this young age.

I felt so exhausted at the end of the day. When it was time to leave school, I shouted 'bye' and forgot Amal and everyone else; I rushed out the doorway towards our car. As I was getting into the car, I saw Amal waving her hand and smiling; I sat in the car and ducked my head so Amal would not see me, but I asked the chauffeur to slow down a bit. I turned around to see to whom Amal was waving; it was a lady with two small children getting out of a car. The lady gave Amal a big hug as if she had not seen her in many years; then the two young ones also began hugging Amal. They all went into their automobile, that same old car I saw parked in front of the neighbor's house. So this must be Amal's mother and the twins who came to pick her up. Poor people, I thought; they have no housekeeper, no chauffeur, and the car was not even theirs. Moreover, here I am—yes, me—how fortunate I must be, to have everything, and all, such comfort, or so I thought; but

I was somewhat dismayed when I tried to compare the mother's hugs and kisses she showered upon her daughter to the chauffeur lifting up his hat and bowing his head upon seeing me. I was also comparing the noise and laughter of the small children in the back seat of the car to the deafening silence in the back of our luxurious vehicle. By the time I reached home, I concluded it was I who lost, in comparison, and it was I who was poor, and not Amal.

I returned home, somewhat dejected; my mother was waiting by the door, and she began by asking me a barrage of questions, but I did not feel like talking much.

"How was your day?" she asked.

"Good, Mom."

"Was everything to your liking?"

"Not bad, the first day is always difficult and exhausting."

"What about the teachers?"

"Not bad, Mom."

"Is it going to be a difficult school year?"

"You forgot that I am Dalal, and you're my mother, and I am the daughter of Salah Abu Suleiman? Nothing is difficult for me, even if it was, I would be able to overcome it, right Mom?" I was up to the challenge, and needed to keep my sense of humor.

My mother applauded my response and felt proud. "That's my girl," as she continued her questioning. "You didn't tell me about your classmates; there are ten in your group, right?"

"Yes, there are ten."

"And all are older than you, I suppose?"

"Yes, Mom, they're all older, except one; she's three months younger."

"You mean she is barely sixteen?" My mother shouted, "And also in the advanced classes? She must be quite intelligent, who is she? I am sure you must have met her; which family does she come from? Do we know her parents?"

"She's the neighbor's daughter, Mom."

"Those neighbors who rented the house across the street; they have an honor student in your school?" she asked. The tone in her voice was more of surprise. This bothered me, and I found myself defending Amal.

"The neighbor's daughter, Amal, is so kind, congenial, and a very beautiful girl, Mom; she and I hit it off really well; we stayed together all day, as though we've known each other since childhood."

Irritated, my mother stood up and said, "I know you Dalal; you are a sociable person and love to be around people, but I don't want you to judge others prematurely. I'll ask around about the neighbors to see who they are and what they're doing here and also to see if they are worthy, and then you can befriend her."

"Mom. I told you she's the nicest girl I spoke to today; just imagine that she speaks fluent Arabic, despite her being born in the United States to an American mother. Moreover, I don't like your use of the word worthy!"

I have no idea why the people of the East have this complex about the West; we usually get enamored by western foreigners—even my aristocratic mother. When she heard that Amal had an American mother, she quickly changed her attitude, calmed down, and apologized.

"How could she speak fluent Arabic if she was born in the United States to an American mother?" she asked. "Her father must be Middle Eastern then, right? Did you know what family he comes from, and what her father does for a living?"

This is also an important status symbol to the Lebanese; what a man does is just as important as the family name he carries, the education he has, or his wealth.

In less than fifteen minutes, my mother knew everything I knew about Amal and the Shaheen family. The important thing, to my mother, was the fact that the father was not a 'nobody', but instead he was quite educated with a good position; moreover, the mother was American, and the daughter was in advanced classes despite her young age. That was enough for mother to give me the green light if I wanted to befriend Amal.

My relationship with Amal initially was nothing beyond being classmates, no more, no less; but she annoyed me by her incessant thanks to the Lord for every little thing! Of course, I had no objection to thanking God, but not every couple of minutes. I used to get embarrassed whenever we had lunch together, for she was the only one around to close her eyes as if she was praying—or so it seemed—before every meal. I had not asked her yet why she would go through the same ritual every time we wanted to eat, what religious background she came from, or whether she knew of my own religious background. I was certain she was Christian, since she had a little cross on a chain that she always wore around her neck. Many of my mother's best friends who were Christian wore either gold or diamond crosses around their necks, but I never saw them pray before their meals, or even mention God in their conversations, except when they wanted to swear that they were telling the truth. No, Amal does not seem to be like them; she was different—somehow—even her behavior was different from that of my other Christian girlfriends.

Three months went by, examinations was looming. I studied a lot; the results showed it. Amal and I were in the top of the class, yet everyone seemed to heap praise upon me. I took this to be normal because of my family and the many friends we have; Amal was simply the new kid on the block. I was happy and proud of my success and of the praise heaped on me, but nonetheless, I felt sorry for Amal because I was treated better than she was. I did not like it, and to be honest, I was very upset that her accomplishments were overlooked. My relationship with Amal was now developing from just being 'classmates' into a deep friendship. I was beginning to feel proud to have her as a friend, I felt that it was no longer a big deal if she thanked God, and was no longer a big deal if she prayed before a meal; in fact, it was a nice habit, I rationalized. Such a behavior used to bother me at first, but now I became used to it, and even liked it enough that I also wanted to do the same thing.

Winter break arrived; it was what Christians refer to as 'Christmas' vacation. Three days into our break, my parents and I flew to Paris and returned just two days before school resumed. Every time I traveled, I would buy some gifts for everyone; but this time, I added another person to my list—my newly found friend Amal—as well as toys for the twins and a bottle of perfume for Mrs. Shaheen. I had not visited Amal at her house yet, nor had she visited me. Upon my return from the airport, I asked Abu Wafiq to let Amal know that I was back from Paris and wished to visit her; the gifts were a good excuse to make that first visit. That was a custom that I learned from my mother; we only visit people by appointment and do not just drop in unannounced. Abu Wafiq tried to tell me that it was not necessary to do so, since the new neighbors were not as pretentious as other people we know, and it was OK to just drop in on them anytime. I insisted that he should do as I asked, and I waited for him to let me know. The neighbors were available. As I approached their front door, Amal rushed out to greet me, followed by the twins and their mother. Amal and I hugged and kissed as though we have not seen each other for months. Mrs. Shaheen also welcomed me warmly, put her hand on my shoulder, and led me into the house.

Compared to our mansion, their house and the furnishings were quite ordinary, but I felt, more comfortable, sitting there than in any other house before. Despite the humble furniture, it was tasteful and quite cozy. Soft music played in the background, everyone seemed happy and content, and the twins were playing with some toys.

"I missed you so much," Amal said with apparent sincerity. It broke the wall of silence that befell us for few moments.

"Me too, I missed you so much."

I looked at her with intent and reached for the large bag I was carrying, and I proceeded to give her the gift. The twins rushed to see what it was, and stood before me as though waiting for theirs. With a big smile, I took out their presents and handed them their toys.

"My, how beautiful. How lovely. That's impossible." Amal was shouting as she looked at her gift, which was a green jacket with a matching black skirt and black hat, as well as black leather gloves. She seemed in need of such an outfit as her mother indicated.

"Thank God, He knows how much you needed a winter outfit like this one, so He presented it to you through Dalal's hand." Then she turned to me and said, "Thank you my dear," but before I could respond that it was nothing, just a simple gift, I heard the twins shout giddily over their toys; this gave me a feeling of indescribable joy. It was the first time I presented a gift to anyone other than our maids and workers and received such appreciation. When we exchange presents with the family, gifts are generally considered a form of obligation rather than an act of love. It all boils down to 'I give you a gift and you give one back to me'—no indebtedness nor loyalty; but today, my presents to Amal, her mother, and the children meant a lot to me because I did not expect anything in return. We sat around for almost an hour, chatting and eating sweets made by 'Auntie' Nancy, as she asked me to call her. Later on, Amal took me to her bedroom—simple but tidy—where we sat on her bed making small talk, nothing in particular. Amal got up to try on the new clothes I had brought her, she put a belt over her small waist and the hat over her head—she looked like a super model. As she took off the outfit and was busy thanking me, repeatedly, for this beautiful gift, her hand knocked off something that was on the table and dropped onto the floor. I reached to pick it up for her—it was a frame surrounding a portrait of a young man in a graduation cap and gown. Out of politeness, I did not take a hard look at the picture, but I heard Amal laugh, saying, "My poor brother, I almost broke him."

"Your brother?" I asked with a tone of surprise. "This is your brother?"

"Yes, it is. He is my brother Samir," she said looking at the picture with such love and tenderness saying, "I miss you, brother."

"You didn't tell me you had another brother."

"There are many things I haven't yet told you, Dalal; perhaps we will talk some more on other occasions as we get to know each other more, Lord willing."

"So, where is your brother now?

"He is in the United States."

"In the United States? In the United States and you're all here?"

"Yes, he is studying in the state of Maryland."

"What is he studying?"

"Medicine, at Johns Hopkins University."

"How old is he, if I may ask?"

"Samir is five years older than I—that makes him twenty-two—and Lord willing, he should graduate by the time he's twenty-five."

"Looks like intelligence runs in your family. No wonder you're in the advanced classes and your brother will become a physician at such a young age."

Amal laughed at what I said because it sounded like a joke about her intelligence.

"I am nothing compared to my brother Samir, you would not have said that had you known him."

"So, there are four of you then—two boys and two girls—how lucky you must be; I am the only child in our family, with no brother or sister." I said with a hint of sadness. I wanted to tell her more about me, but she cut me off, saying, "Your 'Uncle Abu Wafiq' always talks about you; he must love you so much. He told me your life history from A to Z, that's why I am not asking you too many questions about yourself; I already know so much—may God bless you."

I returned home as the jet lag from my trip began to take its toll. I had a light dinner, and then retired to my room. I was feeling elated, for after sixteen years, I now had a true friend.

As was my habit when retiring to bed, I would begin to recall all that happened that day, analyze, and summarize, until I reached a conclusion. The first thing that came to mind was my visit to the neighbors' house, which lasted over two hours. Mrs. Shaheen seemed to be a respectable woman, her smiling face was clear of any wrinkles, despite her age. She had natural beauty, without the help of make-up, and clear blue eyes, like summer skies. She was a bit shorter than I was which still makes her quite tall; her clothes were simple, yet elegant. The twins—who were five at the time—seemed so cute, quite lively, and intelligent. They came into being by sheer 'accident' as their mother said; but, in fact, were a gift from heaven, eleven years after Amal's birth. "They are the joy of the family," Mrs. Shaheen added. Their features were mixed. The boy, Walid, had blond hair with almost blue eyes, and Rima, the girl, had almost black-hair, and brown eyes. The father-whom I had not met yet, seemed quite handsome from his large portrait that hung on the wall. Amal seems to have inherited her mother's fair skin, and her father's Middle Eastern features, which gave her a stunning beauty. I do not know why I lingered a moment or two to analyze what Mrs. Shaheen said earlier to Amal upon opening her gift from me, "God knew how much you needed these clothes, and he gave them to you through Amal's hands." It seems that God knows our every need, takes care of us, provides for us, and uses other people as instruments to carry out His provisions.

I liked this idea, but when I wanted to apply it to myself, it fell short. In all my life, I never needed anything, everything seemed to come to me on a silver platter; I never experienced wanting. Despite that, I caught myself saying, "God gave me wealthy parents, and through them, I am able to enjoy the good life, so God also takes care of me, but in a different way."

That same evening, before I slept, I said in my heart—not with my lips, "Thank you God for my mother and father, and for everything you gave me through them." It was the first time ever that I uttered such words.

Chapter 3
MY TUTOR

*In the weeks that followed my visit to Amal, and when the second semester of school began, everything seemed to have become more difficult: homework, tests, and extra-curricular activities increased, which required both additional effort and time. Consequently, my grades in chemistry—my weakness—began to drop; it was not that I failed the course, because my grades were still higher than most in the class, except Amal's. When my mother saw my grade, she panicked and immediately wanted to find me a chemistry tutor. When I told Amal that, she exclaimed,

"A tutor? What for? Come to our house this evening and every evening and my father could help both of us; he's better than any tutor your mom could find."

"That would be great, but perhaps your father—Don't you think you should ask him first before you volunteer him for such a task?"

Amal replied assuredly, "You don't have to worry about that, my dad loves to be needed. He finds great pleasure in teaching, and at any rate, he will be tutoring me, as he always does with many courses; how do you think I would be able to achieve such high grades? Do you think I am just that smart?"

We both laughed, and I thanked her for this wonderful offer; then she whispered, "We'll be waiting for you this evening."

I liked this idea a lot; it made sense, and I felt sorry for my mother spending all day long searching for a tutor when I already had one next door. As soon as I arrived at the school, I went to the nearest phone to tell her the news and spare her the search.

"Amal's dad is willing to tutor me, and as you may already know, he is an accomplished chemist. He will be tutoring me and Amal at the same time every evening."

"I have no objection, because he, undoubtedly, will be a great tutor, especially that he will also be teaching his daughter. But we need to pay for his effort, so you could tell him that."

My mother always brought up money and wages; everything must have a price; perhaps because she was a businesswoman; but in my view, we could not offer the money; it might be offensive to Amal's father—as well as to Amal—after all, we are best friends now.

"OK, OK, mother, don't worry about this now, we'll talk later."

"And when will you start?"

"This evening."

"Good luck sweetheart." The conversation was over.

Mother was not home when I returned from school, but she left me a note saying that she and father would be coming late. After dinner, I took my books and went to Amal's house, accompanied by 'Uncle' Abu Wafiq. When I entered the house, all the family gathered, and in the middle, was a small table with some beautiful lilies, red roses and pink carnations in a very fancy basket. If this had been our house, I would not have been surprised, because I am used to seeing flower arrangements everywhere. I began to wonder if my mother had anything to do with it. Before my wild imaginations could take me any further, Dr. Shaheen spoke, "Welcome, Dalal, I am happy to make your acquaintance; I already heard so much about you," as he extended his hand to shake mine.

"I am happy to meet you too, Dr. Shaheen. I can't believe it's been six months and we, neighbors, haven't met yet; it just doesn't happen in our community. I feel so glad and privileged that you're going to be able to help me with my chemistry, and I thank you for it."

"Your mother has already thanked me by sending this beautiful arrangement; she's so considerate. Let's not waste any more time, let's get to it. Get your books, girls."

Dr. Shaheen—who asked me to call him by his first name—'Uncle' Najeeb, was very patient with me, and, as well, kind and understanding. He tutored Amal and me at our level and beyond. After every session, I would feel so ecstatic at the knowledge I gained from him; I even began to love chemistry. What a difference a good teacher with a special caring can make. Every now and then, we used to strike up a conversation about other subjects and sip orange juice, have some fruit, and other snacks.

We also ventured to talk about God, whom the Shaheens always referred to as 'Lord'. We would talk about how He loves humanity and wants to save it from the pits of hell. Sometimes, we would get into deeper and more important discussions, and even mention Jesus Christ a little bit, then resume our studying.

We continued this schedule until the end of the school year. The exams showed how much I benefited from 'Uncle" Najeeb's tutoring that I even received a tad higher grade than Amal. I came in at the top of the class and the region that year. My parents were so elated by this success, and they wanted to show their heartfelt appreciation to Dr. Shaheen—from the heart—and the pocket too. However, Dr. Shaheen would not have it. At this point, my mother invited them for a dinner party at our house, so we could also be better acquainted, and strange as it may sound, my parents had not actually met the Shaheens or Amal.

Finally, the two families meet; I was elated. That day was one of the happiest in my life. I counted the hours and minutes for the Shaheens to arrive. I prepared some games for the twins to keep them happy and busy. My mother noticed my care towards them, so she approached me and said something with a hint of criticism, "I had no idea you were interested in children to spend so much time in order to please them."

"Mom, you know, I do not do this with all the kids, but these twins are special; I've gotten to love them so much." I noticed a tear that my mother wiped away with the tip of her finger; she stroked my hair, saying, in a tender voice, "You wished you had brothers and sisters, sweetheart, don't you? Do you feel disappointed that you have none, that you're an only child?"

I immediately realized what was going through her mind. For all these years following my birth, she was not able to conceive. I wanted to change the subject, so I looked at her clothes and all the jewelry she was wearing as if she was going to a ball, and said, "These clothes you're wearing, Mom, will cause some embarrassment to our neighbors; they just don't fit the occasion."

She did not take my advice into consideration, and even let my father know that he could not wear casual clothes; it was the first time, after all, she rationalized—and she was also teaching us the art of entertaining. She believed first impressions were important and not easily forgotten.

Precisely at seven, the Shaheens arrived at our house. Ordinarily, the housekeeper would open the door first and lead them into the living room; after a minute or so, my parents would come to greet the guests. This time, however, I wanted to change the custom a bit, get the door myself, and treat these people as they would treat others. I felt that I should do this because I came to love them and wanted to treat them as guests of honor par excellence.

I always felt proud whenever people would visit us, so they could see all the luxury of wealth inside our house: from imported furniture, Persian rugs, to rare pieces of art, exquisite paintings, and tasteful décor—except this evening, when I felt awkward. I carried on as if to apologize for all this ostentatious wealth, expecting our guests to drop their jaws in awe and express admiration as many others who were just as wealthy as we are did before. To my surprise, none of the Shaheens seemed to be in awe of anything they saw. In a few minutes, my parents, who were over-dressed for the evening, entered the living room to greet our visitors. The meeting was quite cordial; after all, my parents had something to be thankful for, Dr. Shaheen had helped me excel in chemistry. This was a big deal for my parents, especially for my mother. Anything having to do with the success and happiness of her daughter received priority.

We all sat down to chat for a few minutes before dinner, and one of the kitchen staff came in, pushing a teacart full of all sorts of imported drinks. My father grabbed a bottle of French wine, looked at it against the chandelier lights to show that he was a wine connoisseur, saying something to this effect, "This bottle is 1950's French vintage, quite soft and aromatic." It made me feel good that my father was trying to please them, but we had no idea that they did not drink alcohol. This came as a surprise, as all our Christian friends had no problem drinking. Dr Shaheen surprised me when he said, "Thank you, Mr. Abu Suleiman, but none of us drink alcohol, perhaps some soft drinks or juice will do."

"Cigarettes?" My father inquired further, carrying a tray full of all kinds of brands of cigarettes, as is the custom in Lebanon, so nobody would accuse you of being 'cheap'.

"No cigarettes either, thank you very much."

My father chuckled a bit and asked, "If you don't drink or smoke, what do you do for pleasure?"

"We eat and thank God for it," Amal shouted in her merry voice and sweet laugh. At the sound of 'food', the twins cried out, "We're hungry! We are hungry!"

Everybody laughed, including my mother, who was closely observing this family's behavior (so she could give me her assessment later on), especially since they had become part of my life.

Finally, after having soft drinks and fruit juice, we all sat around the dinner table to eat, with the food being served in the order my mother had designated. We were all hungry by now; the server began to go around the table with all sorts of appetizers; Hummus, tabouleh, hot pita bread and meat-pies in addition to roasted chicken, rice, lamb chops, and my dad's favorite dish 'spicy fish'. Everybody was about to begin eating when we heard Walid, one of the twins, shouts, in his broken Arabic, "Dad, we did not say Grace."

One could hear a pin drop at the silence that followed; it was an awkward moment with everyone looking at the other, but my father broke the silence in his diplomatic way, saying very politely, "If you're used to praying before eating, please Dr. Shaheen, feel free to do so in order to please the little boy."

"We thank you Lord for all your blessings upon us, for the health you've given us, so we could enjoy the food placed before us. Bless this food and the hands that prepared it, and provide it to those who are needy. We also ask you to remember the sick, the infirm, and those who are suffering. Bless this house and each of its members, and protect them, according to your mercies and care. This we ask in Jesus' name, Amen."

"What a beautiful prayer." I exclaimed. "I never heard anything like it before, thank you so much."

"You're most welcome." Dr. Shaheen replied.

Everyone was now eating with voracious appetite—hunger reigned supreme—except for me. I was thinking about the prayer we just heard, is this what they call a 'prayer'? These were just ordinary words, a man talking with God and simply asking Him to bless the food and provide for the hungry. Is this how Christians prayed, no gestures, hand movements, signs, or kneeling and standing? It was the first time I heard such a prayer, and certainly the first time, in this house, before a meal.

I ate, laughed and engaged the guests with small talk, but most of the time I thought about this short and simple prayer that affected me. I then wondered why Mother taught me everything else; the etiquette of eating, how to dress, how to walk and talk, how to greet guests, and so on, but never taught me how to pray and thank God for His provisions, perhaps we did not need to pray?

Dinner was over, and everybody went back into the living room for the rest of the visit; the twins played with some of my old toys. My father and Dr. Shaheen were getting along fine in their discussions, especially about a certain scientific subject that Dr. Shaheen was undertaking. It seems that, in an indirect way, my father was tapping into Dr. Shaheen's experience and knowledge. My father was sitting in his chair, having removed his jacket and necktie that my mother forced him to wear; he wanted to feel more comfortable talking with his guests. I knew too well when my father was feeling happy and enjoying the conversation. This evening, he was doing just that. He used to smoke a few cigarettes after meals, but tonight he did not reach for a single one; it just did not seem the appropriate thing to do around our guests. My mother—the socialite—well known for her art of conversation, was sitting by Mrs. Shaheen, having difficulty striking up a conversation. Finally, Mrs. Shaheen said, "Your house is beautiful, and quite tasteful; may the good Lord bless it."

"Thank you, you're very kind," my mother replied.

"I visited your boutique with Amal and found it to be so exquisite and wonderful. You are truly a courageous and smart woman to take such an undertaking."

"Oh, thank you so much for your kind words," my mother replied. This was the second time my mother repeated the same words in less than one minute. What was the matter with her? Why couldn't she begin the conversation as a good hostess should; she was usually in control of the conversation? Why was my mother showing weakness and lack of confidence before this humble woman? My mother entertained princesses and wives of presidents, and spoke to them with full confidence, but her behavior that night was bewildering. At this point, I took the initiative to move the conversation and open it up between my mother and Mrs. Shaheen, so I said, "Mother, do you know that Mrs. Shaheen has a master's degree in musicology, and was teaching it until the birth of the twins—Rima and Walid?"

My mother's eyes opened wide because she loved music; I now felt that I struck a raw nerve as well as an expanded conversation between the two. I felt good. Amal and I took the children to another room so the adults could freely discuss whatever subject they wished. I asked the twins what they would like to do; they indicated that they preferred

42

watching some home videos of my birthday. I told them that I have movie clips from all my birthdays, beginning with my first birthday through my sixteenth. "Which one you'd like to see?" I asked.

"Amal wanted to watch my last birthday, which also included my crowning as a beauty queen, whereas the twins wanted to watch my fifth birthday—their age now. I had not watched my fifth birthday movie for a long time, and could not remember what was in it, but as we all watched it, I remembered that evening as being very long. My father had invited a well-known singer and personal friend to my party to entertain the invited guests, and a lavish dinner was presented and went into the wee hours of the night. We watched in silence, except for when I would make a comment here and there, on certain clips. By now, I noticed the twins were yawning, so I asked if they were bored, but Rima asked,

"When are we going to watch Dalal's birthday?"

"But this was Dalal's birthday." Walid shouted back.

"This? Dalal's birthday? But where are the balloons and horns, and party hats? Where are the kids?" Rima asked, wondering.

"True" said Walid, "But who did Dalal play with? Who sang 'Happy Birthday'?"

Rima replied in anger, pointing to the singer who was singing to me as I was cutting the cake, "That man?"

She then got up, held my hand, and hugged me saying, "Poor Dalal, I feel sorry for you, you must have been bored, poor Dalal."

At this point, the lights came on and the movie stopped. I felt very emotional hearing these words; I was not able to decide whether what I heard from this child saddened or offended me. All my life I did not hear anything but admiration and compliments on my birthday parties. I always felt that everybody I knew wished that he could have been in my place or had a fraction of what I had. However, for this innocent, young child to say, "Poor Dalal" was too much to bear. Perhaps Amal, being intelligent, must have noticed what I was thinking, so she suggested we go back to our parents to see what was going on. It was a timely move, as Amal's parents were ready to go home and the dinner party was over.

Before each of us retired to his room for the night, I heard my father say, "Your friends are very nice people, Dalal. Dr. Shaheen seems to be quite an intelligent and congenial fellow, in fact, all the family is quite charming, and Amal seems to be a good choice for a friend." He said this while tapping my shoulder, "Good night, sweetheart."

"Good night, Dad; I am so glad that you had a good time and liked our neighbors," turning to my mother in such a way as to retrieve a comment from her, but I had no idea why she took this negative attitude by saying, "Dalal, don't think or imagine that Mrs. Shaheen and I could ever be friends. Although she earned my respect, we are quite opposites and not from the same mold. She seems to be one of those Christian fanatics who have extreme positions and ideas about life that I cannot fathom, or like. Although I have several Christian friends, no one is like her, and therefore, I cannot see that our friendship with the neighbors would go beyond this evening."

I stood bewildered, jaw dropped, listening to what my mother was saying, especially when she continued, "And I have a feeling that her daughter, Amal, is exactly like her, and I warn you not to get too friendly."

She said this and wanted to go to her bedroom, but I took her speech to be a threat; what the little girl told me earlier at seeing my birthday movie still bothered me. Yes, I'd say it was 'boring', for tonight I looked at it as a child would and found it to be 'ugly and full of boredom'; I felt furious and said to my mother in a voice filled with anger, "You have no right to talk this way about the Shaheens; I thought I understood you, but at times, I cannot make sense of your declarations."

"Nothing I said could be any clearer, and you're supposed to be more intelligent than that, Dalal," she said as she continued to walk away. But I screamed, nervously, "This is shameful; why then do you want me to lose a friend whom I grew to love and cherish?"

"Frankly, I fear her influence on you."

"And am I that weak to fall under her influence that simply? I thought you raised me to be independent with my views; if that is the case, what are you afraid of?"

I did not wait to hear another word. I rushed to my room, shut the door, and threw myself on the bed. It was the first time, ever, that I went to sleep crying.

I only wished that this evening could have gone smoother from beginning to end. I might have slept better if Mom had gotten along well with a family who I loved tremendously. My mother wields more influence in our family than my father does. She was the one that actually ran the affairs of everyday life in our house. I remained lying on my bed for several hours, tossing and turning, trying to fall asleep and forget about what happened. I wished that my mother would come into my room to wipe my tears and comfort me. This was also the first time I went to bed angry with my mother. I had no idea what went wrong between her and Mrs. Shaheen that caused her to say what she said. I am certain it was not because of religious differences, as my mother was not religious herself, and she could care less what anyone's religion was. She had quite a few Christian friends; at least that's what I thought. Of course, these friends were not as strict or as serious as Mrs. Shaheen was about her Christianity. Consequently, I eliminated the religious difference as the cause. It could not have been in regard to educational differences, since my mother knew that Mrs. Shaheen held a master's degree in music, and taught at a university. It could not have been looks, for Mrs. Shaheen was quite beautiful and looked well in her tasteful clothes and make-up; so what was the problem? What happened? What did Mrs. Shaheen say that ruffled my mother's feathers so badly that she couldn't ever be friends with Mrs. Shaheen, and thus, which could also affect my relationship with Amal? I wished I knew, right there and then.

Was my fifth birthday—same as the twins' now—a joyful one for me? Did I play with kids my age and throw water balloons at each other? Did I dirty my clothes and have cake and ice cream all over my face? Did I also paint other kids' faces with cream as I saw in the twins' birthday pictures? Did we laugh, hit each other, fight, and quickly make up? No, nothing of the sort. My birthday was a joyous event for grown-ups, as they came together to laugh, gossip, and show-off their new clothes. It was also another social opportunity for my parents; my mother would find it an opportunity to give my father another push towards his political future. So why would they invite children—to disturb the peace and quiet they needed? Why give them a playground to mess up the house?

With these thoughts, I went to sleep that Thursday evening. Friday morning, I woke up with my severe menstrual pain and could not go to school. Of course, Mom knew about it, and hurriedly came to my bedside and sat on my bed. She tenderly caressed my hair and began to kiss my forehead. This made me feel guilty about my thoughts and, consequently, my anger disappeared because I had so much love for her. I sat in bed, leaned over, and gave her a hug and kissed her. This went on for a few seconds until I heard her say, "If you can't go to school today, ask your friend Amal to bring you your assignments, and perhaps you can study together this evening if you're up to it." I then looked at her intently, as she smiled a smile only I could understand; but before I could say a word, she continued, "And if Amal would like to stay the night, I have no objection. What do you think sweetheart? Is it a fair deal?"

Fortunately, I had those cramps that made me cry in anguish; otherwise, I would have cried because of joy at Mom's suggestion. The pain was my only weapon allowed me to hide my joy, and therefore, not to appear victorious, behaving foolishly.

My mother left and I did not waste a single moment in calling Amal. Amal was truly shocked to hear my voice; I would be the last person she would think of, calling her so early in the morning. She was even more surprised when I invited her to sleep over, yet she sensed some urgency in my voice, and was worried. I told her everything that had happened, and then hung up after she accepted the invitation.

It was the first time that I welcomed pain so I could stay in bed and avoid looking in my mother's face, for I did not want to reveal my joy over what had just happened. My short friendship with Amal was almost snuffed out last night, and today, it was miraculously revived.

Soon afterwards, the pain disappeared abruptly, and I got out of bed around noon, only to find my mother had left the house. I felt like taking a walk in the garden to enjoy the warm, early sun. As I walked, I arrived at the high wall that separated us from our neighbor's house. I could hear the twins play. As I approached the gate, I called them, and they came running towards me, screaming. Mrs. Shaheen was not too far behind; she, in turn, came towards me smiling and thanking me for a nice evening at our house. I took one of the twins by the hand and asked Mrs. Shaheen if I could take them to the playground where I used to play as a child. The playground was located at the other end of the garden.

"Auntie Nancy, if you'd like to have some time for yourself to do something special, go for a visit, or go shopping, I'll be glad the take care of the twins for a couple of hours."

In a voice not lacking surprise, she asked, "Do you mean that?"

"Why, of course, with pleasure. There's nothing better I like to do than to spend time with Walid and Rima." I said with all sincerity.

"Would your mother agree to this? She may disapprove."

"And why would she? She knows how much I love them."

My doubts began to re-emerge after first having left me, because of what happened last night. I found this to be a good opportunity to investigate further.

"Why do you think my mother would disapprove, Auntie?"

"Oh, nothing important dear, it's just a notion that came to mind. But if you insist, I'll take you up on your offer because, in fact, there's something important I have to do without the kids around."

She left in a hurry, leaving the kids in my care. I took the twins to the playground, and I could see their eyes widen and jaws drop at what they saw; swings, seesaws, and basketball nets, among other things my mother designed for me a few years back. She did not spare any money in buying whatever she thought would amuse me and keep me entertained. I spent hours with my nannies, relatives, and some friends playing here, but I could not remember too many children, my age, because by the time I arrived into this world, all my family's friends' children were already ten years or older. But today, at sixteen, I shall make up for it. I asked Salwa, our head mistress, to stay with us and take some pictures. I had no idea what mysterious force has awakened my childhood. Salwa was ready to take some pictures, so we started to play around with what was out there. We fell, dirtied our clothes, got scratched, played hide and seek, and even covered each other with sand, all the time laughing, screaming, and hugging each other. The twins were exhilarated, and so was I. In a way, I was recapturing a somewhat-lost childhood with other children.

I did not realize that the two hours had gone by so quickly, so I asked Salwa to prepare some snacks for us, as everybody began to feel hungry while I was washing the kids' hands. As she returned with a large tray full of tasty food and fruit, we all rushed to eat. There was so much food on that tray; the twins thought that was dinner. As usual, they closed their eyes, bowed their heads, and began to murmur something in English; but I was able to make out the last sentence, "Bless this food. Amen." They looked so lovely eating, laughing, and enjoying themselves. I then asked them, "Do you always pray before eating?"

"Yes, we pray before eating and before we go to bed." Rima replied, but with a tone of voice wanting to say more,

"Before we go to bed, all of us gather together, Dad opens up the Bible, reads something, and then we pray."

"Who usually prays?"

47

"Mother prays first, and then Amal, then Walid, then I, and finally our dad prays last"

"When Dad prays, we know it's time to go to bed," Walid added as he was reaching for another sandwich.

"And what do you usually pray for?" I asked inquisitively. "Do you repeat the same prayers every night?"

"No," Rima said. "We ask God for whatever we need for that day, as well as we thank Him for everything."

"We also pray for our brother," Walid interjected, as though he was trying to correct Rima by implying that praying for our brother Samir was a given, "He's in the United States, and we pray for him every day."

"Every day?"

"Yes, every day," Walid replied, but Rima the great detailer, added, "We also pray for you, Dalal."

"For me? I asked in a tone of surprise. Walid nodded in agreement and said as he was sipping some juice, "Yes, especially last night after we returned from your house."

"And why last night? What happened last night that you felt you must pray for me?"

"Because Mom said you were in trouble," Walid replied innocently.

How innocent children could be, as well as their beautiful, expressive ways. I wanted to inquire further into this special prayer for me, but I did not get the chance, as Salwa interrupted to inform us that Mrs. Shaheen was here for the twins.

I had a rough time convincing the children to leave because they were having such a great time here, and wanted more of the same. However, when I promised them I would bring them over again and again, they reluctantly agreed. Mrs. Shaheen looked happy. As she was leaving, I heard her say these words that brought tears to my eyes, "Because of what you did, sweetie, I was able to visit a sick friend of mine in the hospital. She was quite happy to see me near her, and when I left, she was feeling so good. So for this, thank you again, sweetheart; may the good Lord bless you."

I wanted to ask her why they prayed for me last night, and why they thought I was in trouble, but she was already on her way home. I stood there looking at them leave until I almost could see them no more, then and at the last moment, Mrs. Nancy looked back, smiled, and said as she disappeared behind the wall, "I wish you and Amal a very pleasant time this evening."

Amal arrived at our house at five o'clock to spend the night with me. So to get an opportunity to chitchat and entertain ourselves, we decided that we would first finish our homework—and we did. When Mom entered our room to check on us, she was quite surprised that we were studying so seriously, and hardly talking or laughing. She gave us a smile of approval and left the room almost immediately. We continued studying non-stop until eight, when both my parents walked into the room to say good night, since they were going out for the rest of the evening.

Amal and I were now the masters of the whole house; we were in control. This was the first time I had ever invited anyone to spend the night. I called the housekeeper to prepare a room for Amal, but Amal objected quickly, "No need to call the maid to prepare anything; we'll both sleep on the floor."

"On the floor?" I said with a surprised look. "I never slept on the floor before; this is new to me."

"Well, Dalal; this will be your first time."

The idea did not sound so bad; in fact, I was eager to try it. However, I did not ask Amal to sleep in my bed, which was large enough to accommodate, at least, three people. Sleeping on the floor felt more adventurous to me, so I did not resist. After we prepared everything needed for our little 'adventure', I wanted to ring the bell for the housekeeper to prepare dinner for us, but again, Amal objected, "Let's not bother anybody; we will prepare our own dinner." Here, I protested, saying that I have no idea where the food is, nor what we have in the refrigerator, and that perhaps we should forget about this 'adventure', but Amal was adamant, "perhaps it's time you begin to learn how to do these little things, Dalal."

I had no choice but to comply. We both went to the refrigerator to see what could possibly be there to eat and came out of the kitchen with a large tray full of food and soft drinks that we took to the balcony to eat.

The cool evening breeze was so refreshing after spending so much time indoors. We could hear the willow leaves rustling in that breeze, and the lights shone over the pond in the garden to reveal the little waves reflecting lights dancing in water. I felt so enchanted by all this. We ate voraciously, like never before, and talked on different subjects so much that our jaws began to ache. This was our first chance to spend so much time together and alone. We talked about the other girls at school, who was like us and who was not; we spoke about the different teachers' personalities, our parents, relatives, and friends. I spoke, at length, about my cousin Majdi—the closest to me of all my relatives. He was the youngest of four children—all boys. He had no sister, just as I had no brother; so each of us loved the other as sister or brother; I felt good when he was around. He was five years my senior, and everybody felt that one day he will have a bright future in politics. Then, in turn, Amal talked about her brother Samir. It was the first time she talked about him at length; whenever she mentioned his name, she did so excitedly, as if he were some kind of an exceptional human being. We spoke about love, marriage, and young men, each giving her own frank opinion on these subjects. But the subject of marriage took the lion's share of our chats. I shared with Amal, a few names of young men who were interested in me; and I spoke about what the bright, happy, and secure future is holding for me. Amal did the same, but with a different twist; I never heard the like before. She said, "No one can guarantee their future, Dalal. Only God knows our future and every detail it holds. Money, prestige, power, and beauty cannot guarantee a happy future and cannot promise a secure and peaceful life if God's peace is not in our heart. I always pray that God will lead and guide my life and future, including the man in my life, if I submit to His will. For it is God who knows our past, and holds the present, and future in His hands; His hand is always the rudder of my life, steering me to the safe shore."

"And you leave the selection of your future husband to God? You let Him decide such matters?"

"For sure. Who is more faithful, more caring, and knows what's best for me than God? We don't know what tomorrow or the day after holds for us, but God does. We often think we know what is best for us, but more often than not, we fail because we depend on our limited human knowledge

"And when you submit to God in choosing a husband, as you say, how would you know that God is the one who chose him?"

"Good question. I would know if this husband has the qualifications given in the Bible. I cannot say this or that husband is God's choosing if he does not believe what I believe and does not walk the talk—as the Word of God commands. It is as simple as that. But this pertains to me as a Christian young woman."

"How about me?"

Amal has a ready answer for every question; but why did she hesitate here, not knowing how to answer such a simple question. Finally, and after more hesitation, she replied, "God reveals His will to that person who is willing to obey and leads him on the right path in his quest to make the right decision."

"So your condition for marriage is a Christian husband?"

"No Dalal, don't misunderstand me. My foremost condition is that my husband be a genuine believer in Christ, believes in God's Word found in the Holy Bible, and lives according to its teaching, and not just anyone born in a Christian family."

"Isn't the Bible for all Christians? Don't all Christians believe in Christ?"

"The label 'Christian' is not sufficient to make a 'Christian' a follower of Christ. In fact, Dalal, Christianity is not a religion."

"What? What are you saying, this is news to me."

"I am saying that Christianity is not a religion in the real sense of the word, but rather a personal relationship with Christ the Lord—a way of life between man and God."

"You mean between an individual and God?"

"Precisely! A personal and individual level."

"Do I understand you to say that there are two types of Christians?"

"Yes Dalal, you got it right. Some are nominal Christians who only know the name of Christ."

"How? I am afraid I do not understand you, here."

"If a so-called Christian lies, swears, utters foul language, gets drunk, commits adultery, kills or steals, brings shame to Christ and Christianity, he or she may not be a true Christian, because the name of Christ is a great and Holy name, and His life and teachings are also Holy. If anyone is to carry His name, he must be worthy of such a name, and to be worthy, he must be willing to live according to the tenets that God provided for us in the Bible; otherwise, he will not be spending eternity with the Lord."

"This is strange. There are many Christians that my parents have as friends, but I never heard them talk like you. They live neither the way you mentioned nor the way you and your family live. You are the first Christian I have ever met that lives and talks this way. The ones we know smoke, drink, and use foul language, do you think they go to hell? Does a nominal Christian, as you define them, go to hell?"

"No, Dalal, I am not sending anyone to hell, only God is the judge of that; that's His domain. There is no reason to differentiate between the kinds of Christians here, for God has no labels, religions, or denominations; do you agree?"

"I guess, I don't know, but go on."

"In God's sight, my dear friend, and according to the teachings of the Gospel of Christ, there are two kinds of people, those who believe, and those who do not, or more accurately saved and unsaved, a child of God or a child of Satan. The former spends eternity in heaven, and the latter in hell."

"In your view, Amal, who is a believer? Who is a child of God? Am I a believer?"

I noticed that Amal became tense at my question; I was wondering why she became uncomfortable, and couldn't answer every time I asked her a simple question related to me. I did not relent, uncomfortable or not, I pressed on with my questions, "Amal, do you consider me to be a believer? Am I a child of God?"

Before she could reply, the door opened and my parents walked in. When they saw us standing on the balcony, they rushed toward us, surprised that we were still awake; it was nearing 2 a.m. I could smell alcohol as they came closer to us; it was the smell of whiskey, which I detested. They asked us to go to bed, and then left the room. Amal and I were also astonished we stayed up until this late hour; time just flew by because we were having such a good conversation. Amal began to collect the dishes and whatever food was left, but I told her to leave them for the help, they'll take care of them in the morning. But again, she refused, telling me that since we brought them here, we should take them back ourselves, which we did. We lay down on our mattresses on the floor and turned off the lights but continued our chat, "You know, Amal, this was a very enjoyable evening; I can even say it is one of the best I ever had."

"Me too, and I owe you an answer to the question you asked me earlier—whether you're a believer or not. I don't want to rush my answer; we'll talk tomorrow; good night Dalal."

"Good night, Amal."

Amal did not go to sleep right away, she sat in bed, head bowed and eyes closed, mumbling some words I could barely hear. I figured she was praying, as usual. She went on for about ten minutes, and I was wondering what a person could say for ten minutes? When she finished her prayer and put her head on the pillow, I asked in a whisper, "Amal, did you pray all this time?" She whispered, "Yes."

"God gives us twenty-four hours a day, don't you think He deserves at least a few minutes from us?"

I could not respond to what she said; I tried to sleep, but sleep would not come, as I tossed and turned in bed. A few minutes later, I asked her again if she had prayed for me.

"Yes Dalal, good night."

"Really, you prayed for me?"

"Yes, I did. I always pray for you."

I was silent again; Amal thought I had slept, but again, I asked her in a whisper, "Did you pray for me last night, after our dinner, together?"

"Yes Dalal, I prayed for you and all your family, now go to sleep."

"Amal?"

"Yes?"

"Why did you pray for me last night?"

Amal sat up again, and with a stern tone of voice, she said, "This is the last answer for tonight; I am so sleepy now, and I'd like to catch a wink before the sun rises. We prayed for you because we love you. After we went home that evening, Mom and I felt that we should pray for you especially after my mother spoke with your mother about religion. Mother felt that your mother might have been irritated, a bit, by what she said; at least that was how it seemed. We were afraid you might take the blame because of us. So, we decided to pray for that special situation, and that everything will come to pass in peace."

"Let me understand this clearly, Amal. You thought mother was irritated by something your mother had said and were afraid that I would get flack for it because the invitation was my idea? Is this what led you to pray for me? Is this correct?"

"Precisely, you must have read my mind, now will you please go to sleep?"

"Amal, just one more question; I promise it'll be the last. How did you feel when I asked you the next morning to come over and spend the night?"

"We were all thrilled, and we thanked God for having answered our prayer. Good night."

"Good night."

I thought, perhaps it was not my tears and sadness, after all, that changed my mother's attitude towards the Shaheen family, from one of anger and disdain to an attitude of love, as well as saving my friendship with Amal, but it was the prayers of the Shaheens—it must have been.

Amal did not keep her promise to answer my previous question (about me being a believer or not), at least not yet. I did not like to think she was ignoring me or that she could not answer me. One cannot ignore such an important issue, but I gave Amal the benefit of the doubt by thinking that it was all due to our preparation and hard work for the final examinations, which indeed did not leave us the chance to be alone or free.

Final exams were over; both Amal and I were among the top three of the class. I was certain mother was preparing a big bash for my seventeenth birthday, as well as celebrating the high grades I received. Surprisingly, she was not as excited as usual, even up to the evening of the birthday party on June 25. That day, Mom slept until almost noon. She later got up and asked me to go with her for lunch near her boutique, and walk a little to window shop downtown. We spent an exaggerated amount of time at her favorite restaurant, and afterwards, she took me to boutique 'Dalal' to show me the latest fashion arrivals. It was getting close to eight o'clock in the evening when we decided to head back home. I must admit, I was a little apprehensive about mother's surprises; my hunch was that my birthday would not take place at our house, since we both spent most of the day outside it. My mother must have something completely different, other than the usual, for my birthday.

When we arrived home, it was darker and quieter than normal. There was no one in the kitchen, which was also quite unusual, and any smell of food was absent. Suddenly, our housekeeper, Salwa, came over to tell us that father was waiting for us in the garden. As soon as we reached the stairs leading to the garden, a big shout startled me, "Surprise! Happy Birthday, Dalal."

The lights were turned on, and more shouts were heard. Hundreds of balloons took off into the sky amid the applause. I looked around with amazement, yet extremely pleased to see everybody I loved—my parents, relatives, classmates, and friends; all the household employees, including our Gardner Abu Wafiq were all there. Of course, Amal and the twins were there, too, cheering and, seemingly, quite happy.

I was just thrilled to see all of them. I had no idea what happened to me at that moment, but I stood there stunned and crying. My father came running towards me to take me in his arms, "You're crying, and I thought you'd be elated instead?"

Wiping my tears away, I said, "If there are tears, Dad, these are my tears of joy. I cannot tell you how happy I am this evening, especially since everybody I love and care for is present at this occasion."

I looked around, further, to see if Amal's parents were present, but I could not spot them. I looked at Mother intently; one look is worth a thousand words; then I said to her, "Thank you, Mom." Then, and before I could ask Amal about her parents, two clowns appeared from behind a tree. They did things clowns normally do, and everyone was laughing and enjoying himself, especially the children who were screaming with laughter, as expected. I was extremely happy to see all the people who never had the chance to attend my birthday parties before, and invited this time, especially our household help and gardener. These people meant so much to me; they cared for me since my birth and loved me as much as my parents did. What a wonderful idea that they were invited; this was the first time Mother did this. So I went to her and gave her the biggest hug I could muster and told her exactly what I thought. She backed away a little, as though to take a breath from my suffocating hug, yet she did not respond to what I said.

The world could not hold me for the joy I was experiencing, despite the fact my mother was not looking so happy; something was bothering her, and I could not put my finger on it. I thought perhaps she felt pain because of my strong hug, but did not realize it might have been a real pain of pride masked by fake smiles—I did not want to extend my fertile imaginations any further, so I continued mingling with the guests to share my joy. The clowns gave me the lion's share of attention because I was the main attraction. In a couple of minutes, they took off their masks and to my surprise and, apparently, everyone else's—including my mother's and father's—they were Dr. and Mrs. Shaheen. Those alone added so much more to my joy that evening and made me realize that Amal had planned this whole party. Even the food was a surprise. There were no tables full of the usual feast for the occasion; everything was American, down to hamburgers, hot dogs, ketchup, and potato chips! What was even stranger, everybody was eating this fast food with an insatiable appetite; even those who were used to the finest foods. By now, it was obvious that the Shaheens, and in particular, Amal, were the ones who prepared and organized all this. I kept my gratitude down to a minimum, lest I upset Mom again; I avoided looking her in the eye.

I loved hot dogs, but we hardly ever ate much of them, since we thought they did not measure up; but that evening, I was eating them as though I were famished, or in a famine area, and not counting any calories. Even my father was eating them with a great appetite; I think he had missed eating this type of food since the time he studied abroad. When dinner was over, Amal suggested I open my gifts; everybody was jostling to sit around me to get a prime look. All had those ridiculous looking hats on their heads, with even sillier noisemakers in their mouths. 'Uncle' Wafiq looked especially funny. The atmosphere felt more like a New Year's celebration than a birthday party. A very simple cake was brought in, compared to the skyscraper cake I used to get. For sure, Auntie Nancy baked it. It had the shape of a rabbit with the candles stuck in the ears and belly. As I tried to blow the candles off before the wind beat me to it, a beautiful voice suddenly filled the sky; it was Amal's voice. "Where did she get a voice like that?" I wondered. That was another surprise of the evening; I wanted to stop her to ask her why she kept this a secret. Amal never told me she could sing, but I let her continue. I blew out the candles; once, twice, and a third time, to no avail; this must also be one of the Shaheen's tricks, again. By then, all realized the trick except 'Uncle' Wafiq, our gardener, he volunteered to help me blow them off, so he took a deep breath and almost blew the cake off the table, but nothing happened, as the candles only grew brighter. Everybody was bursting with laughter, until he realized what was going on; he never heard of such candles before.

That unforgettable evening, the evening of my seventeenth birthday, I'll always remember. Dr. Shaheen, that sweet and intelligent man, and his lovely wife, were accepting congratulations from everyone for their hilariously clownish performance. My grandmother would not leave to go back to her house unless we promised to take her to visit Auntie Nancy. My classmates said this was the best birthday party they had ever attended; my cousin Majdi was so happy to be around Amal all evening, apparently thinking of some future possibilities. My father looked at least ten years younger, wearing casual clothes, coupled by the joy he was experiencing. Even Mother, who I was able to read like a book, was also happy, laughing, and being amused, even though she must have felt outdone by the neighbors who made the evening memorable. This also showed her that a little expense could match her extravagant undertakings, and that money alone could not buy joy & happiness!

It was a truly memorable evening for me; I did not want it to end, nor did I want the laughter and smiles on everyone's faces to ever stop. I just wished I could stop time, so that evening would continue, forever.

Chapter 4
FIGHT EVIL WITH GOOD

*O*ur annual summer vacation was fast approaching, but this year, we decided to skip Europe, and instead, go to the United States to visit my Aunt Sue, and her children, whom I had not seen in a long time, in Los Angeles, California. I had been to the United States when I was six years old, but I could not remember much of what I saw or did. Two years ago, I desired to go to the United States, but this year it felt more like a punishment to me because I really wanted to spend the summer with Amal. This idea, however, was not feasible. When departure day approached, and we placed all of our luggages in the trunk, I ran towards the Shaheens to bid them farewell and give them some pictures taken at my party.

Prior to our trip, Amal and I spoke at length about the time we would have to spend apart to prepare ourselves, psychologically, for the impending separation. We agreed two months was a long time, but they soon would become history, and we would be back together. We also agreed to communicate by phone or mail at least once a week. Furthermore, we agreed that none of us would cry at time of departure, and so on. Nevertheless, that was not to be; we began to cry uncontrollably. I then made a quick exit to lessen the pain, forgetting to give them the pictures. I went directly to my bedroom and dropped face down on the floor, next to my bed, crying my heart out. As I was turning over, my eyes caught a book between the nightstand and the wall. I grabbed it and it felt like a raggedy old book; somebody must have used it a lot. I opened it, and I saw the name Amal Shaheen written on it. I wiped my tears so I could take a good look at it and saw the title of the book, which said, "The Gospel of John." I wondered what this book was doing in my room under my bed and how did it get there! Then I remembered that Amal may have forgotten it here when she stayed the night over. "What should I do with this book?" I wondered. I thought of three options, and I must immediately exercise one of them as my mother was calling me to hurry and come down so we could leave for the airport. The first option was to take the book and give it back to Amal and give her the pictures, the second option was to give it to Abu Wafiq to deliver it, thus avoiding another round of a tearful good-byes. The third option was to take the book with me to remind me of Amal, and then return it to her upon my return from vacation. I chose the third option, placed the book in my handbag, and headed down to the car.

If I had kept my composure and was no longer crying, I thought to myself, perhaps the Shaheens would have prayed for us for a safe trip, but I am sure they have done so in their hearts. Soon enough, we were airborne.

Now I was thinking, "Where and when do I start reading Amal's book? I wanted to take it out and begin reading it to pass the time on our long trip to California. However, I did not want to upset my mother and jeopardize Nancy Shaheen's favor of being on mother's list of acceptable people, despite being on the lower rung so far. For his part, my father had no reservations or any concerns of my reading anything that belonged to the Shaheens, because he trusted them fully and liked them wholeheartedly. I was certain that he would admit to that if I were to ask. They expressed no envy, hatred, position-grabbing, foul language, profanity, backstabbing, or any political ambitions. How comfortable it was to be around such people without having to worry about talking or discussing things freely with them, as well as having to worry about the consequences. My friendship with Amal was a genuine friendship of love and respect with no ulterior motives or hidden agendas As for my family's wealth, Amal did not have a shred of envy in her, for wealth was the last thing on her mind, and for me, I only wanted her love, friendship, and companionship—for she seemed to be the sister I never had. I did, though, let my imagination wander, thinking I could still have the chance to become her sister-in-law, if through a twist of fate, I were to marry her brother. At this point, I had to stop my wild imaginations from straying any further, for I did not intend to marry anyone I had never met before. Even if I did meet and fall in love with him, the Shaheens and us were of different religious persuasions, and generally, in Lebanon, inter-marriages are not acceptable and not practiced widely. This taboo is rarely breached. That said, I do love the Shaheens and envy the spiritual calm and peace that fill their hearts. What type of envy was I experiencing? Perhaps I should not call it envy, but a 'desire' would be more fitting. Yes, I do desire to be like them. These thoughts raced through my mind as we landed in London. Two hours later, we were on our way to the United States; in a few hours, we would land in Los Angeles to see my aunt and her family.

We had an awesome meeting at the airport. Everyone commented on what a beautiful blossoming lady I turned out to be, showering me with many redundant praises.

My oldest cousin, who seemed to pay me a lot of attention since he set his eyes on me, said, "It's true that we have many pictures of you, Dalal, but they do not do you justice; you look far superior."

My aunt had four children, two boys and two girls. Mona, the youngest, was twenty-two, and Suheil, the oldest, twenty-eight. They all seemed bright, gentle, and good-looking—none was married yet. We had a great reunion at my aunt's house a little more than a block away from the Pacific. We mainly spent the evening discussing family matters, achievements, future plans. Then my mother asked with a bit of laughter, in her Lebanese way, "What's the matter, guys? Are there no eligible men and women in America? Why has none of you gotten married yet?" She then turned towards my aunt and with a serious tone of voice as though chiding her, "It's entirely your fault, Sue; yes, it's entirely your fault. If I were you, I would have found them spouses a long time ago, especially the girls; they're so beautiful. Why are they still single? How could this be?"

Everyone laughed, especially Mona who joked, "Thank God, Auntie, you're not our mother, poor Dalal."

We spent a good deal of time talking about this subject. Finally, Suheil put his hand on my shoulder, drew me close to him, and looked me in the eye saying, "And what shall we do with this beauty here? When shall we find her a husband? Who will be the lucky man to win over this flower?

He said this, as he pulled hard on my arm, hurting me a bit. My blood rushed towards my face, and I tried to pull myself away from his firm grip, but he was determined to get to know his cousin quickly and surely, whatever the cost. As the evening progressed, each began to go back into the house to retire for the night, tomorrow was another day.

Suheil, who like most American young men his age, lived alone, stood up and planted a kiss on my cheek as he was leaving, a kiss I had hoped was just an innocent, brotherly kiss.

We all went to our respective bedrooms; my room happened to be Suheil's old room, it had that masculine touch to it. My parents slept in the guest room on the upper floor, away from me. I tried to sleep that evening, but I could not, and as usual, I began to analyze the events of the day, fearing what might develop as long as Suheil was in the picture. Perhaps I was wrong, and his behavior was all too innocent. I tried to dismiss it as such, but without much success; the way he behaved, still bothered me. I then remembered Amal's book, and thought that was a good time to start reading it; it might be the cure for my insomnia. I got up, brought it into bed, and began leafing through. I wondered how anyone could read such a book; it was full of scribbles, highlighting, and underlining. I did not want to read it in any serious manner now, but was planning to read it later, when I felt more comfortable, more focused. However, my curiosity was stronger than my feelings, so I began to read the first page, especially concentrating on the highlighted lines. The first sentence read, '**In the beginning was the Word, and the Word was with God, and the Word was God.**'

I could not understand what this meant, but Amal had drawn circles around the word 'Word,' and written 'Jesus' above each. This translated as such, "In the beginning was 'Jesus,' and 'Jesus' was with God, and 'Jesus' was God."

I began to understand what I read, and I liked what I read. The words cut deep into my heart and mind. I then began to repeat them, and every time I did, the word 'Jesus' sounded so sweet, that it left me with some semblance of exhilaration. I began to love this name— Jesus—although that book made Him God, which was a no-no in our religion, I still felt He was close to me, and I loved to hear that name, even when I did not know much about Him. I did not want to read any further that night, but was satisfied with that what I had read thus far. With that, I fell into deep slumber with those words still echoing in my mind.

After having had a good night's sleep, I woke up the next morning at the sound of laughter and chatter. I went to the window to see what was going on. Everyone was on the beach; they looked like they were sitting on water. I showered and put on my bathing suit and went to join them. As I walked out, I remembered something and ran back to my room. It was Amal's book (Gospel of John) under my pillow. I had no idea who was going to make my bed, and did not want anyone to discover it, so I put it back in my handbag remembering the sweet words I memorized the night before. I believe these words caused me to sleep comfortably, so I began to recite that same verse, but could not stop there. I then opened the book and read some more, hoping to find similar words like the ones I liked, so I could repeat them and make my day a happy one. I read until I reached the verse that says, **"All things were made by Him; and without Him was not anything made that was made. In Him was life; and the life was the light of the men. And the light shineth in darkness; and darkness comprehended Him not."** Amal had also circled certain words she deemed important. 'All things' was circled, and replaced 'Him' with 'Jesus', so the verse read as such, All things were made by Jesus; and without Jesus was not anything made that was made. In Jesus was life; and the life was the light of the men. And the light shines in darkness; and darkness comprehended the light not—or Jesus. I folded the corner of that page, put the book in my handbag, and began to repeat the new words I just read. I stood by the window, again pondering the vast ocean and this huge universe that Amal's book says that Jesus had created. How about me? Did Jesus create me, too? If I am included in 'all things', then He must have created me—He must have given me life—my life. How Jesus the man could be God, I wondered. I was lost here; I felt in need of more clarification, but nonetheless, those words also sounded sweet, and I left the room, although somewhat confused, but feeling quite happy and content.

All stood up to greet me as I headed towards them, but they waited until I finished breakfast before presenting me with an agenda for our first day in California. My father was in the habit of relying on my mother for whatever she arranged on our travels. However, this time, they both decided, since this was my vacation, I should prepare the plan for our daily activities, so everybody looked at me to hear what I had in mind.

"If it were really up to me, my preference would be to stay here today, relaxing, and lying in the sun on the fine sands of the beach. So if you want me to be comfortable, that's what I would like to do," I said that as I plunged into the surf. My parents liked the idea, as both loved the beach, except perhaps, Mother, who was afraid the sun might add a few wrinkles.

As my father soaked in the sun, Mother told him to use sun block to avoid a burn. As she began rubbing cream over his body, and at the same time, talking with my aunt, she abruptly screamed, "What's this?"

Everyone looked in her direction, and my father quickly jumped up to see what was going on.

"What's what?" My father asked in bewilderment.

"This lump here," pointing her finger to a little lump she saw near his waist.

My father got up and looked at where mom's finger was pointing, and felt it with his own finger. We all worried a bit, but were at a loss not knowing what to do, particularly my father, who despite his manly personality, was a true 'baby' when it came to his health. Suheil's arrival, with his vitality and loud voice, distracted us from father's 'lump.' No sooner had my cousin arrived, than he began to tease me and joke around.

In reality, I did not know my cousins at all, except from the pictures they used to send us occasionally. I learned that Mona, who recently graduated from college, worked as a nurse at some local hospital. I found her to be so congenial and sweet, which was a perfect fit for her career. Mona was also frank and open. She was the type of person who called a spade a spade, and always invoked the name of God. Had she mentioned Jesus' name, I would have asked her if she were one of Amal's friends!

Her brother Ashraf, older by two years, was a computer engineer for a large corporation. Although he was born in the United States, it seemed the western culture did not affect his Middle Eastern culture and behavior much—only his accent was quite American. Leila, twenty-six, was exactly the opposite of her siblings; she had a striking resemblance to my mother—beautiful and attractive—with a flair for fashion and elegance. She also had a strong personality, and did not seem to care for anything having to do with religion or Lebanese traditions. She even had a boyfriend whom she dated regularly without her parents' consent and without any regard to Middle Eastern traditions and culture. Furthermore, Leila worked at her father's business in new home construction. As for Suheil, I did not have to ask much about him, since his parents never missed a chance to talk about him and his accomplishments as a successful engineer in his father's firm.

My first impression of my relatives, so far, gave me the following conclusions: Ashraf, Mona, and I are from the same cut and expect to become real friends. Mom and Leila will spend a lot of time together; what Mother does not know, Leila does, and vice versa. My father will have to put up with my aunt's husband—for his sister's sake—who is always proud of his accomplishments and accumulated wealth. My aunt will do her utmost to make me her daughter-in-law, while Suheil will do his best to win me over. Similarly, I will do my best to avoid him. My mother will make sure to keep everybody worried about the lump on my father's waist.

My predictions were all realized. Ashraf, Mona and I became best friends, and were always together. Since Leila was nine years my senior, I did not get close to her as much as I did with the others. Suheil's behavior was more or less along the lines I expected or imagined. He often told me that he fell in-love with me at first sight, at the airport. He followed me around like my shadow, trying to win me over, and would often bring me flowers and gifts. Moreover, every time we went somewhere, he would insist I sit by his side. He even moved back into his parent's house so he could get to know me better. Everybody seemed to notice his behavior, which became somewhat out of the ordinary.

My mother worried so much about my father's lump, which distracted her from noticing what was going on, or if she did notice, that was not her priority, now. She turned into a bundle of nerves when the doctors told her that it would be advisable to have the lump removed.

My aunt was well aware that her son was chasing me around, and she encouraged it. At first, I thought I was making too much of his actions towards me, after all, he was eleven years older, and in a few weeks, we would be returning to Lebanon—everything then would come to an end. His behavior, however, could no longer be characterized as brotherly, or that of someone who is trying to entertain a cousin he had not seen since childhood. My fears were confirmed when one late evening he took me home, intoxicated, after a jolly party we both attended, despite my objections to his driving in such a condition. I hated the taste and smell of alcoholic drinks, apart from my religious convictions. I always felt that alcohol debased people who drank it, and they were no longer in control over of any their senses. As Suheil drove home in his convertible, erratically, he was singing loudly along with the radio at full blast. His looks seemed strange, that made me feel uncomfortable! I pleaded with him to turn down the music, which was giving me a headache, but he did not heed my pleas. We almost had a terrible accident, but he did not notice. We finally made it home, as the car screeched to a halt, to my relief. He then proceeded to pull down the cover. At that point, I promised myself never to go anywhere with him again. However, before I reached for the door handle to get out, I felt two strong hands grab my arms; Suheil then took me by surprise, when he abruptly held me and kissed me, uncontrollably! His awful liquor breath only added insult to injury; I attempted to extricate myself from his strong clutch, but failed. I felt he was turning into a beast, so I began to cry out inadvertently, "Jesus, Jesus, Jesus, help me." I pushed him away with all the strength I could muster, which I never knew I possessed, and I ran out of the car.

As I ran, my foot slipped, and I fell on the gravel. I got up, not minding the fall; all I wanted to do was to enter my aunt's house before he could follow me.

I did not know whether it was my fortune or misfortune that nobody was at the house. The only person present was Mary, the housekeeper, who opened the door for me and looked dismayed by my disheveled appearance. I ran to my room and into the shower to remove the stench of liquor and smoke that hung on my skin and hair; and hopefully, the water would remove the painful memory of that evening. The cut on my knee was worse than I had thought, initially; it was bleeding profusely and required attention, as dirt and gravel lodged under the skin. I called Mary to ask her help in cleansing the wound, but she remained silent all throughout the ordeal—she did not even ask what caused the cut. However, her heavy silence was very telling; she truly might have understood what happened. She seemed very concerned as the treatment ended with a silent, "Good night."

I could not sleep at all that night, nor did I read The Gospel of John as I did the nights before. I was terribly concerned and worried about how to behave the following day.

Should I tell my mother and create problems in my aunt's house, or should I tell Mona and her brother Ashraf about Suheil's behavior? On the other hand, perhaps I should let my father know and exclude everyone else, I asked myself? I was confused; I did not know what to do. Suddenly, I remembered something that made my heart stop with fear. My mother had told me that morning about her going with my father to Washington, D.C. to see a physician there, Dr. Munther, an old friend of my father's, who practiced medicine at Johns Hopkins University; he would be the best choice to look at the lump on my father's waist. She had already made all the necessary arrangements to fly there and see the doctor. Our initial plan was to spend a month and a half in Los Angeles, then my parents would fly to Washington,

D.C., for some business, and I was supposed to stay behind at my aunt's house until they returned. This very thought that I would be alone here for any further harassment from Suheil made me shudder; in fact, it made me cry. I tried to rationalize that, perhaps, what had happened with Suheil, was due to excessive alcohol, but I wanted to make certain that nothing of the sort would ever be repeated that might cause problems at my aunt's. Yet, this rationalization did not help matters; I felt that I needed Amal by my side, and I wished she were here; at least I could give her a call and tell her all that happened. I needed to talk to someone; I needed Amal's advice. Then as though I heard her voice within me saying, "Pray, Dalal, pray." But to whom do I pray, and what do I say? Then I remembered when I felt in need and in danger, how I cried out "Jesus, Jesus". In my subconscious, I felt Jesus was the only one who could really answer my prayers and keep me safe. I knelt down and prayed to Jesus, asking Him to lessen my pain and give me a good night's sleep. This prayer made me feel much better, and I slept like a baby, only to wake up in the morning with my menstrual pain. I took a tablet to ease the pain, and then I went back to sleep, intermittently, until my mother's voice woke me up.

"Are you still in bed? This is the result of staying up late."

When I did not reply, Mother sat on the bed near me and stroked my hair with her loving hand saying, "Dalal, I want to tell you something very important that perhaps you didn't notice, so please try to understand. I know that Suheil is a wonderful gentleman who possesses traits that every mother would love to have for her daughter's husband, but he does not seem good enough for you; besides, he's your first cousin, and he is several years your senior; simply, he's not what I expect for you."

I wanted to lift up my head and ask her why she was bringing this up. Moreover, I wanted to know what traits, what husband she was talking about. Just the mention of Suheil's name at this moment disgusted me; I, however, remained silent, mainly because my mother never stopped talking, and the excruciating pain has not abated. I was not able to move; but she continued, "It seems your aunt and everyone else are happy about the chemistry between you and Suheil. I could see it in her eyes as you and Suheil went out last evening; she even hinted that she'd like to have you as his bride. I am just telling you all this so you will be aware of what's going on. And now, get up, or have you forgotten?"

I had really forgotten, so I asked her, "Forgot, forgot what Mom?"

Mother kept repeating, "We're having lunch at Danny Thomas's, the famous American-Lebanese actor, have you forgotten? Isn't this your dream to meet him? We were barely able to make this appointment, and you're asking; "What? You forgot?"

Yes, Danny Thomas and how could I forget? After such a long wait to meet him and now, I forget! This was truly a dream to meet this world-famous comedian and actor, as I was proud that he accepted to meet us, for lunch! My mother immediately realized that my period came at the wrong moment; she knew how painful my periods always were, and how paralyzing they could be. Then, as she got up to leave, obviously irritated, I muttered to her, "Mom, please take me with you to Washington, I don't want to stay here another day." Then I began to cry, incessantly. My mother panicked at what she heard. She came back running, asking me for an explanation. I told her everything that happened between Suheil and me, and that I did not ever want to see his face again. Then, I showed her my injured knee and told her how painful this bad experience was.

For a second, I thought Mom would turn the world upside-down, because of what I had told her, especially in regard to Suheil's. I was shocked when she quietly asked if anyone else knew about this. When I replied in the negative, she said, "Good, let me arrange things, and don't worry about staying here, you'll go with us to Washington on one condition—that you would not tell your father about the incident; he has enough problems now." Then she left the room.

How strange it seemed for my mother to behave in such a nonchalant manner. How could she have kept her cool at such news? How will she go have lunch with Danny Thomas when her own daughter was almost killed the night before in a car accident, and whose a close relative almost assaulted her daughter, as well? I could not understand her attitude except from this angle: that she did not want to create problems in my aunt's house while we were staying there. Nevertheless, I was more than content and relieved that she would be taking me along to Washington.

Everyone felt badly for my illness, but despite everything, they all went to have lunch with Danny Thomas. Just a little less than two hours after they left, I left my room, still in pain, limping my way towards the kitchen. I saw Mary, the housekeeper, reading a book while sipping coffee. Mary was a tall African-American woman, probably in her late forties, with a sweet, kind, and congenial personality. I did not communicate much with her, save for a few words we exchanged since we came here. I learned she was a widower who'd worked at my aunt's house for over ten years. I wanted to ask her to make me a cup of tea to drink with my medicine, but I did not want to distract her from her reading and relaxation that she probably needed.

I walked quietly and stood behind her where she could not see me, in order that I could peek at what she was reading; it turned out to be similar to the book I had seen at the Shaheens'. The sight of that book delighted me and made me forget my pain for a minute. I greeted Mary with a polite and formal, "Good morning." She immediately closed the book and stood up to ask me if I was feeling better. I told her I was feeling a little better, and I asked her to bring me some food with a cup of tea.

While Mary was preparing the food, I sat in her chair and randomly began to turn over the pages of that book. The title on the cover read, "The Holy Bible". The Holy Bible! That was the first time I held that book — the whole book — not just a portion of it, like Amal's book. When Mary saw me leafing through it, she said, as she was placing the food on the table, "This is my Bible — the best friend I have. When I am down or sad, it comforts me, when I feel weak, it gives me strength — I don't know what I'd do without it."

I did not know why I decided to pray before eating; it just came to me, spontaneously, upon seeing the food. Perhaps I wanted to thank God for his provisions, just as Amal used to do, or maybe I wanted Mary to see me pray. Perhaps with such a gesture, she would open up to me and talk about this book — and about Jesus.

I was so eager to learn more about Jesus and welcomed it at any occasion. I closed my eyes and bowed my head without uttering a single word. When I opened my eyes, I saw Mary looking intently at me, expressionless. That look was special, but I was unable to interpret it. Mary then gave me a huge smile that added charm to her looks, and sat opposite me at the table, as if each of us were waiting for the other to say something. She finally broke the silence and said, "You had me worried last night, Miss Dalal; I knew you must have had a bad day, so I prayed for you."

"Prayed for me? How nice of you Mary. Thank you so much — I needed it, indeed."

Mary kept looking at me, expecting me to say more; she sensed there was something wrong and wanted me to share it with her. I was about to tell her, when I changed my mind and asked her about the Bible instead, which I was still clutching in my hands.

"I am so sorry I interrupted your time of relaxation with your best friend. Will you forgive me and tell me something about it?"

Mary chuckled when I used her own expression, 'best friend', and joy seemed to flush over her face; this must have been a golden opportunity for her to tell me about her beloved friend. She somehow managed to explain to me that the Bible has sixty-six separate books, and is divided into the Old Testament and the New Testament. The Old Testament deals mostly with the history of the Jewish people, as well as the many prophecies concerning the coming of Christ, the Messiah. The New Testament, on the other hand, summarizes the fulfillment of these prophecies, the birth of Jesus, His works, and His eventual second coming. It also consists of the four gospels known in Arabic as *"Injeel"*. Additionally, it tells us about the birth of Jesus, His life on earth, His teachings, His death and resurrection, as well as the miracles He performed. The remaining books talk about His apostles and the epistles they wrote.

Mary explained all this to me, as though she was lecturing to hundreds of people at a seminar. From what she explained, I understood enough to ask her where the gospel of John falls; she said that it was one of the four gospels, in which the author speaks about the divinity of the Christ. It is the only gospel that begins with this fabulous verse: **"In the beginning was the Word, and the Word was with God, and the Word was God."** Of course, Mary recited this in poetic English, streaming softly and sweetly out of her mouth; I felt our spirits were united, speaking the same language. This gave me a great deal of satisfaction that exuded with trust in her person. I told her I had a lot of questions that I would like to ask her, but in confidence. I made certain I mentioned Amal and the relationship that developed between us, including the deep impression her family had made on my life. Moreover, I told her about how I happen to have Amal's copy of the gospel of John. Furthermore, I also found myself telling her that I loved Jesus and would like to know more about Him. Finally, after having gained her trust, I spilled out my deep secret regarding Suheil's behavior the night before, without holding back from telling her everything that took place. Just because I knew she was a real

Christian—unlike those nominal Christians—as Amal would say, I opened up my heart to her and gave her my love and trust. This African-American woman, despite our differences, felt closer to me than I could have ever imagined. We barely had anything in common: race, status, language, age, culture, religion. I might have probably never bothered to acknowledge her existence under different circumstances, but at this point, I regarded her as a dear friend and a confidante. It is certainly amazing how Christ can bring people together and change their feelings and attitudes.

Mary and I spoke for several hours; I asked her questions, and she gave me answers; I sought, and she guided. I was the blind woman, and she was the cane leading me through darkness. Telephone calls from my mother inquiring about me, as well as calls from Suheil who was dying to talk to me, sporadically interrupted our discussion. Perhaps he did not believe Mary when she kept telling him I was not feeling well and could not speak to him. Suddenly, the door swung open and Suheil barged in. He seemed to have been surprised at my unkempt hair and my appearance in general, especially the paleness in my face and the agony it reflected. He stood like a statue, staring at me with expressionless eyes. I apologized for my appearance, excused myself, went into the bathroom to at least comb my hair, wash my face, and put some clothes on. I wore a long skirt to hide my scraped knee, combed my hair into a ponytail, and applied some blush to hide the paleness of my cheeks. I returned, with confidence, to face my cousin who was pacing the garden, his shoulders somewhat slouched, grim-faced, with signs of embarrassment and remorse.

I was feeling good, except for some pain in my knee and the limp that I was trying to mask. When he heard my footsteps, he looked at me and noticed my limp; then he rushed towards me, asking why I was limping. I told him it was due to a misstep that I took, and consequently, fell down and hurt my knee—but there was nothing to worry about. I gave no hint that it was due to his reckless behavior the night before. I was sure he knew, as he asked me, almost sorrowfully, "Tell me, what really happened? Tell me that you fell running away from your disgusting cousin, that the pain is not in your knee, but because you lost my trust. Rebuke me with the harshest words, do not spare me your anger, for I deserve more than this."

He fell to his knees in an effort to kiss my feet and apologize, but I did not allow him, as I suddenly felt pity for him and how the same glass of wine, which energized him the night before, humiliated him a day later. I thought, if I had the chance to rebuke him last night or even this morning, I would have given him a load of my anger and chastisement. Somehow, I was not prepared to tell him anything now. No, I was not ready, not now, nor later, after the long talk on forgiveness and the love of Christ, I just had with Mary.

"Let's forget about what happened; I forgive you; besides, we're cousins, and I love you like a brother. Let's just behave as if nothing happened, before I travel with my parents to Washington, soon."

Undoubtedly, Suheil was expecting the worst from me, but he stared at me with frozen eyes. Mary had advised me earlier and explained how I should behave with Suheil if I wanted to win the battle, and that a kind word is sharper than a two-edged sword. I was now reaping the fruits of her advice because I could sense victory. Perhaps Suheil was suffering more now than he would have had I chastised him and hurled at him all sorts of insults. I was sure of that. My forgiveness was his condemnation, for he began to hit his head, saying, "You gave me nothing but suffering since I first set eyes on you, and I was even satisfied with it, but now you're killing me with your kind words and forgiveness; all my hopes are dashed."

After Suheil said this, he left hurriedly, almost bumping into Mary who was watching us. She then looked at me and smiled. I raised my head towards heaven and thanked Jesus because He first helped me in dealing with Suheil properly, and second, because He gave me a new friend called Mary Graham.

My mother kept her silence regarding the incident; she was planning to deal with it in a manner that would not cause any problems. Everyone was under the impression that my parents would soon be traveling to Washington leaving me behind at my aunt's house. She would have to break the news that there was a major change in plans, but how would she go about letting my father know? I did not want to bother much with the issue, so I decided to leave it to my mother to carry on with her plan since she always had a way. I felt good that I would be traveling with my parents, thus avoiding any further confrontations with Suheil. At the same time, however, I felt very sad and wished to stay longer at my aunt's house so I could learn more from Mary, as well as further explore with my cousin, Mona, her interests in knowing Christ as Mary had suggested earlier. I felt intrigued by this prospect, seeing how the two of us became interested in Christianity. Unfortunately, or maybe fortunately, I did not dare to hint that I wanted a change in my mother's latest plan.

Suheil did not fully stay away from visiting and spending some time with the family, but these visits became increasingly scarce and low-key. His conversations with me, in the presence of others, were quite polite and short, but whenever he found me alone—a rarity because my mother always made sure I was not left alone—he behaved differently. One day, he came to visit when my mother was not around and badly wanted to mend things between us. He begged and pleaded for my forgiveness and wished I would give him another chance to prove he never meant to behave in such an improper manner, and that what had happened was due to alcohol. He also promised never to touch another drink as long as he lived. However, when all his effort to regain my trust failed, he became uptight and hot-tempered at the slightest irritation, especially towards his sister Mona who was always with me. It seemed he wanted to take it out on her instead of me. Everyone noticed his new, strange behavior; especially my aunt, who it seemed, had a long talk with him behind closed doors. As she came out, she remained silent but gave me those long, hard looks that were obvious expressions of blame and displeasure. There was no argument or any question-answer session; her behavior toward my mother and me—especially me—drastically changed for the worse.

I had no idea what transpired between her and her spoiled son, Suheil that caused this sudden change in her behavior. I did not think Suheil told her about what happened that evening, but I was sure he must have told her how cold I had become towards him, and no longer paid him any attention. No wonder no one was surprised when at breakfast the next day, my mother announced we would all be travelling to Washington D.C., and from there, fly directly back to Beirut. This solution sounded agreeable to all, considering, the situation that had developed, and no one seemed to mind or object. The only person who expressed any surprise was my father, but he would not question my mother's decision nor object to it. My cousin, Mona, on the other hand, was the only one who tried to say something, but was evidently overcome with emotion, as she left the room crying and headed towards the beach. I promptly followed her, and on the warm sands, we both cried silently. I was crying because I was not leaving my cousin Mona of the past, but my friend and sister of today. I was also crying because I knew I may never see Mary again, and hear her tell to me about Jesus and His wonderful teachings. Mona was crying because she was going to miss not only a new friend in me, but also a sister who understands her and shares with her the same sweet feelings. Although we did not articulate such thoughts, they, nonetheless, were in our hearts. We did not mention Jesus when we were together, not once, but we both knew we were seeking the same truth of Jesus.

The few remaining hours at my aunt's were tense, especially when my mother told everyone there was no need to accompany us to the airport. Silence was so thick and heavy, and conversations were short and dry. The worst moment was when Mary and I were saying our good-byes when we were alone in her bedroom. I cried on her shoulder while I removed a gold bracelet from my wrist, and I quietly slipped it on her wrist, as a token of gratitude and love. She then got up, went to the closet, and brought me something wrapped in gift paper and asked me to hide it well in my suitcase. I was almost certain it was her mother's Bible that she promised to give me earlier when I asked her about one that looks exactly like Amal's—with black and red underlined verses. I took it from her and pressed it against my chest as I was wiping away my tears and preparing to leave.

I did not find it awkward to bid farewell to my aunt's husband nor to Leila who gave me a cold kiss on my cheek. I neither had a problem in bidding my aunt good-bye, but felt her kisses were genuine, so I reciprocated likewise. I found it difficult to bid farewell to Ashraf; we were both crying. One day he would know the truth about what ensued between Suheil and me, and his brotherly love will return towards me as it had always been; he apparently did not know the whole story, the way it happened. It took nearly five minutes to bid farewell to Mona, as we both were engaged in a lengthy hug, at times crying; and, at time, laughing and promising each other to keep in contact by phone and mail. At that moment, Suheil suddenly appeared, hurriedly, and shook hands with my parents. As soon as Mona and I unlocked our hug, we stood there looking at him to see what he was going to do next. I noticed that Mary was looking at me, smiling, as if this would be the last time she will ever see me; perhaps through her anxious smile, she was trying to tell me something. It was certainly an awkward moment. Then all of the sudden, I mustered enough strength to go and give Suheil a hug and a good-bye kiss that I planted on his cheek. He looked stunned, as he certainly did not expect such a gesture from me! He hugged me back, and with some cautious hesitation, gave me a tepid kiss on the cheek. I looked at him and smiled to assure him that all was well with me, and forgave him his transgression—he understood. He then stood by me, still holding my hand and said, "At this moment, I feel I owe everyone an apology, especially my cousin Dalal. I would have never said what I am about to say if it were left to my pride, but I feel compelled to confess and say that I behaved irrationally and stupidly with Dalal. I had no idea what values my aunt and uncle instilled in their daughter, but I never met anyone before who resisted evil with good, blame with forgiveness, and hate with love. I congratulate you for such good upbringing."

With much courage and remorse, Suheil went on to tell everything that had happened on that ill-fated evening, with me. Heavy silence hovered over the hall as he ended his speech. I could see Ashraf wiping away the tears from his cheeks, as he looked at me, begging my forgiveness for his misinterpretation. My aunt sat down, wearily, on a nearby chair, her head hanging between her hands, and wept, uncontrollably, without saying a word. Her tears said it all. Her husband stealthily slipped out of view, losing himself in the big house, not saying a single word; he must have been shocked. Leila stood by her brother, patting him on the shoulder, to reassure him his 'heroic' admission of guilt; despite the huge embarrassment he caused himself and the family. My mother, with a dropped jaw, looked at me, wondering who might have taught me to be such a forgiving and loving person, resisting evil with good. My poor father's eyes widened as he heard Suheil, and looked at my mother with a transfixed gaze of dismay. Without uttering a single syllable, he headed straight to the car. No one noticed the beautiful smile of victory on Mary's face, except me, as she waved to me for the last time. In my heart, I could hear her repeat those beautiful words from the Bible, **"Therefore, if thine enemy hunger, feed him; if he thirst, give him drink: for in so doing thou shalt heap coals of fire on his head. Be not overcome of evil, but overcome evil with good."**

The airplane took off at one o'clock in the afternoon and headed towards Washington, D.C. Less than half an hour after takeoff, I closed my eyes in an attempt to get some sleep, but instead, I began to rehash the events of the day in my mind. It included lots of smiles, and obviously, some tears. I awoke twice during the six-hour trip, once to drink a glass of juice, and the other due to a heated conversation between my parents. My father's tone was that of anger; he was visibly upset and his words were harsh. I was able to gather that he was upset because my mother had kept from him all that happened between Suheil and me. I heard him say he felt slighted, as though he did not exist, and he was the last to know. For the first time, I heard him talk harshly to my mother, in a voice that was, at times, somewhat threatening!

"When it comes to my daughter's safety and integrity, or her future, it does not matter how trivial or serious the issue might be, I must be the first to know — It is then up to me to make a decision, is that clear?"

I pretended I was fast asleep and did not move a muscle. Nevertheless, I deeply felt proud that my father reacted in such a manner, and always wanted him to be the master of the household. I suppose he was all along, but he shunned confrontations, which I took to be a weakness! I kept pretending to be asleep until the conversation and the anger slowed down and heard my mother apologize, though explaining why she kept him in the dark. She promised she would never again hide anything from him that had to do with me. After that, both became silent when the captain announced the landing in Washington.

After our arrival, we went to the hotel; my mother promptly went to bed, pretending she was tired and had a headache. My father took advantage of her absence and asked me to change my clothes and wear something 'chic' so he and I could go to a nearby restaurant to have dinner and talk. I liked the idea, and in less than an hour, we were inside the fancy restaurant, where the owner was waiting for us. He led us to a choice table, close to a dance square, where a live musical band was playing beautiful music. The cozy and elegant atmosphere made my father forget all he had to endure that day, and was back to his old happy disposition. He asked me for a dance, but I told him, "After we have dinner," as dancing on an empty stomach did not set well with me. We both laughed and began looking at the menu. When the waitress came to take our order, I asked if they had any hot dogs. I like the simplicity with which Americans approach things; if I had asked for a hot dog at a fancy restaurant in my country, I would have probably gotten a haughty look and a knee-jerk reaction, as this lowly hotdog would be considered insulting! Nonetheless, the waitress told me that even though hot dogs were not on the menu, they would be more than glad to prepare me some, although she also might have wondered about my choice, but without showing it. Anyway, I ordered one all-beef hot dog with French fries. That was what I really craved and wanted to eat. When it was my father's turn, I thought, for certain, he would select the choicest seafood they had, as he usually does; but instead, he told the waitress he wanted the same, including a glass of red wine. By then, I was certain the waitress was wondering why these people came in here, just for hot dogs, but she never even as much as raised her eyebrows. We both chuckled; we were so nicely dressed only to order hot dogs!

Soon enough, we changed our conversation and talked about Amal and her family, and my last birthday, which came to mind. I told my father about my desire to see Amal and her family, and that I missed them; I was counting the days to see them again.

"My goodness," he said, "That family must have won your affection, what is it Dalal?"

I told him that their character and certain habits they had—like praying before every meal, while holding hands, had really impressed me. I also mentioned how nice it was for a person to thank God for the blessings He provides. I had no idea how I mustered enough courage, then, to ask my father, "Why don't we pray before our meals—or even afterwards Dad? Why didn't we thank God for arriving safely from California, as there are so many dangers, flying? There are many people around the world who go to bed hungry every night, some even die of hunger. Can't you see how short we fall in this respect? Don't you agree we don't thank God enough, Dad?"

I could not tell whether my father was irritated or pleased by my questions, but he seemed deeply affected, by the way he kept looking at me, until the waitress brought us the food. How the aroma of food can influence the hungry; as soon as the food was on the table, I dug into it as a hungry wolf would. "Aren't you going to pray first, Dalal?" my father asked, to my astonishment.

The mouthful of food almost chocked me, and I felt embarrassed; at the same time, I was surprised my father cared enough to remind me of what I had just preached; nonetheless, I smiled and said, "How about you pray for both of us, Dad?"

I said this, knowing he would not do so in public, but, he bowed his head and began to pray with his eyes open, "I thank you, the all merciful and all benevolent God, for all your blessings upon us, and for our safe arrival."

He uttered this simple and short prayer as best as he knew how and began 'devouring' his hot dog from evident hunger. He raised his glass of wine to tell me, "To your health sweetheart," and asked me if I wanted a little sip.

"I hate the taste and smell of wine, Dad; you know that."

He then remembered what I went through a couple of days ago, because of alcohol, and he looked the other way with obvious sadness and anger. The words I heard Dad ranting to my mother on the plane, and chastising her for covering up that ill-fated incident with Suheil, he repeated to me, but with a different tone of voice, a tone of hope, rather than blame. He took my hand, squeezed it tightly, and he told me to look him straight in the eye, "Promise me, Dalal, that you will never hide anything from me; promise that I'll be the first one you come to with any problem that might come your way; you must trust me in and with everything."

As he told me this, the band began playing a beautiful song I liked so much. What he said touched me deeply, but I dared not open my mouth to say a word, lest I become emotional and ruin the evening. Instead, I got up, took him by the hand and led him towards the dance floor. We danced to the beautiful music while I buried my head in his broad chest, and I felt he must have understood my love for him, even without uttering a single word.

My mother's pretense of a headache took longer than expected and became problematic. She was somewhat still upset with my father when he raised his voice, once in his lifetime, and expressed his displeasure with her. Although he apologized numerous times after that, she apparently was punishing him in a passive-aggressive way, by refusing to accompany him to his official visits or even go sightseeing. Now it was up to him to show me around Washington, which he gladly did. We had a great time sightseeing in this beautiful city, visiting all those wonderful and historical monuments. On our last day of sightseeing, a congressman, and a friend of my father's, accompanied us on a visit to tour the White House. It was a truly grand place to visit, where history continues to be made. It is also a place where the most influential world personalities live and visit, at one time or another.

There was nothing left for us to do in Washington except for one more reception the Lebanese Embassy had planned in my father's honor. The list of guests included a plethora of influential and successful Lebanese émigrés, Arab politicians, and other foreign and American dignitaries.

It was Saturday morning when my father and I were having breakfast, while my mother was away at the hairdresser, in preparation for the evening. We sipped hot coffee, laughed, and had a good time, when, suddenly, my father sighed deeply and said, "I miss you Dalal."

This took me by surprise and I retorted, "Miss me? You see me every morning and evening, what do you mean you miss me?"

"I didn't know you that well; before, I mean I never spent any quality time with you to get to know you better. I feel that I have just gotten to know you for the first time this week, and now I feel that every moment I don't spend with you goes to waste. Life is short, it is a travel station; we're here today, gone tomorrow, not knowing what will take place in between. This is the reason I like to spend more time with the most precious person I have. You suddenly grew up and matured; the important thing is that you became a new person to me this week."

We were both silent for a while, then he asked, "Tell me Dalal, what prompted you to treat Suheil so nobly, holding your tongue about the whole episode? It is unlike you to be silent and forgiving, over-coming evil with good, blame with forgiveness and hatred with love. I had no idea you were like that; I don't think it was your mom's influence, so — what happened all of the sudden, can you tell me?"

I did not know how to reply. I was afraid to tell him that I read it in the Bible, but when he insisted, I said, "I heard a voice within me telling me, **'Be not overcome with evil, but overcome evil with good,'** and that's what happened."

"If this is true Dalal, then I must also do likewise; I should call your aunt in California and let her know that nothing has changed between her and me and that I still love and appreciate her just as much as I did before. What do you think?"

I did not reply, but instead got the phone, dialed my aunt's number, and handed it to him. They spoke for a long time. Of course, I was not able to hear what she was saying, but I could make out the gist of the conversation from his replies. In summary, my aunt apologized for her son's behavior with much emotion and tears. She was elated that my father was not angry and had made amends with her, without any further negative feelings. She also told him he was so fortunate to have a daughter like me. The strategy of forgiveness worked, it proved the best weapon against revenge.

My father seemed happy and relieved after his conversation with his sister; he told me I was right — we should overcome evil with good, then he looked at me and said that whoever becomes my husband is 'one lucky guy'. I naughtily agreed with him, but asked if I will be as fortunate? Only the future could answer this question. To this, my father sat up in his chair, crossed his legs, and clasped his hands together.

"What qualities do you wish to have in your future husband, Dalal, and what conditions would you require of him?"

"What a difficult question to ask, Dad, especially coming from a father to his daughter."

"I know you are still too young and don't have anyone in particular at the moment, but it would be nice to give me an idea of your opinion of the man you would desire for a husband."

I got up from my chair, sat on his knees, put my arms around him, and whispered in his ear, "My wish is to have a husband with your qualities, Dad: loving, generous, kind, noble, good-looking, and quite intelligent. I need him to be confident of himself so I can honor him; truthful, so I can trust him; strong, so I will not fear for him or be afraid of him."

I saw a tear trickle down my father's cheek, and to relieve the tension of an emotional moment, I mixed a serious moment with some humor, "Another important quality of the man of my dreams is that he prays before meals and likes to eat hot dogs!" We both chuckled, albeit my father retained a serious look, sighed, and said, "Do you think I'll live long enough to see you become a bride and give you away to the man of your dreams?"

What he said is a common question every parent asks his daughter, but the way he said it sent a shiver down my spine, "Dad, are you OK?"

"I am afraid."

"Afraid?"

"Frankly, yes; in two days I'll be going to the hospital, and—"

"Dad, this is not like you; you are Salah the son of Suleiman— afraid? You're afraid of a small lump on your waist? It is nothing, Dad; you'll be out of the hospital in a couple of hours after you check in."

"You're still a child Dalal, these things should not be taken lightly, size means nothing, and lumps begin small then grow larger, soon enough, and it could become malignant. I am not prepared for anything like that; there are so many things I still have to do; besides, I hate doctors and hospitals."

I wished I had been able to comfort my father, other than with the usual words of comfort—the likes of 'do not worry, everything is going to be OK,' for such rote clichés would only increase his fears. I wanted him to look up to Almighty God, our only hope and comfort; I then remembered a verse I had read in the gospel of John, **'All things were made by him; and without him was not anything made that was made. In him was life**—' I wished that I could say this to him, and point out the source of life—Jesus—but unfortunately, my knowledge, experience, my courage or lack of it, did not help. I did not want to open a Pandora's Box at this critical time. Then, a bold idea clicked in my mind; I held my father's hand tightly, and in a voice full of confidence said, "Don't be afraid, Dad; I'll be praying for you. I'll ask God to touch the lump and remove it completely, and that He will give the physicians wisdom and guidance to do their work, properly, so you can be out of the hospital in no time."

I had no expectation and could not foretell his reaction to my words. He did not draw me closer to him, nor did he squeeze my hand or embrace me, as usual, whenever I said something good or intelligent; but he did not show anger, nor did he smile. He did not even thank me for my concern, my feelings, or my abundant love for him; but at the same time, he did not ignore what I said. He finally looked intently at me and said something that shook me up, "I was like you at some time in my life: simple-hearted, innocent as a child, when I became your age, my heart was full of faith—your words about prayer and the assurance your words display, awaken precious memories in me. I need your prayers, Dalal, I believe in prayer, or at least I used to—keep on praying for me, Dalal."

"I promise, I will keep on praying for you, and you too, keep praying for me, Dad."

Our last evening reception in Washington was one of the classiest and best-organized events I have ever attended. My father was in good spirits, mentally and physically. He looked so handsome and self-assured, as he mingled with all the dignitaries. He looked even better when he took to the podium and delivered his speech. I thought he was going to deliver a fiery political one and show his well-known oratory skills that always rang with substance. I also thought that the audience would strongly applaud him, for he loved his country so much, he was willing to give his life for it. However, he began his speech with a question, "What can I do for my country that I love so much?" Then he built on this question.

What kind of introduction was this? The idiom was completely different from what I had expected. I expected usual clichés or expressions that cause people to explode in applause, but today was different; the speech was balanced and emotional; he sounded like a father challenging his children to love each other before anything else, 'for here where the love of one's country begins.' He continued, "Violence has made us weary, and has exhausted us in every way. Hate became our master, and vindictiveness tied us up; although selfishness steers us, it will not give us a clear conscience, and if this is lacking, we cannot reap the grains of sacrifice, but rather, the fruits of evil. When we reap evil, we cannot offer goodness to build a free country and become a sovereign nation. Moreover, we deceive ourselves and shout, "We built a nation. No, my dear brothers, nations cannot be built this way."

He spoke at length, and freely, on this subject, from a true and sincere heart, as he terminated his speech with another question, "What must I do to build a true nation, and not a hollow structure of a nation built by fancy words?"

He answered his own rhetoric with clarity, "To build a real nation, we must replace violence with kindness, vindictiveness with purity of heart, and harm and hate with true love." To my surprise, his last words were, "**Be not overcome with evil, but overcome evil with good.**"

I was the first to begin a standing ovation for what my father said from the bottom of his heart. There were no loud cheers, or great applause, but his speech certainly stirred the audience, as they were overcome with emotion, including my mother, as nearly everyone wiped away tears they tried to hide, without much success. The tears, accompanied by reserved applause, were tears of appreciation and agreement with the substance of this emotionally charged speech, which will likely be remembered for a long time to come. It was a speech of vision, free from embellished vocabulary. I alone knew what inspired this speech; he thought I gave him the idea, and I thought I got it from Mary, my aunt's housekeeper; and she, in turn, knew she got it from her Bible; but in fact, the inspiration came from Jesus, Himself, who overcame evil with good.

Chapter 5
THE LOST FRIEND

*O*ur next destination was the city of Baltimore, barely an hour's drive from Washington, where the famous Johns Hopkins University Hospital is located. I was sitting in the backseat of the car observing how my mother stroked the back of my father's head, a gesture of reassurance. She kept reminding him of how much she enjoyed last night's reception, and how great his speech was. Then I heard my father tell her how fortunate he was to have a wife like her and a daughter like me. I had no idea how or why the thought of death came to my mind at that instant. The image that death could take my father away, as well as how life would be without him, made me shudder. I let out a scream, completely involuntarily, "No, No." My parents were startled and looked back at me. I tried to compose myself but did not tell them the real reason—that I may be having anxiety attacks at the thought of my father's mortality—so I made up something about seeing a near-miss accident on the highway; they seemed convinced and went on with their conversation.

I tried unsuccessfully to drive this anxiety away. I attempted to think happy thoughts about Amal and the joy and excitement we would share, when I would call her later that evening to let her know I was at the hospital where her brother was. I also tried to picture how I would meet her brother, and wondered how much he knew about me. Did Amal tell him about her new friend? None of these happy thoughts seemed to be working; death had lodged itself in my mind and remained with me until we reached our hotel. I wanted to share my seemingly unreasonable anxiety and fear with someone other than my family, so I took advantage of my father's early retiring to bed to call my aunt's house. I had hoped that Mary would answer the telephone, and in case she did not, I would make up something to ask to talk to her. Luckily, I did not need to make up that excuse—Mary picked up the phone. She was excited to hear my voice, but before she could say a word, I asked her, "Mary, is this a good time to talk to you? Are you alone?"

Yes, Miss Dalal, I am alone," she answered with her usual gentle voice. "I am all ears, and am listening to anything you have to say, how is everything with you Sweetie?"

I felt relieved to hear her, and I began recounting the events of my trip so far, including the speech my father gave at the embassy reception, which was indirectly inspired by the words she shared with me about evil and good. I tried to contain my excitement so my parents would not hear me. "Believe me, Mary, I was feeling so happy; I felt joy and strength engulf me—and—and—but suddenly—"

Sighing, Mary interrupted me, "The enemy came to sow the seeds of doubt and fear in your little heart in an attempt to reverse your victory with your Dad, and change it to defeat, see, he always wants to change your strength into weakness. He attacked you through a tiny opening in your mind, entered in, and wreaked havoc with your thoughts. Isn't that what, exactly, happened, Miss Dalal?"

"Yes, Mary; that's what exactly happened, but how, how did you know, and who's that enemy you're talking about?"

"He's the 'debil', Miss Dalal."

"The devil? God forbid. Why would the devil try to fight me? What have I to do with the devil?"

"Because he doesn't want people to get close to the Creator; he does not want us to trust in God and worship Him; it is for this reason he fights us tenaciously and creates doubt in our minds. His only job is to drive us away from God; that's what he tried to do with you."

"But this is scary."

"Of course it is, as long as we are ignorant of his evil ways and schemes. But when we become aware and familiar with his intentions, then we can fight him back with the weapon that God provides for us to fend his attacks and defeat him."

"What do you mean, we should know the devil as he really is? I'm afraid I don't know what you're talking about."

"The debil is a coward and flees right away when we resist him."

"But how should I resist him?"

"We can resist him by the greatest name—the name of our Lord Jesus Christ—the only wonderful and Holy name that brings terror to the debil and causes him to flee."

"And how do I know the thoughts that bother me are from the devil, so I can fight and defeat him?"

"Because Jesus does not torture us and confuse our minds, nor does He leave us pray to the debil. He promised to give us full joy and peace that no one can take away from us; and anything that tries to take these away from us, is from the debil. And when we mature and become strong in spirit, we can easily discern which thoughts are from him and which are not."

"But how can I grow and become strong in the spirit?"

"How does a baby grow?" I thought Mary's question was somewhat naïve, but as a student stands before his teacher, I replied, "He drinks milk, eats baby food, and sleeps to get rest, as babies do."

"Ezzactly. It is the same way a baby believer grows, he needs to eat spiritual food—which is the Word of God and the rest, comes from our dependence on the Lord. What happens to the child if he doesn't eat, drink and sleep?"

"He will die," I said sheepishly.

"The same thing happens to us, Miss Dalal, if we also do not get fed and rest on a daily basis, we begin to become spiritually weak. Then doubt, fear, worry, hate, hypocrisy, lies, and all kinds of sins will attack us and leave us spiritually sick. The debil then becomes happy."

"What is the point of all this, Mary?"

"Nothing scares the debil away like praying to God; this is the secret formula for defeating the debil. Prayer is a line of communication between you and God; it opens up His throne for you. It is the vehicle by which to solve the problems which might encounter in our daily life. But hear me well, Miss Dalal; for God to answer our prayers, there's a requirement first—you must make a decision to surrender your life to Christ."

Mary kept on talking for a long time, teaching me to rely on God's promises. She did not leave me be before she gave me certain passages that I should read in the Gospel of John and go back to them whenever I was troubled. She also told me that the only real friend I would always have, in times of need, is the Word of God. Mary also promised to pray for my father's health, both his spiritual and physical wellbeing. She promised she would never forget to pray for me as long as she lived. I was not sure what she meant by some of the things she said—such as surrendering to Christ—but it was getting late, and I decided to ask Amal to explain them to me when we met.

Five minutes after our phone conversation, I heard a cough and footsteps. My mother walked into my room, she seemed to be coming down with a cold or suffering from some sort of allergy. She asked me if I knew where the handbag filled with medicine was. I got up to help her look for it so she could have a restful night. Before she left, she advised me to sleep soon so we could all get up early in the morning to accompany my father to the hospital. I tried to get some sleep, but could not. How could I go to sleep when I was so curious to read the passages Mary told me about? I said to myself, "My friend John, as much as I would like to read what you've written in your gospel, please forgive me if I just read them quickly tonight, but I promise to study these passages, and also memorize them soon."

I opened to John 1:29, according to the list Mary gave me, and began to read, **"Behold the Lamb of God, which taketh away the sin of the world—"** Then followed by John 1:34, **"And I saw, and bare record that this is the Son of God."** I noticed that Amal had underlined this verse and circled the word "this" and wrote 'Jesus' above it, so it now read, **"And I saw and bare record that 'Jesus' is the Son of God."** As I reached the third chapter of John, I read verses 3-5, **"Jesus answered and said unto him, Verily, verily, I say unto thee, except a man be born again; he cannot see the kingdom of God. Nicodemus saith unto Him, how can a man be born when he is old? Can he enter the second time into his mother's womb, and be born? Jesus answered, Verily, verily, I say unto thee, except a man be born of water and of the Spirit, he cannot enter into the kingdom of God."**

This passage was quite difficult for me to comprehend, but nonetheless, I continued reading only to see what the content was rather than trying to study it. I began to read John 3:16-18 which had so many highlights in different colors and circles here and there that it was barely legible. I finally was able to read it as follows, **"For God so loved the world that He gave His only begotten Son, that whosoever believeth in Him should not perish, but have everlasting life. For God sent not His Son into the world to condemn the world; but that the world through Him might be saved. He that believeth on Him is not condemned: but he that believeth not is condemned already, because he hath not believed in the name of the only begotten Son of God."**

I paused here to look at my watch; 1 a.m. I was not able to read further, what I read gave me enough food for thought for the time. The words struck deep down in my heart with their richness and eloquence. I wanted to reread them and try to understand them fully, and read what Amal had notated all over the margins and between the lines. Moreover, I was eager to find out why she had scribbled her name all over the page, so I began to reconstruct the sentence until it read, "For God so loved 'Amal' that he gave his only begotten Son that if 'Amal' believes in Him, Amal should not perish, but Amal has everlasting life."

I then understood that the phrase "For God so loved" was a personal kind of love, and that I could also put my own name, where Amal had put hers. The verse would then read, "For God so loved 'Dalal', that he gave his only begotten Son that if 'Dalal' believes in Him, Dalal should not perish, but 'Dalal' has everlasting life."

"I liked that." This verse began to mean something personal to me, and I felt so 'special'; I loved hearing my name inserted in there; it sounded so good and sweet; in our religion, there is nothing like that. I then put the Holy Book under my pillow, closed my eyes, and began repeating this verse until I memorized it. Furthermore, I tried to replace my name with my father's name to see if the name Salah would also fit well within the verse. It also sounded as good and sweet. I now really understood the meaning of 'whosoever'. I also began to try other names in place of 'world'; I tried the names of known criminals and wicked people of past and present to only realize that the love of God, the richness and the beauty of this verse never changed. I then became certain that God did all He could for the benefit and salvation of man, and that any if man should perish in hell, it would be his choice and not God's. I finally fell asleep while repeating John 3:16.

I woke up the next morning only when the phone rang; I was still half-asleep when I offered a drowsy "hello". I was surprised to hear my mother at the other end asking me with some anxiety, "Are you all right, you had me worried, this is the third time I called your room."

"Where are you, Mom?" I asked with a voice of surprise, "Where are you calling from? It is still dark."

"What dark are you talking about? The sun is going to set shortly; open your eyes, open the curtains, and look at your watch."

I hopped out of bed, and in panic looked at my watch, "It is 1:30 p.m., Mom. Why didn't anyone wake me up? How could you go to the hospital without me?"

"I wanted to wake you up, but your dad refused when he saw you in deep sleep and felt that a cannon could not wake you up."

"But I wanted to be with Dad—"

"Believe me, sweetheart, this day is not for you or even me to be there. I've been anxiously sitting here in the waiting room since the early hours of the morning and have not seen your father yet. I have a bad cold; the doctor advised me not to get too close to your father, as they would not want him to catch my cold before surgery."

"They're going to operate?" I was beginning to panic.

"I'll let you know when I see you later; I'm on my way to the hotel."

My mother returned to the hotel, her face flushed, and could barely talk. She took some medicine to bring her temperature down; it seemed her cold was not a mere cold, but a full-fledged flu. She hurried to bed to get some rest so that she could get better soon, and we could both go to the hospital. It was a sleepless night for my mother—and me. The morning did not bring any hope as she was in a terrible condition. I had no choice but to go to the hospital alone.

My father burst into laughter when I told him about my mother's fears for me of taking a cab and coming to the hospital by myself. He also felt badly when I told him about her illness. In a moment, he held my hand tightly to reassure me that my presence was the greatest gift he could ask her, and he would not exchange it for anything in the world. He then asked me if I had prayed for him as I promised; I responded with an emphatic yes, and went on to reassure him that I would continue to pray for his well-being. A few minutes later, they took him to the operating room and upon a special recommendation from my dad's friend Dr. Munther, a nurse came and accompanied me to his office, which was close to the lounge where nurses and staff take their breaks so I will not be completely alone and overcome. It was also close to a small cafeteria if I needed to eat or drink something.

I had not had breakfast yet; the smell of food coming from the cafeteria made me realize how hungry I was. I went and got a piece of toast, butter, and a cup of coffee and sat at a small table eating and observing the movements around me when I noticed a young physician in a white coat sitting at a table close to mine. He seemed to be the center of attention, almost everyone who passed by stopped to chat with him; and those who did not, either waved at him, calling out his name, or just yelled out, "Hi Danny," or "Good morning, Dr. Roper," or just a simple "hi". He was sipping coffee and reading a newspaper.

He did not seem to mind the interruptions at all, but I thought he was either disinterested in what was in the paper, or too congenial and kind to ignore his colleagues. My mind was wandering again, thinking whether it would be appropriate to start a conversation and perhaps inquire about my friend Amal's brother. Why not, that wouldn't be too forward; I am here, so I might as well. With that, I turned and gazed in his direction, until I caught his attention. He smiled cordially; with that I immediately spoke my rehearsed words, "Doctor, may I ask you a question?"

He broke out into a big smile, and said, "Of course you may, but that does not mean I have a correct answer."

I replied equally cordially, "My question is quite simple; it only requires a yes or a no."

"And what might your question be, young lady?"

"Do you happen to know a doctor by the name of Shaheen—Samir Shaheen?"

"Yes," he said, looking at me quizzically, which made me feel a bit uneasy.

"You said yes? Continue please."

He laughed and continued: "You just said your question requires a yes or no, and I am saying yes—my part is done."

When he realized my sullen reaction, and the fact that I was not amused by his joke, he continued, "Yes, I know Dr. Shaheen—Samir Shaheen."

I moved from my chair, got closer to his, and showed the excitement that was building in me, "Yes, that's the man I am looking for; how well do you know him?"

Paper tossed aside, he said, "You might say I know him well; he studies and works here."

I was now intrigued and trying hard to contain my excitement, but went on asking, "Could you please point him out to me?"

He knitted his eyebrows, folded his arms in a defensive posture and seemed to be questioning my investigative approach. I felt I needed to explain. I finally broke what seemed a long awkward silence, and without wanting to divulge too much information about myself, I said, "I do not know Dr. Shaheen personally, but I've heard so much about him, and would like to meet him."

He lay back in his chair, and I found myself sitting in the other chair. He then laughed mischievously, and with a twinkle in his eyes and a lilt in his voice, he said,

"You must first take a number and stand in line; there must be at least a dozen girls ahead of you."

His nonchalant, haughty manner bothered me, and I realized what I said could have been easily misunderstood, so I needed to clarify, "I'm afraid you misunderstood what I was trying to say; Dr. Shaheen happens to be my best girlfriend's brother."

That must have changed his silly tone, as he replied, "Oh, you're Amal's girlfriend. You're Amal's girlfriend?" He asked repeatedly.

"So you know Amal, as well?" I asked.

"I do not know her personally, but I heard so much about her from her brother, and I would love to meet her one day."

I saw a golden opportunity to give him a taste of his own medicine and said in a quiet voice, "Then take a number and wait in line."

"*Touché*" he replied,

At this, we both had a good laugh.

"Where were we? Yes, although I have not met Amal or her parents yet, but Samir happens to be a good friend of mine; in fact the best friend I have ever had."

While we were making small talk, he repeated as if talking to himself, "So you're Amal's friend then?"

"Yes, I am. Amal is also my classmate, and more than that, she's my next door neighbor."

At this point, he exclaimed loudly, slapping his leg, "I don't believe it. I can't believe this; it's getting too good to be true!"

"Believe what?" I retorted.

He did not reply, but instead roared, "You must be Dalal?"

Now, I was bewildered. The blood rushed to my face, and I wondered how he knew my name when I did not remember introducing myself. I kept staring at him in total disbelief. I half-seriously asked him how he knew my name. To lessen the impact of what he said, and to put me at ease, he drew closer to me and whispered in my ear, "I recognized you from the picture. I have your picture." He laughed aloud after telling me this, expecting me to do the same, but this only added to my bewilderment. He was surprised to see me stone-faced and confused, which prompted him to change his demeanor and speak in a more serious manner to put my mind at ease, "Listen—Samir and

I are roommates, we live in an apartment close by; I know how much he's attached to his twin siblings (Rima and Walid), and how much he loves them. Their pictures are plastered all over the walls. He recently received some new pictures of the twins, and you were in most of them. As usual, Samir hung these pictures on the walls. I was forced to look at you morning and evening until your picture embedded itself in my memory."

My mind began racing, "The pictures? The pictures? Yes—yes—I remember the pictures that were recently taken with the twins, running, jumping up and down."

"And how many of these pictures are hanging on the walls?" I asked with a bit of sarcasm.

Laughing, he replied, "Oh, lots and lots of pictures, don't even ask."

I was not upset by any means. How can one be upset with such a congenial young man? He continued, "Sorry, but I didn't ask why you were in the hospital."

I told him about my father's condition, as well as my mother's illness at the hotel. My eyes welled up as I talked about my father's illness. He gently got up, walked towards me, and patted me on the shoulder to comfort me,

"You're not alone here anymore, consider yourself among friends. I am with you and willing to keep you company, that is, as long as you permit me."

His gentle tone and sincere words comforted me; it felt like I had known him for a long time, so I did not hesitate to take him up on his offer; in fact, I was quite happy. We then decided to head back to my father's room chatting along the way. Samir kept coming up in our conversation, and the prospect of meeting him was still on my mind, "Since we're done with surprises and the mystery of my identity was solved, can you now introduce me to Samir, or obtain an appointment for me to see him in the next couple of days? It would be unthinkable not to see him and explain it to his sister that I came to where he works and did not meet him?"

Astonished, Danny looked at me and said, "Seems that surprises are not over yet, there's another one—"

I cut him off, "Please, no more surprises today—all I'd like you to do is introduce me to Samir, so when I get back to Lebanon, I could tell Amal and her parents that I met him—no more, no less. Please, don't complicate matters."

"Well, as much I'd love to comply, it's not possible at this point in time to meet him; see, he happens to be in Beirut now with his parents," Danny replied with a chuckle.

"He is where? What did you say? Samir is in Beirut? You've got to be kidding, right? I had no idea; Amal did not tell me."

"He left two weeks ago; I am surprised that with you two, being so close, as well as neighbors, had no idea!"

"But we left Lebanon about a month ago; I have not spoken to Amal since the day we left. Strange, Amal didn't mention anything about this upcoming trip."

"His trip to Lebanon this summer was not planned," Danny replied. "It was an impromptu trip. He received an invitation to be the main speaker at a youth conference there."

"Main speaker? What youth conference? What are you talking about?"

Danny was speaking as if I knew what he were talking about. Then as we walked, he stopped and leaned against the wall, and became more serious; as though talking about his dear friend necessitated more respect on his part. In less than an hour, Danny told me more about Samir than Amal had told me in one year.

Before Danny's exposé of Samir, I was under the impression these two friends must be two peas in a pod, especially since they were roommates. To get along sleeping under the same roof requires it, I reasoned; but Danny's narration about Samir was completely the opposite. He said Samir is a dynamic speaker who constantly receives invitations from various churches for speaking engagements. He was a role model for many young people, and he took that role very seriously, in addition to being a successful, upcoming physician, who also took that vocation seriously.

Danny also told that Samir was a consummate Christian, who loved the Lord deeply, and who walked with integrity in his Christian faith, to the point of becoming a medical missionary serving his Lord and Savior in poor countries. Danny was talking to me in a language he thought I knew, as he had no idea I was not born in a Christian home, nor knew much about the Christian faith.

Danny was very serious when he talked about Samir's life, both his profession and faith. He curtailed his humorous side every time he spoke about his friend Samir, and his eyes widened, reflecting the pride and respect he had for him. Danny's own personal faith in

Christ resulted from Samir's ministering to him, he told me. Time was running short, but Danny told me he would tell me the story of his coming to Christ and the role that Samir played, later, in bringing him back to Christ.

At the end of our conversation, I felt as if I was at some sort of a religious service or just returned from a pilgrimage to some shrine. All the anecdotes I heard about Samir, who was thousands of miles away, at the time, made me more eager to meet him.

"Well, it looks like meeting him now is out of the question," I said with a deep sigh, "I only wanted to meet him so I could carry his news to his parents when I returned to Lebanon. But now, after all I heard about him, I could only wish to take a number and stand in line, as you suggested!"

I thought he was going to make fun of what I said, but he replied as if to diffuse my anxiety, "Oh, he might be coming back soon; perhaps you could meet him after all."

I shook my head, "I don't think so; we will be leaving Washington as soon as the doctor allows my father to be released."

"Perhaps you'll meet in Beirut," Danny replied in excitement, as if he invented the wheel; "He is not expected back before the 16th of August," he confirmed.

"No, we won't go back to Lebanon right away because we will be spending ten days in London, what a shame."

"Yes it is, but who knows, perhaps God has a different plan." he replied with optimism.

Our conversation was over, and I headed to my father's room. Danny left after we agreed to meet the next day, so I could introduce him to my father. A nurse came to let me know the surgery was over, that everything went well, and my father was in the recovery room. When they allowed me to see him, he looked fine and seemed in good spirits. He told me he would always be OK as long as I prayed for him. I sat close to him, held his hand tightly, and told him about the pleasant surprise I just had.

I recounted my meeting with this young physician, who turned out to be Samir's roommate.

"Samir, who?" My father asked drowsily.

"Why, Amal's brother, of course."

"Yes, of course" my father replied wearily.

My father had no idea that Amal had a brother, let alone one who was a physician at Johns Hopkins.

I went on to tell him almost everything that had just transpired; and, come tomorrow he would get to meet him.

"Meet who, Samir?"

"No Dad, you're not listening, meet Danny, Samir's friend."

"Ah yes, what did you say his name was?"

"Danny Roper."

"Good, good, tomorrow then, I will get to meet this doctor?"

"Yes Dad. He's also willing to help us with anything we need."

I spent more time with Dad, and when I was sure he had come around, completely, and was going to be fine, I left him and headed back to the hotel. The doctor would let us know the results of the biopsy and other tests they were conducting the following day. Today is over, and it ended on a high note.

My mother was feeling a bit better, but felt she must spend another day in bed so she could fully recover and prepare for our return trip, in addition to the newly-added responsibility of having to take care of my father. She was going to be quite busy in London over the next few days. We had dinner, together, in her bedroom, and spoke about different things; but contrary to what I did with my father, I avoided telling her about Dr. Danny Roper. I had no idea why I felt the need to conceal this information from my mother; it just felt natural not to tell her anything. I kissed her good-night, but felt I must at least share part of what was going through my mind.

"Imagine, Mom, had Suheil not acted improperly with me, I would have not been able to be by Dad's side while you were sick in bed. It is amazing how God's ways are, and how He permits things to happen for our own good." I caught myself talking like Amal here! Of course, nothing can justify what Suheil did, regardless.

She looked strangely at me but did not comment; all she said was, good-night.

Despite struggling to fall asleep, I had a very good night's sleep. As usual, I stayed up late with my newly found best friend—the Gospel of John. It became so dear to my heart that I memorized portions of some passages. Of all the verses that I liked, I loved best the one found in John 14:14, which left a deep impression on me; it comforted me and gave me a new outlook on life, **"If you shall ask anything in my name, I will do it."**

Reading these verses always brought me memories of Mary, my aunt's housekeeper. What a wonderful woman she was, and how fortunate I was to make her acquaintance and become her friend. Yes, what wonderful words they were—Jesus, the almighty God, promised me, Dalal, and told me that He would do anything I ask in His name. This promise and privilege I received gave me strength to carry on. I then asked, in His name, to give me good news of my father's test results.

I was up early the following day, and by ten in the morning; skies were dark and indicated a possible storm. Weather conditions added a feeling of melancholy to that day. I entered my mother's, room, sporting a large smile on my face; but she looked concerned about my father's condition. She also looked completely consumed by upcoming test results. The dark morning worsened, and Mother felt even worse about her illness at that critical time. She complained that this was her third day in bed with no improvement. In other words, my mother felt depressed; and that made me feel badly that I was not able to offer her any consolation. I wanted to tell her about what I read in the gospel of John, but was afraid that she would blame Amal for it. Do I tell her not to worry about my father's condition because I prayed for him and he was going to be just fine? I pondered this for a while, and then decided to do just that. I was being overly cautious with what I wanted to say, as if only Christians pray, but we pray too, worship, and fast. This thought gave me some courage, so I moved closer to her bed and said, "Mom, I know that you love Dad so much, and you fear for him—" However, before I could finish my sentence, she interjected with a question, "And you, Dalal, aren't you afraid and anxious about your dad?"

"No, Mom; in fact, I am not because I prayed for him and asked God to intervene. I am certain God will answer my prayers, and everything is going to be just fine."

Contrary to what I had expected, her reaction was completely subdued, as she mumbled, "*Allahumma* (our God), you are the one who hears and answers. May God hear your prayers, Dalal."

God has already answered my prayers, I thought.

Chapter 6
OUR LITTLE SECRET

❦

I was glad I would be seeing Dr. Roper later on, to introduce him to my father. When I arrived at the hospital, as planned, Dr. Roper and I went into my father's room; we found him sitting on his bed. Dr. Roper approached him, extended his hand and said, "Dr. Roper—I am glad to meet you, sir."

"Salah Abu Suleiman—glad to meet you too, please have a seat; Dalal already told me about you. You said your name was Roper?"

"Yes, Danny Roper."

"I once had an old friend with the name Roper; at one time, he was one of my best friends."

"The Roper surname is widely scattered in the United States, how long ago was that, sir?"

"Oh, long time ago, when I was nineteen; it was the first year when I left my parents and my country to study in England."

"Oh, you studied in England?" Danny asked after he complemented my father for his acquired British accent, then he added with a chuckle, "My father studied in England, too, for about two years, but his accent remained southern USA."

My father was looking at Dr. Roper closely, as if giving him a physical exam when he asked, "What school did your father go to in England, Dr. Roper?"

"Cambridge."

"Cambridge? I too studied there. What is your father's name?"

"William Roper, but everybody called him Billy, and because he was somewhat overweight with some girth, some called him Belly Roper." He said laughing.

I joined Danny with laughter, but my father did not. He kept staring at Danny, which made him a bit uncomfortable.

"Did I say something wrong?" Danny asked, puzzled.

My father assured him, "Please, Dr. Roper, do you mind my asking you your mother's name, as well, because I am developing a strange feeling."

Comforted, Dr. Roper replied, "Sandy Roper—"

My father, wide-eyed, and with a voice rising in surprise, "Is her maiden name Henry?"

"Yes, it is—"

"I can't believe this, I can't believe it," my father exclaimed. He rose from his bed, barely able to walk, and rushed to hug Dr. Roper.

"You are my friend's son—you are my friend's son, Billy Roper."

I responded to my father, in Arabic, as he was wiping his eyebrow from resultant perspiration of excitement. I then sighed and continued, "What are you talking about, Dad?"

"When I first set foot in England, to study at Cambridge, I felt lonely; it was the first time I left my parents and my country. One day, as I stood lost before a large building, I heard some noise and singing coming out of the building. Then I saw a group of young men and women forming a circle. I walked towards them, out of curiosity, and saw a blond, blue-eyed, handsome young man about the same age as mine, but somewhat overweight with a protruding belly. He was playing the guitar, singing, and encouraging the crowd to get closer to one another and become one family, especially foreign students. He spoke of love and friendship in his mellow voice, and I wished I could become his friend, or at least meet him and get to know him.

It did not take long for my wish to come true, because we both lived in adjacent dorm-rooms. It made me happy to become acquainted with him, a young man with an immense sense of humor, and wit, always ready with a joke."

"Billy was the first person I met at the university," my father continued down memory lane, "He was a big help to me in just about everything, as well as my guide to the various buildings, centers, and classes, as that was his second year of college."

We became good friends, and I loved him like a brother. I, Salah Abu Suleiman, an only boy in the family, acquired a brother, as our friendship became deeper and deeper. Then there was the British young woman, Sandy, who he loved so much—we three became inseparable. She was the one who first called him 'Belly' instead of Billy. I must say that this period at the university was one of the best years of my life; but as you probably know, your grandfather was a diplomat and had to travel from one country to another, as most diplomats do. That same year, he had to move to Germany, and Billy had to leave with his parents. This sudden separation from Billy was hard on me, and the university was not the same to me after his departure. I had difficulty coping afterwards, and I, in turn moved back to my country.

During that time, I lost all contacts with him and Sandy. The following year, I returned to England to study at a different university, but all these years, I did not forget my friend and 'brother' Billy. I tried, in vain, to locate him, and I had lost all hope of ever finding him again. That is why when I heard the name, Roper, I could not believe my ears. The nickname, Belly, was the clue. It took me back thirty-six years."

My father took a sip of water, as if to cool down. As Dr. Roper and I were looking at each other in utter disbelief; my father was shaking his head and smiling, also in disbelief, and injecting his narrative with the words 'unbelievable', and 'strange'.

"Come on, Danny; tell me everything about my friend. Do you have any brothers or sisters?"

"This is an incredible story, Mr. Abu Suleiman! Yes—I have a younger brother, John, who is twenty-four years old, and a sister Lillian, who is a couple of years younger."

"Where does the family live today?"

"They all live in North Carolina."

"Tell me Danny—what does your father do these days? If I remember correctly, he was studying to be an engineer."

Here, Danny sat up straight in his chair, as though talking about his father required a great effort. With a smile, he replied, "True, he studied mechanical engineering and graduated with distinction, but he never worked in this field for more than a year. As you may know, since you were a close friend, he is a believer who loves the Lord and loves to serve Him by preaching. Do you still remember?"

What Danny said seemed to have caused a knee-jerk reaction with my father. It was an innocent question, since Danny had no idea of our religious background. My father nodded affirmatively, and after jogging his memory, said, "Yes, I remember he was in charge of a youth group that was held every Friday evening where he played music, sang, and then delivered some sort of lecture. I also remember how he used to make your mom and me—whether we liked it or not—sit for a long time to listen to his lecture to acquire the appropriate training."

Danny laughed and said, "Tell me about it. Yes, I know; he still does the same thing to my mother and siblings."

He looked at my father and drew closer to him as though he was going to whisper something, "Why do you think I live in Baltimore, and Dad in North Carolina?"

My father chuckled at this joke, and said, "Although you did not inherit your father's physical stature or likeness, you have certainly inherited his quick wit."

I was still in disbelief at what I was hearing. I was picturing my father sitting for long hours listening to his friend Billy preach weekly, for a whole year, probably day and night, about Jesus, the Bible, and the Christian faith. This revelation intrigued me, and I sensed a parallel between my father listening to his friend Billy, and me to Amal, about the same subject. I thought that, perhaps, his friend might have influenced him, as I was influenced by Amal. However, one thing I was sure of was that my father must have known about Jesus, and still does, as well as about praying and the Bible. I was now ready to analyze every aspect of this new revelation about my father and Billy Roper, but for now, I had to rejoin in the ongoing conversation and leave the analysis for later, then I said, "I don't know where North Carolina is, or how far it is from Baltimore; perhaps we may have the opportunity to meet your family?"

My father liked the idea and insisted he see his old friend, Billy. Danny said that North Carolina was a bit far from Baltimore, and that his brother John had informed him, yesterday, that their parents went away for a two-week vacation. My father expressed his sorrow that the opportunity might not materialize to see his old friend, "Oh, that's too bad. I was hoping to meet my old friends, or at least hear their voices, but perhaps at another time, when I visit the United States again."

I was listening and noticing how Danny, who seemed to be thinking hard, suddenly stood up, as though he just remembered something he had to do, excused himself for a few minutes, when the phone rang. It was my aunt from California wanting to talk to Dad.

I sat there, continuing to contemplate how I should face my father with the new revelation I just heard. I did not know what to say about all he had concealed from me. What would Dad say about all he heard from his friend Billy concerning Christ and Christianity for over a year? Has he forgotten it, or did he choose to block it out of his mind? Will he tell me that he knows about Christ and even the gospel of John? How will he explain to me this period of his life? Should I ask him about it? So many questions were racing through my mind; I was excited, yet anxious, as I waited for my father to hang up the telephone. However, the conversation took its course and I felt bored, and I got up to look for Danny. Soon, I saw him with a broad smile on his face, carrying what looked like a movie camera.

"If your father can't see or hear my father, I'll show him both my parents. I have them on tape."

My father was in the bathroom when Danny and I entered his room; he took advantage of his absence and set up the film so it would be ready when he returned. Soon enough, the movie clip showed a tall man singing behind a podium. My father sat, uncomfortably, in a chair, trying to figure out what he was seeing. I cannot begin to describe my father's reaction at seeing and hearing his old friend. There was a mix of laughter, tears, nervous reaction, and shouts of joy, as he continued to watch the clips.

Billy Roper looked exactly as my father had described him earlier, a tall, overweight man with an aura of gentleness surrounding him, and a touch of grayness that added dignity to his old friend. As I listened to that religious song, as Danny referred to it, the lyrics captivated and comforted my whole being. The camera was now panning the audience, and towards the back of the hall, a woman was sitting in the middle; and to her right, a young lady and a young handsome man; to her left, another young man. Danny stopped the movie and asked my father, "Do you recognize this lady?"

My father took another good look, rubbed his hands together, and shouted, "It is Sandy. Yes, this is Sandy—incredible. That's her smile, and she still pulls her hair back with a ribbon as she used to, thirty-six years ago. After a moment of silence, he continued, "This handsome, young man wearing the white suit must be your brother, John?"

"No, he's not my brother John; it is my friend, Samir, who delivered the sermon at my father's church in North Carolina that evening; my brother is the one sitting to the left of my mother."

"Your father is a pastor of a church?" my father asked surprise.

"Yes, he is. The church has a little over 5000 members. He spent many years as a traveling evangelist, but at the behest of my mother who got tired of traveling, he decided to settle there and become the pastor of that church."

My father did not pay much attention when Danny mentioned Samir; all his attention was directed at his old friends—Billy and Sandy.

"And who is this beautiful young lady sitting next to your friend?"

"That's my sister, Lillian."

"Wow, she is so beautiful; that's how your mother looked at the university; she's her carbon copy. No doubt this young man must be taken with her beauty, as they both look good together," he went on to add.

"I sure hope so; there could be no better person for her than Samir."

Lillian was truly a beautiful young lady; the lights were projecting on them as though they were a prince and a princess. He looked so distinguished, and she exuded femininity and natural, soft beauty. While my father was engrossed with his old friends, I focused my attention on Samir and Lillian. Although I never met Samir except from an old picture when he was fifteen, which I picked up when it fell from Amal's nightstand, I felt a strange feeling. I could not believe that I, Dalal Abu Suleiman, would feel this way. I was not able to figure out whether the feeling was a feeling of jealousy or envy or completely something else. Samir was certainly handsome; nonetheless, I could not explain the feeling that overcame me then. I had not been aware that the clip moved on to another scene and my father was now intently listening to his old friend's song, as it was winding down.

After that, Billy said a few words I didn't understand, but it sounded like it was a humorous anecdote that caused the congregation to explode in laughter. Danny commented that it was his father's style to always end his sermon with a touch of humor.

"That's my friend," my father proudly declared.

I do not think my father was actually listening to what his friend was saying; he was only listening to his voice and living old memories. He did not even seem to pay attention when he introduced Samir as guest speaker.

Samir, as Danny described him, seemed to be a dynamic speaker with a serious tone of voice. He began his sermon with a voice full of confidence and assurance as he was basically preaching about a Biblical passage, **"For what shall it profiteth a man, if he shall gain the whole world, and lose his own soul?"**

Danny then whispered something in my ear, "You said you'd like to meet Samir; well, here's your chance young lady; this is one way to get acquainted."

Yes, that's what I want; but what Samir was saying, apparently, did not impress my father so much, as he asked Danny to fast forward the clip until where Billy begins to speak again. Danny seemed to be quite familiar with the tape as he went on to wind it only to show his father and the rest of the family. I wanted to scream at Danny for forwarding the film so quickly, thus depriving me, of hearing what Samir was saying. How could I ask him to take me back to where Samir, who captivated my whole being, disappeared from the scene? I had no choice but to remain silent until Samir's message was nearing the end and stepped down to go and sit by Lillian. Soon afterwards, Danny's father, with a smile on his face, took to the pulpit to thank Samir for the wonderful message he had just delivered. He then exhorted the congregation to take to heart what they just heard from this young preacher and surrender their life to Christ. However, certain things he said grabbed my attention, "What will your fortune, wealthy men, your beauty, young ladies, your strength, young men, your education and intelligence, learned men and philosophers, your position, political men, your might, leaders, and your authority, judges, do for you one day when you approach the grave and stand naked before the seat of judgment? For what shall it profit you, if you should gain the whole world and lose your own soul—a precious soul that Jesus died on the cross of shame to save? Do not delay or put off your decision to take Christ as your personal Savior, for the Word of God says, '**Today is the accepted day of salvation.**' No one can know the time or day when they will leave this world. Only one heartbeat separates life from death, so hurry to Jesus Christ, your redeemer, and ask Him to have mercy on your soul. You'll find him stretching His arms to meet you and take you in his arms to cleanse you from all unrighteousness, by His Precious Blood. He will save you and give you eternal life, for as I said earlier, you will profit nothing if you gain the whole world and lose your own soul."

Before the doctor walked into the room, accompanied by a nurse to check on my father, Danny quickly removed the equipment, said good-bye, and left the room. I followed him and he stared at me questioning, "Are you OK, Dalal?"

"Yes, I am." I replied softly, but he kept looking at me as if trying to read my mind.

"Are you sure? Your flushed face and tone of voice indicate something is wrong. Did I behave improperly?"

"No—not at all. I am just fine, but I was affected by what I saw and heard, as well as by both our parents' story. That's all."

Danny seemed convinced, as he also was emotionally affected by the story of our parents and said, "If anyone had told me this, I would not have believed it; and had I known that the movie clip would bother your father, I would not have shown it to him—"

After a moment of silence, he continued, "I thought he would have loved seeing his old friends and family and revive his memory of old times. I wanted to surprise him, but now I don't think it was such a good idea, because towards the end, while my dad was speaking, your father was breathing heavily, wiping away some tears, and he put his hand over his heart."

"You saw him cry?" I asked. "Did you really see him wipe away his tears?"

Somewhat surprised, Danny wondered at my insistence to know that my dad indeed cried, I continued, "Listen, Dr. Roper; there's something I'd like to tell you. We are not like you—" I said that taking a deep breath in an effort to get his reaction, but instead, he simply said, "I too was not a believer; I only took Christ as my Savior just two years ago. You said you're not like us; this shows that you are truthful with yourself, and God can deal with a truthful heart."

His comment told me that he did not understand what I was trying to get across to him, so I made it clear to him or so I thought.

"You mean because you were not born in a true Christian family?"

"No, Danny—we come from a different religious background."

"Oh, I didn't know that; I thought you meant you came from a nominal Christian home. At any rate, Jesus is not only for Christians, for John 3:16 says—"

Here I cut him off because I knew what he was going to say next, so I continued for him, **"For God so loved the world, that he gave his only begotten Son, that whosoever believeth on Him should not perish, but hath everlasting life."** "Isn't this what you wanted to tell me? I asked.

"But how do you know this verse?" Danny asked with a look of surprise.

"Because as you said, Jesus is not for Christians only, but for the whole world, and the Bible is for anyone who's willing to read it—right?"

At this juncture of our conversation, I gave Danny a summary of my life that began when I met Amal, including Mary Graham in California, and my cousin, Mona. I stressed my mother's role in our family life, and indirectly told him to avoid talking about religion or the old friendship between his father and mine, in her presence, if he happened to meet her. I had no idea why I wanted to protect such information, or even why I wanted it to remain a secret. Danny respected this and promised he would be careful if it ever came up. I also asked Danny if he could kindly make me a copy of that movie clip, but he laughed in a sly way, "Don't tell me you were taken so much by my father that you want to see him again, eh?"

I did not reply, but the blush on my face gave him the answer, then he bid me farewell.

I felt awkward as I re-entered my father's room, for I had no clue in which mood he was. When he saw me, he asked, "let us take a little walk because I feel tired of lying down."

"Sure Dad. Can I help you with anything?"

"No. Thank you, I am fine"

"How long will you stay at the hospital? Do you have any idea?"

"No."

"How are auntie Sue and the family?"

"Fine."

"What did she tell you?"

"Nothing."

We walked a little bit, but he did not say much; we then headed back to the room. He sat down and began to read a newspaper without saying anything, so I said, "Since you like to read, I think I'll go back to the hotel and spend some time with mom."

My father threw the paper away as if I had said something to hurt his feelings, "I know exactly what's going on in your mind. I know you must have a thousand questions you want to ask me, but I am not ready to do so today, understand?"

My father's harsh tone took me by surprise. How could he talk to me this way when I did not do or say anything to upset him? I remained silent, looking at him with tenderness, realizing he was going through a period of emotional stress and personal struggle, and that something bothered him about his old friend Billy.

I called a taxi and prepared myself to return to the hotel, but before I left, I heard him call my name asking me to sit next to him. He held my hands, looked at me with tears welling in his eyes, and said, "Sorry Dalal, it was not appropriate for me to talk to you like that; you didn't deserve it. What happened today, wreaked havoc with my emotions, and made me tired. Sorry, sweetheart."

"I thought you'd be happy to see your old friend, Billy, and meet his son."

"Of course I was. Inasmuch as I was happy with such a surprise, I was also saddened and pained."

"Why are you sad, and why were you stressed? I feel guilty because I caused this."

"No, you didn't cause anything; it was mainly my doing. You and Dr. Roper helped me a lot. I promise, one day I'll tell you all about that chapter in my life with the Roper family, and answer all the questions you seem to have."

"How did you know I have questions, and why do you think my questions are about that period in your life?"

"Because they're written all over your face; and I can see myself in you these days, feel your feelings and read your mind. You and I have a common denominator, because today I see you going through what I went through some thirty-six years ago."

"I think you might be right, Dad; I have many questions I'd like to ask you, but not today or tomorrow. I'll just have to wait for the right time when you'll tell me without my asking."

He gave me a tight hug and a kiss to let me know he appreciated my understanding of the situation; but before I slipped out of his hug, I said, "From now until we bring up Billy Roper again—as we saw him today—this will remain our little secret."

My father felt comfortable when he heard that, as if a burden was lifted off his shoulders, and he did not question the word 'secret', but gave me a look I understood too well, and told me how much he loved me.

I returned to the hotel but did not find my mother. When she returned, she looked a lot younger with her new short hair style. It surprised me that she trusted a total stranger for a hairdresser, other than her own hairdresser in Beirut. She told me she wanted my father to see her with a new look after having been ill for the last few days. Poor mother—she thinks a new hairdo will do wonders for her mood. I felt sorry for her, and I left her to prepare tomorrow's program. Only a few minutes earlier, she told me my role was finished, she was now in full control.

Although it would be crass to confess this, I thanked God for her illness so I could get closer to my father, and in this strange way, reconnect him with his old friend, Billy. Who can know the mind of God and the hidden wisdom He exercises in our lives? Could this little secret between Dad and me determine our fate one day? Who knows?

What I expected and prayed for came through. My father's lump turned out benign, and, hence, the doctor removed it. We thanked God for answering our prayers, and my mother rushed to hug and kiss me, warmly, at this great news, saying, "God has heard your prayers, my sweet little angel."

I can describe the days after my father's release from the hospital as the best days of my life. We did not know anyone in Maryland, considering my mother kept my father's condition a tight secret, but in accordance with the doctor's instructions, we extended our stay in the United States, until my father recuperated and was ready for travel.

We were elated, as Aunt Sue surprised us when she arrived from California, accompanied by her daughter Mona. I considered Mona's presence for another week with us a gift from heaven. I soon introduced her to Dr. Roper, who made it a habit to see us every evening after work. Mona stayed in my hotel room that had a second bed, while aunt Sue checked in an adjacent room. We broke up into two groups: my parents and aunt, with a chauffeur, and Mona, and I with Dr. Roper, in his car. In a few days he became one of the family. Both my mother and Aunt Sue liked him and gave him a hearty welcome, especially my mother, after my father told her, in his own words, about his friendship with Danny's dad.

My mother did not find Danny to be detrimental to our friendship for two reasons: first, he was Christian, and therefore not eligible, and second, because he was at least nine years older than I was. That said, Mona did not find these two obstacles to be real issues, as far as she was concerned, and in a couple of days, she expressed to me her admiration for Danny.

Mona and I spent hours in our room talking about everything. Naturally the Shaheen family was the topic of our conversation, and my friend Amal in particular—even Samir, whom none of us knew had a special part in our conversation that centered mainly on religion and the Christian faith, which I learned about from Amal's family. What I learned about Christ and Christianity, I witnessed in their daily life, as well as the love that Mona witnessed in her housekeeper Mary Graham's life. The name of Jesus ceased to be a mere thought in our mind or a secret in our heart. He became the focus in my discussions with Mona.

I can never forget the evening while we were having dinner at a restaurant when I asked Dr. Roper to tell us about how he became a true Christian, and what role Samir played.

For two whole hours, he expounded on his glorious experience of accepting Jesus as Savior and Lord over his life. He told us how fortunate he was to be born in a Christian home where he lived a decent life, praying, read the Bible every day, and went to church. What struck me most and what I did not quite understand, was when he told us that practicing all of these, did not make him a true Christian, as he continued to explain his point, "The word Christian alone does not make any person saved from the pits of hell, even if one is born into a true Christian home. I am a good example of that. Going to church, fasting, praying, reading the Bible, and doing good deeds do not provide salvation; the only way for salvation is by opening our heart to Jesus Christ and accepting Him as personal Lord and Savior. Regardless of the position one holds, or to what denomination or religion he belongs, unless he surrenders his life fully to Christ, he will never go to heaven, but will spend his eternity in hell—according to what the Word of God says. God is not interested in man-made religions or the names thereof; He is only interested in two kinds of people: saved by Grace or not saved."

Mona and I sat there speechless, and at the same time, bewildered by these revelations. Most were news to us, as we never heard such things before. Danny went on to tell us about his life without Christ: his alcohol abuse, drugs, sex, and the bad company he kept. Such behavior almost put his future as a physician in jeopardy. Moreover, he told us that although he was highly intelligent, he wasted two years before he could continue his medical studies when he was undergoing treatment for drug abuse. He went on to tell us about his rebellion towards all he heard from his parents, and how he broke their heart in the process. He also told us that, at one time, he belittled and mocked God and His Word, as well as his father's preaching until he met Samir at Johns Hopkins a few years earlier. It was God's will they were both roommates, so Samir could witness to him about the love of God and the way to salvation. Samir's serene life, his love for Jesus, his forgiving attitude, and his non-judgmental style, opened up his eyes to his sinful ways, which pierced the hands and feet of Jesus on a daily basis.

He continued, "The impregnable fortifications that Satan built between me and the love of Jesus and His mercy began to crumble; I then took refuge in His cross, confessed my sins, sought His mercy, and accepted Him as Lord and Savior. From that moment on, although I still feel no older than a two-year child in my faith, and although I fall and stain my life from time to time, I have the assurance that I have eternal life with my heavenly father, who holds my hand and guides my steps in my Christian faith." With this, Danny ended his story, or testimony, as he called it, while Mona and I were wiping away our tears.

For a whole week, my aunt and cousin, Mona, stayed with us, but the days went by quickly, since we had to travel to London. Danny had told me Samir was going to return from Lebanon in six days, and I had wished my mother would postpone our travel for another week, just to meet him. Of course, I did not reveal this to her, but I pretended I wanted to spend more time with Mona. I begged and pleaded with her to stay here another week, but she did not relent. She insisted we leave on Friday because of a previously scheduled meeting with a famous designer in London.

Thursday was a difficult day of farewell; neither Mona nor I slept well. We read some passages in the Gospel of John and promised we would correspond and stay in touch by phone. Moreover, Mona promised to attend my graduation ceremony in Lebanon the following summer and spend the rest of the summer with us. This lessened my crying and sadness at this parting, for we became quite attached to each other. The moment of farewell came too soon at the airport; it turned out to be a lot worse than I'd anticipated, especially when I bid Danny farewell. I did not feel embarrassed or awkward in front of my parents when I gave him a big hug and kissed him on the cheek; I felt I left behind a dear friend and brother, just as I left another dear friend in California by the name of Mary Graham. Furthermore, I left, in the United States, so many sweet memories, as well as a little secret between my father and me.

Chapter 7
AT THE CAMP

❦

The plane took off at 9:30 in the evening from Washington D.C. and landed in London at 8:30 the next morning. It was raining; the dark London sky looked depressing, ominous.

The trip was neither difficult nor pleasant; I knew what to expect in the city that I did not particularly care for, anticipating the boredom that awaited me there. I knew my mother would be on a fashion spree, going from one show to another, and my father from one meeting to another. With such anticipation in mind, I did not sleep a wink on the airplane, nor did I eat or drink anything, but silently cried thinking about Mona and Danny. I wished I had more time to get to know them better, especially when I discovered that Mona would be spending another week in Baltimore in Danny's company, while I spend my time here in London alone. I would have felt elated, had I been traveling to Lebanon to see Amal and meet her brother Samir who captured my heart; but now, as it stands, I am in neither place and may not get to meet him anytime soon.

We settled into the taxi, but I let my imagination and foul mood take hold of me. I felt, forsaken, and went on a self-pity binge. A voice inside of me whispered, "You went to Washington expecting boredom, but you had a great time. Do you remember the nice evening you spent with your father, and his awesome speech? Did you not worry about your father's health but God made him well? Did you not get to meet a new friend, Danny, who brought joy to your heart and your father's? So you must trust God and allow Him to direct your paths in His special way, and not rush things." The words were crystal clear and sounded quite real so much that I had to turn around to make sure the voice was not audible to anyone else. My anxious anticipation left me promptly, and I was already feeling better. I took a deep breath as hope replaced dread; perhaps I can expect similar experiences in London as well. Who knows?

We arrived at the hotel around 11:30 a.m., and I headed straight to my bedroom to relax and catch some badly needed sleep. Whenever we traveled, my father would usually contact his secretary to inform her of any changes in his itinerary or calls to confirm he had arrived at his destination. He would also provide an update of phone and fax numbers when and as needed. A couple of hours later, I awoke to my father's voice updating his secretary with his whereabouts and the details of his trip, as well as other issues. I lifted my head, looked at the bedside-clock, and went back to sleep. A few minutes later, I heard the phone ring, but this time the ringing did not wake me up because I was now wide-awake. At first, I thought it was my aunt, from the United States checking on us, but as the conversation progressed, I heard my father mention my cousin Majdi who was in Beirut. His tone was different with a deep sense of urgency. "Did I hear the name Majdi?" I asked myself.

I sat up in bed somewhat worried and tried to concentrate on what was coming through the door. I'd already established that my cousin Majdi was on the other end of the line calling from Lebanon. The conversation was a serious one, but I could not decipher its content. Then I heard my mother's voice inquiring quietly, "What happened, Majdi? Tell us?"

My mother was on the listening end of some long explanation my cousin must have been offering, but her last sentence seemed revealing, "Salah will be on the first flight to Beirut," she said.

My heart beat faster than I had ever experienced in my life, it seemed to me the situation was more serious than I thought, then I heard my father ask, "Heart attack? Oh Dad, I hope I can get there before it's too late."

The pieces were coming together; my grandfather had a heart attack. I did not move at all, but remained silent in bed, attentively listening to my parents make plans and discuss the new events that were unfolding.

"Huda, let us prepare to leave either today or tomorrow morning at the latest."

"No, Salah, I cannot go with you today or tomorrow; I cannot just cancel the appointments I worked so hard all year to make; you know how important they are to my business."

"You want me to stay here with you for your business appointments while my father is dying?"

"Don't raise your voice; we don't want Dalal to wake."

I felt awkward as I laid my head on the pillow, closed my eyes, pretending to be asleep, but still trying to hear what was being said. For a few minutes, there was total silence. Soon my mother broke the silence as she continued, "Why don't you go to Lebanon tomorrow morning with Dalal, and I'll follow in a few days?"

"You want Dalal to accompany me at such a time? The whole family will be at the hospital, what if anything should happen to my father and Dalal is with me?"

"Dalal is a mature young woman; she spent a whole week with you at the hospital and proved that she could handle everything quite well. Regardless, it would be better if she were to be there with you than here all by herself."

"Why don't we ask her and let her decide; perhaps she'd rather be with you here, if not, she can go with me, if she so chooses."

"No, I don't want to provide her with a choice, this is not an either or. Let her go with you; I want her to be with you—I prefer it that way. I then do not have to worry about her all alone in this place, and at the same time, I would be able to concentrate on my business and finish early. Dalal is asleep, so I'll call the airline to reserve two tickets on the first available flight to Beirut."

"No, Dalal was not asleep," I said to myself, but though I had my head buried in the pillow; I could not stay sedate. I wanted to jump and shout for joy, but had to suppress my excitement. I would be in Beirut soon. I felt guilty that I did not feel any concern about my grandfather, my father, or my mother. My only concern now was to meet Samir before he leaves for the United States. How shameful! Nevertheless, I went back to sleep only to be awakened by my mother's voice,

"Great, you slept well and long; it is now six o'clock, aren't you hungry?

"Six p.m.? Of course, I am hungry."

I got out of bed, washed my face and felt refreshed; then I remembered a little from the conversation between my parents, I thought it was a dream. When I was ready to go down to the dining room, my mother motioned that I sit next to her on the bed, "I have a surprise for you, Dalal, but I am not sure if it is pleasant or not."

"I am always worried when you have a surprise, Mother; what is it today?"

"You'll be leaving to Lebanon tomorrow morning with Dad."

"But why?" I feigned concerned reluctance.

"Your grandpa had a heart attack and was taken to the hospital in critical condition."

"How about you; aren't you going with us?" I asked in agreement.

"No, not tomorrow, but as soon as I am done with my business meetings and appointments, I will. Your dad will let me know if I am needed there."

"Will Grandpa be OK?"

"We don't know; Majdi says he's in a coma or semi-coma."

"Where's Dad now? He must be quite upset."

"Yes, he's worried, but he had to go and meet somebody before he heads back to Beirut in the morning. You have to be at the airport by six and the flight is at eight."

"This means Father will see Grandpa tomorrow at five in the afternoon Beirut timing."

"Yes—God willing you will be in Beirut by then."

I thought, I too, would be seeing the Shaheen family later that evening and be able to meet Samir; I will also be seeing them Monday, as well for a little bit on Tuesday. 'How great God is and how wise His ways are—of course if these were really His ways,' I thought a little selfishly, perhaps these were my ways and not His'

I tried to cheer my father up, but to no avail. I hid any signs of excitement about the prospect of seeing my friends again, especially Amal, and expressed genuine concern for my grandfather's condition. Just twenty minutes before landing in Beirut, as the plane was circling over the capital, my father turned to me and asked, "Dalal, have you prayed for your grandfather?" Apart from few exchanges during our four and a half hour flight, we spoke very little during this trip. This question caught me completely off guard, and I felt myself formulating an acceptable answer without resorting to tell a lie. I blurted out as best as I could, "Not really, but I promise you that I will, and I'll also ask the Shaheens to pray."

My father smiled, squeezed my hand, looked me straight in the eye, and said, "Yes, please do; I am sure God will hear your prayers and theirs. My father's life is so precious to me, and I would not want anything bad to happen to him."

I could certainly sympathize with him as he tried hard to suppress his tears. He loved his father just as much as I loved mine. I began to remember how I felt when they took my father to the hospital just a few days earlier. I wanted to make it easy for him, but I did not know what to say. Suddenly, a comforting thought came to my mind: could it be that God permitted my grandfather to fall ill because that was a way in which I would be able to return to my country. With what little knowledge I had in such matters, as well as my child-like understanding, that was the only thing I could think of at that moment. My reasoning led me to the inevitable conclusion that, for sure, God was going to heal my grandfather. I voiced this to my father without any doubt; I was even surprised when I heard my own words, "I promise you, Grandpa is going to be fine by this evening."

I was not surprised when my father asked, "How could you say this so assuredly, Dalal?"

"I don't know what to tell you, Dad, but all I can say Grandpa is going to get well. How, I don't know, it's just a feeling—I really don't know."

My father laughed loudly at my answer that was solely based on 'don't know'. That was the first time I heard him laugh since we received the sad news. At that moment, the captain instructed us to keep our seat belts fastened as we taxied to the gate at Beirut airport.

Our chauffeur was at the airport waiting for us, and so was my cousin Majdi. My father asked me whether I preferred to go with him to visit my grandfather, or continue home. This way, the chauffeur would take him to the hospital first and I could ride on with my cousin to go home.

The truth was, I wanted to do neither, I wanted to go straight to see Amal; so I hesitated and kept looking for the right words, I did not want to sound like a selfish irresponsible little girl. While stammering and trying to find the appropriate words, my father said, as if reading my thoughts, "Oh, how could I forget your friend Amal? I forgot you have been eagerly waiting to see her. So if you'd rather go see her, I wish you a good time with her and her family—and—don't forget to pray for your grandpa." That caught me by surprise, and it also made me realize how sympathetic my father was and sensitive to my needs.

With these words, our conversation ended with a gentle kiss on my forehead, and my father went to the hospital with our chauffeur. I rode with my cousin Majdi, who in his turn, asked me, "Where should I take you, the house in Beirut or the house in the mountain?"

I answered, "Neither—just take me to Amal's."

"Amal is not home today." He simply said, as though he knew Amal and all her schedules. His response took me by surprise, "What? What do you mean she's not at home today? Where is she?"

"She's in the mountains with her family, on vacation."

I felt my blood freeze in my veins; after all the long waiting and anticipation, my hopes were dashed because I had reasoned that my grandfather's illness was to my advantage. I was very disappointed, to say the least; my eyes welled up out of frustration, yet I was able to keep my composure and asked calmly, "Do you know when they'll be back?"

"Either tomorrow or the day after." Unaware of how I felt, he started the car and asked, "So, where are we going?"

I did not respond because I was confused, I asked nervously, "Tell me, how you know all these things and details about Amal? Were you seeing her in my absence?"

Majdi was surprised at my question and tone of voice, as he replied, "Oh, I saw her couple of times while talking with Abu Wafiq in the garden."

"Really? So when you saw her, she ran to you to tell you about her plans for the summer, and that she'll be back tomorrow or after tomorrow—just like that?" I asked with a hint of sarcasm.

With the same tone of sarcasm, he continued, "When she saw me, she asked me to come in and visit with the family at the house; then she told me all about her plans. Are you now satisfied with my answer?"

I felt there must be more to his caustic response, and that something must have happened during my absence, when suddenly, my memory took me back to my last birthday party when my cousin was following Amal all over the place.

"Really now, and I want the truth this time, what prompted you to visit the Shaheen family?"

"I was in the neighborhood one day and went to convey your greetings to Amal."

"I never asked you to do that, but this is not the time to question you—Majdi, do you really know where the Shaheens are, and where they are spending their vacation?"

"In a place not too far from here; it's not what you call a summer resort, but more like a camp." He was silent for a moment then shouted with excitement, "I have an idea."

113

"OK, let's hear it, because I have an idea too, but let me hear yours first."

Majdi is not only a cousin, but we also became good friends since we grew up together. We were able to read from the same music sheet and agreed much of the time. I knew what he was going to say, so I was not surprised to hear his idea,

"How about it if we surprise them at camp this evening? I'll be tickled to see how Amal is going to react when she sees you."

I gave Majdi a big hug and began to shout with excitement. He felt embarrassed as we were beginning to attract undue attention from passers-by; my cousin freed himself from my clutch, got hold of the steering wheel, and drove to camp.

Majdi looked so content; he never talked about my grandfather nor asked about my trip to the United States. I wanted to ask him about the goings on during my absence, as well as whether he had met Samir yet, but because I was not supposed to know that Samir was even around, I refrained from asking direct questions, so instead, I said, "You conniving fox. You were using me to convey my wishes to Amal, weren't you?"

I thought Majdi was going to laugh, but because he was caught off-guard by my question, he turned to me and said, "Don't you dare tell Amal or anyone else about this, or else I would lose Amal's respect and her parents'."

"I was only joking; you made it sound so serious; you'll never become a good lawyer if you can't get a joke right away" I said teasingly.

"Not to worry about my professional success, but did you know that Amal has a brother called Samir, studying to be a surgeon in the United States?"

"Yes, I know; Amal told me."

"Of course, you don't know that her brother is here, do you?"

"Really? When did he come; Amal did not tell me about this?"

"Amal didn't know either, he surprised everybody."

"Have you seen him, I mean have you met him yet?"

"When I went to Amal's house to convey your greetings two weeks ago, she was so happy and told me about her brother, and that she'd like to introduce me to him; and that's what happened."

"Looks like you already know about the Shaheen family more than I do; you know Samir, and I don't."

"You'll get to meet him tonight; believe me it was an honor for me to meet him; he's a very respectable and impressive person."

My heart began to flutter as a dove trapped in a net. I was afraid Majdi might exaggerate in describing Samir's traits and besides, I already heard enough from Danny that I changed the subject. However, Majdi's ignorance of my anxiety to meet Samir, kept him talking about Samir's personality, eloquence, his reserved demeanor, and above all, his love for God. He went on to tell me in detail how the friendship between them grew so fast—in less than one week—and how they had spent so much time discussing important issues pertaining to life and religion, especially Christianity and its so many denominations.

"You know," Majdi said, "I Was totally ignorant of what Christians believe. I had not heard, read, or known anything about true Christianity, the way Samir explained it to me. It made me more eager to learn more about Christ and the Christian faith; Samir was quite obliging."

Majdi was talking with a lot of enthusiasm about his discovery. His face brightened every time he spoke about Samir; he was stoking the fire that I already had about Samir without even meeting him yet. I think I was obsessed by then, just from hearing about him and seeing his face in a movie clip. Majdi sped up on those sharp curves, it scared me. I pleaded with him to slow down, but all he could say was, "I don't want to be late for the opening, as Amal is going to sing a solo."

"Oh, so you've been attending the camp with them too?"

"Yes, I have every day of the week, until Grandpa got sick."

"You've been attending the camp with them?" I repeated my question to him, somewhat surprised.

"What's wrong? I already told you I attended; Amal invited me and said this conference was for everybody, and that Samir was going to be the main speaker. You'll get to hear him tonight, since that's going to be his last meeting before heading back to the United States, Tuesday morning."

Majdi did not tell me anything that Danny had not already told me. Here I was, disappointed at Samir's departure before even having met him, tears welled up in my eyes. But why was I so obsessed? Maybe when we even meet, we may not have the chemistry, and nothing may materialize; silly and foolishly sentimental teenager, I thought! I wished Majdi would change the subject, but how would he know what I was thinking. He continued, "I can't imagine how Amal is going to react when she sees you sitting next to me; she's been counting the days and hours, waiting for you to return from the United States, she kept talking about you to her brother and wanted to introduce you two to each other so badly."

"She told her brother about me? What would she tell him? I hope he is not disappointed when he sees me."

Majdi laughed as he told me about when Amal showed him my birthday video.

"And how did Amal get a hold of that video; I don't remember giving her a copy, nor did I lend it to her. Is this also one of your tricks?"

"Sorry, you'll have to forgive me. Your birthday party is so dear to me because that's when I met Amal. Have you forgotten?"

He said this to me with a tone that reflected his feelings towards Amal, so I did not comment. Soon enough, Majdi opened up his heart and told me how much he liked Amal and how much he admired her. After this admission, I felt uneasy and feared for Majdi. I warned him the repercussions of such an attachment and the possibility of her rejecting him, because not only was she unlike other Christians, she was also a true, strict, committed Christian. I then asked him if Amal's feelings were mutual, but he dejectedly shook his head, sighed, and said, "I don't know, not sure. I become more attached to her every day, especially after I met Samir. What a nice family." We both sighed and remained silent until we reached campgrounds.

The campgrounds were just beautiful, sitting on a high hill surrounded by the Mediterranean, and the umbrella of pine trees. It was not luxurious, but rather rustic and somewhat primitive, with graveled inroads. Everything was dark except for the main hall where meetings were held.

We arrived a little late; nonetheless, the hall was already full, some standing along the walls or outside. There was no music, nor was there anyone speaking; silence prevailed with all heads bowed. "They are praying," Majdi explained in a whisper. When he mentioned the word 'prayer', I remembered my promise to my father that we would pray for grandpa. I wondered how I could let Amal know.

Majdi was walking ahead of me to the front of the hall. He kept on walking until we reached the front rows, where there were three empty chairs. This surprised me because many were standing, yet these seats were empty. I thought, perhaps, Amal had reserved these seats for her and Majdi. We sat in the second row, to the extreme left of the hall, as

I began to look around for Amal or anyone related to her. Most conference attendees were young people and a few older folk, but no children in sight; I was also looking for Amal's twin siblings. Perhaps the children were in another room. I noticed most were wearing ordinary, yet modest, clothes. None of the jewelry or excess make-up—a common sight in Lebanon—was to be seen. I felt out of place and began to wipe off my lipstick surreptitiously. I settled in my seat, observing when I saw Amal's mother walk towards the piano. Oh, how much I missed this lady and her music. Then I saw Uncle Najeeb—Amal's father—handing out books to the people, but I had not seen Amal, yet. It did not take long, I noticed her walk in from the front entrance with a young man tagging behind her. They sat in the front row, on the extreme right, where I was able to see them quite well.

"That is Samir." Majdi whispered in my ear.

Of course, I did not need Majdi to point him out to me; I had already seen him recently on the tape, in addition to his pictures here and there. "What a handsome man he is!" Mrs. Shaheen was at the piano playing; Amal took her place behind the podium to sing a beautiful song that added to the worshipful atmosphere. Her eyes did not move, as if focused on one thing; Majdi volunteered to tell me she was not singing from her mouth, but from her heart, as she focused her eyes on Jesus.

From time to time, I would glance at Majdi while Amal was singing, to see his reaction and how taken he was by Amal's voice and presence. I looked at Samir, but could no longer see his face, as he hid it between his hands in a prayerful stance. After a while, Amal began to move her eyes, panning the audience until she saw me. I slightly waved my hand at her, which drew a reaction of surprise; I saw it on her face. I did not know the song, or whether to determine when it came to an end. Apparently, this was the end of her solo because she began to talk to the audience.

"I have a word I'd like to share with you." Samir raised his head to listen. "As you may already know, this is my brother's final night among us at this blessed conference. He will be leaving us Tuesday morning. At first, I did not feel like singing this evening, but the conference leader insisted. So I sang, but not with the usual fervor, as I am saddened by the thought of my brother's departure soon. I also noticed a very dear friend who has been vacationing overseas, but has apparently returned; I see her sitting among us, this evening. Seeing her removed much of that sadness, and it gave me an added impetus while singing. I'd like to welcome my friend Dalal to our midst," she concluded with a smile on her face, as she pointed me out.

Amal was talking about me in such a sincere tone of voice, full of love. At the mention of my name, I noticed Samir turn his head to look where Amal was looking, in an effort to see me. He saw me sitting next to Majdi, whom he already knew to be my cousin; his eyes met mine, and he gave me a slight smile of acknowledgment. Amal was already by my side, squeezing my hand and planting a kiss on my cheek. When the song leader asked everyone to stand, Amal and I hugged each other with tears of joy, streaming down our cheeks. She kept looking at me with her hands, rubbing my back, as if making certain I was there in the flesh, thanking God for my safe return. Even at such an inopportune time, Amal did not hesitate to complement me on my new curly hairdo. After the warm exchange between us, I whispered in her ear to pray for my grandfather. She promptly said, "Majdi told us already about your grandfather's condition, and we all prayed for him. At any rate, I will ask my father to remember him in his prayer once more time."

Before Amal left, I whispered in her ear again, "Please, do not mention my grandpa's name; you know how sensitive this issue can be."

"Oh, not to worry, Majdi already made that clear."

While Amal's father was praying, I looked at my watch: it was 8:30. I wanted to know the exact time, so I could tell my father we prayed for Grandpa at that time. Soon afterward, Samir was behind the pulpit. He stood there, scanning the hall from end to end; Amal was holding my hand the whole time, not letting go, as though afraid I might vanish. She squeezed it repeatedly, as though telling me, "That's my brother. My hero."

I thanked God that Samir did not surprise me that evening, for Danny already told me what to expect, apart from also seeing and hearing him on tape. At this point, I wanted to rid myself of any childish feelings or thoughts and clear my head, so I could concentrate on the message and not the speaker. I truly wanted to hear the word of God tonight; I wanted to hear more about Jesus, as well as wanting to feel assured about my own salvation. I was now enamored with the Christian faith because I never heard such thoughts before; it was akin to being in total darkness then suddenly seeing the light! I felt Satan was waging a war on my thoughts; he usually attacks in our weak areas. I closed my eyes and sincerely prayed to God to help me overcome Satan's attack by driving away any improper thoughts I may have had, so I could listen to His Word without any distractions. Samir began his message in an intelligent way.

"Good evening dear brothers and sisters, and welcome to this evening of worship. You heard my sister Amal, earlier, relay to you a simple experience she had this evening, and how she felt sad as this conference was about to wind down along with my last message to you, and how the Lord has turned her sadness into joy, as she saw her friend in this hall after months of absence. I must admit, I felt the same way my sister did about the conference, leaving all the good people I met and the new friends I made. The Lord, however, gave me joy instead of sadness. The joy He has given me is not about seeing old friends return, but the return of so many precious souls to Christ in the last few days. Souls Christ paid His own life for on the cross, to save those who genuinely repent and seek His mercy. Yet, there are other souls here tonight who have not accepted God's gift of salvation, but may be willing to do so before they leave this hall tonight. That's what gives me joy. The salvation of even one soul tonight will make me forget the pain I will endure, as I prepare to leave behind so many precious friends. Christ said, **"I say unto you, that likewise, joy shall be in heaven over one sinner that repents—"**

Samir choked up and was unable to speak for a few long moments. Amal let go of my hand to wipe away tears that found their way down her cheek. I also noticed other people wipe their tears away, especially Samir's father, Dr. Shaheen. Upon seeing people cry, especially Amal, I also began to cry. The words I just heard pierced my heart For a few more moments; silence prevailed over the hall until Samir was able to resume his speech. All he could see before him were precious, lost souls that he wanted to bring to the knowledge of salvation through repentance.

Most of the passages he read were taken from the Gospel of John— my favorite book—I had already memorized many of its verses. Whenever he began reciting or reading a verse, I would finish it in a soft voice that made Amal tug on my arm to say, "I can't believe you learned all these verses. Where and how did you do it?" Even Majdi glanced at me from time to time, during the message, wondering how on earth I memorized all this scriptures.

Samir's sermon was quite clear and eloquent; his presentation was dynamic, similar to what I have already seen before on the tape Danny shared. He then asked,

"Are you a child of God? Are you ready to meet your Creator? What's keeping you from becoming ready? What stands between you and our Lord Jesus this evening?"

Samir spoke about God's love for all people of the earth. I joined in when he recited John 3:16, "**For God so loved the world—**" He stressed the fact that Christ was for everyone, and not just for Christians. His gift of salvation was free to anyone who chose to follow Him. He also spoke of the victorious resurrection of Christ from the dead, as well as eternal life. He mentioned several Bible saints, prophets, as well as great men of God who had already passed on.

"All of these people died and were buried; their graves can attest to that, but Jesus is alive today; his tomb is empty for all ages to see. He rose from the dead, was taken up to heaven, and will one day return, soon. All the world's religions end at the grave, except Christianity—it begins at the grave." Wow, this really stunned me!

Samir went on to exhort those who have not yet taken the step in accepting Jesus as Lord and Savior, to accept Him now.

"**For what profiteth a man should he gain the whole world and lose his own soul**?" He asked.

I felt he was talking to Majdi and me in particular; if he had looked at us, then I would have been sure of that, but he did not. He continued, "Wealth will do you no good on Judgment Day, nor coming from a reputable family, nor youth or beauty, neither strength nor all the degrees you may hold or positions you have assumed; without Christ, all will only lead to eternal damnation."

For forty-five minutes, Samir pleaded and exhorted the listeners not to put off making decisions regarding their eternal destiny another day. '**For today is the accepted day**', the Bible says. Come to Him and repent of your sins, for He will take away your sins and throw them into the depths of the sea, and open the gates of heaven for you."

Again, he asked people to raise their hands to show their desire to accept Christ as personal Savior and become the children of God. I could sense the urgency in his words, his love for the lost in his tone of voice, and the enthusiasm he exuded in doing so. Moreover, I noticed how he never mentioned the word 'Jesus' without preceding it with the word 'Lord', out of respect and awe for His wonderful name.

Every word he uttered moved me, especially the concern he showed for others in an effort to lead them to heaven.

"Dear brothers and sisters, do you know where you're going should you die, God forbid? If you're not sure, it's an indication you haven't accepted the Lord Jesus Christ as your Savior or not sure that you already have, and have become a child of God. For the Word of God says, **'He that hath the Son hath life, and he that hath not the Son hath not life, but the wrath of God shall rest upon him—'**"

I was shocked when I asked myself this question. My answer was, "I don't know." I could not say I was certain of going to heaven, although I thought I became a believer and believed every word Samir was saying. I wanted to raise my hand to indicate my intention, but I could not. Amal was still holding my hand tightly, but when Samir began an altar call, she let go of my hand as though she expected me to raise it, but I still held back. I took a slight peek at Majdi to see if he was going to raise his hand. I loved him as much as I loved myself, and did not want him to go to hell, so I wished that he would raise his hand. I knew Amal and her parents would be praying for us this very moment. Samir then said, "My brother and sister, this is the last call I'll be making tonight; who else will raise his hand to accept the Lord Jesus as his personal Savior?"

Majdi raised his hand; Samir reacted by shouting "Hallelujah," whatever it meant. I was encouraged by Majdi, hence, I decided to raise my hand should Samir ask again, but he never did. I waited, but to my chagrin, Samir did not repeat the question. He then proceeded to ask all those who raised their hands to come forward so he could pray for them and answer any questions they may have. "What a predicament." I thought. I was ready to raise my hand because all eyes were closed, but going forward and marching to the altar was too much, considering my family's background; I just could not do this in public. I felt Majdi was readying himself to go forward, but I held him by the arm and whispered to him,

"Don't do it Majdi—don't. Many of those present here may know us, and they'll tell our parents." However, Majdi ignored my pleas and stood up, and me still pulling on him to remain seated. At this point, Amal walked to the front to join the many young men and women who were already singing what sounded like an invitation. Samir was talking to them separately, and because Amal was singing, I was not able to hear what he was telling them. From time to time, he would signal to her to quit singing so he could talk to the rest and exhort them to come forward. Amal's tears were now streaming down her cheeks, as she was singing; then I said to myself, "Perhaps she heard what I said to Majdi, and how I was keeping him from going forward." I felt ashamed and guilty that I had missed the chance to repent and accept Christ. I felt afraid and heard a voice from within shout, "Coward!" Suddenly, I heard Samir's voice again, "Brethren, please understand that in itself, raising your hand does not save anyone, nor will buy you a ticket to heaven."

Upon hearing this, I felt a little more comfortable, "So I did nothing wrong, the intent was good and more important than raising one's hand," I rationalized. However, Samir continue, "Nonetheless, raising your hand is an indication that you mean business, and that you're defying Satan who does not want you to belong to the body of Christ or declare your allegiance to Him. God knows the heart, and He knows if you have really and truly repented, whether you raised your hand or not."

I truly repented of my sins and believed in Christ as my personal Savior and Lord. I was trying again to convince myself, while Samir continued, "The raising of hand or walking down the aisle indicates that we are not ashamed to receive Christ as our Savior, and that we're not afraid to proclaim our faith in public. Christ was never ashamed of us, but He bore our sins and shame in public and died on the cross for our sake, so do not be ashamed of Him; He loves you."

With this, Samir concluded his message. His words pierced my heart like a sharp sword; my secret and problem were exposed. Yes, I was afraid and embarrassed, but in a moment, I saw Majdi walk down the aisle boldly, his head up, showing no concern whatsoever about being seen by anyone. Samir walked up to meet him as he came closer to the front and put his arm around him, then both knelt to pray. Few moments later, the service was over and people were streaming out. Dr. and Mrs. Shaheen did not waste any time to rush and take me in their arms, welcoming me back from my trip. I had really missed them all, but I was sad and my heart was aching. Amal was now by my side, again, to make me feel welcome. I wondered whether Amal was disappointed because I did not march down the aisle as my cousin did. She was very happy and certainly did not express any disappointment in me, but rather complimented me on my ability to memorize so many verses from the book of John. She was still excited and wanted to know what had prompted me to do that. I did not want to be evasive, but felt that this is a topic better saved for later, so I replied half-seri-ously to her insistence, "Not now, Amal—it's a long story and needs a special session." She understood and now was eager to introduce me to her brother Samir.

With my strong personality, I always seemed to manage to leave a positive impression on people I met for the first time. What I lacked in clever argument, I would always make up for in congeniality and finesse; in that respect, I had no worries; but in that instance, I was experiencing an—I am not quite myself—feeling. I was anxious to meet Samir, and expected he would rush to meet me after the service and remain by my side late into the evening, talking to me. However, nothing of the sort happened. Samir was basking in some sort of happi-ness while totally engaged with the people who attended the service, talking and listening attentively. Apart from glancing in my direction a couple of times, I seemed to be completely invisible to him. I was not used to being ignored in such a manner. This made me feel disap-pointed and miserable. Amal broke her grip and left me all alone to go to talk to Majdi, a huge smile drawn all over her face. The excite-ment over seeing him and talking to him gave her a glow of joy and a sparkle in her eyes. I kept observing her and noticing how happy she was—or perhaps some sort of love in her eyes---or perhaps she was waiting eagerly to see Majdi become a Christian so she could love him with no religious barriers.

I saw Majdi extending his hand to shake hers, his face shining like a full moon. It surprised me that Majdi would display such courage in accepting Christ as Savior so publicly without worrying that his parents would find out, especially at the time our grandfather was on his deathbed. I was beginning to feel indignant, perhaps it was a false sense of indignation, "his behavior is reckless, and it would endanger both of us," I thought. There he was, happily mingling with people and accepting congratulations right and left, as if he were in another world.

The crowds were now dwindling; those who remained were surrounding Samir talking to him and still asking questions. As for me, I was feeling so miserable, tears welled-up in my eyes. Here I expected to meet him in the USA; and now he was a few feet away, yet so far, and didn't seem to feel or care that I was there. I wanted to leave and disappear, so I started to look around for a quick exit. The weather was getting a bit chilly, and the cool mountain breeze caused my tears to dry on my cheeks. There was a wooden bench nearby, underneath a huge oak tree, so I made a beeline for it and sat there. The tree limbs shielded me from the eyes of the people. I sat there, trying to understand my sentiments, a mixture of anger and sadness, pride and humility, childishness and maturity. I tried hard to pinpoint the reason for my misery and anger, when I shifted my thoughts towards my cousin Majdi. The truth was, nobody had offended me or did anything to make me angry. Majdi's only 'sin' seemed to be accepting Christ in public, disregarding any possible repercussions in our harsh society, concerning conversions. Amal was being very courteous to me while Samir was doing what he should with all the people who were listening to him. So why was I angry?

"Dalal, Dalal," I heard Amal calling. I turned around, and there she was with Majdi, looking for me. I walked over to them without saying a word to Majdi about how I felt, regarding what happened in that meeting, and I gave Amal a look of disappointment when she asked me, "Where were you, we were looking for you, you seem to have disappeared? I want you to meet Samir; don't you want to meet him?" It sounded as if I was the one who ignored him, but I coldly replied, "I don't think there's time tonight to meet him; it's getting late and it's time to go home. I am tired; perhaps it would be better if we meet tomorrow."

"What?" Amal shouted, as though what I said was an insult. "You want to go home now? Now? We're going to have a nice evening of music and fellowship outdoors, with a bonfire that will be lit up in a few minutes. You don't want to miss this evening; it will be one of the nicest evenings you've ever had."

She spoke about the campfire, as if it were a once-in-a-lifetime opportunity, an event not to be missed. She and Majdi pleaded with me to stay, even for a little while, and then she added, completely oblivious to how I was feeling, "I am sure Samir will have plenty of free time later this evening; I want you to meet him so badly."

I did not want to disappoint Amal or Majdi, who was very keen on staying; moreover, I really wanted to meet Samir, but did not want to show it; so I agreed.

Amal—as smart as she was—sensed I was not intentionally ignoring her brother, but maybe it was the other way around. With a sharp female instinct, she tried to make amends and create a series of excuses on behalf of her bother, "Poor Samir, he doesn't get enough time to eat or rest; I didn't even have enough time to talk with him alone, not even for five minutes straight; everyone wants to talk to him and ask him questions, as you may have noticed."

Before Amal finished defending her brother's behavior, and out of nowhere, I saw this tall figure extend his hand to shake mine; to my shock, it was Samir! My goodness, what do I do now? Although my height is way above average, his towering stature stood a head and shoulder above mine. He had the face I yearned to see only moments ago; and now, playing coy, I extended a cold hand to shake his, "I am so happy to meet you, Dalal; I have heard so much about you."

Even his words and the mention of my name did not move me; I felt cold — and nervous, "Glad to meet you too, Dr. Shaheen," I replied in a tone that seemed normal to the ear, but no one other than me would be able to sense it was as dry as a bone. Amal sensed my discomfort, and Majdi attempted to make excuses for me because of the long airplane trip I had made today. We moved toward the tent in single file, as the trail was quite narrow. Amal, who was familiar with the camp, with Majdi by her side, led the way; Samir and I were behind them. I was thinking this evening was supposed to be the happiest ever for me; but, alas, I was now walking inches away from the man who captured my imagination, who I also concocted to be my knight in shining armor, riding on a white horse. What I felt did not necessarily mean he was also feeling the same way; being older and more mature than I, may have been the factor that I was not able to acknowledge.

Majdi's obvious elation was bothering me; I felt envious of the joy he exuded and the peace that filled his heart. How happy he was; he did not worry at all for his name, reputation, family, or future; his main concern, now, was to enjoy the fruits of what he sowed at the meeting.

Since the tent was quite a distance from the meeting hall, and the trail was gravelly, it would have been quite difficult to walk, had it not been for the moonlight shining down on us. The shoes I was wearing were not suited for walking on a rocky terrain, and from time to time, I would stumble. Since Amal was walking in the front, she would warn us about possible hazards. Upon reaching one, Samir held my hand securely to help me cross that hazardous part of the trail, without uttering a single word, or even looking at me. When we approached the square where the tent was pitched, we heard loud noises and laughter emanating in the still of the night; the bonfire flames were shooting up, high into the sky, lighting up the whole compound. Joy filled the whole place, and an atmosphere of peace and happiness prevailed. I wished I could drive away the irritating thoughts I had and tell Samir, who was walking silently by me, how I felt, so he could help me. Did not Amal tell me earlier that Samir would do anything for the sake of his Lord? However, before I could muster enough courage to ask him and prepare my words, he turned to me and said, "Is this the first time you attend such a meeting?"

"Yes, it is." I replied without looking at him.

"And how was your impression of this evening?"

"It wasn't the first time I hear about Jesus; I already know a lot about Him—from Amal and from your parents—as well as from a dear woman I met on my recent trip to the United States."

"Dalal," I heard Samir call my name. I turned around to look at him, despite the darkness and because of the light of the fire, I was able to see his features clearly, the blue eyes, and his tender smile. He continued his questioning, "Perhaps you already know a lot about Christ, and I don't doubt it, but my question to you is not what you know about Christ, but whether or not you personally know Him. Do you?"

"And what's the difference?"

"You hear about the President of the United States, but can you say you know him in person? No, you only know 'about' him. That was my question to you. Do you know Jesus Christ as your Lord and Savior? Do you have a personal relationship with Him? Have you asked Him to come in into your life and surrender to Him? He is not the Jesus of Amal, my parents, or your American friend, but *YOUR* Jesus and Lord, as well. Have you genuinely repented from your sins and asked for His mercy and forgiveness?"

I was unable to give him an answer, for I was surrounded with all scary things, darkness, walking through the woods, even in bright light, and insects and, perhaps, snakes are my worst fear. I was also afraid that if I should die, I would end up in hell because I had disappointed Jesus and lost the opportunity to accept Him during that evening. However, what scared me more than all my phobias put together was this young man talking to me. I was completely lost, but sincerely replied, "I don't know—I thought I knew Jesus—but—but."

I could not go on; I raised my head to look at him and began to cry uncontrollably. Samir let me cry and did not attempt to stop me or comfort me, but kept on walking by my side silently. Amal and Majdi were ahead of us at a distance, perhaps it was Amal's scheme to give her brother and me some time alone, I wondered. We were now a few moments from reaching the tent, and the gathering was well on its way.

Since the gathering was quite informal, and people tended to be close together, I did not want any to see me there because many people might recognize who I was, so I told Samir, "Go on alone, don't keep yourself from enjoying this final evening; I'll stay here for a while."

I was almost certain that he would leave me behind and continue on his way. Did he not see me cry and did nothing to assuage my feelings? Did he not walk by me — even when he extended to me his helping hand — and not say a word nor even look at me? Now, after I made a fool of myself and acted like a little girl by crying uncontrollably, he must have been disgusted with me, and this could be his chance to get rid of me by going alone.

I was wrong this time; I felt a tender hand grab my arm and heard Samir say, "Come on, Dalal, let's sit here for a little bit," as he led me we sat on a large boulder.

"I know for sure, there's something you want to tell me, and I'd be willing to stay with you till the morning to hear you and talk to you about what might be bothering you. Please relax, you're upset, and I am here to help you."

His words were sincere and not just a mere attempt to calm me down. I felt comfortable in his company, so I stopped crying and started talking. I began pouring my heart to him and told him everything since I first met Amal, including the story behind the Gospel of John, all the way to California where I met Mary Graham, my aunt's housekeeper. I did not mention the Washington episode or anything about his friend Danny, because I felt it was irrelevant to our conversation. The time will come when I can divulge the Washington tales to him. I told him everything I had in mind, about my fears and disappointment of not raising my hand at the many invitations he gave earlier at the meeting but failed to do so. He was listening intently to what I was telling him, and did not interrupt me, nor did he ask any questions, but he let me go on, "I love Jesus — very much and I want to follow Him and give Him my heart and life. I love Jesus, or the Lord Jesus, as you refer to Him."

"And He loves you too, for He can see your tears." That was all he commented on a full hour or longer of my delivery. The fire outside the tent was down to a few flames, the voices, the noise, and the laughter were gone. Most of the campers had left while I focused on understanding the awesomeness of the moment in which I was absorbed—this life-changing moment. I knew that there would be no turning back for me. Samir went on, "The Lord Jesus Christ saw your tears Dalal, the tears of his children are so precious to Him."

These words sounded so reassuring. So according to Samir, I was a child of God; that revelation gave me a feeling of comfort, "What happened to you this evening is not exceptional, many have felt the same way when they went through the experience of spiritual birth. The intense struggle you faced and what you told me about what happened to you in the last few months, were nothing more than birth pangs."

Samir's down-to-earth examples and analogies pacified me and drew a clearer picture for me to understand. "A mother does not conceive and give birth in the same day, but rather there are associated pains, tears, and often unexpected difficulties, culminating with labor pains. However, when she gives birth she forgets about such pains. Moreover, Dalal, you experienced the same: pain, sadness, doubts, and guilt, and all of these emotions that accompany the new birth—your new birth. Do you believe that Christ died in your place and for your sins, and that He forgives your sins and gives you life eternal?"

"Yes, yes, I believe it, but how can I be sure that God accepts me, makes me His child, and gives me eternal life?"

"Because He said so and made a faithful promise according to His Word, 'For God so loved the world—'"

Before he could continue, I interjected, "For God so loved Dalal that He gave His only begotten Son so that Dalal will not perish but should have everlasting life—" John 3:16, I added laughing.

Danny was wrong when he described Samir as made of steel, for I was able to notice tears well-up in his eyes and shine in darkness. Samir bowed his head, held my hands, and prayed the sinner's prayer, as I repeated the prayer of repentance, after him. We broke the news to my cousin and Amal and the rest of the group. Majdi was first to hug me and give me a kiss to express joy at surrendering my life to Christ. He and Amal must have been observing us, and they both rushed towards us at the end of the prayer to congratulate me and praise God for my salvation.

My own mother must not have been as happy seventeen years ago at my natural birth as Majdi, Amal, Samir, and I in particular, at my new 'second birth'. I shall not say any more about what happened that evening lest I mar the image of this remarkable event that only comes once in a lifetime. That evening, I slept like a baby, comfortably and peacefully, knowing that the peace of God filled my heart as a new child of God.

Chapter 8
THE ROSE

❧

*T*he events that took place at the conference the night before and the physical and emotional feelings that followed, in addition to the earlier, long and weary flight back to Lebanon, left me drained. I was fast asleep and stayed in the bed the following morning until well past noon. When I went out of my room, I saw my father still in his night-clothes, sipping coffee and reading the newspaper. I stealthily walked towards him, came from behind, and put my arms around his neck and said, "At exactly eight o'clock last night, we all prayed for Grandpa."

My father was startled, stood up, and said, "You scared me. While Grandpa is feeling a lot better, you almost gave me a heart attack."

"Sorry Dad, I didn't mean to. I don't know why I did that; I just wanted to let you know we did not forget to pray for Grandpa." I then sat opposite him and asked, "How's his health now? Tell me, I have a feeling he's well; otherwise, you would not be sitting here in your pajamas."

"True, he's well; in fact, it was around eight last night that he started feeling better." Then he was silent for a moment, and continued, looking at me surprised, "Didn't you just tell me that you prayed for him around that same time last night?"

"Yes." I replied.

"It looks like it wasn't the doctor's skill that made him better after all, but the providence of God."

He went on to tell me he was in critical condition when he arrived at the hospital, and the doctors were quite worried about his condition, but were surprised that in a few hours, his condition improved from critical to stable. They relegated this speedy improvement to a psychological effect after having seen his son. My father, however, seemed to think it was because of God's grace. I was happy I told him about the time of prayer; otherwise, he would not have said that. This experience gave me the courage to tell him more of what happened last night at the camp, but did not go as far to tell him about Majdi and me accepting Christ as Savior—not yet, at least. This issue was a sensitive subject that required more wisdom than courage, but nonetheless, I did not have a guilt trip nor was I ashamed about my decision to become a follower of Christ.

My father expressed surprise that I had persuaded Majdi to take me to camp to see Amal, but did not comment on our attending a Christian meeting. Moreover, he did not inquire about Samir, except about the time of his return to the United States. With that, he seemed quite comfortable when I told him Samir would be leaving tomorrow, as though he was thinking his daughter would then be safe from this dashing young man, within twenty-four hours.

We remained together awhile, and then my father got up and went into the house. I was now alone on the balcony reflecting on the events that took place at the camp, as it was the first day of my new life. I felt so ecstatic at the thought, more than anyone could imagine. I thanked the Lord for saving me, giving me eternal live, and making me His child that I repeated this verse, **"He who hath the Son, hath life, and he who doth not have the Son, hath no life—"** 1John 5:12. I knew I had received that life and that Jesus and I became intimate friends that I could now lift up my eyes and speak to Him. I not only knew about Him, now, but also knew Him, and began a personal relationship with Him. I called Amal's house to see if they returned from camp, but no one answered. I called Majdi, but did not find him, either. I then sat down to write letters to my cousin, Mona, Mary Graham, and Danny to let them know about my wonderful experience and my new birth. I called Amal's house again, then Majdi's, and the hospital, in an effort to find them, but still, no answer.

It was around 3:30 in the afternoon, I had not seen our gardener, Abu Wafiq yet, so I went down to the garden looking for him to ask if he had seen our neighbors today. He was nowhere to be found in the garden, so I went to the room where he usually used to rest after a day's toil. I peeked through the window and panicked at what I saw. Abu Wafiq was sitting on the floor on an old, small rug, with some fruit close by, and a young man sitting next to him. I rubbed my eyes to see better and looked more closely, just to make sure it was not a shadow; to my shock, it was Samir! I stepped back, somewhat startled, ran back to my room, and sat on my bed trying to figure out what was going on. Why was Samir with our gardener and where was everybody else—where was the rest of his family? Why was he there by himself?

What made Samir come to our garden, and particularly to Abu Wafiq's room? Who brought him from camp? There were no cars in front of his parents' house; moreover, what did Samir have to do with our gardener? How dare Abu Wafiq invite Samir to eat with him in such a humble room and make him sit on the floor like a common peasant? What could they be talking about? I have so many questions, but no answers. It would not be appropriate for Samir to talk with him about Christ and Christianity, "Is this possible?" I asked myself. "And why not?" I thought, "Samir does not waste his time with anyone without talking to him about salvation."

I felt bad and ashamed that I was still thinking about social and religious differences, and that I thought it was demeaning to us that Samir could care about our gardener in the same way he cared about Majdi and me. I must confess, at first, I resented the fact that Samir would worry about our gardener's soul—just as he did about ours. I remembered how Samir knelt by me the night before pleading with me to accept Christ, just as he was doing now with Abu Wafiq, even making him recite, "For God so loved Abu Wafiq—" Within a moment, I felt as if two strong arms were shaking my body; my heart was racing inside, I could hardly breathe. I then threw myself on the bed crying, "Lord Jesus, forgive my blindness, my selfishness, and my ignorance; forgive me because I have not yet fully understood your love for humanity, regardless of class differences or religious differences, wealth or poverty, learned or unlearned, black or white, sinners, or good people—Majdi, me, or Abu Wafiq—"

My eyes were opened to this truth, and I began to pray for Abu Wafiq's soul; I suddenly felt I truly loved him, and just like me and Majdi, I wanted him to accept Christ as his Savior. Instead of blaming myself, I thanked God that He allowed me such lowly pride, that He humbled me, so He could lift me up to this level of revelation. I got up quickly, washed my face, and ran down to the garden. I did not want to see Samir, but I wanted to see Abu Wafiq who, as usual, was working. When he saw me, he quickly picked a red rose and rushed to give it to me—just as he did in years past. His face shone like never before; so I ran towards him and gave him the biggest hug I could muster. I felt a strong force and new love drawing me to him, which I never felt before. He was so happy to see me, as he showered me with kind words and expressions of eagerness to see me again. We spoke for a while, but he never mentioned anything about his encounter with Samir earlier. I did not think he would. I thought, because he did not, Samir must have told him about Christ. Of course, I did not want to put him on the spot, so I returned to my room, thinking of an excuse to go to the Shaheens to have a talk with Samir. I then had a clever idea; I went into my father's room, took a small velvet box containing a gold pin, gift-wrapped it nicely, took it along with the letter I wrote to Danny, and headed towards the Shaheen house. I entered the house through a back door, adjacent to our garden. To my surprise, I saw Samir sitting, sunning all by himself. I greeted him from afar, he then got up and came rushing to greet me. He told me everybody would be back from the camp a little later. He stood there, looking at me, wondering why I was still standing there, and knowing it was contrary to our custom to be alone with a man! He must have seen the gift in my hand, so I quickly explained to him the reason I was there,

"Can I ask you a favor?" I asked with a little trembling voice that he must have detected.

"But of course, of course, what can I do for you?"

"During my recent visit to the United States, I met this nice young man who did us great favors we'll never forget, so I wanted to express our gratitude to him with this small gift and letter, and I thought to send it with you, if it's no bother."

Samir looked at his watch, knit his eyebrows and wanted to say something, but before he could say anything, I explained, "This gentleman works in the same hospital where you work—Johns Hopkins."

"Johns Hopkins?" He again checked his watch and asked as his jaw dropped. "And whatever took you there, and who's this gentleman you're talking about? And—did you know I worked there all along?" I replied sarcastically, "If you stop checking your watch and if you let me come in for few minutes, perhaps, I would tell you a beautiful story the like of which you've never heard."

Samir blushed with embarrassment as he invited me to sit in the garden, grabbed a chair and sat beside me, mumbling a few words of apology. He then took his watch and handed it to me, saying, "Here, you have all the time in the world, keep this watch as long as you need."

I indeed took the watch and began telling him the story in detail, beginning with my cousin Suheil in California who was the reason for my travel to Washington, and consequently, meeting Danny Roper.

"Danny?" Impossible. What a small world." He exclaimed. When he heard Danny's name, he felt more at ease, became a little less serious, and appeared more ebullient. He began to inject some humor in his conversation—a far cry from yesterday's preaching. He asked me one question after the other, and wanted to know everything that took place. I spoke about Danny all the way from when my father met his father many years ago, and at the end, how it all culminated with viewing the old film footage at the hospital. Samir put his head in his hands saying, "Praise be to the name of the Lord; I've never heard a story like this in my entire life; if someone had attempted to write it, he would not have been able to arrange its exciting events the way they took place—Praise God."

I had wished time would stand still while we were recounting all those amazing events, but since my excuse to be there had expired, I gave him the gift and letter, and made a quick exit. However, before I entered our house, I heard Amal calling me from the garden. I happily ran to meet her and told her I had just come from their house.

"Where were you? I asked quizzically. "Did you just jump out of a helicopter?"

Amal laughed and said, "You are so kind and thoughtful; your gift to Samir says it all."

Her reply left me perplexed; how did she know about the gift so quickly? I felt she must have not been talking about Danny's gift, because I just came from their house and nobody was there except Samir.

"What do you mean, Amal? What says it all?"

She ignored my question and said, "You tell me Dalal, how did you know?"

"Know what?"

Amal then became confused when she saw me perplexed and attempted to explain herself better, "I saw Samir carrying a gift, and knowing you, thought for sure it was a gift from you for his birthday."

"Whose birthday?" I asked, feeling there must be some kind of a mix-up somewhere. I then sat on the stairs, took a deep breath, and explained to Amal everything about the gift, and since it was a long story, I told her the details would have to wait for another occasion.

"But I had no idea it was Samir's birthday."

Amal apologized for the mix-up and said, "The truth was that it was Samir's birthday last night, and we wanted to surprise him with a party at camp around the fire—but—"

I interjected, "Looks like I spoiled your party last night?"

Amal grabbed my hand and said, "No no, to the contrary, Dalal; when I spoke to Samir to tell him we're sorry about his birthday party, he told me that the evening was the happiest in his life, and the salvation of Dalal and Majdi were the best gifts he could have ever received on his birthday."

Tears welled-up in my eyes—a sign of an incoming storm of tears—but our housekeeper saved the day when she came running to tell me someone was on the phone for me. I ran to answer; it was Majdi on the other end informing me my father asked him to come and take me to see Grandpa, and he would be here in half an hour. I relayed this information to Amal, but she did not seem too happy about that and said in a sad voice, "What about Samir's birthday; I wanted to make it up to him this evening with a small family party and ask you and Majdi to be with us."

I could not disappoint Amal or see her sad, so I promised not to stay long at the hospital, and promised I would do my best to return in time for the party. To give her more assurance I added, "Listen, Amal. Do not go to the trouble of making a birthday cake; you must be very tired from camp; you can prepare other things if you wish, but leave the cake to me—I'll take care of it. Wasn't it I who spoiled the party last night, I'll make it up to him," I said with a wink.

Amal easily agreed to my offer, but told me not to be later than 8:00 o'clock. I made a dash to the phone, dialed the bakery that my mother uses, and asked the pastry chef to prepare the best cake he could muster, and to put the letter "S" on the top. He chuckled, thinking the cake was for my father Salah.

Majdi was not at all surprised when I told him it was Samir's birthday, as I was looking for a nice gift for the occasion. He replied with a bit of sarcasm that his invitation came much earlier and that he had already bought him his present. I looked at him somewhat surprised, and shook my head wondering about his recent revelations, but did not comment. Within a few minutes, I found a silk shirt stashed away in my bags, which was originally my gift to Majdi. I will also include one of my father's many unopened leather belts, with the letter "S" on the buckle. I gift-wrapped these two items, put them in the car, then off we went to the hospital.

Majdi warned that we must leave the hospital by 7:30 p.m. so we could make it to the party by 8:00, but as soon as we entered the hospital, there were many security people searching inside and outside. As soon as we reached the floor where my grandfather was, we were told that the brother of the king of a Middle Eastern country and his nephew—the heir apparent—were paying my grandfather a courtesy visit. Without asking for permission to enter, I walked right to my grandfather, kissed his hand, and said to him, "Thank God you're fine, Grandpa—I love you so much."

Grandpa was so happy to see me; he kept holding my hand, not letting go, as he proudly introduced me to his visitors who I formally greeted. When my father's turn came, I introduced myself, "Dalal Abu Suleiman." Everyone chuckled, including the distinguished visitors, as well as the king's brother who gave my father a look of fake reprimand, "Salah—you have such a beautiful progeny and you keep her to yourself? Goodness, such beauty."

My father was taken aback, not knowing what to say, and decided to go along with the joke; he put his hand on my shoulder, laughing, and pulled me towards him in a hug of appreciation, and jokingly said, "I had no idea I have such a beautiful daughter."

I thought my father's expression would put an end to the uncalled-for compliments; but, to my surprise, it continued and began to take a different line of insinuation. The visitors began a plethora of questions that indicated an interest in me as a prospective bride that would be added to the harem of their family. The prince, who sat there silently, looked attractive and modern; he wore fashionable western clothes, unlike his uncle who was wearing the familiar Arab *thob* (garb) and a checkered head cover. From what little that he said, I concluded he was quite educated and fluent in English; I figured he must have studied abroad.

From time to time, I would see heads peeking into the room. It was getting late, nurses came in and out, and the visitor asked just about every question he could think of, and I was duly replying the best I could. The only question he did not ask was my age. I felt he did not know my age nor was he able to guess an approximation other than my being young. His line of questioning left no doubt in my mind, he was looking for a bride for his nephew, the prince. I wanted to make it clear to him, once and for all, first pointing to my father then grandfather,

THE ROSE →

"I don't know if my opinions and philosophy in life will change after I am eighteen; but as for now, I have not had enough of life's experiences. So until I reach maturity, I shall remain the pampered little girl of this man Salah Abu Suleiman and his honorable father, who I call Grandpa."

I knew how to hit two birds with one stone. First, I pleased my father and grandfather, and second, I let the distinguished visitors know I was only seventeen and would not contemplate marriage for a long time to come. Did I make myself subtly clear? Did the young prince agree with his uncle's inquisitiveness, did I embarrass him? I asked myself these questions as I was bidding them good-bye.

I could not believe, that finally, I was in Majdi's car driving towards the Shaheen's house. It was a little after eight, and we still had to pick up the cake. Majdi was driving fast and incessantly complaining about being late. Along the way, I told him I would like to go and see Grandpa again when he was alone in his room. I told him how I felt about our grandfather's eternal destiny and was afraid he might die without having received Christ first. To my surprise, Majdi had beaten me to this and had already spoken to Samir regarding my grandfather's salvation.

"What did Samir say?" I anxiously asked Majdi. I really wanted to know how Samir felt about this subject and what advice he would give us. It now appears Majdi has become as zealous as I have, to tell others about the joy and assurance of our salvation.

"Frankly, Dalal, the time I spent with Samir this morning was of great value to both of us. Since you were not with us, Samir showed a great interest in you by asking me to pay special attention to your spiritual well-being. He made me promise I should read the Bible with you and pray together whenever the opportunity arises, so we can strengthen each another in the faith. He promised to correspond with us, send tapes, and keep in touch. He also told me Christianity would not be a bed of roses, for at times, we would encounter thorns of trials, tribulations, even persecution from family and friends, alike. Moreover, we should exercise wisdom in averting defiance or provoking anyone to anger because of our faith; otherwise, we might find ourselves in unnecessary problems. He also intimated we ought to grow and mature spiritually first, and become stronger in the faith before engaging in any potential battles. True Christian life is a message and a living testimony worth more than thousands of empty words."

Samir's words related by Majdi left a deep impression on my heart, as well as on Majdi's, who kept talking about Samir. I was anxiously waiting for the time to go to bed, later, in the evening, and rewind today's events in my thoughts, and analyze all that happened, including Samir's words.

I wished Majdi had accepted Christ either before or after me, but not on the same night, so I would be able to tell whether Samir cared for me and not just my soul. His elation seemed to cover both of our salvation, as well as that of Abu Wafiq's, which threw me off, and hence, I could not tell. When Samir said that the last evening at camp was one of the best in his life, and Majdi's salvation and mine were the two most precious gifts he received on his birthday, would he have said the same if it were only me? I had no idea, nor would I ever know, because from that moment on, every concern Samir showed would be about both of us, together. "I really should not worry about this, at least not tonight; my salvation takes priority over my silly teenage crush!"

We were now about to enter the Shaheen's house. The party was not exclusively for the family, as I had thought, but there were many other people. I later learned these guests were their close friends from church who came to say good-bye to Samir.

The weather was beautiful on this last day of August; everybody was in the garden—some were singing, while others were sitting down, chatting—the twins were playing at the far end of the garden.

I had barely taken my first step inside the garden behind Majdi, who was carrying the cake; a loose ball hit me in the face throwing me off balance and caused me to fall. But before I hit the ground, two strong hands grabbed me to keep me from falling down and led me to a chair, where I sat down in a complete daze. Samir was standing next to me, applying an ice bag to my face. I had not then realized the extent of what the ball did to my face, as the pain became more intense between my eye and nose. Within moments, everyone rushed to my side, expressing how sorry they were for my misfortune. Bewildered, Samir asked all to move away, my nose was bleeding, and my face was throbbing with pain. He was now administering first aid, wiping away the blood with some paper tissues in an effort to stop the bleeding, and applying ice to my eye to keep down the swelling. I could not remember how much time had lapsed since the ball hit me; but now I could not feel the pain anymore, despite the hard hit my face took.

By then, I was totally taken by Samir tenderness and care; the look of concern in his eyes seemed to ease the pain. However, lest I go off on a wishful-thinking trip, it immediately dawned on me that any physician would show the same concern and care for anyone needing medical attention. I quickly dismissed entertaining any romantic thoughts. After some period of silence, Samir asked, "Do you feel better, Dalal?"

"Oh, sorry, looks like I ruined your birthday again."

Tears welled-up in my eyes and streamed down my cheeks. I felt his hand wipe my tears away, and at the same time, he told me not to ever feel sorry or even think I may have ruined his birthday. He said he was the one who felt bad seeing me in this condition. He repeated that as far as he was concerned, last night at camp, was one of the best birthday celebrations he has ever had. Hearing this made me feel better, particularly that he did not include Majdi's name at that instant, but was talking to me and me alone. Soon, I felt better, got up to join the party, which had gone almost silent after the accident. I saw Rima peek at me with Walid behind her, so I called them because I had not seen them since my arrival from the trip. They both ran to shower me with hugs and kisses, but Samir told them to go outside and not disturb me. No one remained in the room except Majdi, Amal, and Samir. The bleeding ceased and I went to the powder room to check on my face. I had a black eye, as expected, and my face looked awful, so I retreated in panic. Majdi attempted to mitigate the situation with a bit of sarcasm, "If the king's brother could see you now, he would immediately ask for your hand in marriage for his nephew!"

Majdi nearly fell back with laughter while Amal and Samir looked at him, wondering why all this laughter. Despite the humorous sarcasm, I did not laugh, but chided Majdi for laughing so hard when I was still in this condition. He apologized and told me he could not resist it. Amal now wanted to know the story behind the heir to the throne. At her insistence, Majdi finally, but briefly, told them. They all laughed except Samir who wandered away in a world of his own, without making a comment on what he had just heard. He finally said, "As long as you're feeling better, why don't we cut the cake and feed all those waiting outside?"

Amal jumped to open the carton containing the cake and exclaimed, "Oh my, what a cake! It has your first initial on it, Samir, come and have a look at this masterpiece."

Amal gave me a box of candles and I was more than happy to place all twenty-three of them around the cake, while Samir was standing next to me, watching. I then raised my puffy face, looked up at Samir, wanting to say many things, but ended up with a simple,

"Happy birthday, Samir."

Amal carried the lit-up cake, and we all went out to the garden where Samir could blow out the candles, then cut the cake. All the lights were turned off, except for the candles that looked so pretty, giving off their exquisite, dancing flames in the breeze. As Amal began to sing "Happy Birthday," everyone joined in. At the end of the song, Samir blew out the candles, sliced the cake and said, "Thank you again, Dalal, for this lovely cake, I shall never forget that the three of us were born on the same day — August, 30 — I, a physical birth, Majdi and Amal a spiritual birth."

Samir never passed an opportunity to inject spiritual analogies or the name of Jesus on every possible occasion. He expressed the great love he had for the Lord Jesus and the extent of his love and gratitude for Him in all seasons. I wished I would be like that one day. At that moment though, rather than learning from Samir's love and devotion to Christ, I felt jealous on two counts. First, I was jealous that I had no such deep emotions toward Jesus, and second, I was jealous he could not display similar emotions towards me. I felt like a little child who wanted to be loved beyond anything else. Of course, what I was thinking was probably the last thing on Samir's mind, because after much fun and mirth, he, naturally, would not let this evening pass by without spiritual encouragement and preaching.

When everyone stood up to pray at the end of the party, Samir's father asked that we all form a circle and hold hands to show unity in Christ. I happened to be standing between Samir and his younger brother Walid, and there was no escape but to hold his hand. Dr. Shaheen prayed a very touching prayer that brought tears to my eyes, but at certain moments, I would let go of Samir's hand or Walid's on the other side, to wipe away my tears. As Dr. Shaheen continued praying, my emotions betrayed me, and hence, began to sob uncontrollably; however, Samir kept squeezing my hand in support and understanding of the moment. I thanked God it was dark, so no one would see me in such a condition.

We all let go of each other's hands after the prayer ended, then Samir said a word of farewell to all those present. Majdi and I prepared to leave, but we agreed not to say good-bye now because we will be seeing Samir one more time the following morning, since Majdi, had volunteered to take him to the airport. Samir looked at me and said, "It might be a good idea if you took some medicine to relieve potential pain, and I'll be seeing you tomorrow, Lord willing."

I took some pain medication before going to bed that night, and it completely knocked me out, leaving me exhausted the following day. I looked at my watch and was utterly dismayed when I realized the watch on my wrist was not mine, but belonged to Samir. He had given it to me in the garden to indicate his total attention to the story that I told him earlier. He never reminded that I still had his watch, and it completely slipped my mind. It was 7:30 now; he should be leaving to the airport in half an hour. I got up like a mad woman, put on my housecoat, and ran out without first looking in the mirror. As I reached the garden, I saw Samir giving our gardener a hug, carrying a small bag in one hand, and in the other, a red rose. I thanked God that he was still there and shouted his name to make sure he heard me.

"Samir, Samir. Wait a minute."

He turned his head in my direction and walked towards me. He placed the bag on the ground only to notice my teary eyes; he then took a tissue from his pocket and gave it to me so I could wipe my tears away. Instead, I began to weep profusely that I became speechless. All I could do was hand him his watch back and take the red rose that he gave me, also without saying a single word. I ran back to my room, no one seeing me, except Abu Wafiq who was also teary-eyed over saying good-bye to his dear friend.

As I looked into the mirror back in my room, I was horrified. My face was black and blue and swollen, and my hair was unkempt. I shuddered at the thought that this was the last image Samir would remember me by. I slipped my body underneath the covers, lay my head on the pillow, and remained there until I heard Amal's voice, as she walked in and sat at the foot of my bed. I looked up and saw her face looked much worse than mine did. I knew that a loose ball caused my condition, but what caused Amal's face to look like that? It was pale and her eyes swollen, apparently, from crying. As soon as her eyes met mine, she threw herself on my shoulder and began to cry.

Poor Amal, she was not going to find solace in me because I needed more solace than she did. If her brother's departure saddened her, in comparison, he broke my heart, especially, now I had met him, and had become even more enamored by his person. If she was crying freely, I was trying hard not to shed a tear, lest I give my feelings away, at Samir's departure. My tears could not be justified, but I finally managed to say, "But that was not the first time your brother leaves, Amal, why all this crying?"

"True, it's not the first time, nor will it be the last; I thought I got used to it, but it's different this time." She replied as she was wiping her tears away.

"In what way is it different? What changed? A brother remains a brother, and travel remains travel."

"I felt he was not feeling well this time, and that he got tired of travel and wanted to stay with us. When we waited for you this morning, and before he rode in the car with Majdi, he went to bid good-bye to your gardener. When he came back, however, I saw sadness in his face, and some signs of tears in his eyes. He remained silent all the way to the airport. That broke my heart because Samir never cries, as he always puts on a strong front."

I did not comment, and Amal had nothing more to say; she said good-bye and left. Then I began to wonder why Samir never told them anything about our encounter earlier. Why did he not tell his sister—my best friend? Why did he cry after bidding Abu Wafiq farewell? As usual, I began to think, dissect, and analyze all Amal told me. I smiled to myself thinking, "Samir must have shed his tears because he was saying good-bye to me." I felt so much better with these thoughts, though they may be the extension of wild imagination, but all indicators seemed to be in my favor. Or were they?

Now, a plane in the air flying above Lebanon is carrying a piece of my heart. All of a sudden, an overwhelming avalanche of emotions overcame me, and I sat there in my innocent adolescence, thinking about how would I carry on without having Samir around? The days ahead seemed to create a great divide, and months would pass before I would be able to see him again, not to mention the thousands of miles that separated us. School will sure help me overcome the void I felt that morning. I opened the book of John and caressed the red rose I put within its fold, thinking, contently, the red rose will have to do for now.

It was not easy to explain to my father that my blue-black face was just the result of a simple accident; good thing my mother was not there. All I could hope for, now, was that my face would heal before my mother returned from England. My father did not comment further on the accident, and it was soon forgotten.

Despite the sadness I was feeling, the two days that followed Samir's departure, were quite memorable. Amal and I were always together. I wanted to take advantage of the situation before my mother returned; because, although I missed her, I knew things in my life would change, drastically, upon her return. That is why I asked Amal to sleep at our house those two nights—we had a lot about which to talk.

One of those days, we asked Majdi to come and have dinner with us around the small pond in our garden. Amal promised she would take care of the cooking. It was during that evening that I told them all the details of my trip to the United States, beginning with the story behind the Gospel of John, until we met again at camp. It took me over two whole hours to tell all, because Majdi and Amal kept interrupting and asking questions about certain events, finding some parts of my story quite incredible. Amal commented on the story behind the Gospel of John, and jokingly called me "The Bible Thief". She said she left no stone unturned in the house looking for that book. I was happy that Majdi was present, to hear about my trip, so that I would not have to repeat it to him, later. I could then, talk about Danny, Mary Graham, and Mona as one family. Majdi took a special interest in the story of my father's old school mate, Billy Roper, whereas Amal took interest in knowing more about Mary Graham, her personality, and her love for Jesus—She also wanted to see the Bible Mary gave me. I said to them while opening my bags, "I am still quite impressed by the book of John and the way you studied it, Amal. Had it not been for the lines, circles, and notations with which you marked, I would have understood very little of it; that's why I asked Mary to give me a similar one with such markings, if she had any. She promised to give me her deceased mother's old Bible."

"I did not circle or underline Bible words that seemed important" Amal replied, "But I also wrote what God has spoken to me about. I wished Mary would have given you a new one, so you could do the same with it, and hence, become your own personal Bible."

I was listening to Amal and looking for the Bible Mary gave me. Amal's statement was true and logical, Majdi was quick to agree with what she said, and added, "Me too, that's what I am going to do, as I study my own Bible. Just give me one year to study this great book and then see me again, so I can give you wonderful reports of my studying." He said proudly.

I did not comment on what Majdi said in any way, I felt no need to encourage him nor discourage him, neither did I feel like I should congratulate him on his new endeavor, not that I was being indifferent, but because, at that moment, I was too absorbed in finding Mary's gift, wrapped in colored paper. I tore off the wrapping expecting to see the old dilapidated Bible, but instead, there was a brand new Arabic Bible bound in a leather case, with a zipper! I screamed in disbelief and called on Majdi and Amal to help me solve this puzzle. Why did Mary change her mind about the old Bible and gave me a new one instead? She never told me, and I had no idea why she did that. Why an Arabic Bible and not an English one, and how was she able to find an Arabic Bible in the United States?

So many questions raced through my mind; I began with one single question, but quickly my questions were multiplying exponentially. Finally, Amal took the book away from my hand and opened it. There she found a letter and said, "Here, don't bother yourself with questions; this letter should provide all the answers."

"Dalal, I know you must be surprised, now, that you opened my gift to you; instead of my dear mother's old, dilapidated Bible—as I had promised you—you found a brand new one. Do not think I changed my mind because my mother's Bible was a dear memory from her, and that I had decided to keep it; the truth is, I wanted you to begin with your own Bible so you would not be robbed of the joy of beginning to study in your own Bible. You could also mark it as you see fit, and as the Holy Spirit leads you—just like my dear mother did with her Bible, and as Amal did with hers. On the inside cover, I pasted a daily Bible reading schedule so, within one year, you'd be able to read it from cover to cover. Now you may wonder how I got hold of an Arabic Bible. Who could know about it except your dear cousin Mona? She knows of an Arabic church here in Los Angeles, through which I was able to get you this valuable book. I wish this Holy Book to be a blessing in your life and that it becomes your friend in need and out of need. Memorize this verse and repeat it as often as you can, **"Thy word have I hid in mine heart, that I might not sin against thee."** I will stay in touch and keep remembering you in my prayers."

"What an expressive letter." These were Majdi's and Amal's almost first similar words after having read the letter aloud. Then they chose to leave me alone in the room to continue unpacking, and I held the Bible close to my heart. "Thank you, Mary, for this precious gift, and thank you Lord for the joy you have brought my way today."

The days that followed were full of activity, as my mother returned from London and my grandfather was released from the hospital, as well as traveling to our mountain house to spend the few remaining days of summer. Seemingly, my mother found out, soon, about the king's brother who came to visit my grandfather, accompanied by his eligible nephew at the hospital, and was very interested. Every time we sat together, she would repeatedly ask me the same question, What did he say, and what did you reply? What did he ask? What did you say—*ad nauseum*? Her questioning really bothered me because I was able to see where she was going with this line of questioning.

A few months ago, this attention would have made me very happy, amused me, and fed my ego, but today was different—I had changed. I could not remember that any of the Shaheens ever asked or told me how to behave or not behave; they never dictated a "Do" or "Do Not Do list." I began to hate loud parties and felt I did not belong there, among people who reveled in dancing, smoking, drinking, or irreverent partying. In fact, I began to have self-awareness when I put on immodest clothing—such as mini-skirts—or even dancing with men. I began to become disgusted with young men hovering over me, like flies around honey, making all sorts of cheap, embarrassing remarks. I began to feel lonely and out of place in such company.

What bothered me more in staying at the mountain house, even for such a short time, was being unable to have fellowship with Amal, as I had become used to in the last few weeks. Even Majdi, who was the only one in the family I could feel comfortable with, limited his visits to us. I was certain he was spending his time with the Shaheens, profiting more from their deep spiritual walk with the Lord; it made me count the days and hours, to get back to school, and our home in Beirut.

The schedule Mary provided me for my Bible reading would take me one whole year to read from cover to cover, but my thirst and hunger for God's word made me read more than what the schedule required. In less than two weeks, circles, highlights, and notations in different colors covered the many pages. To my surprise, I even found that reading Old Testament stories was of great interest, such as the story of Esther, Ruth, Joseph, and many others. The Psalms of David became one of my favorite books to read that I even memorized the

23rd Chapter by heart, according to the schedule, **"The Lord is my shepherd, I shall not want..."**

The schedule included reading both testaments—the Old and the New—and Psalms, beginning with the Gospel according to Matthew. I reflected long on the story of Jesus' humble birth and compared it to my own birth and the fanfare that followed. The comparison touched my heart and moved me to tears; here, God Almighty, Creator of this universe, would be born in a humble manger meant for animals? I was now eager to see how the Shaheens would celebrate the coming Christmas and then compare it to how other Christians marked the occasion. I found the celebrations to be very different from the Biblical story. I knew Christians exchanged presents, gave lavish dinner parties at Christmas; many would spend the evening in nightclubs dancing, drinking, and doing everything else to please themselves instead of the One whose birthday they were supposed to celebrate. Christmas was a commercial success; we even began to decorate a Christmas tree in our house with the most expensive ornaments even though we were of a different persuasion, altogether. Moreover, it was a great profitable occasion for my mother's boutique, 'Dalal', where society women would not hold back to buy the fanciest and most expensive clothes to wear for that evening or to give as presents. I did not know why the Christmas story kept popping in my mind and the way many Christians celebrated it. I could not wait to see how 'true' Christians, such as the Shaheens, commemorated it.

Despite my great craving to read the Bible every chance I got, I would sometimes close it, put it near me, and begin to rerun the events of the summer up to that point. I would begin with our travel to the United States, meeting Danny, London, our return to Lebanon, and meeting Samir, including the memory of the red rose he gave me. Although there were no visible signs I was on Samir's mind, or even occupied a tiny, little corner of his heart, I was, nonetheless, able to draw conclusions and build on some words he uttered here and there. I loved to think he harbored some feelings towards me. After all, most young men I met felt the same way, so why not Samir? The biggest sign came from Amal who told me she saw his eyes get misty when he was bidding me good-bye. As we say in Arabic, "If we need something badly, we try to hang by strings of air."

Meanwhile, my mother was preparing a grand party at my grandfather's house to celebrate his recovery after surgery and his release from the hospital. The party will contain the usual routine, dancing, drinking, and showing off flashy clothes that bordered on immodest. Not to mention the presence of that young prince I met earlier at the hospital—and who my mother was told was such a good 'catch' for her daughter. Just the thought of attending the party worried me; I dreaded it. Despite that, I was overly happy that this party would announce the end of summer, our return to Beirut, and the beginning of the school year. This meant I would be joining Amal and visiting her family quite often. That was exactly what happened; it felt so good to see the neighbor's house again and its occupants, especially Amal. We began our last year of high school, but I somehow felt that that year would hold a lot of happiness, as well as pain.

Chapter 9
THE CHRISTMAS STORY

❦

*T*he sickness and heart attack which beset my grandfather stirred my mother's old dream that one day he would relinquish his leadership role and my father would take over. In turn, she would officially become the wife of the undisputed leader of the clan. She was already preparing for such an eminent title, even though my father did not see that happening in the near future. My feeling was he had no desire to take over as leader, which meant immense responsibilities, mundane ceremonies, visitations, meetings, and other equally boring duties. My father wanted to live a simple life with his wife and only daughter. I could overhear their discussion—often heated—that would frequently end up with my mother storming out of her bedroom, slamming the door, and going to sleep in a different room.

Since my father's illness in the United States, then running into Danny who turned out to unfold a bigger surprise in finding out his father was an old friend, I felt my dad was undergoing some kind of deep psychological struggle. He became very moody, losing his temper over the slightest irritation. He would always try to find me alone, but without bringing up the "Christ" element, but instead, he would indirectly invoke a spiritual topic. For example, he would ask about the Shaheens, their faith, and the discussions we had when I was at their house. I always hoped that in my mother's absence, my father would come to me and tell me all about his university experiences some thirty-six years ago, as he had promised. What happened the year my father and Billy Roper were together? I found it strange he never mentioned him since we returned from the United States; equally strange, he never asked about him, called him or corresponded with him. I began to wonder why he was acting this way, and what was bothering him that made him so miserable. I wished I were able to lead him to the only true friend who said, **"Come unto me, all ye that labor and are heavy laden, and I will give you rest."** I felt that was what my father needed at that point in his life.

It was no coincidence my mother had to go on another business trip to London just before the onset of the Christmas and New Year's holidays. She allowed me to spend as much time as I wanted with Amal and her family, for she now trusted our neighbors. My excellent grades were the icing on the cake that convinced her I was safe; and on this premise, she flew to London. The trust she had in the Shaheen family pleased me, and if my relationship with Samir had any shape other than what was running in my imagination, I would have been the happiest girl on earth. There were absolutely no signs from him, and only wishful thinking on my part, in addition to the few straws I tried so hard to hang onto. Such straws, however, are not strong enough to hold up to reality. Samir never dropped me a note, or even conveyed his regards to me via Danny who regularly corresponded with me. All his letters were sermons or replies to questions from Majdi. If any person had treated me with such indifference, I would have forgotten him in no time at all; but Samir's behavior intrigued me and made me more attached to him. What irony! This situation lent truth to the old saying, "A woman is like your shadow, follow it and it runs away from you; run away from it, and it follows you." Except here, it applies to the man and not the woman.

In the few days that followed my mother's absence, my relationship with my father became stronger than ever, and instead of a parent-daughter relationship, it became more of a friendship. One evening, I went into my father's study to wish him 'goodnight'; but to my surprise, he did not kiss me as he always did. There were several papers in front of him, written in English, but I was not able to read any of their content. He kept looking at them without even acknowledging my presence, so I became worried and asked him, "Are you OK Dad?"

He did not reply; and when I repeated my question, he replied with a loud voice with some anger, "What makes you think I am not? Of course I am OK. Good night."

I promptly left the room before he could realize what he said hurt me. I went into my bedroom, shut the door, and sat on my bed, worrying. His behavior was not normal, there was definitely something wrong, more than I could imagine. Something in these papers must be the reason. Who was the author? What was their content?

The truth was, although I was his pampered daughter and he ever hardly said 'No' to me, there were some 'forbidden fruits' I was not supposed to touch. I was not supposed to go into his study when he was not there or go through the drawers to read anything that did not concern me. There was an old understanding between the two of us that I never broke, but I felt certain the paper he was perusing caused his moodiness. The more I thought about it, the more I felt the urge to taste the forbidden fruit. What a dreadful thought. The temptation got the best of me, and I found myself stealthily walking by my father's room to check whether he was sound asleep. He was snoring, and the lights were out.

I ran to his study and started searching through his drawers until I found what looked like the papers I had seen, earlier, on his desk. My heart was pounding so loudly, I could hear the beats like drums; I went through them hastily with my eyes racing over the words. I was now breathing heavily, and my hands were sweating with one eye on the door and the other scanning the papers. There was a small night light in the corner of the study, and I began to read these papers by that dim light. I did not want to turn on a brighter light so as not to wake any of the housekeepers, either. I nearly fainted when one of the letters was from Billy Roper; I was able to gather, it was the third letter from him after having received a call from my father, after our trip to the United States. Billy was asking my father why he had not returned his call, but I skipped all the portions about old memories, in an effort to discover the source of all the pain my father was hiding. I finally made the discovery that I always wanted to know about his life at Cambridge; I was just intrigued. The words leapt from the letters and came to life as they hit the dim light that came upon them, "Salah, you happened to accept the Lord and experience the taste of Jesus Christ as your Savior, my dear friend. I was with you when you knelt down to pray and asked Jesus to forgive your sins and invite Him into your heart. What caused you to walk away from Him and deny Him, as Peter did before he heard the rooster crow? What have you gained from your neglect of His great salvation? My friend, remember that message that shook your being, **"For what profiteth a man if he should gain the whole world and lose his own soul…"**

Before I could take another breath to give me more strength to read any further, I heard a slight cough coming from my father's room. I had almost finished reading the whole letter, when I suddenly read my name, and now I became more curious, but I was not able to read all the sentences that followed, except this, "As far as your daughter Dalal is concerned—"

My hair stood on edge as I heard the squeaking noise of my father's bedroom door and footsteps approaching the study. There was no room for escape now. I thought such events only happen in the movies. I ran and hid behind a bookshelf as I held my breath and prayed to God he would not to discover me. I also asked for forgiveness that I would not never ever again disobey. My father did not stay in the study for more than a few seconds that seemed like ages to me. I was not sure what he wanted from the office: Did he want to reread his friend's letter or just to take some medicine from a cabinet he kept there? Whatever the reason, God saved me from a huge mess. My father returned to his bedroom and closed the door behind him. I then ran as quietly and as quickly as I could, to return to my bedroom, and I locked the door.

I knelt down crying and thanking God for saving me at the right moment from being caught. I poured out my heart for the new revelation I had just discovered about my father. What a bombshell that was! I did not have enough strength to get up and sleep in my bed, so I remained lying on the floor all night long. I was too exhausted to think about what happened or to analyze the content of the letter, especially my father's past encounter with Christ. My only concern now was to fall asleep. I finally fell asleep around 4 a.m. before my father knocked on my door to wake me up three hours later. I jumped up from the floor unto my bed, pretending I was asleep. My father knocked again and called, "Dalal, may I come in?"

I wanted to reply, but every time I tried, my voice betrayed me; it seemed I developed what I thought to be a sore throat. Then he spoke again with a voice of sadness that broke my heart, "Please Dalal, open the door; I am sorry about last night."

I quickly remembered I had locked the door and felt guilty my father was standing outside, pleading with me to forgive him when I actually offended him and betrayed his trust, although he knew nothing about it. I lazily got up and opened the door; he walked in and gave me a hug, then looked me in the face, rubbed my head, and said, "Are you OK? You're not sick, are you?"

I wanted to tell him I was fine, but my vocal chords would not cooperate. I had completely lost my voice. He noticed I was trying hard to reply, so he put his hand on my forehead only to feel high fever. He panicked and immediately called our family doctor who came hurriedly, examined me, and said with a smile, "Nothing to worry about; it's just a symptom that will soon go away. Physically, your throat seems fine; take this medicine, and in a couple of days, your voice will return to normal."

My father asked, "What happened, what caused this? There was nothing wrong with her last night."

The doctor shook his head, and said, "I don't know; sometimes these things happen when someone experiences shock or fear; but this does not apply to Dalal of course. I am sure she did not experience any of these, but other causes might apply, such as sleeping in a draughty place. The important thing is there's nothing to fear, and she soon will return to normal."

The doctor wrote a prescription that our chauffeur promptly filled at a nearby pharmacy. Meanwhile, I thanked God for having lost the ability to speak to avoid answering some would-be questions. Besides, I would not be obliged to tell Amal about what happened, either, should she ask. From that moment on, and until my condition improved, I would stay in bed and try to discover the mysteries of my father's past, as well as let loose my imagination in analyzing the contents of the his friend's letter.

I did not go to school that day, or the following two days. Amal was spending much time with me keeping me up-to-date on my schoolwork. Her mother was checking on me twice a day, whenever my father went to work, only to check on important issues, then would rush back to the house to be with me. He stopped talking to me or asking me questions, to keep me from aggravating my vocal chords. He, however, would sit, open a book, and pretend to read a while then glance at me from time to time. I knew he could not concentrate on reading with all that was on his mind.

It was late October; there was a much steady rain, accompanied by unusual cold. The wind was creating strange symphonies as it pushed the rain in different directions. However, I was feeling warm, quite warm, under tons of covers, with only my head sticking out, watching my father's facial gestures, to see if I am able to figure something out that may be on his mind. The more I looked, the more love I felt for him—even more than I had thought I would. The letter I read last night increased my love for him and caused me to sympathize with him, yet feel sorry for him, at the same time. My poor father—I had mistakenly assumed he did not contact his old friend after having found him and knew where he lived. The letter indicated there must have been two previous letters, but I had no idea how many letters there were, nor did I know what was in them.

After the few scary moments last night in my father's study, I had no desire to try the same stunt again. What concerned me the most was my knowledge of my father's salvation and his second birth that took place many years ago, but were they genuine? He must have passed through the same experience Majdi and I went through; he, therefore, must be a child of God. Then a thought struck me: when we are born to our parents, we will always continue to be their children; we cannot reverse that procedure, once a child, always a child, no matter what the circumstances are, even if we ever wished to disavow them or vice versa. For example, I, Dalal Abu Suleiman, daughter of Salah and Huda Abu Suleiman, born 17 years ago, will always be their daughter, even if I did anything that might bring shame on them. Now, would this apply to my father and his heavenly Father? I wondered. Will God forgive him for all the years he lived away from Him, and maybe even denied Him? I remembered what Billy Roper wrote in his letter to my father when he was exhorting him to 'return to the Lord on his own accord lest God uses the "stick" on him to bring him back into the fold.'

I looked at my father who was sitting across from me, pretending to read a book, and I thought about his situation. It must be a difficult one. How could he declare his Christianity while he is the well-known politician of a renowned family, son of a political leader and feudal lord who is able to shake a whole country? Moreover, who will soon inherit his father's title? How will the family react? What will my mother say and do if she found out that her husband once privately declared his faith in Jesus Christ but never practiced his newly-found faith, and now might want to declare it in public? Was all this possible, or was I again allowing my imagination to wander off into oblivious wonderment? I panicked at such thoughts. My father had only two choices to make, either to please God or man. If he opted for the first choice, he would certainly anger his family, his society, and his political followers; if he chose the second, he would sadden his heavenly Father. He cannot please both. Needless to say, it was not that simple to change. This decision required a lot of courage, and above all, wisdom. Therefore, what could I do, how would I play my role— and more important—what is my role in this predicament?

I tried to remap the roots of my father's dilemma. Did I cause this seismic event from unfolding by going with my parents to Baltimore and meeting Dr. Danny Roper? Did I bring to the surface the lost relationship between both our fathers? Was it Danny's fault to bring such a sensitive issue, albeit innocently, to surface? On the other hand, was it Amal's fault to ask me to look up her brother while I was in the United States? Suddenly, I realized the futility of this line of reasoning. It was nobody's fault, after all. Things happen for a purpose. At that point, I asked myself what God's purpose was in all this. Has He no part in it? Is not my father His child? Does not the Father do good things for his own children? I thought about how much my father loves me and would never cause me any harm. I also thought how Dr. Shaheen must love his own children and would do the impossible to provide for them. Then I thought how much more and better our Heavenly Father provides for his children? Then it must not be anyone's fault; God simply loves my father—his child—so much that He will provide him an opportunity to repent and return to His fold where He put him at an early age, regardless of any consequences. My father's reputation, his political leadership and influence, his standing in society, and even his immense wealth were unimportant when his soul was at stake, I thought. God, the Father, was now—through all these events—shaking up my father so he could wake up from this lull and return to make amends with Jesus.

I pondered about all such thoughts that floated in my mind while still in bed with my eyes shut. I always found being in bed was the best time and place to reflect on things, especially events that were rapidly unfolding before me. When I opened my eyes, I saw my father nodding off in his chair, with the book still in his hands, on the same page. My hoarse voice could not ask questions, nor was any comfort for him, but then I thought,

"Sorry, Dad that I referred to you as 'poor Dad'; you are not poor at all. Poor would be the one without a heavenly father. Not to worry, Dad, I will pray for you, stand by you, and will keep this revelation about you confidential, until you choose to proclaim it yourself in public. I am also prepared to suffer with you, if you have to suffer from any pain, insults, or persecution that may come your way from those around you. Persecution would be inevitable from those who consider your conversion an aversion to what you were taught or practiced all your life. Not to worry, Dad, you will come out victorious with God's help. I love you so much and proud and happy to be your daughter."

Since my voice was still silent, I deliberately made some noise to wake him up. When he opened his eyes, I held a piece of paper on which I wrote, "I love you Dad."

***

The relationship between my parents became more complicated, as none of them had much patience with the other. They did not talk gently, anymore, but anger seemed to make its way into their conversations—or perhaps I should say arguments! Every exchange grew louder than usual, even over trivial matters. The once-happy life we enjoyed became a thing of the past; our dinners together became silent and tedious. My father was turning down many social invitations and stopped holding official dinners. He ceased to be the 'life of the party' and quit smoking except on occasion, just to please others, and I hardly ever saw him hold a drink in his hand. It was evident he was struggling with himself. I had hoped the letter from Billy Roper was behind his recent behavior; this letter, should have been a source of peace and joy in his heart instead of misery; but he seemed to have become more agitated, he would blame my mother for every little thing. I was now lost between them, as each was showing more love to me than the other did, in order to win me over, or perhaps to spite each other. I was a tool in their battle that had turned me into their captive. Not knowing how to deal with them, I sadly became accustomed to the situation that was getting worse as the days passed.

Christmas and New Year were just around the corner; I was eagerly awaiting these two events. One day I was at Amal's house while her mother was away shopping. When she returned, she was carrying a bundle of music sheets, as well as many other items. She told us she was planning to form a small group of people to teach them Christmas songs.

Christmas? Yes, that was what I had been waiting for, impatiently, so I could see how this family celebrates this event. I listened, carefully, to every word Mrs. Shaheen was saying about the way they observed Christmas in the United States, and how she directed choirs and recitals at different churches and places. Then she said, "Although I realize we cannot organize a large choir here, Jesus, nonetheless, could bless a small group and magnify our minimal efforts as long as we do it in His name and to His glory."

Here I interrupted her, "Why can't you do it as you used to in America? Our Lord Jesus deserves a huge event."

"It's true, sweetie, but we lack the means here; moreover, we are so short on time, we should have started much earlier. In the United States, preparations begin in late summer, and now we're in mid-November' we still don't know who can join the choir."

"If it's a matter of money, I can manage to provide it."

"No doubt my dear Dalal that money is a major element, but we also need a pianist who can read music."

"You can; that's your specialty, isn't it?"

"Yes, it is; but I cannot lead and play the piano at the same time."

"Don't you have pianists in your church, Auntie Nancy?"

"Yes, but most play by ear, and I need someone who can read music and is willing to help. Practice is very important, and even if I were able to find someone who is willing to spend time in practice, then I believe we can have an appropriate performance; otherwise, I'd have to settle for a small choir where I can simultaneously play the music and lead at the same time."

Mrs. Shaheen went silent, and so did I, but my heart, within, was restless. I studied piano since I was six, and I excelled—including reading music. I had the best teachers and received different certificates and diplomas to attest to that. An inner voice told me, "This is your chance, Dalal; to serve your master, Jesus, and contribute in an appropriate performance that befits Him and His birth." At the same time, an inner voice was telling me, "This requires a lot of time and great effort; how will you manage both your studies and practice?" Then I would hear my heart tell me, "You can easily do this; God gave you a talent not only to use for the enjoyment of politicians and dignitaries who come to visit you on occasion, but also to glorify the name of the Lord Jesus Christ who loved you and died for you."

However, my mind kept its threatening tone, "Even if you were prepared to sacrifice your time and effort, your mother and family would not allow you to participate in a Christmas concert."

There was a struggle going on between my heart and mind, each pulling me in the opposite direction. I finally overcame my fears and told Mrs. Shaheen, "Auntie Nancy, if the problem is going to be the pianist, I'd be willing to play for you. I am sure you will be happy with my playing; I have many years of experience, and this is my chance to give the Lord Jesus His first birthday present from me."

Mrs. Shaheen's jaw dropped, and so did Amal's. They were both now looking at me with disbelief that I really meant what I said, and even had the courage to embark on such a commitment, considering my non-Christian background and the potential consequences of such a public display. My character and my upbringing, however, would not keep me from doing what I thought was right. So after some concerns expressed by Mrs. Shaheen, she agreed on the condition that I obtain my mother's permission first. Frankly, I had not thought how she would react if I told her, or whether or not she would allow me. I was counting on my father to help me directly or indirectly. Regardless of whether I get her permission, nothing was going to stop me from playing the piano at this precious occasion. By now, I was simply engrossed in the Christian faith.

I began to practice in earnest, playing the cantata music so I could offer my best. I told Majdi of my plans and expected him to ask me with disbelief. "Did your mother agree to this?" However, he said nothing of the sort; but instead, he encouraged me and expressed pride in my spiritual growth. After much thought, I first approached my father and told him of my intention, but only after he saw my excellent grades in chemistry. I told him that I would like to return the favor by playing the piano for Mrs. Shaheen's choir. I told him they were looking for a pianist, but could not find one. He did not exactly give me a negative answer, but he immediately asked, "But what about your mother, how do you intend to convince her?"

"By praying; I'll pray and the Lord will answer my prayers to provide the proper solution."

Shaking his head while looking at me, my father, curled his lip, as though he was saying, "That's faith." He then wished me good luck and abruptly walked away.

I really did not need much luck and did not take a great effort to persuade my mother. I carefully built my case and basically told her I would be playing in a large hall at the American University of Beirut before hundreds of Lebanese personalities, and what not. She immediately agreed—as I thought—and considered it a golden opportunity that her daughter would be playing before so many people. Not only that, but she also promised that she would also attend the event!

"Thank you, Lord for your faithfulness; I knew you would come through." I exclaimed. He gave me more than I bargained for. All I wanted was my mother's permission, but He gave me the bonus of my mother's attending the event as well. This indeed calls for a celebration. That said, I did not volunteer any more information about the concert lest I gave her any room for second thoughts, and she did not ask any further questions. She probably thought I would be playing secular music! That was great, for I did not want to tell a lie or make up some story. The first thing I did was to run to Amal's house with the good news. The whole family was having dinner, so I took the music sheets, sat at the piano, and began to play as though it was a do or die audition. I wanted to reassure Mrs. Shaheen of my playing ability, so I selected the most difficult piece. When it was over, I turned around, bowed my head, and said while laughing, "Dalal Abu Suleiman will play for the choir with her mother's permission."

Everyone applauded and shouted with joy as tears ran down my face, promising the Lord that I would pay Him back what little I could offer for His great love and providence for me.

I had a great time practicing with the choir despite the hard work and time required; but the joy I felt at the piano for hours on end was the best reward I ever had. There was laughter, exhaustion, complaints, errors, corrections, and all what practice entails, but everyone was ecstatic performing a simple task for the Lord Jesus.

Saturday, on the day before the recital, we spent many hours practicing. While we were performing the final rehearsal, the door opened, and I saw my father take a seat in the back of the hall. I ignored him for fear that I would lose concentration and continued performing well until the end; then everyone went home to get some rest before the recital on the following day. I rode back home with my father, and on the way, he praised my playing the piano at such a high level with such feeling. He also told me how great everything sounded, including the voices not forgetting to heap praise upon the efforts each member put out, especially Mrs. Shaheen's dedication.

"Jesus deserves our best, and since it is His birthday, what better gift to give Him than the best we have; my playing the piano is my gift for Him at this occasion; what will you give Him, Dad? I nervously asked.

This was the first time I mentioned the name of Jesus to my father. We always used to substitute His name by saying 'Lord,' but after my concert, I became filled with courage to invoke the name of Jesus freely. We played John W. Peterson's Night of Miracles cantata. It was the first time for me that I heard these songs; they carried me to new spiritual heights I'd never experienced before. It was an unparalleled feeling, save for the day I accepted Christ as Lord and Savior that evening at camp. I did not mean to offend my father, but I asked him that question, not expecting a reply. I wanted him to start thinking about the whole issue and the consequences that might follow. I wanted him to feel that Christmas must not pass without our proper acknowledgment for what the Lord has done for us. It would sadden me if my father would not have any room in his heart for Jesus. Perhaps having accompanied Amal on the piano while she sang, "Have You any Room for Jesus?" prompted me to ask him all these questions. I memorized the enchanting lyrics Amal sang; and while my father was driving slowly, with his eyebrows knit, apparently thinking about something, I began to sing,

"Have you any room for Jesus, He who bore your load of sin?
As He knocks and asks admission, Sinners, will you let Him in?"

I repeated this stanza several times until we reached home. All the while, my father kept to himself, silently driving, as I expected, but I did notice some tears streaming down his cheeks. He was trying hard to wipe them as inconspicuously as possible, taking extra care I would not notice. In times like these, tears of silence speak more eloquently than thousands of tongues uttering the most articulate words.

After we arrived home, I went directly to my room, leaving my father to respond to a barrage of questions from my mother. I could overhear her ranting on with the usual line of interrogative style, "Where, who, when, how, and what? Who else was there? Did any of our friends see us, and from where did he pick Dalal?" All her questions were asked in vain; my father ignored her, as he did me, earlier, and his only response was a terse, "Good night."

The evening episode made it clear to me that my father was facing a ferocious spiritual battle against Satan. My father's soul was at stake; Satan was throwing everything he had at my father so he would continue on this path of denial and fear. Satan is very powerful, and can use our weaknesses and vulnerabilities to gain a foothold in our minds to keep us from worshiping God. His abilities would only be successful when we are weak and alienated from God. We cannot face his ruthlessness on our own, as I heard from Samir's preaching earlier. The drastic change in my father's behavior was an indication that he was succumbing to Satan's ploy. Both my mother and I noticed this change, but particularly my mother, when he snapped at her, and when he kept his conversations with her to the bare minimum.

I decided I must do something after the Christmas program and the end of the holiday, to get him back to where he was spiritually when he surrendered to Christ, long ago. I thought about the letter from his old friend, Billy Roper, and what secrets it held. I thought perhaps I ought to share those secrets with somebody—maybe Amal. I soon discarded such a notion because I thought Amal was still too young to be of any useful help with such a thorny issue. I thought of confiding in my cousin, Majdi, but soon dismissed that idea too, as he would not be a good candidate to talk to my father at this time because of his recent conversion. Finding out about both our recent conversions, might turn my father against both of us, but I could not be sure.

I thought of writing Billy Roper a letter to let him know I read his letter, and to share with him the way my father was dealing with it. I also wanted to ask him for some advice regarding this dilemma; while at the same time, I did not want to expose the fact I had read my father's private letters without his permission. I wished Samir were still here; he would have been the person to talk to in his calm and collected style, as well as his objectivity. He alone, I thought, would be able to have a deep spiritual opinion in regard to that tricky situation. Then I thought of writing Samir to explain to him the situation and get his input. The idea kept brewing in my mind, until I felt quite comfortable, and I began to prepare for it, running words and expressions through my mind, I would include in my letter.

I lay in bed trying to sleep with all these thoughts running through my mind. I woke up Sunday morning even more tired than the day before, because I had many a restless night thinking and analyzing. I was worried that I might get sick during the day and spoil the Christmas program later in the evening. I felt certain Satan was waging his war against me this time around. He wanted to paralyze my will and take away the joy that filled my being. I remembered what Mary Graham had told me, earlier, that we should not be ignorant of Satan's ploys; we therefore must not let our guards down, but be wary and vigilant at all times. At such a thought, I knelt down by my bed and prayed to the Lord to give me the strength needed to perform well, including a special prayer for Mrs. Shaheen, the choir, and the audience, so that everything piece of the performance would glorify the name of Christ.

The time came for us to be on our way to the concert hall at the American University of Beirut. But before heading out, I tried on a yellow and green dress in front of my mother, who expressed her approval and told me how lovely I looked. She gave me a hug, wished me good luck, and promised me she would attend the recital. My father, on the other hand, kept to himself, so I avoided talking to him and did not ask him whether he would accompany my mother. I did not wish to add to the turmoil I was sure was ripping though him; besides, I wanted to prepare myself mentally, physically, and spiritually to do my best for my Savior.

The program was quite successful—even better than expected. The concert hall adorned for the occasion with lovely Christmas decorations, and with dignitaries, diplomats, clergy, professors, and many university students in attendance. Mother sat in the front row, next to the Lebanese Minister of Tourism, my father's friend; but I was not able to see my father. Before the start of the program, I played an interlude that received thunderous applause. I must say that my heart was racing at full speed, as this was the first time I performed before such an audience. I kept focused on my playing and avoided looking at my mother. When my fingers hit the keys, I was praying that they would be the fingers that would make a psalm of music for my Lord, and express the sentiment in my heart that would confirm my love for Christ.

The program lasted two hours and the cantata was superb, and everyone gave their best. Amal's solos were angelic, and the readings from the Gospel of Matthew were anointed with a special blessing. The entire time, I kept my eyes fixed on Mrs. Shaheen while she conducted the choir. The first time, I looked in my mother's direction to gauge her reaction; I noticed non-other but the "charming prince" standing next to her, smiling, and applauding with vigor. "Whatever brought him here; why was he standing next to mother. Did she invite him? Did she know he was going to attend?" The questions were rushing through my mind.

At this moment, without paying much attention, I began to play the postlude when I thought I heard my name being called, and the public was up on their feet in an apparent standing ovation. However, I froze in my chair, not noticing I was expected to stand up and take a bow. I then heard Amal whisper my name and motion to me to stand up and take a bow; I immediately jumped up, took a bow, and went back to continue the postlude, all the while cameras flashing in my face, blinding me. As I hit the last note, and the music sheets were turned for the last time, I sighed in relief.

As the concert ended and the congratulatory expressions deluged the place, I was beginning to experience a pounding headache, which may have been the onset of a migraine that used to beset me, from time to time. Amal was the only one to detect my condition. Majdi suggested driving me home, but before I could gather my belongings, my mother was hugging, kissing, and showering Mrs. Shaheen with all kinds of compliments for the beautiful program.

This was a big social occasion for Mom and an opportunity to show me off as well. I was almost certain she probably mostly enjoyed my playing the piano and did not understand the lyrics, nor likely cared for them. She was so excited to the extent she'd invited the entire choir for a party at our house. I almost dropped to the floor upon hearing this, not quite sure I had heard it correctly. I hated to have all the group come to our 'mansion' and discover all the extreme lavishness, extravagance, and luxury in which I lived. I wanted that part to remain innocuous as long as possible, if not forever. I was ashamed of that part of my background. Before long, I motioned to Mrs. Shaheen, Amal, and Majdi, to help turn down my mother's offer, especially now that I had this severe migraine. However, my mother would not take a 'no' for an answer, so I had to pull her aside to tell her I was not feeling well; and, therefore, would not be able to spend any time with the guests. She finally succumbed to my insistence and told Mrs. Shaheen she would postpone the party for some other time. Then she asked me, "The Prince would like to see you to offer his congratulations, what shall I tell him?"

"Just tell him what I told you, and that I'll see him on another occasion. Now please let me go home, my head is about to split."

Thus, the Christmas program ended, along with the good time I spent practicing and performing with the choir, and giving Jesus back a fraction of what He gave me to please Him on His birthday. However, the most reviving event, thus far, as far as I was concerned, was the final rehearsal when my father attended and I played whole-heartedly to honor my Savior. That was the true Christmas celebration.

***

With only five days remaining until Christmas Eve, the Shaheens — young and old — were relentlessly preparing for that big evening and

Christmas Day. They were wrapping so many presents and gifts that included all kinds of foods, clothing, toys, and medicine. They asked us to lend a hand, and we had to ask some of our house staff to help in this endeavor. Abu Wafiq had the large boxes to wrap and could not have been any happier, as though the presents were all for him!

Initially the scene at the Shaheens left me completely disillusioned. The living and family rooms, kitchen, and every corner of the house, were overflowing with boxes of all sizes and shapes, wrapped in a rainbow of colors. I thought the Shaheens were different from other Christian families and they would not celebrate by exchanging that many expensive presents. I was truly disappointed and saddened, and Dr. Shaheen noticed my disenchantment. He pulled a chair and sat next to me, and without my asking, he started a long conversation with me to clarify, "Dalal, Christmas is a very dear holiday for us. The Lord left heaven to come down to earth to be born in a humble manger and dwell among us, where He grew, preached and taught, and finally died for you and me on the cross of Calvary. This loving God, who taught us humility, giving, and sacrifice, deserves that we celebrate his birthday in this fashion that He loves."

I was nodding in agreement silently, but I objected loudly before he could finish his little talk, "But why so many presents?" I asked in disbelief.

He laughed and continued, "If you call Abu Wafiq and some of your housekeepers to help us, I'll give you a complete answer."

I complied, and he fulfilled his promise. He made everybody sit down wherever space was available, and he began to tell the story of Christmas in his appealing style, as it is was reported in the Gospel of Luke. He told us of the host of angels that proclaimed the birth of Jesus to the shepherds who were tending to their sheep by singing, **"Glory to God in the highest, peace on earth, and joy to the world..."** He continued the story in an attractive story-telling fashion that made all stop their work and listen, attentively, to things some have never heard before. Even I, who already read the Christmas narrative several times, was intently listening, as if I was hearing it for the first time; nonetheless, I was eagerly awaiting his answer about all those presents.

Dr. Shaheen expanded his narrative, especially why Jesus came to earth, and how if He had not become flesh like us, He could not have saved us from our sin. The Justice of God required that man must die because **"The wages of sin is death..."** Sin entered the world when

Adam disobeyed God and death was the consequence. The cross was to be ours, but Jesus' birth from a virgin, the God who became man for only one reason—to die in our place, on the cross, and save us from God's justice that required death." Dr. Shaheen continued, "Compared to the indescribable and unlimited love of God, the Creator, for each one of us, we appear so small, like a drop of water in an ocean. Since God knows we cannot ever pay Him back for His love, or perhaps, do not know how, He gave us several commandments in this regard."

Since I always carried my Bible with me, especially whenever I went to the Shaheens, Dr. Shaheen asked me to turn to Matthew chapter 10 and read, aloud, verse 42, to all who were present in the house. I read, **"And whosoever shall give to drink unto one of these little ones a cup of cold water only in the name of a disciple, verily I say unto you, he shall in no wise lose his reward."**

After having finished reading, he asked me to turn to chapter 25 of the gospel of Matthew and read from verse 35 on, slowly and clearly because of their importance, so I continued, **[35]For I was an hungered, and ye gave me meat, I was thirsty, and ye gave me drink, I was a stranger, and ye took me in. [36]Naked, and ye clothed me, I was sick, and ye visited me, I was in prison, and ye came unto me. [37]Then shall the righteous answer him, saying, Lord, when saw we thee a hungered, and fed thee? or thirsty, and gave thee drink? [38]When saw we thee a stranger, and took thee in? or naked, and clothed *thee*? [39]Or when saw we thee sick, or in prison, and came unto thee? [40]And the King shall answer and say unto them, Verily I say unto you, Inasmuch as ye have done it unto one of the least of these my brethren, ye have done it unto me.**

Dr. Shaheen did not ask me to stop reading, but I was not able to continue because something I read shook me. I must have read this passage before, but now it seemed I understood it better. I was shaken because I realized that when Jesus was talking about those strangers, the sick, the thirsty, the hungry and the rest, He was referring not only to people, but to Himself also. When I choked up, Dr. Shaheen took over and finished the rest of the chapter. By then, my eyes were opened and I realized what the Shaheens were planning to do with all these presents, and there was no need for any further clarification. Dr. Shaheen clearly answered my question. He resumed his talk for the sake of all those who were present, "Jesus does not need our gifts, for He is the Lord of glory, creator of the heavens and earth, '**All things**

were made by Him; and without Him was not anything made that was made.' He is the almighty, everlasting God, who has all the wealth of the universe, as He is generous who opens his hand and showers all those who seek to please Him with His richest blessings—material and spiritual. He does not need our money, gifts, or offerings, but what pleases Him is what we do for the poor, the sick, the hungry; He considers it done for Him as well. This is our chance to serve Him."

Dr. Shaheen then turned around, looked at the wrapped boxes, and said, "Not too far from the luxuries of our homes, there are people who are homeless and hungry, while we are overfed. There are the sick that are suffering and have no money to buy medicine to ease their pain. There are children who have no milk to help them develop healthy bones; neither do they have toys with which to play. Christmas is a time of giving; it is Jesus' birthday, the Lord of love and giving; what we do for those poor people is our present to Jesus."

With this, Dr. Shaheen concluded his eloquent presentation of the meaning of Christmas. I sat there holding unto my Bible, rereading that beautiful passage and wondering what I myself could give Jesus on His birthday. I wanted to feed Him and quench His thirst, clothe Him, visit Him, and give Him the medicine He needed. I kept thinking, as long as we did so for our less fortunate fellow man, we would be doing it unto Him. From now on, I would not hold back anything from Him, but give Him all I had.

When I returned home, I could not bear to look at the extravagance of our house, and know that, not too far from us, there were all those suffering people that Dr. Shaheen mentioned.

The next day, I told Mrs. Shaheen what was going through my mind, to repay Jesus a fraction of what He did for me. She proudly beamed at what she heard and said, "Why Dalal, how sweet of you; Jesus, who knows what is hidden in our hearts, saw your good intention and your willingness to do anything for Him. In fact, it was as if you already did it for Him."

She walked towards the kitchen table and brought some papers that gave them to me. "If you really insist on participating in this project, you will find a list of the presents we were not able to provide because we ran out of the money allotted for Christmas."

Mrs. Shaheen had organized the list according to priorities. They were necessities such as food, clothes, and medicine, but no toys or games. I brought this fact to Mrs. Shaheen's attention. Her reply was,

"You are so right, Dalal. Children love toys, but when they're hungry and cold, toys would not be their priority."

"Ok then, I'll be willing to use the money my parents provide me as allowance to buy the toys for the unfortunate children and put a smile on their faces."

The next day, I put on a Santa Claus suit, sat with Amal in Majdi's car loaded with all kind of presents for the children. I contemplated on the words of our Lord Jesus Christ, **"Inasmuch as ye have done it unto one of the least of these my brethren, ye have done it unto me."**

Chapter 10
THE SHOCKING NEWS

☙

*T*he holidays were over. I was especially thankful the nightmare of the New Year's Eve dinner party was now history. Our family was invited to a friend's house for the evening, but to my utter surprise and chagrin, the Prince *(Emir)*—my mother's dream husband for me—was also present. My description of his highness may sound flippant, but in all honesty, he was quite a charmer in the worldly circles. He was erudite, sophisticated, and a highly intelligent man, a definite 'catch' in all sense of the word, for many eligible women.

Despite all his assets, material and intellectual, he was not my *'prince charming'* dream husband. My heart, at that moment, belonged to another man, albeit a one-sided attraction—so far. Nothing had changed or developed since Samir and I said a quick good-bye earlier last year, when no romantic involvement materialized. Samir's silence and indifference towards me did not change; in fact, I felt those imaginary sentiments, though, they had no chance of seeing daylight. The news of my participation in the Christmas pageant and my piano playing had apparently traveled the Mediterranean across the Atlantic all the way to Baltimore! Danny sent me a card congratulating me for piano playing at the Christmas recital when, on the other hand, there was no word from Samir—not even a sign of acknowledgement, or just a simple postcard to wish me a happy new year. Furthermore, what equally perplexed me was why Samir and I could not be, simply friends, and at least exchange holiday cards like other people did? Why would he completely ignore me? "How rude," I thought. Miserable and negative thoughts raced through my mind which made me suffer in anger, but how could I be angry with the one with whom I was smitten—my own prince charming? I 'rubbed my wound with salt' and buried my head in my books, in an effort to take my mind away from such inanities, but how could I forget or bury those feelings that kept reminding me of him on a daily basis? I tried to rationalize different scenarios for his behavior, but none were convincing enough.

It was early spring; Amal and I were on our way to school with everything around looking so bright and cheerful. Amal must have been the happiest girl on earth by then, since she and Majdi seemed to be 'up to their eyeballs' in love. Of course, she did not tell me she was in love, although we were best friends. I wondered why. Aren't best friends supposed to be the first to know about their romances, secrets, and other things they normally keep away from their parents? Well, she must have her reasons, and I am sure she will tell me sooner or later. Nonetheless, this did not stop me from being happy for both of them.

I thought a union between families of different faiths was impossible. In fact, the question never came up; a question a person would never and should never ask. It was a given that a mixed marriage for a member of the Abu Suleiman family would never take place. In my cousin's case, this would be a first, should it materialize, and no opposition is encountered along the way. If, for any reason, the marriage were to take place, then a precedent would be set. Despite such complications—I, nevertheless, tried to picture them as bride and groom, but I had no idea how to do it; neither did I have an idea how I suddenly saw Samir and me in that same picture! How did this happen? I had no idea. Amal's voice brought me back to reality when she said, "Oh, I forgot to tell you, Samir called last night and told us about a friend who would be arriving in a week's time, and that we should take care of him and invite him to stay with us. He also mentioned he would be sending things with him, including some materials from Danny to you—things you had requested earlier. His voice was not very coherent since he called after midnight, Beirut time, and I was half-asleep while talking to him. I hope Dad did not rely on me to take down the flight number or time of arrival."

My response was marginal, and I just felt I must say something here, "You're right, I also hate those late and untimely phone calls. Sometimes my mother does that when she's away—and as the Arabic saying goes, 'The talk of the night is erased by the break of day.'"

Amal and I did not talk much that morning, nor did we see each other much during the rest of the week. The days went by, and the arrival of Samir's friend was fast-approaching. I was curiously waiting to see what Danny had sent me, even though I'd forgotten what I had requested. Although Danny and I corresponded regularly, he never went into details, even in answer to some questions. Anyway, I enjoyed reading his amusing letters and we became good friends through all this correspondence. Despite the fact that sometimes his letter would include a flirtatious phrase or two that annoyed me at times, he always made it a point to inject some humor in it, to ease my mind. Surprisingly, he never mentioned my cousin Mona in his letters, although I was under the impression that they had become a couple, and that she had moved from California to Baltimore to be near him. I never asked because I did not want to sound nosy; besides, this was none of my business. I was content with the friendly exchange between Danny and I, and the fact that it opened a tiny window to Samir's world.

I was at Amal's house when Dr. Shaheen came back from the airport, accompanied by a handsome middle-aged, gray-haired man. The moment he saw me, and even before we were introduced, he said, "You must be Dalal." We were all taken aback. Puzzled, Ammo Najeeb promptly asked him, "How did you know who she was. Have you two met before?"

The gentleman—Dr. Williams—as I later found out when we were introduced laughed and said, "No, actually we've never met before, but I recognized her from her pictures."

This was a strange déjà vu for me; Danny was able to recognize me the same way, from my picture with the twins at Samir's apartment. Dr. Williams noticed our puzzled looks but was quick to explain the mystery, "Danny and Samir are among my best friends—I was their professor and mentor, and often visited them at their apartment. I recently saw a large picture of a beautiful young lady hanging on the wall in Danny's bedroom, and I said to myself, "Here he goes again, putting up photos of models on his walls. But Danny told me it was a picture of a girl whose name was Dalal that he had recently met, and went on to tell me how he met you."

Neither Dr. Shaheen nor I commented on what we just heard. There was an unexplained silence, as though everybody were waiting for more clarification, so he continued between sips of coffee, "Samir and Danny are opposites. Danny likes to joke, even to a fault, and we all know where Samir stands on the seriousness barometer—also to a fault—but the two of them are the best of friends and colleagues; they sort of balance each other." Then he looked at me intently and said, "Danny was right, you are a very beautiful young lady, in fact, your photo doesn't do you justice; it is no wonder that Samir and Danny quarreled daily over your picture." I was shocked at this new revelation and retorted with visible surprise, "What do you mean quarreled over my photo?"

"Yes, it seems your picture has become a source of contention. Samir thinks it is not appropriate to hang pictures of beautiful women in a bachelor's apartment, other than a girlfriend or a fiancée, of course, and always asked Danny to take it down..."

I was somewhat irritated at what I had just heard, both at Danny's liberty of hanging my photo and at Samir's self-righteousness and indignation at something I had no say in or control over. Still, I did not know how to take either stance, in regard to Samir's point of view. At such confusion, I blurted out, "And why does Danny hang my picture in his bedroom? We took pictures for memory, not for display."

Dr. Williams, somewhat taken aback, did not utter a single word in response to my question, but in jest to change the subject, he opened one of his suitcases and handed me several items that Danny sent me with him.

"Here, these are from Danny. Forget about what I just told you, think no further about the picture, maybe he was just proud to have a friend that looked like you."

That was certainly easier said than done, with my mind running at the speed of light, all I could think of was that both Samir and Danny were quarreling over my picture, or was there something else to it? I excused myself to leave, to give the guest and the family a chance to rest. I then carried gifts, thanked the guest, and hurriedly returned home. I kept trying to make something out of this and analyze it ten different ways, typical of my line of thinking, in situations both simple and complex. Majdi suddenly showed up but I did not even notice him come in; he noticed I was a bit irritated and inquired about the cause. I told him everything that took place at the Shaheens, but he calmly replied, "I think Samir is right; a picture of a beautiful young lady in a bachelor's bedroom can be used by Satan to tempt the heart and the mind." He then took out a pocket-sized Bible he always carried, and read a few verses from Matthew 5:27-29, "**[27]Ye have heard that it was said by them of old time, Thou shalt not commit adultery. [28]But I say unto you, That whosoever looketh on a woman to lust after her hath committed adultery with her already in his heart. [29]And if thy right eye offends thee, pluck it out, and cast it from thee: for it is profitable for thee that one of thy members should perish, and not that thy whole body should be cast into hell.**"

That was not the first time I had heard those frightening words, but the method and the occasion that presented themselves, caused me to understand the passage in a different light. Of course, this passage does not infer Danny's motive at all, but the principle is, nonetheless, true. My eyes were opened a little more to truths of which I was not aware. Perhaps that took care of one of the reasons Samir was asking Danny to take my picture down. I asked Majdi what he would do if he had such a picture hanging in his bedroom. Majdi wasted no time in giving me his answer, "I would get rid of it immediately, but then this is our Middle Eastern mentality vs. a western one. The Word of God, however, is clear in that respect, and it warns us about being exposed to anything that could lead us into temptation. It is the thought that begins this process, and therefore, God commands us to flee from such temptations. It does not say we should stay away from them or avoid them, but an emphatic command to *run* away from them. In another place, the Bible says, **'Keep yourself pure...'**, but then again, since I am sure your picture is quite proper and reserved, it can't be very tempting," he said with a smile.

Majdi went on to tell me how, one day, Amal suggested I bring the old videotape and watch the Miss Mt. Lebanon beauty contest, which I had won two years earlier, and Samir turned his head away, saying that, whatever we see, hear, or do, that does not glorify the Lord's name or spiritually uplift us, we should avoid it.

I was certain Majdi did not mean ill towards me when he told me this, but he wanted to lend support to his point of view by giving me a clear example. I knew it was not inappropriate for me to watch a two-year old tape that meant so much to me, and that was a source of pride at the time, but nonetheless, I wondered why Samir was so strict in his behavior. What did Samir have to say about the tape? I started crying when I began to think what he might have thought of me, a conceited, empty-headed beauty queen. No wonder he was ignoring me the whole time he was there, I rationalized. I would not be surprised if he even was disgusted with me, as well, but then he must have known I had entered the beauty contest before my newly found-faith, and, there-fore, did not have to be upset with it!

Majdi looked troubled by my reaction; he tried to calm my fears by telling me it was not as I thought, he was only trying to show the video in an honest gesture to show off his dear cousin. He also added, Amal was so happy, after all, "to watch you and see you win the contest," but all his attempts to convince me that Samir was not unhappy with me, were futile. I was certain Samir had ignored and avoided me because of the tape that he did not even attempt to watch, and in fact, feared my worldly background. He must now be cautious, even after I had accepted Christ as my Savior since, perhaps, he still thought my vanity was rooted too deeply to suit his taste, in any would-be future mate. That was how I tried to rationalize his rejection of me; it was a mechanism, which minimized my pain at that time. The funniest thing, however, was Samir was oblivious to all of what was happening with me!

Majdi left me swallowed up in waves of sadness and struggle. I felt lonely, as never before, until my eyes shuttered into a restless slumber. The following morning, I went to school reluctantly, and was very aloof even towards Amal, and showed total lack of interest when she tried to talk to me about their guest, Dr. Williams. I dryly told her I was not interested in him or in stories about her brother, or anyone else in the United States! "Can we change the subject, please?" I could tell Amal was taken aback at the unexplained attitude I had exhibited. As a result, Amal avoided me all day, and even when we returned from school, we mechanically said our good-byes, unlike our daily routines of spending more time together to review the events of the day. I went to my bedroom and began to sob. Tears seemed to cleanse my mind from the fog-like layer that covered them, and made me come back to my senses after I realized that my behavior was juvenile and outlandish. Although I was who I was, I sometimes behaved like a little child. I realized I had overreacted with Majdi and felt pain at behaving in such a non-Christian manner towards Amal for no fault of hers, so I decided to make it up to them and apologize. Even though it was getting late, I called Majdi at his house but could not find him. When I saw Amal in the morning, she seemed pale and sad, so I rushed to her, gave her a hug, and said to her, "I apologize for my behavior yesterday. Something was bothering me, which led me to behave the way I did. Please forgive me, will you?"

Amal did not need all this explanation to forgive me, for she forgave me there and then and asked if she could be of any help, "Dalal, you are like a sister to me, what grieves you, grieves me, and what makes you happy, makes me happy. I hate to see you suffer alone, allow me to share your suffering. I know you're upset about something, but I don't know what. All I know is I love you and ready to help you if I can. Tell me if you trust me, and as usual, I am all ears."

I thanked her for her love and kindness and told her I was fine now. I promised that from then on, I would share, with her, everything that bothered me. As for Majdi, as soon as I saw him again, I also apologized for my behavior, with tears welling in my eyes. He felt badly for me and assured me he was not angry with me, but that my reaction scared him, and that he was still trying to figure out what caused me to be upset.

"Dear cousin," he said, "be frank with me, and tell me the secret of that picture; I am sure it has something to do with your behavior."

Majdi promised, before the Lord, that he would not tell anyone about my secret. I hesitated as I began to stammer, but then the flood gates opened, and I told him how I felt about Samir—the story of the picture was only the straw that broke the camel's back—I did not want Samir to think there was something between Danny and me. I waited for Majdi to offer me a solution to this problem, but his response came as severely disappointing.

"I was afraid of that, Dalal; I had been praying to God to spare us such a situation, yet here you fall in love—or become infatuated, I should say! And with whom, Samir of all people, only to bring on yourself, and all of us, a problem we don't need." He then sat in a chair, put his head between his hands, and said, "I can't believe it—I can't believe what I am hearing." He then began to mumble unintelligibly, I could not understand anything he was saying, except that I was in trouble, and that I had chosen to love the wrong person! I assured Majdi that I had done my best to prevent this from happening, even prayed to God to help me forget him, but I was finding myself becoming more attached to him by the day. The more he seemed to ignore me, the more I seemed to love him. "You can call this 'infatuation' if you like, Majdi, but whatever you wish to call it, it is real. Time might prove it is only infatuation, but for now, that's the way I feel. Time will tell."

I was now crying, uncontrollably, and Majdi felt sorry for me, attempting to calm the tempest he had created by telling me that Samir and I were not compatible, personality or otherwise, especially in regard to differences in customs and backgrounds. He went on to tell me Samir was preparing to become a missionary physician, somewhere in a developing country such as Africa or India, serving among the sick and the poor. He was very frank with me, to the extent of announcing this painful declaration, as he told me,

"Even if he were to fall in love with you, as you may hope or fantasize, do you think he could see in you the wife of a missionary who might go to the African jungles? Do you think he would find you a helpmate in his ministry? Even if he should fall in love with you, I am sure he would do his best to forget you by staying away from you in order to avert a potential disaster for both you and him."

Tears were flowing down my cheeks as Majdi was persistently trying to yank me back to reality. However, he later was less harsh in volunteering these cold facts by injecting some humor to allay an already painful scenario, "When you returned from America, and before we went to camp, I told you, see if you can face the challenge of resisting this young man, but I was only joking; I had no idea you would take me seriously! Look, you are still very young, and I am sure you will meet someone with whom you'll fall in love, as I am sure many young men would give an arm and a leg to gain your attention."

At hearing this, I was able to force a faint smile. My cousin continued giving me all kinds of advice; he even jolted me with the possibility that Samir was in love with another woman?

The next day, on the way to school, Amal told me that Dr. Williams informed them that Samir would like to return to Lebanon as soon as he graduated, and that he would like to practice medicine for two years in the land of his ancestors at the American University Hospital, or some other hospital in Lebanon.

"It's good to have this guest at our house to tell us of Samir's future plans. My brother hardly ever declares his intentions to us, and is quite discreet about his private matters, especially when he's still unsure. Dr. Williams told us to get any news out of Samir is like pulling teeth!"

I laughed at this, but did not comment about his persona, in case I said something to give my thoughts away about Samir. I just resorted to head-nodding or exclaimed by widening my eyes, Amal became bored with me, and with a surprise-look on her face, she asked me if I the cat had bit my tongue.

That day was a beautiful spring day, just as Khalil Gibran once described spring in Lebanon—spring is beautiful everywhere, but more so in Lebanon—and it so happened that we were off for the afternoon. I suggested we take advantage of that, and go downtown window-shopping. Amal agreed, and we took a taxi there. For the first time in my life, I had to stand in line to buy some "falafel" from a folksy fast-food kiosk. We were happy and laughed at what we were doing, until we began to draw people's attention. Afterwards, and after much walking here and there, we went to a sweet shop, sat at a small table in the corner, and ordered some sweets first, then some ice cream.

"Amal," I said, "You are heaven-sent to me; I have no idea what I'd do without you; you are not just a true friend, but also the sister I never had."

"And you too, Dalal, you are more than a friend; you are a cherished friend, and I am proud to have you as a friend. I don't know what I'd do without you, either, should we ever separate, God forbid."

"Amal, did you ever think of such a day, and what will happen to us?" I asked with a tear welling up in my eye.

"No, I never thought, nor will I; all I want to do is live this moment, and think about how I will ever finish eating what's on my plate that you forced on me."

We both laughed so hard, and suddenly she stopped chewing—as if she remembered something—looked at me and asked, "Whatever made you think of such a day, Dalal, we just met? I cannot stand the word 'separation'."

"Separation" I seriously replied, "does not necessarily mean travel or immigration that will physically separate us by thousands of miles, but that which could be caused by differences in our personalities, character, or outlook on life. It could be that one of us gets married before the other and moves elsewhere, or even if we lived on the same street, the attention will turn to the spouse or children, and eventually lessen interest in each other. Sometimes, these things happen."

"Please, Dalal, don't jump the gun and invoke useless assumptions that may never come to pass; let's just enjoy the sweets and the ice cream now, and let marriage wait."

There was more loud laughter; and, now, everyone was looking our way again, to see what was going on with these two silly girls.

Despite the growing friendship between Amal and myself, I never asked her whether Majdi meant anything to her. I brought up the subject of marriage, hoping to extract some information about the two of them. The atmosphere of mirth we had created became conducive to letting our guard down and opening up to each other when Amal said, "When I had first met Majdi at your birthday party, I found him to be terribly annoying. His excessive attention to me bothered me, and his consistent flattery felt too flattering to be real. In this case, and contrary to what is said of first impressions, I guess it was wrong this time. After having known him a little longer, I found him to be quite the gentleman, particularly after Samir came from America. I felt both respect and admiration towards him. As time went by, the more I knew him, the more I began to like him. I began looking forward to seeing him and felt more comfortable upon seeing him—and before you knew it, we had become good friends. We were talking more often, and I found myself looking for excuses to start a conversation.

When Samir came here last summer, Majdi hung around our place more than he had before, and his friendship with Samir strengthened. Samir spoke very highly of him, as well, as he was also instrumental in bringing us closer to each other, but as you may already know, the biggest hurdle in a relationship like ours is our religious difference. As far as I am concerned, the fact that he was not a believer in Christ like me is a definite no-no. Apart from the difference in our backgrounds, the issue of faith is extremely important to me. On the other hand, I did not want Majdi to be interested in faith only because of me or as a way to get to me. I began to pray and seek wisdom from God on how to behave and carry myself around him without losing his friendship or hurting his feelings. I wanted to make certain he wouldn't show interest in the Christian faith just to please me; in other words, I was able to suppress my real feelings and disguise my sentiments towards him as brotherly. Even today, I continue with our friendship until the Lord gives me a certain peace about him. At any rate, I am still young and have four years of college coming up. It's too early to think any further. Who knows what God has in store for both of us or any of us for that matter?"

"What about Majdi? You may be causing him to suffer; I believe he loves you so much."

"That's what he told you?"

"Yes. He told me on several occasions, especially after I returned from the United States."

"I don't think he's suffering, for his faith and trust in the Lord is now so strong, which leads me to believe that God will lead him to the right person in His timing. If I should turn out to be the right person, then he will have me despite any obstacles."

"I envy you, Amal. I've never envied anyone in my whole life except you for the peace you have in your heart."

"Usually, the one who envies knows he cannot attain what the other person has or is. But as for you, my dear friend, you are in a position to have this peace and enjoy it—just like me and Majdi— without having to envy."

Amal's intelligent answer silenced and shamed me; she must have gathered that I still did not have such peace in my heart, and hence, she became a little preachy. She also cleverly and subtly knew how to trap me during our discussion, when she asked if I had ever fallen in love with anyone before; or if I were in love then, or infatuated? She was able to sense it from what little I said.

I wished I would be able to tell Amal what was going on in my mind and heart, but what could I tell her, that her brother stole my heart? What a predicament! Here I tried to trap her, but I was hoisted by my own. However, this was Amal; she just would not give up.

"If you do not wish to talk, no problem, but let me talk and discover who prince charming is; I know who you're talking about; it is this guy you mention a lot—my brother's friend, right?"

"Danny? I exclaimed, and then burst into laughter.

"Yes, it is Danny, isn't it?"

"Nooo...Danny is the last person I would fall in love with. I love him like a friend or a brother."

After Amal pondered my answer for what seemed a long time, with obvious disappointment of reading me wrong, she screamed, "Oh, what a fool I am—I forgot, the prince; it must be the prince, isn't it? But be careful Dalal, not that I encourage this choice, he's not a believer, and you undoubtedly know, by now, the Word of God discourages a marriage between born-again believers and non-believers. That said, it does not mean that we do not, at times fall, in love with non-believers, despite God's admonition."

My stern looks must have given Amal the clear notion it was not the prince, and that I was not about to reveal to her my prince charming. She sighed when I told her I clearly understood what the Word of God says about marriage. At this, she yelled, "Who is it then, come on, Dalal; stop teasing me. We are best friends, after all! I think I know all the young men that you know; is it someone you met in the United States you didn't tell me about?" She then began to name people I had met during the summer, as I had told her about them, among other names she knew, but I was afraid she might name her brother, and thus reveal my secret love. If she asked, I would not have a choice but to tell the truth.

177

"Let's see, it is not Danny, nor the prince, neither some young man in our church, or anyone in the United States, who is it then? Who is it? Hmm. You also met Samir, but no—it can't be him."

I paused a little at the mention of Samir, as my heart sank, then she softly whispered,

"No, no, no, please tell me it's not Samir; we must remain friends." She pleaded with laughter, but when she noticed I was not engaging in her laughter, she felt she must have hit a raw nerve. She stopped laughing and became more serious, as she sat up straight in her chair, and gulped the whole cup of juice, as if to energize her for further questioning.

After a lengthy, complex introduction, and a solid promise that she would not tell anyone, I had no choice but to tell. I started from the very beginning, telling her how even before I had met him in person; I had a funny feeling about him. When I met him in person, I was so ready and ripe to fall in love with him, I couldn't help it. I really wanted to make a strong impression on him, and the fact I had failed, is causing me all this pain and suffering. I explained how, in spite of my interest, he has only given me a cold shoulder; moreover, I have had nothing but total silence from his side. I ended my confession with a plea and a request for help, "If you were not my best friend Amal, I would not have uttered a single word about this; but since you now know, I'd like you to help me get over this obsession, infatuation, or love, whatever you want to call it. I know it a disaster waiting to happen. Besides, I can't stay in this one-sided imaginary relationship with someone who doesn't even know about it."

I expected Amal to lecture me the way my cousin Majdi did earlier, since there was a vast chasm between Samir and me—especially our religious backgrounds, my upbringing, and the worldly sophistication our family exuded. Contrary to what I expected, Amal, was quite understanding; her kind words comforted me and were exactly what I needed to hear.

"Anyway, how do you know Samir doesn't care for you? You only spent less than two days with him. By all standards, except for those who fall in love at first sight, two days is hardly long enough for anyone to remember someone's name, let alone fall in love. If you were basing any conclusions on the fact he ignores you, never writes you, or calls you, then you are mistaken and aren't able to read him right. In my case for instance, although I like Majdi, I ignore him deliberately and keep my emotions checked so neither of us will be heartbroken, if things don't work out. I play it safe. So don't count on me to help get over whatever it is you feel towards Samir. If he's the person God chose for you, then nothing would make me happier, and nothing will stop it, for God will take you by the hand and guide you through a potential maze of thorny obstacles. We are both aware of that. In addition, you're still so young to really know if this is real love, obsession, or infatuation. This goes for me too; we first need to mature, then we can decide. Yes, we can fall in love at our age, but real love comes after maturity, right? Moreover, you need to finish school first; and then, who knows what the future holds.

Meanwhile, submit to the Lord fully, and He will certainly see you through, as Proverbs 3:5 says, **"In all thy ways, acknowledge Him, and He shall direct your paths."** More than that, Dalal, please don't be offended by what I have to say, your romantic love may be one-sided, but I am sure Samir has some special feelings for you, or have you forgotten that you are his child in faith? There's a special bond between a father and a child. Be certain Samir has a special love for you, if for nothing else, it is because he led you to the Lord."

That was the first time I had heard this expression "child and father in the faith". I liked it. Faith is the new birth, and whoever leads a person to accepting Christ as savior, is a parent in taking part in his/her birth, in a spiritual sense. At least, I will always have Samir's love as his child in faith, and no doubt, he loves me because of this, if nothing else—now or later.

In the midst of all the emotional mayhem created by Dr. Williams' visit—the story behind my picture, and the long conversation I had with Amal—caused me to forget informing Majdi about the package Danny and Samir had sent with Dr. Williams. The package contained tapes, books, as well as the tape Danny showed my father and me at Johns Hopkins. There was another tape from Danny for my father; I am guessing it might be about his friend Billy. When I told Majdi and Amal about the package, they were furious with me, "Why now, miss thoughtfulness, you could have told us much later?" they said sarcastically.

I gave the cassette tapes to Majdi, who took them like a thirsty man in a desert would take water, and he quickly disappeared. My guess was he went to his room, shut the door, and began listening to the tapes in earnest. I suggested to Amal we watch the footage of

Samir preaching, by ourselves; I saw this same tape when I met Danny in Baltimore. We agreed to watch it the following evening, while her parents took their guest out to dinner. I went home looking forward to the evening, when I could watch Samir freely, even in Amal's presence, since we had already revealed our little secrets to one another. What a relief that was.

The evening of the next day came ever-so-slowly, but as we watched the video, Amal began to tease me at the sight of her brother behind the pulpit and said, "I can't blame you, Samir is such an irresistible fellow."

Nine months had gone by since that morning when Samir had given me that red rose. These nine months seemed like nine years; I missed him so much. Seeing him in the video only increased my desire to see him again, especially after that evening at camp when I accepted Christ as my Savior, through him. I thought Amal might talk and comment all throughout the film, but silence prevailed as we watched Samir and the Roper family. Amal stopped the video at my request, for I wanted to take a good look at Danny's sister, Lillian, who was sitting next to Samir when he was not behind the pulpit. I took a good long look, Amal, no doubt, noticed; then she asked, "Is there anything you saw that bothered you?" My response was another question "Is there any romantic relationship between the two?"

Amal assured me she had no idea about her brother's personal life, and that he never mentioned anything about a relationship with a woman. Moreover, she told me just because someone sits next to a person does not necessarily mean romance; otherwise, there would be so many uncalled for weddings!

Her assurance was somewhat comforting, but she was not sure! We went on to watch the rest of the film, which, between stopping it and talking, took us a whopping three hours to watch! I did not take the video with me, but left it with Amal. That same evening, I watched the film again, but in my memory. I prayed to God to relieve me from my weakness—and if it was His will that Samir and I eventually walk down the aisle, He would remove any obstacles, and if not, to help me forget him.

I now began to entertain the thought that Samir may not be available. There might be a slight possibility he and Lillian could be more than just friends, or he could meet someone else, since he was older than I was, and was already eligible. Many things could happen by the time I finished my studies in four or five years. Such *possibilities*, nonetheless, bothered me; but I had to be able to face such potential situations.

My first test came when I met Dr. Williams again—two days after Amal and I saw the video. We were sitting in our neighbor's garden, and I was feeling good about myself; I thought I would accept anything in good spirits. Majdi, who was also present, had come to say good-bye to Dr. Williams, who was leaving to the U.S. the following day.

Soon enough, Dr. Williams asked me if I wanted to send anything to Danny. I immediately answered negatively and added, "You might as well suggest to him, in an unobtrusive way, that my picture is not to be exhibited in his bedroom, nor should it be a source of friction between him and Samir, and quite frankly, I am not pleased with either of their behavior over my picture. But please, do so in an indirect way, without hurting their feelings. They're both precious friends."

Everybody noticed my seriousness about this subject, but none commented. Dr. Williams took what I said further, "Poor Danny, do you realize he loves you very much?"

What I just heard brought me shivers and goose bumps, all over, I promptly asked, "What do you mean by 'poor' and 'loves you'?"

"He thinks you do not love him more than a friend."

"And that's precisely the way it is," I firmly replied.

"But you always correspond with him and send him gifts. I think he's up to his ears in love with you."

"What? Then perhaps I should stop writing him."

Majdi interrupted me, and by doing so, he saved the day, "Dalal is only kidding, Dr. Williams, that's her style."

However, Dr. Williams kept looking at me and continued his barrage of questioning,

"Then you don't love Danny? I mean, romantically?"

I nodded without saying a word.

"This is very intriguing, isn't Mona your cousin?"

"You know Mona? You know her?"

"Of course I know her; she's one of the kindest human beings I've ever met. The poor girl is in love with Danny, but Danny is in love with you; what a dilemma!"

Dr. Williams started laughing and turned to look at Dr. Shaheen, saying, "Young people amaze me, and love is so fickle; here is a case *par excellence*; Mona loves Danny, but Danny loves Dalal, and I have no idea who Dalal loves, and so on. Such convoluted and mysterious lives young people live these days."

What he said certainly shocked me. I sensed from some of Mona's letters that all was not well between her and Danny, and that she would be going back to California, soon. I asked Dr. Williams if he could rectify the situation gently and diplomatically when he got back. I promised him I would write Danny a detailed letter explaining every-thing; but only after he paved the way to prepare Danny for my revela-tion. I would also be writing Mona to explain the situation further. At that, I said my good-byes and returned home.

I hardly slept that night, thinking about the misunderstanding I'd caused by my behavior.

I confessed, in my heart, I did write Danny many letters, and perhaps showed him some tenderness only to make Samir a bit jeal-ous in a way to win him over, but I guess my behavior seemed to have backfired. I had used Danny to my selfish advantage. One of the cruelest ways to use people is to play on their emotions. I did not think of myself as being cruel, however, I guess the sense of rejection I suffered because Samir had been ignoring me made me, behave in an irrational manner.

I sat there weighing the results of my juvenile scheme. On one hand, here were two staunch friends living under the same roof, and one of them was hiding a little secret from the other. What if Samir really liked me and was under the impression his best friend was in love with me? What if Samir had been ignoring me because he assumed Danny and I were in love? What about my cousin Mona who was in love with Danny and had to face rejection because of my behavior? Mona certainly did not deserve the heartache. It appeared like I had created a chain reaction—a surely terrible situation, a nightmare, for all involved. Lord, help me to deal with this situation; help me to solve this problem; Lord, please forgive me.

It did not take me long to write Danny a long, detailed letter asking him to forgive me, if I had been leading him on in writing or behavior. I made it very clear to him that I loved him like the brother I did not have, and that it was an honor for me to consider myself as his sister. I also implored him to maintain our relationship as two friends and to take good care of Mona, a treasure he should preserve. I realized it was not easy to tell a person how he should feel; that was not how feelings work; they develop under favorable conditions. All I could do was take measures—regardless how harsh—in the hope time would heal all wounds. I wrote another letter to Mona asking her to understand the situation and reconsider her relationship with Danny.

I was not feeling at ease until I received letters from both, Danny and Mona, who basically informed me of their renewed friendship. In his usual humorous style, Danny told me that the past was nothing but a beautiful dream. Furthermore, Mona assured me she planned to attend my graduation. The letter, dated three weeks prior to my graduation, meant I would be seeing her in three weeks, and I could explain the situation better, if needed.

***

One day, Dr. Shaheen asked me to bring over the Billy Roper tape so he could show it to the church leaders at his house, including Majdi, who was deeply involved in all church activities and decisions. Majdi later told me there would be a week-long youth conference for people between age eighteen and thirty-five—to be held in July. They were looking for a good speaker. I also understood Samir recommended Dr. Billy Roper to be the main speaker. As we all sat to watch the tape and discussed certain aspects of it, Samir, as the conference leader, appeared on the podium, to introduce Dr. Roper who then delivered an awesome sermon. The committee gave it a high point of approval. After everyone left, Dr. Shaheen and Majdi sat there discussing how to invite Dr. Roper to the conference and how to take care of him, while in Lebanon.

I heard Dr. Shaheen mention something about finances and expenses; they had also planned to invite Samir. I was afraid Dr. Shaheen might leave someone out, due to excessive expenses, especially air tickets, and the expendable one would be Samir. I did not want to take any chances, so I immediately offered to ask my father to pay for airline tickets, since Dr. Roper is an old-time friend, and we would love to see him.

Everybody was surprised at the generous offer, even Majdi ran to me and said, "You mean it, Dalal? Will you ask your father and let us know as soon as possible, so we can extend the invitations? You will be doing us a great service if this materializes."

It did not take me long to give them the answer, as I hurried home and fortunately found my father sipping on a cup of coffee on the balcony. I rushed towards him, gave him a hug, and showered him with kisses, then sat across from him. He was nibbling on some fruit, so I started my conversation directly, by cutting to the chase.

"Dad, did you by any chance contact your friend Billy Roper after we returned from the United States?"

"Why are you asking this question, and why are you concerned about him a year later, all of the sudden?"

"I was wondering if you missed him enough to want to see him."

"Of course, I miss him and would love to see him again; but my gut feeling tells me there must be some other reason for your question, so what is it?"

"How much would you be willing to pay to see your friend?"

With a smile on his face, he asked, "What kind of games are you playing? OK I'll play along. You ask how much I'll be willing to pay to see him. I say, whatever it takes."

"No, I am not interested in whatever; I only need the cost of an airplane ticket."

My father eyes widened upon hearing this veiled statement. I then told him the full story behind my question, "This is your chance, Dad, to participate in the work of the Lord, and at the same time see your friend." He thought for a while, knitted his eyebrows, and said, "No, sweetheart, I cannot do this."

"What? You cannot pay for an airplane ticket, the price of two pairs of shoes from London's fashionable district?"

"You know money is not the problem, Dalal." He said, as he continued to read the newspaper and coldly sip on his coffee, as though the whole thing was a done deal. His attitude so irritated me, I yanked the newspaper out of his hand and angrily said, "Give me one good reason for your refusal."

He took a deep sigh then retorted, "There are several reasons. First, we should not invite him without his wife Sandy, who is also my friend; second, I don't think they would want to leave their children behind; thirdly ..."

"What a wonderful father you are, Dad." I said as I was kissing his hand and head, "You are the best father in the world."

He asked me to bring his checkbook, and without a moment's hesitation, he signed his name on a $10,000 check. When he handed me the check, I pinched myself to make sure I was not dreaming.

"Dalal, I think this amount should be enough for five people, including spending money. Are you happy now?"

"Of course, you are the best father..."

He cut me off, and asked, "Do you remember the day when we were returning from the Christmas recital, and you asked me what I will give Jesus on His birthday?"

"Yes, yes, I remember quite well, Dad."

"Well, consider this check to be my present for Him on His next birthday."

I did not try to analyze this statement, nor commented on it—at least, not now. I took the check and ran to our neighbor's house. Majdi was gone, but the family was at the dinner table, as I knocked at the door and entered, triumphantly shouting, "Great news, great news." I cheered.

Everybody stopped eating, wondering about this great news and my abnormal excitement. Without saying a single word, I walked over and handed check to Dr. Shaheen. With eyes as wide as an ocean, he inquired, "Ten thousand dollars? Who's this for, and where did it come from?"

"It's for you, for the conference you have planned for July."

"Yes, but we only needed $2000, not ten..."

"Yes, ten thousand dollars. It is simple. My father wants to invite the whole Roper family to the conference—his old and dear friends."

All I heard then were shouts of thanks and praise to the Lord, accompanied by applause. The sound of the phone, ringing, silenced all the raucousness the check had caused. Walid picked up the telephone and hollered, "Mom, Dad, it is Samir!"

Mrs. Shaheen took the phone, but I was able to understand everything in the conversation from her answers and questions.

"We have no idea how she was able to persuade him; she just came in a few minutes ago."

"No, it was her suggestion; she assured us her father would comply with her wishes."

"What? Oh yes, ten thousand."

"Yes he wants the whole family."

Samir then spoke with his father, then with Amal. I did not feel badly he did not ask to talk to me, but was just ecstatic God had answered my prayers. Then, suddenly, Amal handed me the phone and gave me a wink. What was going on here? What a strange coincidence. Soon

185

enough, I heard Samir's unmistakable soft voice on the other end, "Hi Dalal, I am so proud of you, God bless you and your father. I thank the Lord for you and your love for Him and His service. I always pray for you to keep steadfast in the faith. I shall be doubling my prayers from now on, that He can give you many other opportunities and privileges to serve Him. **"And For whosoever shall give you a cup of water to drink in my name, because ye belong to Christ, verily I say unto you, he shall not lose his reward."**

"Thank you Samir and thank you for your prayers; please also remember my father in your prayers; he is in great need."

"Truth is—somehow the Lord put your father on my heart and I began to pray for him; I even asked some members in our church to remember him in their prayers. I have also been hearing your news from your letters to Danny."

"Dad is on some crossroads in his life; he is in dire need of encouragement and determination."

"At a crossroads for what, Dalal?"

"Remember the camp? What you told me about labor pains before the second birth, just as in the first birth?"

"Of course, I do remember everything. I can never forget that evening."

"My father is undergoing second-birth pains—I think; it is coming soon, Lord willing."

"Wow, that's great news. Are you constantly praying and reading your Bible?"

"Yes—the Bible is the most precious friend I have, and I experience the power of prayer, day after day." ('Our conversation is an answer to my prayers,' I thought.)

"Please Dalal, convey my best wishes to Majdi; Danny also says 'hello' as well as his sister—even if you both have never met—she will be staying with us this week. She heard a lot about you, as Danny doesn't waste a moment talking about you. I can't wait to tell the Ropers the news; I just hope they'll believe it."

"Say hello to Danny for me, and also his sister, and tell them I can't wait to see them."

"I will; may God be with you; it was good to hear your voice and your news again—Good-bye my....."

I inadvertently kept the receiver in my hand, as I stood there stunned. Was this a dream or reality? I had no idea how long I stood there, but it seemed like eternity before Amal came to take the receiver from my hand, but not before she rolled her eyes, smiling mischievously.

As usual, I ran home to be by myself and analyze every word, expression, and breath we took during our conversation. My line of thought began with, 'what did he mean when he told me he would never forget that evening at camp?' 'Why did he pause when he told me 'it was nice hearing your—voice'. What was he going to say, your beautiful voice or your sweet voice? At the end, he told me, "it was good to hear your voice;" and he does not lie; but then, why did he let it be known that Danny's sister would be staying with them? Is it to tease me, or to let me think there was some romance going on between them? Oh goodness, when I try to plug a hole, another one appears. However, before I fell into analysis paralysis—my pastime— my mother walked into my room to pull me out of my silly, adolescent thoughts. She was carrying what seemed to be tons of papers, going over the list of invitees for my graduation party.

I knew my mother was preparing a big party on June 24 for this event, since graduation falls on June 23, and my 18th birthday on the 25th. She seemed to be planning to combine the two events together. I tried, to no avail, to persuade her to wait until tomorrow to discuss these events, but instead, she presented me with about 150 names of friends, including the "his highness" the prince who topped the list, at which I asked, "Scratch this one, please."

"This one? This one has a name." She retorted. "What happened to your manners? He's a prince of an important country, and maybe some day you'll marry him."

I cracked up laughing loudly at hearing this absurd notion, which annoyed her to no end.

"What's so funny young lady? I see no reason for..."

"The expression 'may be some day you'll marry him'; and who said I would marry him?"

"And why not? He seems to be the best person for you, so far."

"Mom—please, let's not start again. There are tons of reasons for not marrying him. One, I am still too young to think about marriage; two, I'll be going to college next year; third, I don't love him."

"Still young? That's ludicrous, I married at nineteen."

"I thought you wanted me to graduate from college and live this beautiful, rich experience."

"And who said I changed my mind about college? By the time you get to know him and get engaged for a year or two, and then marry, you will have finished college."

"Mom, I have a lot on my mind right now to prepare for graduation; we'll talk about this after graduation, OK?"

"As you wish, I was only trying to put you in the picture of things to come. We'll talk about this after graduation, for sure."

Reluctantly, my mother did not pursue this subject any further, but she would not fail to mention the prince on a daily basis, that he must be counting the days for my graduation. She also told me he always calls to ask about me. I would get irritated at the mention of his name. Moreover, she would not stop telling me about my surprise graduation dress that was hand-made in Paris, in the best fashion house of haute couture. I was beginning to worry about my dress, since I suspected it would be a bareback of immodest design. I have worn such dresses before with pride, but after my conversion, I would hesitate to wear such revealing clothes Amal or Lillian would not wear. I had no idea; moreover, if it were immodest, then I would have no choice but to wear it, since it would be too late then. That was something I would have to deal with in due time, hoping such a dilemma would not come to pass.

The Ropers were on the list; my mother was happy when my father told her about his friends who were coming to visit Lebanon. She reserved hotel accommodations for all. The Shaheens, of course, were on the list, with the exception of Samir. I did not put his name on the list; my mother probably had no idea the Shaheens had even an older son. One person would not make much difference, so I decided to keep him as a surprise.

I still wondered whether it was a good idea to invite all the Shaheen family, or only Amal. What if the dress showed lots of skin and Samir should see me wearing it? What if my mother forced me to apply heavy make-up, as she always did? I became more agitated, worrying so much about many things as the time drew closer for the big day that I began losing weight due to loss of appetite. When I told Amal about my apprehensions, she told me I worried too much, too soon, over trivia, and to just let the Lord take care of things we cannot do ourselves—and if the dress was rather immodest, we'd take care of it. She also pressed upon me this fact—since I am the class valedictorian; I ought to worry more about my speech. "Let's now go and prepare for graduation and put off worrying about the dress and what Samir might think; he may not even show up, as you may well know. He's arriving on graduation day and might be too exhausted to attend, so let him be for now."

At the mention of 'let him be'. it reminded me of our last phone conversation that I used as fodder for my fertile imaginations; I began to rattle off some of what I deduced from that conversation, which made me happy of course from my own vantage, but Amal was not listening anymore, so I stopped talking and said, "What's wrong Amal?"

"Samir called two days ago and asked my mother to take good care of Lillian and her mom, as they'll be arriving first. I understood from Mom that he couldn't wait to introduce Lillian to her—at least that's the way Mom must have understood it."

Amal's words hit me like a ton of bricks; I forgot everything I learned about the will of God. It seems that we accept God's will only when it is convenient—at least that was how I felt upon hearing such a declaration. My head began to spin and I felt nauseated, but I was still able to control my emotions by pretending to laugh it off, "Your brother is sneaky; he used my money to bring Lillian along to introduce her to your mom. Smart guy."

Although I tried to pass it off as a joke, Amal realized I was just pretending, and started pleading with me not to complicate matters, and that I should get Samir out of my system and let God be in control. Of course, what she said was easier said than done, but some pieces of advice do not seem to work in matters of the heart. Nonetheless, I promised her several times I would do just what she suggested, but I failed miserably every time. Now I was arguing with myself, saying, "Dalal, you are bigger than that, where's your pride? Young men are dying to be near you; you are Dalal Abu Suleiman." I felt Satan was attempting to further confuse my mind and cloud the atmosphere in the days to come.

One day, Amal asked me if I would mind spending some time with the twins while she went out with her mother on an urgent chore. Playing with children seemed to take one's mind off adult matters, but it did not seem to work for me that day. Even though I was around the twins, I could not shake off the worry or the anxiety surrounding graduation, the guests, and the party. I was afraid I might falter when I deliver my valedictorian speech if Samir was sitting there, watching me. Despite what Amal said, I was adamant on leaving a positive impression and looking my best to attract his attention. I even wished he would arrive in a couple of days after the event, so I would not have to worry about anything. I sat in a pensive mood watching the twins play when suddenly the phone rang, "Hello," I answered.

"Hello, is this the Shaheen residence?"

"Yes, it is; how can I help you?"

"You must be Dalal, but I don't think I dialed your number by mistake."

I immediately recognized Samir's voice. His last question made me laugh and I could not resist a little sarcasm, "Do you know that habits are second nature, Samir? Because you had been calling me so often, you thought you had dialed our phone number by mistake?"

Ignoring my sarcastic remark, although he chuckled a bit, he said, "Good evening, Dalal; are my parents there?"

"Your father has not returned from work yet, your mother and Amal went out of the house to run some errands, not sure when they'll be back. Would you like for me to convey any message when they return?"

With some hesitation, he finally said, "Truth is, I wanted to talk to either of them in person to apologize for Amal because I am not sure yet, but it looks unlikely I'll be able to make it on time for her graduation, and I feel very badly about this."

"Really?" I shouted happily.

Oh goodness, I think I made a blunder, not so easy to correct, even when he asked, "Dalal. Did you hear what I said? I thought you'd be happy if Danny and I would be present. Is there anything wrong?"

"No, no, not at all."

"But you seemed thrilled at the news, weren't you?" he asked, perplexed.

I felt badly and realized I must have offended him, and regretted my apparent joy. I apologized if I seemed joyful and told him I did not mean it as he took it. However, I did not think he actually believed me; and before he finished his phone conversation, he said,

"As I said, I am still not sure whether or not I'll be able to make it on time, considering how happy this might make you if I didn't, but please let Amal know I'll do my best and leave the rest to the Lord to take care of—until then, good-bye."

I sat down, put my head in my hands, and said to myself out loud, "You're stupid, Dalal. You're stupid. I wish you had bitten your tongue."

When Amal returned, I relayed to her what Samir had said, and I went home, somewhat distraught and disgusted at myself; but—I didn't mind giving him a taste of his own medicine!

Chapter 11
GRADUATION

The morning of graduation, which was supposed to be a happy moment for me, was not. Amal was sad her brother had not arrived yet and would not see her march in her graduation gown, to receive her diploma, with distinction. I was sad because Mona and my aunt had not arrived either; they were to have arrived the night before. Amal and I were talking about our mutual disappointments, as we were putting on our red gowns and caps. We were as ready as could be for the event. The school selected my mother to be one of those to hand out diplomas, and my father was going to be a guest speaker.

As the convocation music played, we entered the large hall amid "Pomp and Circumstance" and took our assigned seats. I was able to see the Shaheens with their guests, Billy Roper, his wife, their son Billy, Jr. and daughter Lillian. I did not look towards my family, lest I see anything that might upset me before giving my speech, which I could not wait for it to be over.

Amal took to the podium to sing her song, as my eyes followed down the aisle to the podium. I glimpsed my cousin Mona sitting by the side of her mother, Aunt Sue. I turned to look again to make sure I was not hallucinating. I wanted to leave my seat, remove my gown and cap, and jump in their direction to hug a precious person accompanying them. It was none other than Mary Graham. Yes, Mary in flesh! What a wonderful surprise. My beloved friend and mentor had come all the way from California to see me graduate. There she was, unmistakably. How did this happen? I realized, I was told Mona and her mother had not arrived yet because they wanted to surprise me with Mary. What a pleasant surprise.

I was so elated I did not notice Amal, almost done with singing the school song. I then looked her way to hear the rest. The moment she was done, thunderous applause met her. She then made her way to sit next to me, her face shining like a bright star, to whisper in my ear, "Did you see them?"

"See whom?"(Thinking to myself she did not know my aunt and cousin.)

"Samir and Danny."

"Who?"

"Samir and Danny."

"Samir and Danny are here?"

"Yes Dalal—yes they are here—thank you, Lord."

I looked towards where the Shaheens were sitting and saw them both. Danny was seated next to Mrs. Shaheen, and Samir next to Lillian. They must have arrived and come directly from the airport. They still had their travel clothes on. It surely must have been God's grace that I saw Samir before I took to the podium to deliver my speech so I could compose myself, catch my breath, and regulate my heartbeat. I could hear it beating in my ears like distant drums. Amal kept encouraging and advising me to take control of myself after seeing me in that pathetic, flustered situation. Then I heard my name and the announcement that I was first in my class, graduating with distinction. The applause was loud; it lasted for what felt like eternity, particularly in light of the fact I was Salah Abu Suleiman's daughter. I glanced in the direction where Samir was sitting, but he was not applauding, "How can someone applaud if his hands are behind his back?" He looked a bit disoriented to me. I had wished he knew why I did not want him to be at my graduation and wished he would forgive me.

As the noise of applause was still ringing in my ears, I prayed God would touch my speech and make it successful and beneficial to all those who were about to hear it. All the while, as I prayed, I had my friend Mary Graham in my sight of vision; I felt I was alone in this hall, and that Mary was my only audience as I began a slow delivery. Some of what I said was, "I will leave this school with my future life's luncheon box: culture, education, knowledge, and precious friendships. This school has changed my thinking and outlook on life."

I was sure Amal's family knew what I meant, so I continued to mention things I learned; honesty, faithfulness, and humility; and whoever wants to be a master, he must first be a servant. Furthermore, I also mentioned I was privileged to be the daughter of the family to which I belong, but without pleasing and honoring God in our lives, all is vain, akin to grasping the wind in our hands. A loud applause interrupted several portions of my speech.

Majdi was right when I showed him my speech a week earlier; he said it would be a success. Before I concluded, I paused for a few moments as a professional orator would, took a deep breath, and said aloud, "Let us all remember the fear of the Lord is the beginning of wisdom," and I returned to my seat.

Amal grabbed my hand and squeezed it tightly, as acknowledgment of a job well-done. At this point, I dared to look Samir's way and saw him beaming; I smiled back and nodded a thank you, after he signaled to me a thumb's up. I then looked at Danny and saw him beaming, as well; he made a sign pointing to his head that he did not understand a word I said. I smiled back and nodded a thank you. I also did that to Amal's father and his guests, seated next to him.

I really did not care what might have happened after my speech. My mother presented each graduate a diploma and a red rose. Afterwards, my father delivered his speech, but I cannot remember anything he said except, "If I had known what my daughter Dalal wanted to say, I would have excused myself from my speech, for she said it all, and there is no need to add anything." He indeed delivered a short speech, and right after that, the ceremony ended.

I was not able to get close to Samir or any of the Roper family, to welcome them to Lebanon, because at that time, my whole family surrounded me, smothering me with hugs, kisses. I saw Samir with his arm around Amal, making their way out, slowly.

As they reached the outer door, Amal and Samir waved at me. I was not able to reach Mary yet because of a long line of friends and family standing in line to congratulate me. Additionally, I had to stand alongside the "Prince" for over five minutes, who was apparently taken by my speech. To my discomfort, he kept holding my hand while my mother looked at him with amazement and joy; but soon he said good-bye, and promised he would see me the following day.

After I greeted everybody, it was time to greet Mary. I fell all over her, hugging and kissing her, all the while, crying from joy. Same thing happened when I greeted Mona; I held both their hands for the fear of losing them in the swarms around us. We finally arrived home, where we spent the rest of the evening until the late hours of the night, talking, laughing, and, of course, recapping the ceremony.

After everybody went to bed, Mona and I slipped to Mary's room where we spent whatever time was left of the night, chatting and talking, about every subject that came to mind. I learned it was Mona's idea to bring along Mary, and that my aunt took care of the expenses in agreement with my mother, to surprise me.

We did not have enough time to take Mary and Mona and introduce them to the Shaheens before the graduation party, so we waited until the evening for that meeting to take place—the time for the big party. Meanwhile, we spent some time with my aunt, who I did not get to see much the night before. My father joined us, later, and kept reminding me how proud he was of my speech. My mother asked who helped me write it, at which, I gave her a look that spelled, "what are you talking about, Mom?" I then sarcastically asked her if she thought I needed someone to help me write a speech. She did not stop there, but continued to tell me she sensed the speech had some language and other thoughts of influence from the Shaheens, and perhaps Dr. Shaheen might have assisted me. She went on to say, that the important thing was that everyone liked the speech, especially the 'Prince.'

"By the way, please don't ignore the 'Prince' this evening at the party; I want you to spend as much time with him as possible."

I completely ignored what she said and did not respond or comment, but rather turned towards Mary, who had no idea what was going on and said, "You're fortunate, Mary, you don't understand our language to know what is going on—like a deaf person at a wedding ceremony, as we say in Lebanon."

Everybody laughed, including my father, who thought it was a cute joke, except for my mother, who was offended by my remark. She then rose from her chair and left, pretending she had some things to take care of.

There were only a few hours left before the party—and up until that moment—I still had not seen the dress my mother had bought for me to wear. The evening was quite enchanting, and the weather, superb. My mother had tents raised to cover our garden. The tables were full of all kinds of scrumptious foods and properly arranged around a dance floor. Attendants, dressed in uniforms, were busily applying the final touches.

Although my aunt's house in California was quite opulent and did not lack any luxuries, what Mary saw tonight was beyond what she could imagine. She kept following me around, everywhere I went, amazed at everything she saw, and could not understand this grandiose celebration for just a simple high school graduation party. I told her, "This is the Lebanese way!"

Finally, my mother showed me the surprise evening dress. It was made of beautiful, green velvety material, obviously meant to be tight enough to highlight my physique, and split on the side from the toe to a good part of the thigh. The upper part of the dress, unashamedly, was low cut, and the upper back was almost missing except for only two crossed strings holding it up. I wore the dress, which in fact, was quite a piece of art. I thanked God I had lost some weight in the last few hectic weeks leading to graduation, that it seemed somewhat loose. My mother was with me in the room as I was putting it on, as well as her own hairdresser who she asked to lift my hair up above my head, so as not to conceal my back. Of course, I refused and wanted it down as to cover the bare back, which led to an intense argument between us. I did not dare tell her I felt indecent with my hair up, but instead told her with the hair down, I would look more feminine; but my mother did not buy it, and she continued to argue with me, which prompted my father to come into the room and intervene. He took my mother by the arm and led her out of the room, in an effort to calm things down. After a few moments, my father returned to my room and asked the hairdresser to do my hair the way I liked it. He smiled and said, "All is well." He remained in the room until the hairdresser finished the job and left. When we were alone, my father told me, "If you behave in such a manner Dalal, you'll always lose; be wise with your mother, so we can keep peace in the family."

I then moved my hair up, exposing my back and angrily said, "Is this the way you want me to appear, half-naked?"

He promptly said, as if he had it prepared, "You always dressed that way before, and you had no problem, so what's happened now? Tell me the truth, is it not because you don't want to appear like that in front of the Shaheens and Ropers?"

"That was in the past, Dad. I had no idea then, but it is different now, and for your information, I do not dress to please anyone, I do it to please the Lord."

My father stood, speechless, for it was him who did his best to please me by convincing my mother—which was not easy—and he knew how to by telling her, "Huda, let her be. Otherwise, she may not talk to the Prince if you aggravate her."

I felt sorry at my blunt reply and was quick to apologize to my father; he then planted a kiss on my forehead and said to me, "Don't let little matters like these spoil your great party; I want to see you happy—Happy birthday, sweetheart."

The guests began to make their way towards our house. My mother's plan was to wait for all the invited guests to arrive first, and then for my grandfather's entrance who accompanied the Prince to head the celebration. I would come down the stairs as the music played, like a princess. I did not like such an arrangement, even though I had the last word regarding my hair-do, but to ask for more was too risky, so I reluctantly complied. After a while, Amal arrived wearing a simple, yet elegant dress that made her look very attractive. I introduced her to Mary and Mona who she smothered with hugs and kisses; then she looked at me and shouted, "Goodness, Dalal. This is way too much."

That was the last thing I wanted to hear; no one had the freedom and courage to tell me such things except Amal. I then pleaded with her that when the party was over, to go home and tell everyone, directly or indirectly, that I had not seen the dress prior to the party, and that my mother and I had an argument over it because I refused to wear it. I also impressed upon her to say these things in Samir's presence; but she replied with a stern yet honest words, "I just wish that instead of worrying about what Samir or my family might think, you ought to direct your worry as to what Christ might think, and that you ought to do things to please Him, and no one else. Samir did not die for you on the cross, but Jesus did; make sure you never forget this fact, and act according to this standard from now on; moreover, before you do or say anything questionable, just ask yourself, would Jesus do it or say it? If you follow this little precept, then it will not matter what Samir or others might think."

Amal did not give me a chance to reply; even if she did, what could I have said? All of the sudden, the music began to play, and my mother signaled for me to come down the stairs. At that moment, I wished the earth would split open to swallow me. I could hear the loud applause gain momentum, and everyone chanting 'Happy Birthday'. I began to descend the stairs, slowly, to the first row of guests to greet them.

Traditionally, I began by kissing my grandfather's hand, who then stood behind a microphone welcoming the guests, "Today is the happiest day of my life, since most of my loved ones, relatives, children, grandchildren, and dear friends are present to celebrate my beloved granddaughter's graduation and birthday."

197

My grandfather made a brief speech and ended by saying he had three wishes for the evening, "My first wish is for my son Salah and my granddaughter Dalal to have the first dance."

At once, I felt a burden falling off my shoulder, for there was nothing I liked better than to dance with my father at this time. My father took me in his arms and began to dance with me. All eyes were focusing on how I snuggled in his arms, with my head nestled in his bosom, looking left and right, as he twirled me around. I saw Samir looking at me, but he did not seem to be annoyed; instead, he seemed happy, as he smiled at me; his smile comforted me and somehow sent me a signal he was not upset about anything. The dance was over, and we waited for Grandfather's next wish. Meanwhile, I resumed welcoming the rest of the guests, but I had not seen the Ropers, yet. The Prince shook my hand, heartily, and flattered me about the way I looked. Moreover, he commented on how fabulous my dress was, as well as my great dancing ability. I politely side-stepped him and reached where my friends were sitting. They all stood up to greet me, and I hugged and kissed each one of them, beginning with Mr. and Mrs. Roper, then Lillian and her brother. Danny received the lion's share of my welcome, for I had really missed him. Finally, Samir extended his hand to me, and I shook it; but because of his reserved personality, he did not take any step further—not even a brotherly hug or an air kiss— but I was understanding. Without much thought, I gave him a hug and a peck on the cheek, but why not, he was no different from the others. Well, like it or not, he had no choice but to give me a light hug saying, "Congratulations, Dalal, may the Lord bless you."

Before I could respond, my grandfather's voice came hollering through the microphone to announce his next wish. We all waited, anxiously, as I prayed in my heart that his wish would not be impossible, but rather acceptable, "I'd like for my son Salah and his lovely wife Huda to take to the dance floor, as well as Dalal and my friend's son, the Prince."

"What a devious man you are, Grandpa. "I thought. "This is not a simple wish, Grandpa. Let us suppose it was your own plan, but with mom's blessings for sure, how could I escape this predicament?"

The idea was no doubt a welcome suggestion for the Prince; this was much easier than his having had to ask me directly. However, before he took my hand to dance, he took a gorgeous-looking necklace that he resumed to put around my neck. The necklace felt more like gallows around my neck, but this action put me on the spot, and I could not refuse. The music began as we took to the dance floor, but he danced with me in a respectable, reserved manner and did not utter a single word that was out of line; he was the perfect gentleman. What surprised me was his confession of his utter ignorance of my grandfather's announcement—he sounded sincere, "I am extremely sorry, Dalal, that you were not prepared to dance with me, as I obviously see you were put on the spot. Just give me the sign, and I promise not to bother you the rest of the evening."

I could not believe what I heard, what a real gentleman he was; he earned my respect. I expressed my disdain for such tricky ways that people would take to accomplish their wishes. I did not know why, but truth be told, I felt comfortable around him. I told him that my mother had bought the dress without my knowledge, and that I refused to wear it with my hair up to uncover the bare back. He abruptly stopped dancing to look at me, not believing what he just heard, and said, "I now feel I can never live up to your expectations." I knew he was referring to marriage, so I took the opportunity to give him a summary of the qualities of my knight in shining armor, perhaps in an effort to scare him away. He, however, seemed pleased with what he heard and said that we ought to continue this conversation another time.

The dance was almost over, but all the time I danced, I never lifted my eyes off the floor to look at anybody. I knew my mother must have been elated; she probably felt it was a lifetime opportunity to see her daughter being prepared to marry a prince—perhaps soon—and perhaps, later, the prince would become a king.

"Where was Samir?" I thought. "What was he doing? Did my dancing with the Prince—or just dancing—annoy him?" I then noticed he was still sitting by Lillian, the expressions on his face unchanged, with a glass of juice and his plate of food on the table, still untouched.

Once more, during a break from music and familial duties, I mingled around my dear guests, and briefly sat here and there; yet so far, Samir never complemented me, not even once. My mother came and welcomed the Ropers and the Shaheens again, but not before she whispered to tell me there were other guests who need my attention. Then without thinking, I asked if she had met Dr. Shaheen. She gave me that usual annoyed look and asked, "Dr. Shaheen? Are you trying to be funny? Do I need you to introduce me to him?"

"Mother, I am talking about Dr. *Samir* Shaheen, his son and Amal's older brother. He just arrived from the United States yesterday, to attend Amal's graduation and spend a few days here." Then without any further hesitation, I took the initiative, "Dr. Samir, this is my mother—Mother, this is Dr. Shaheen."

Samir stood up, bowed his head slightly, shook my mother's hand with both hands, thanked her for her generous invitation, and told her how happy he was to make her acquaintance. I had no idea how my mother became tongue-tied. There must have been something in that young man that seemed to scare her. She wanted to get away from him, so she mumbled a few words, and walked away holding my hand only to say, "You did not tell me Amal had an older brother in the United States studying to be a doctor."

"I didn't? Well, you didn't ask me before."

"When did you meet him?" she asked inquisitively.

"Last summer."

"Did you spend much time with him?"

"Oh, I'd say less than twenty-four hours altogether."

"I don't believe you, Dalal."

"You're free to do that, but this is the truth."

"Now I know why the Shaheens are so kind to us; they could find a future rich wife for their son."

"Mother, stop this nonsense. I am the last person on their son's mind. Believe me. Besides, who told you they'd want a non-Christian wife for their son?"

However, my mother seemed not to hear what I had just said, and continued her barrage of comments and questioning, "It's all very clear that kindness and friendliness are not for free, but they come with a price." I reiterated my words about Samir, "I only wish he would want me for a wife; it would be more than I would ever hope for, but in fact, he doesn't know I even exist."

"What did you just say?" My mother shouted in dismay, not believing anyone in the world could have the gall not to notice her daughter. I then told her that Dr. Samir Shaheen is not one to marry a girl who appeared half-naked at her graduation party. These words hit my mother like a bolt of lightning! She became hysterical, took me to my room, and began to warn me. She then left the room, fuming, while I remained in my room for a while, talking to Mary about what had happened between my mother and me. The more I told her, the more she seemed concerned and wished she had not witnessed this.

I went back to the party, after a while, and, I noticed Mona, Amal, and Majdi were looking for me and wondering where I had been. Perhaps Amal may have noticed my reddish eyes and tried to question me, but I was quick to tell her "not now." Amal knew the problem was worse than she had thought but did not pursue it any further.

Later that night, my grandfather stood up, with his golden cane in hand, (similar to the cane my mother had broken once before when she was angry with him), to announce his third and final request. I wished that whatever the request might be, it would not cause me to break his cane this time around. I was feeling miserable, but how could I not be when Samir was sitting close-by, totally ignoring me, and a prince, who thought he was in love with me and might one day be my husband, sat craving my attention? Between these two young men lay my misery that night. I stood by my father holding onto his arm, as if seeking his help and protection while I listened to my grandfather speak, "My last request, which I will not leave here tonight unless it is accomplished, is to see my pretty granddaughter carry this cane and dance the special 'cane dance' — a Lebanese custom." He then gave a signal for the music to start and returned to his seat with obvious pride in his eyes, to sit next to the prince, while caressing his moustache and feeling certain that nobody dared turn down his request.

I promptly noticed Samir get up to leave. No doubt, he would not stay to watch a woman wriggle her body in a provocative way before all those spectators. Furthermore, this type of dancing — similar to belly dancing — would not please the Lord, if I wanted to apply Amal's reasoning earlier. My blood began to boil, as I walked towards the microphone. I gave a signal for the music to stop and said in a loud but rather calm voice,

"Grandpa, with all due respect, I am afraid I'll have to disappoint you and turn down your request, tonight. Your first two requests were doable, and I did them with pleasure, but the final request is not. I am so sorry, but I am not a belly dancer. Make any other request, and I shall be glad to comply."

I returned to my seat between my grandfather and the prince, who was apparently taken by what I said. I lifted my grandpa's hand, kissed it, and apologized.

"Isn't this kiss better than a belly dance, Grandpa?" My grandfather did not protest, nor returned my kiss, but carried his cane and asked one of his aides to take him home. A hush fell over the place, as some began to leave, as well. I noticed Amal whisper in my father's ear, and he walked up behind the microphone to say, "The evening is still young, and we should take advantage of this opportunity as Dalal's friend is about to surprise us."

"What might be going on?" I wondered.

"What will Amal and her brother do? He's talking to the band, and now he's taking the guitar from one of the band members. What on earth is he doing?" Amal then walked towards the microphone and said, "Dalal is a very dear friend; she is more like a sister than a friend. I'd like to take the opportunity to give her a special gift, somewhat different from the other gifts she received or will receive this evening. It is a joint gift shared by all members of my family—a song, if you will. My father wrote the lyrics, my mother composed the melody, my brother will play the guitar, and I will sing."

In the stillness of the beautiful evening, Samir's music began and sent shivers through my body; it was such a beautiful melody, which penetrated the inner depths of my heart. Amal proceeded to sing her soul through lyrics that came from the heart; they spoke about a young woman who stole everyone's heart and filled life with love and beauty. It was not a long song, but was really the highlight of the party and the best gift I'd ever received.

The evening passed without any further public display or power play. I received whatever gifts remained, said good-bye to my guests as they started leaving, and said all the right things. After the last of our guests left, I sat there expecting a quarrel. There was my mother, ordering the attendants to clean up and put everything back in order. I know her; she was hurrying so she could have time to talk to me or talk "at me" in this case. I did not think my refusal to comply with my grandfather's request upset her, but the culprit was me—I was able to sense she would have loved to see me dance before 'Prince Charming'.

My father, on the other hand, was not in his usual pleasant mood, but did not chide me for standing up to his father. He was walking alongside my aunt, who defended my decision; I could hear her whisper, "But she has the right to refuse; Dalal is not a child anymore; my father should have asked her prior to making his request public. Dalal apologized gently and courteously, and Dad should not have left the party in such a manner." I was able to hear my father agreeing with her, but said, "Dalal is gutsy, with a strong personality; she does not do what she is not convinced of, but she did not have to break my father's pride in such a way—a man of such influence and power. She could've walked in a little swagger, pretending to dance; my father did not ask that she undulate like professional belly dancers; all she needed was a little more wisdom. I personally do not care, but she may have a problem with her mom, just wait and see."

"No, my dear brother," my aunt responded as she walked into her bedroom, followed by Mary.

As for me, I took my haute couture dress off, threw it on the floor as if I was ridding myself of a painful experience, and I put on my nightgown. Then I sat in bed, with Mona in the same room, readying myself for a big showdown; I heard my mother call my father while walking outside my bedroom door. Before she came in, the phone rang; it was 3:30 a.m., I wondered who could be calling at such a strange hour. My mother answered, and from the tone of her voice, I could tell there was a big problem, or rather, a catastrophe. I heard mother call my aunt, and from her response, I figured what might have happened. My mother entered my bedroom and saw me still sitting in bed, with my hand on my mouth, to keep a shout from emerging. Mona was also sitting in her bed, looking bewildered, while my mother came over to me, and like a mad-woman shouted, "Are you happy now Miss Dalal? Your grandfather had a heart attack and passed away. You killed him." She immediately left the room. I heard my father chide her for her crassness, and entered my room. When I saw him, I cried, uncontrollably.

"I love my grandfather—I did not kill him. I loved him," I said, now crying, hysterically. My aunt tried to calm me down, so did Mona and everyone else, especially my father who wanted to go see his father without having to worry about my condition. Before he left, he asked Mona to call on Amal and see if she could come to be near me; but my mother went crazy at hearing this suggestion.

"All our problems resulted from Amal, Amal's family, and Amal's brother—may the hour we met Amal and the Shaheens be damned," she shouted.

Oh, what a terrible nightmare this evening had turned into; each time I remembered my mother's words, I felt deep pain, resumed crying profusely, and shouted, "No, it wasn't my fault," and then buried my face in my pillow. I suddenly felt a soft hand, gently tapping my shoulder, and pulling the pillow away. A voice said, "Please Dalal, try to control yourself, and listen carefully, sweetheart. It is not your fault at all, what you did was not wrong, but in fact, you did the right thing. God has His own timing in our lives; He's the only one who decides when our time on this earth is up. Whether you dance or not, your grandfather's time was up, precisely at that particular moment."

I felt a strong hand around my shoulder, trying to prop me up. I looked up, not to see who it was, but to make certain I was not dreaming. No, it was not a dream; it was Samir; somebody must have called him to assuage me.

There were no words to express the comfort and peace I felt upon seeing my loved ones surround me: Amal, Mary, Mona, and Samir. I was wishing Samir would look at me and talk to me, and now he was tapping my shoulder, giving me comfort and kindness. I would not, for a moment, pretend to think it might be more than that, and the relationship between Samir and Lillian is still unclear to me; however, I am at peace with what God has willed for me. After a while, my mother called in to check on me since she felt she might have been too harsh on me.

By habit, Mary took the call since, as a housekeeper; she was used to answering telephone calls. I heard her say I was fine and innocently added that Amal and her brother were with me. Thinking that would put my mother's mind at ease, Mary also told her how happy I was that they were with me and that I was smiling and having a good time.

I wanted to pull my hair upon hearing her explain to Mother that I was beginning to calm down. However, words, once said, cannot be unsaid; it was too late. I did not ask Mary about my mother's reaction, nor did Mary make any comments in that regard.

I thought all went well. I, therefore, pulled the curtain of forgetfulness over this episode. However, Samir's words of endearment, although, commonly used and are actually meaningless the way they are spoken in such situations, sounded like music to my ears, for a long time to come.

***

I knew the youth conference was to begin July 1. Preparations were underway. I wished I could attend, but I was not sure I would be able to. Things changed drastically. My grandfather's funeral was a state affair. People pledged allegiance to my father, akin to 'The king is dead, long live the king," and carried him on their shoulders. There was an abundance of poetry and speeches, to either praise or to eulogize. There were people from all segments of the region, from presidents, princes, dignitaries, and other officials, down to the commonest people who came to pay their respects. After the mourning period, my mother's picture was in every newspaper, donned in her black mourning attire and matching hat. They referred to her as, "The wife of the 'Za'eem' (feudal lord) Salah Abu Suleiman." Her dream was finally fulfilled, and she was probably secretly happy, thanking me that I refused to dance that night, and was in her estimation, instrumental in my grandfather's passing, so she could now be the wife of the next 'Za'eem'!

The next few days, following the funeral, the youth camp began. I asked my mother if I could go for a short outing with the Shaheens, but before I could finish my sentence, she interrupted and replied with an emphatic, "No." I wondered how she would have reacted, had I said, "to a Christian camp."

The first three days of camp passed, and my mother would not as much as permit me to mention the word 'camp'. She refused, despite my pleading and tears to even allowing me to go out with Mona and Danny for a little picnic. She remained unmoved and warned me about that. What I saw, from her, would not compare to what was to come in the future.

Because of my grandfather's passing, Majdi would pass by the house, from time to time, to avoid any suspicions of where he might have been, and, consequently, avoided talking to me about camp. Every now and then, I would ask him, when my mother was not within earshot, and about Billy Roper's preaching. He would say it was so wonderful, but would go no further, for he did not want to sadden me. However, he said something that brought tears to my eyes, "Just think, Dalal, that all the success, the salvation of souls, and Mr. Roper messages that shook enough hearts would not have materialized had it not been for you—even when you have not attended a single meeting. God will not forget the efforts in making such meetings possible. You were the instrument He used for His glory."

Although what Majdi just said brought joy to my heart, I questioned why God did not permit me to attend the camp and to hear His Word. Why did He allow my mother to harden her heart and refuse to let me go? Why did He allow the death of my grandfather at such an inopportune time—the time when my father was longing to hear his old friend Billy preaching? Now, he has not seen him or been able to spend precious time with him, except for some fleeting moments at graduation, and my grandfather's funeral, when both occasions were crowded—nor did he hear him preach. Why, Lord, why? Questions raced through my mind; Mary was able to answer some of them with sound logic, and at times, not so convincing, but she always said, "I don't know everything, Miss Dalal, but I know one thing for sure—God does not make mistakes—just remember this truth whenever you ask such questions."

Mary reminded me of circumstances that I went through since we met, and how everything turned out to be a blessing and for the good. Of course, I remembered, but I just could not see how this problem was going to turn out for my good. I failed to see any good at that moment. How would my father benefit from not seeing and chatting with his old friend, Billy? I had trusted the Lord that his presence here might be useful in untangling my father's spiritual problems, but now things did not look so rosy. Those thoughts pained and disappointed me. I cried and felt sorry for such an unfortunate circumstance; I even wished the camp would end without hearing one more word about it. My depressed mood was very visible. My father noticed.

One evening, my mother and my aunt went out for a visit, and I remained home with my father. As we were eating dinner, he asked me, "What's wrong with you? You don't look well."

I began to cry; he rose from his chair and came to ask me about the reason. I have no idea how I could joke, when at the same time, I was feeling miserable, but my words came out mixed with my tears, "Imagine, Dad, we paid $10,000 so we could hear Dr. Roper speak, and so far, we have not received a single dollar worth, of his talks, in return.

My father did not even crack a smile; perhaps he had forgotten about the money we paid, or he did not get the joke. I explained to him that the camp was a dream for me, but Mom refused to allow me to go, even once, or even engage in a single activity with Amal and her family and the Ropers.

My father seemed upset with my mother's behavior, and then remembered the money he spent for airline tickets; he also wished he could hear his friend, at least once. At hearing this, I screamed, "Do you really want to hear him, Dad?"

"Of course I want to, but when and where? Didn't you say the camp ended?"

"Not yet, tonight is the last session, and the place is not far from here; I wish we could go."

"It is now 7 p.m.; it must be over by now."

"No, Dad. The last session is always special; it won't be over until late in the evening, anyway, don't they say better late than never?"

"Do you know its location?"

"Yes Dad." I replied as I was getting excited.

"Ok, let's go."

I could not believe what I had just heard, but within five minutes, I was sitting next to my father, driving away to camp. We did not leave a note as to where we were headed, but the guard saw us leaving together, and that is all my mother should know.

We did not converse much on our way, but my father expressed fear that someone who knew him might see him at camp, but I was quick to quell his fears by telling him that most of the campers would be young people. Moreover, lights were dim at the campgrounds, and it was hard to make out faces and recognize them. My father laughed adding, "I must now preserve my position as the new Za'eem, the new leader."

Up until that moment, I did not have the chance to congratulate him on his new role as the new leader, perhaps because I considered such a leadership to be a curse rather than a blessing. Therefore, I said, "Dad, your leadership is worthless at camp, for the Lord of Lords and King of Kings is already there." He seemed to smile at my new philosophy in life but did not comment!

We finally arrived; it was the same place when Majdi took me to, almost a year ago. I told my father we were fortunate that his old friend Billy had not begun his sermon yet. We saw Samir and Lillian go up the platform to sing a duet and I began to feel somewhat uneasy. At this point, I began to say a silent prayer to keep any thoughts from distracting me from the voice of the Lord this evening. I also prayed the same for my father as Billy Roper was now taking his place behind the makeshift pulpit. He opened with a prayer that shook the camp-grounds—a prayer I have not heard the likes before—followed by a song he played on his guitar. My father whispered to me, "Oh my God, I know this song; I must have heard it thirty-five years ago, at a similar youth meeting when we were at the university."

I was able to hear Dad singing along words he could remember, just as I did last year while the preacher read from the gospel of John. The sermon was as fiery as I'd heard, and more. I glanced at my father, from time to time, and noticed how the words were affecting him—seemed exactly as they affected me the year before.

The message spoke to young people, exhorting them not to fall for youthful pride and the lust of the flesh because death could be untimely for the old as well as the young—no one is immune. He alluded to my grandfather's sudden death without mentioning his name and said, "He did not know when he was going to die; death came suddenly for him and did not offer him time for repentance. He had not heard such a message before, and no one cared about his eternal life, to invite him to such a place to hear the Word of God, as you are now hearing, to take advantage of such an opportunity." Here, he paused, laughed lightly, and told us that he is here because of a friend, but without mentioning my father's name either. He went on to say, "It is no accident you and I are here; you are here because the Lord wants you to take this opportunity—perhaps your last—to accept Him as your personal Savior, if you have not done so as yet."

My father said to me, "He saw me—he's talking to me."

I was sure Billy Roper did not see my father, as we were sitting in a place far off, unable to be clearly seen; but I was certain it was the voice of God talking to him. Oh, how I wished I could see Samir, Danny, or even Majdi, whose faith was not known to my father. I just needed someone to pray with me for my father's salvation. Dr. Roper words were very touching; eyes were now closed and heads bowed. I took out a piece of paper, wrote something on it, and quietly made my way towards the main hall until I reached Samir, and as quietly, returned to my seat. My father had his head between his hands, and I could see tears streaming down his face. I took his hand gently, saying, "Let's go and sit among the trees outside."

He got up and walked with me, like a little child following his mother; he was still crying, silently. I could see his tears reflect the light of the moon, just as Samir saw mine last summer. So why would I not do the same with my dad, as Samir had done for me, and tell him what Samir had told me then? Why could I not be the one who led him to the Lord? Why could my father not be my child in the faith? Before I could answer myself, my father asked, "How do I know that I have truly become a child of God?"

I remembered the exact words Samir had told me when I asked the same question; I then asked my father to repeat after me, "For God so loved Salah that He gave His only-begotten Son, that Salah should not perish, but Salah should have eternal life."

When Samir and Billy Roper showed up, I was not surprised because of what I had written on the piece of paper I had handed Samir, earlier, asking them to meet us after the service was over. Despite that, I let out a yell when Dr. Roper—with his massive size—lifted my father off the ground, as if he were a feather. Apparently, they were both listening to our conversation. I left Dr. Roper with my father and walked to where Samir was standing. I did not wait for him to pose any questions, but immediately asked him while evoking a slight laughter, "Don't births happen, sometimes, before the doctor arrives?"

I expected him to laugh and comment on my question, but certainly did not expect him to take me in his arms and give me a hug.

***

In light of all the blessings God had bestowed upon me, I was not overly sad when we moved to our mountain house the following day, to spend summer as we did every year. The very same move seemed like punishment to me, because it took me away from Amal, but I was comforted with the thought my cousin Mona would be with me all summer long, whereas, my aunt and Mary would be staying through the end of July. More importantly, Samir would be staying in Lebanon after he accepted the American university offer for a two-year contract to practice medicine at its hospital.

The Ropers stay was winding down with only a few days left before they would return home. My father wanted to honor their presence, in the best way possible. Despite my mother's wrath at the Shaheen's, she was nonetheless compelled to invite them, according to our customs of hospitality. As soon as the Ropers had arrived, my father and his friend, Billy, disappeared to his study. My mother was being the perfect hostess to Mrs. Roper, whereas Mona took Danny and his brother to the stables to ride horses. My lot was Lillian who expressed her desire to take a tour of the house, and then asked me, "Dalal, how do you feel living like a pampered princess?"

I retorted, "I feel suffocated."

It seemed Lillian blushed from being embarrassed for asking the question, when I replied to her the way I did. I felt my answer may have sounded like that of an ingrate, particularly before almost an-almost-total- stranger. It would also sound as if I was not appreciative for what my parents have provided me, conveniences very few had. I realized my mistake, so I attempted to correct it—and it worked, "I was only joking, I really consider myself more than fortunate the Lord has honored me with much more than I deserve, but at times, certain restrictions suffocate me."

I resumed taking her around the house and showing her all the opulence within, yet all the while, I tried to lure her into telling me her real relationship with Samir, if any. I thought the opportunity knocked when she asked me, "Do you have any college plans lined up, any idea where you might be going to school?"

"Oh, perhaps I'll enroll at the American University of Beirut."

She innocently replied, "Oh, I envy all three of you—Samir, Amal, and you—will be together. Samir and I went yesterday to the university, where he showed me around this beautiful campus."

I sensed a cloud of sadness overcome her, having to leave the one she loved, soon, so I said in a comforting manner, "Oh, Samir will only spend two years here, and it soon will pass, like a dream." She did not reply; I felt the opportunity to find out was slipping away, and my inquisitiveness helped a little. I then hurried to ask, "And you, what will you be doing, Lillian? Are you still studying?"

"I was supposed to have finished last year, but did not because I changed my major, and transferred to a Christian university to study Bible and prepare, myself, to be in HIS ministry."

"Ministry, what do you mean by ministry?"

"Originally, I wanted to become an engineer, but the Lord had other things in mind for me. I observed my mother's life as a preacher's wife, and how she was living in joy and peace, so I wanted to be just like her, and..."

Before knowing what she wanted to say next, I interrupted, "So you plan to marry a preacher, like your father?" I said, hoping to catch the thread I was looking for. I thought if she answered positively, then it would not be Samir, otherwise, Samir would come into the picture, for sure. However, she disappointed me when she said, "Serving the Lord does not necessarily mean a person should be a pastor or a preacher; each can serve in his own way: a physician in his practice, a teacher in his teaching, and a mother in her house. As for me, I am willing to serve with my husband wherever he might be, and whatever he wants to be, even if he should be called to serve in the jungles of Africa or in the comfort of the United States."

"In the jungles of Africa?" I thought. "Isn't this where I heard Samir was going to serve?" By this time, we arrived to my bedroom; what Lillian saw, especially the clothes in my closet, astounded her. She asked if she could look through them, and I nodded in agreement, but still thinking about this African element. I wondered how she could be so engrossed with my evening clothes, traditional Lebanese costumes, and here I was dying to find out the answer to my question.

Again, I felt the opportunity slipping away; Lillian was obviously a shopper. She suddenly saw an Arabesque-looking dress and wondered if she could take a picture wearing it. However, I was in another world, certainly not thinking about clothes. She was being as slippery as an eel; all I wanted to know was about her relationship with Samir, so I led her back to the subject, "You are an attractive young lady, Lillian; there must be a long list of admirers waiting in line for you."

She smiled and replied, blushing, "I believe I have found my dashing knight in armor; we will soon marry."

Oh, thank God, I said to myself, this declaration must give me some reprieve from my anxiety about Samir and finally extract myself of his spell over me. However, I needed more assurances than that. I continued my quest to extract the truth from her, as I was taking her pictures while trying on some of my clothes.

"And what does your 'knight' do, if I may ask."

"He's a physician."

Oh, my goodness; it was an answer I was not looking for. Just the moment I thought my problem was almost solved, it came back to hit me, vigorously. However, why worry; there must be thousands of eligible doctors out there, why should I think of Samir? I then said, while pretending to laugh, "Please forgive my stupid question, but is your friend a Christian believer?"

"I am sure you know Samir Shaheen?"

I almost passed out at hearing his name. Why did she not tell me this before, instead of leaving me to probe around?

"Yes of course, I know him; he's a great guy."

"If the man I plan marry was no better Christian than Samir, I will not marry him, but to answer your question, he is a very good Christian and loves the Lord tremendously."

I was just elated at hearing this, moments after I almost passed out. I did not know how to react, because I did not want her to discover my little secret about Samir, but due to my elation, I opened another closet and told her to take whatever she liked from my clothes. At this point, I did not care if she took all the clothes I liked; I even offered her to take some of my jewelry. Perhaps what I *may* have now, even if it was a little dimmed light of hope, was much dearer to me than all the material things I had.

We drove the Ropers to the airport the next day and wished them a safe trip back to the United States. The thought Samir being available still overwhelmed me. How did I arrive at such a bizarre conclusion that was still oblivious to Samir? I had no idea and did not want to analyze it any further. It was more than enough for me to have a glimmer of hope, regardless how small or insignificant it might turn out.

Chapter 12
THE DANCE OF THE WILLOW

❦

*M*y father provided Danny with a car since he was to be our guest for a few more days. Samir, Amal, Madji, Danny, Mona, and I—and sometimes Mary—went sightseeing together. Lebanon did not lack places to visit and see, ranging from old historical sites, some dating back 4000 years to modern seaside resorts. My father was happy because I was; even my mother did not mind our outdoor activities knowing, in a few days, Samir and Danny would be returning to the United States. I chose not to correct her.

Lillian's admission about her future husband gave me the comfort I needed. However, Samir's attitude toward me remained unchanged. I did not expect him to change overnight and throw himself at my feet, but I expected him to show at least more interest in my Christian walk and the potential problems I might encounter from my family. He often behaved as if I were invisible and did not mean anything to him. I tried to get close to him, yet he remained disinterested. I often thought "who does he think he is, to ignore someone like me?" His behavior frustrated me and played on my emotions. I also felt there must be some reason to cause him to ignore me—something that stood in the way between us. I had to put my finger on the cause.

I confessed these thoughts to Mary Graham on the eve of her departure, as we were taking a stroll in our garden. The night was clear, the air fresh and mild. I poured my heart out to her; she was not at all surprised—she even told me it was obvious. I did not give her any details, but she could read it in my eyes and behavior. She said a blind person could see it—not only from my side, but also from Samir's. I was stunned at what I had just heard. How was she able to detect Samir's feelings? She told me, "I observed him suffer, suppressing his feelings, probably to protect himself."

I reacted, "But why, Mary, why, what is to protect?"

"Perhaps he's afraid of you."

"Afraid of me—me?"

"Not from you personally, but from Dalal, the beautiful, pampered girl, the daughter who comes from a very influential family; that's what scares him."

I felt Mary was reading my mind! "But how is that my fault? I never asked to be born into a wealthy and influential family. I never asked to be beautiful or pampered; it was given to me."

"Of course it is not your fault, dear, nor is it Samir's. Take a good look at this opulent mansion you live in, and all its keepers, chauffeurs, and guards. How would you expect him to behave? I am sure he must have realized, by now, the difference between you and him. Furthermore, this difference in your backgrounds, as well as a more important reason, is involved He probably doesn't realize you hold such feelings for him, enough to accept him as a future husband—or that would be willing to overcome these differences, should he ask your hand in marriage. But then, Dalal, I think it's too early to talk about marriage since you've not even started your first year in college yet!"

"But I love him; at least I think I do, regardless."

"Yet, he doesn't know this. Moreover, he may not know you're the mate God has chosen for him. He must first ask his heavenly Father for wisdom and leading, and as he waits for an answer, he's probably acting cautiously, with obvious trepidation."

"Mary, you talk like you're certain of this—how could you know, and what makes you so sure? Have you spoken to him?"

"Of course not; this is very personal, and I would not. But I prayed for you, and the Lord gave me a clear vision of what might be happening."

"If what you're saying is true, then I have no hope; I cannot turn from princess to pauper overnight."

"I realize that, but you can experience whether or not you can live like a pauper for the sake of Christ. You can honestly ask yourself and answer if you could hold onto the love of Christ, if life changes course for you, or if persecutions should come your way, because of your decision to follow Christ."

"But why would my relationship with Samir have anything to do with my love for Christ? I am not sure what you are trying to say."

"I have no evidence of anything, except what I analyzed and deduced. Perhaps Samir—in spite of your conversion and salvation—is still not sure of...of..."

"You mean, not sure of me becoming a true Christian or capable of carrying the burden of belonging to Christ? In other words, he does not trust that my faith is steadfast and fears it might vanish when the first problem comes my way? Is this what you're trying to impress upon me, Mary? Is this why you think he may not want to deal with all of this?" I asked.

Mary, agreeing, nodded with sadness. She spoke to me for a long time and encouraged me to trust the Lord at all times, for He was in control, as well as a few other expressions I had already heard. They entered in one ear, and went out the other.

What Mary told me, made me ponder during the rest of the day, and until my aunt and Danny returned to the United States. Two months into the summer, it was almost August, and the last Bible camp at hand, which the Shaheens' church organizes, was just around the corner. Mona's presence helped me, tremendously, to overcome adversities; my grandfather's mourning period caused many of our gatherings and parties that we had, during the summer, to be brought to a halt. My mother stopped harassing me about the prince and the exquisite wedding gown she was designing for me, just in case. Consequently, the tension between us subsided, not because either of us changed, but because the situation changed. I didn't see Amal as much; however, my thoughts about the upcoming camp continued to take my time, worrying about how Mona and I would be able to attend—not to see Samir or hear him preach, but because Mona, as I could see, had not accepted Christ's salvation, yet. She still did not grasp, well, the concept of the second birth, although she spoke often about Christ and her faith in Him. When I asked my mother if we could attend the camp for just a couple of days, she went berserk, "Haven't we had enough of the Shaheen camps yet?"

Here, I defied her and said, "If I don't go to camp, I will not attend the charity celebration, nor will I play the piano as I promised. It's either this or that. Take your pick!"

My mother moved her arm, as if to slap me, but stopped short, when she heard my father call her. She left the room, biting her lower lip out of anger, right before Mona, who exclaimed her astonishment, as to why I should take permission to go to camp! She mentioned in the United States, people my age had complete freedom. She then realized we were not in the United States, but in Aunt Huda's jail, as she continued, "Despite your intelligence, Dalal, you still have the mind of a child; you can get what you want without such tantrums and arguments. You must have forgotten that, due to renovations, camp officials changed the location, and now it is much closer to us. I have my own car, and we can use it to go anywhere we wish without 'Mama's' permission, you innocent child."

Yes. Mona was right. Why couldn't we use the car my father provided her while in Lebanon? I liked the idea, so we immediately went on a surprise visit to Amal in Beirut.

When we arrived, we saw Samir and Majdi removing some boxes from their car. We shook hands and entered, to visit with Amal. After a while, Majdi came out and asked if we could help staple paper, to make small booklets, instead of our small talk. We agreed.

At this instant, I remembered the issue of Mona's salvation, so I decided to approach Samir with this subject. I took him aside and asked, "Do you have time to talk about an important subject?"

Laughing, he replied, "Does this subject require a closed room?"

We went into Uncle Nabob's study; I told him what I wanted, concerning Mona, and hoped that perhaps, he should help in this matter.

"Samir, you must not wait until camp to disclose this to her, perhaps we may not be able to attend."

"What?" he exclaimed, "Perhaps? This is a very important camp; you did not attend the previous one, and you should not skip this one."

"You talk to me as if it is my decision to go or not to." I snapped back!

"Then make it your decision," he sternly said.

"We have a religious holiday coming, and our family celebrates it seriously; and since my grandfather passed and my father took the helm, many meetings and appointments are scheduled, as a result; there is no way we can ignore them."

"What does that have to do to do with camp?" he replied.

"My presence at camp is conditional on my presence at my family's events; I just don't think my mother will turn over her special chauffeur to take me to camp on a daily basis."

"I don't understand."

"I must attend at least two gatherings of this celebration..." I said before he cut me off, "And what will you do there, if I may ask?"

"I'll choose the lesser of the two evils."

"And that would be...what?"

216

I felt he asked this facetiously, "My mother is participating in a charity dance that she volunteered me to…"

"Volunteered you to dance, I suppose?"

"No, but she volunteered me to play the piano."

"So where is the evil in this?"

"The event is under the auspices of the prince's mother, which means he will be present and will ask me for the first dance."

"And what do you plan to do? Will you accept or refuse?"

Samir was acting like an investigative official, coldly and dryly asking me questions, as though I were accused of a crime. I came to talk to him about Mona; he switched the topic to me, as he began to preach to me about what it means to be a Christian and what Christian life entails. He then said, "Christian living is a testimony, like any other testimonies; a true Christian is a person whose allegiance to Christ is steadfast, wherever the place or whatever the situation, regardless of any pressure or threats; otherwise, he grieves the Holy Spirit."

He then proceeded to talk to me about Majdi, his love for Christ, and his willingness to lay down his life for Him. Moreover, he spoke about his enthusiasm for Christ and the great work he was doing for His sake. He was also reading Christian books in-depth and studying them with much hunger. I replied with some irritation, "You just don't understand; my situation is not the same as Majdi's."

"Why? His situation, background, and potential problems are no different from yours."

"You've been in the United States too long, Dr. Samir, and have forgotten that we are now in the East, not the West. Besides, I am an eighteen-year-old girl, whereas he is a man—you must know the difference; women are over-protected here. Despite my personality and courage, I cannot refuse my parents' requests, as he can."

"There is no one man or woman, when it comes to obeying the Lord, after we have accepted Him as Savior. You and Majdi accepted Christ at almost the same time; but our closeness to Him and studying His Word, as well as putting Him first in our lives, gives us the courage and the strength to overcome any obstacle that gets in the way."

"You mean I am weak and Majdi is stronger?"

"All I am saying is, the more we love God, obey His Word, and live in His proximity, the better the victory."

Tears were welling up in my eyes. His words hurt me and made me feel weak and cowardly, when he compared me to Majdi, whom

217

he began to consider a beginner spiritual-giant. I regained my strength and said, "Maybe you're right, Majdi is, no doubt, better than I am, spiritually speaking, and you—of course—you are much more spiritually mature than both. It is easy for you to stand here in a friendly environment, where everyone around you is happy, and thank God. But, unfortunately, you seem oblivious to the misery of so many who suffer day and night, not because they are just Christian, but, because they simply want to behave decently and properly."

Samir attempted to interrupt my tirade to tell me I misunderstood him and that he was well-aware of the difficulties facing me, and that he was not as oblivious to my misery or the misery of others, as I had alluded.

I did not let him continue; my blood began to boil, and in defense, I said, "You know, Dr. Shaheen, before every social gathering, my stomach begins to hurt? Do you know how much I suffer whenever I think I am displeasing Jesus in my behavior? Do you think you love Jesus more than I do? He is *all* my life, and to let you say you're concerned about my suffering is simply not true; you have not lifted a finger to build me up in the last year and a half."

"What are you saying, Dalal?"

"Did you not say Majdi and I accepted the Lord at the same time, and you see a big difference between him and me, spiritually speaking? Do you know why?"

"I do not ask about this, I...I...," he began to say.

"But you're the reason; since day one, Dr. Shaheen. You treated us with disparity. You always prayed with him and encouraged him, but seemingly, you looked at me with indifference and non-chalance. For a whole year, you called him and corresponded with him. You sent him tapes and videos, and while you were encouraging him on giving, sacrificing, writing, and studying, you, not once, gave me a single word of encouragement. Do you realize all the preaching, praying, and encouragement you offered me—except for that night at the conference—would not amount to more than a single hour?"

My stomach began to cramp severely; I would put my hand on it from time to time to lessen the pain. Whenever he attempted to talk, I cut him off and asked him to just listen. He did not talk, but cautiously drew closer to me, looking concerned, while my stomach was raging with pain, and said, "Dalal, there's no reason to go on further with this subject; we must attend to your pain; your symptoms scare me. Let me examine you, not as a friend or a preacher now, but as a doctor."

I pushed him away, gently, and asked him to leave me alone. I told him this was not the first time I had experienced this kind of pain, but he refused to leave me alone. Suddenly, I felt like vomiting, so I rushed to the bathroom and shut the door behind me. I stayed there a long time, ignoring anyone knocking. I finally heard Amal's voice asking me to open the door. I opened just to let her in, and lied, by telling her, my period just started. She laughed and said, "You worried Samir and everyone to death; poor guy, he went crazy wondering what was wrong with you."

I then went into Amal's bedroom to rest while Amal, laughing, was putting all at ease by telling them it was only a female problem.

No one knew what took place between Samir and me, but there was a big question mark, when I left the office, in my condition. If my relationship with Samir was on the edge of a deep pit, it must now have fallen deeper into it. I thought, "This is better for both of us."

As I slept in Amal's bed, I could hear the bedroom open from time to time, and a body standing over my head. I could also feel a hand touch my forehead; it was either Amal or Mona…or even Samir, but I was too sleepy and exhausted to find out. After having slept an hour, I called Amal and asked her if I could leave via the back door, without anyone noticing. Poor Amal acquiesced to everything I asked her in silence. As I sat in the passenger seat next to Mona, I saw Samir standing by the door with signs of severe discomfort on his face, but I did not care; it was now my turn to ignore him and give him a taste of his own medicine. Let him suffer a bit, it would not kill him.

I did not wish to disparage Samir in Mona's presence; I must separate my personal feelings from his ministry. All I talked about was my physical condition. As soon as we had arrived at the house, I promptly ran to my bedroom to seek shelter underneath the covers. I did not attempt to analyze, as usual, or rewind, in my head, the reel of what had transpired that day. My disappointment with Samir was greater than I could analyze. Sleeping now reigned supreme.

I woke up the next day feeling much better; I looked out of the window to notice a beautiful summer day. The phone rang; Amal was on the other end, inquiring about my health, "Are you alone Dalal?"

"Yes, I am, is anything wrong?"

In a sad voice she asked, "Tell me the truth, Dalal, what was bothering you yesterday?"

"My stomach."

"So it wasn't your period, like you said?"

"No, it wasn't. Why do you ask?"

"Was this the first time you feel this pain?"

"No, it isn't; but I have been lately feeling such pains."

"Like a year, six months, one month, a week?" she anxiously inquired.

"Why all these questions, are you now practicing medicine?" I said with obvious humor.

"Please do not joke, just answer my question."

"Oh, I'd say prior to graduation, why?"

"You mean all during June?"

"Yes."

"Does it come after sadness, agitation, or anxiety, you think?"

"Yes, Dr. Shaheen," I replied facetiously.

"This is Amal…"

My sarcasm continued, "Seriously, Dr. Amal? What are you up to with this line of questioning, why don't you get to the point?"

All the sudden, I heard Samir's voice on the phone, "Hi Dalal, this is Samir; please don't hang up, I'd like to talk to you. Don't say anything, but listen carefully."

"I am listening."

"Your health now is of utmost importance; what I observed yesterday concerned me. If what you were telling Amal is true, then you should immediately seek medical advice; these symptoms are not to be ignored."

He then proceeded to tell me more about them, as well as the possible consequences should I ignore them, which made me afraid. I promised him I would seek medical advice, and as soon as my promise satisfied him, he wanted to pick up the conversation where we left off the day before. With obvious sadness in his voice that tore my heart, he said, "Can I see you for a few minutes? Please do not refuse my request. I know you were upset with me yesterday."

"Perhaps, I can see you in camp?" I coldly replied

"No, I must see you before, please. Camp is a little far off, quite far off."

I could not break his heart, so I asked, "When is a good time?"

"Now, now," he said, "It is very important, ask Mona or Majdi to drive you over to a place where I can talk to you alone."

"You're worrying me, what's going on?"

"Are you coming or what? Please, Dalal, say yes."

He knew I would not refuse, so we agreed to meet in front of our beach house in Beirut, and from there, we could go anywhere we liked. Within an hour, Mona drove me to the appointed place where Samir was waiting in his car. It was the first time I went out alone with Samir; he was feeling ill-at-ease and confused, not knowing what to do. We drove off from the city, taking a scenic road towards the mountains, with pine trees everywhere on the side of the road. For a good while, nobody spoke a single word, until we stopped by a place full of curious rocky formations. We sat on the rocks, overlooking the Mediterranean, but despite Samir's intelligence and oratory capability, he was not able to start a conversation, so I took the initiative, "Why can't we be friends, Samir, like Danny and I, or Majdi and I? Why can't you treat me like Mona, Lillian, and the others? I don't want us to be more than friends." I said, contrary to my feelings.

Samir raised his voice, almost scaring me and shouted, "Because I love you. Yes I do! Do you now know why? Do you understand?" He said this turning away from me.

I was shocked as well as confused at his confession! I thanked God that he did not look me in the eye to see my face! What I had just heard made me wonder whether I was sitting on a rock or flying in the sky. Was I in a dream or in reality? Was his confession genuine? Did I hear wrong? Was he Samir Shaheen who stole my heart away and made me suffer, over a year?

I was not prepared, psychologically, for this shock? I wanted to say something—anything to break the ice that Samir created. I wanted to get up, but was unable to. Samir still had his face cupped in his hands, and his back turned to me. I did not know what to do next.

I waited and put my head down on my knees, and closed my eyes for a few seconds, waiting for some inspiration from above. It came. I thought of an idea that left me shaken. What if my silence was an embedded message to Samir to let him know I did not feel the same way? I opened my eyes, only to see Samir kneeling down beside me; without thinking, I threw myself at him saying, "I love you too. I have been anxiously waiting for this moment. I love you Samir."

On chest, where I long yearned to rest my head, even for a few moments, I buried myself, as a lost child would, when finding his parents.

When we returned, Mona was anxiously waiting for me. I did not say anything to her, my happy countenance perhaps said it all. I asked her to pass by our garden, in Beirut, so I could pick a red rose from Abu Wafiq's garden.

I told no one what had just taken place between Samir and me; I did not want to share this precious moment with anyone else—at least not just yet. However, I appeased Amal and Majdi's concerns they were worried sick, although surprised to see me in such a good mood. I looked at Amal, smiled, and said, "Trust me. This is much more than I had wanted or hoped for."

I was not able to hide either my feelings or the joy gushing through my eyes. My whole disposition changed. I began to see my hairdo as the best I had ever had; it even felt longer and softer. The smell of lavender at the entrance of our house, became stronger; the sun seemed brighter, the sky bluer and clearer, and the passing clouds happier—I even saw the sad and weeping willow by the entrance to the garden lift up its branches and dance, as a mother would, when her son returns safely from battle.

The new confessed love between us increased the love in Samir's heart for our Savior Jesus Christ. I now felt certain that the more we loved Christ, the stronger our feelings would grow. Samir became my mentor and teacher, guiding me to focus my eyes on Jesus and not look to the world. The camp I was finally able to attend, increased my understanding of spiritual matters in-depth, and gave me immense joy that had eluded me in the last few weeks, when I focused more on Samir's love, rather than my love for Christ. More importantly, the Lord honored me with Mona's salvation, who seriously decided to accept Christ as her personal Savior.

Mona stayed with us for two more days and flew back to the United States. I thanked God that Samir was now filling the void that Mona left; otherwise, I would not have been able to endure her absence, particularly because I would not be able to visit with the Shaheens with the same freedom, because of her departure. Afterwards, I hardly visited them and began to feel lonely. It suddenly dawned on me that I had neglected my poor father lately—the man-child who was barely two-months old in his faith, and no one attending to him. The Lord wanted me to care for him by prayer and Bible study. He welcomed the idea, began to take advantage of my mother's absence to talk about our newly-found faith, and I even made him listen to a tape of Samir's preaching.

Although, I never mentioned, a single word, about my relationship with Samir. My father surprised me, one day, when without any warning, he said, "Are you aware of the consequences of your relationship?" His question caught me off-guard. I was now unable to pretend, so I carefully replied, "I am well aware, Dad—and well-prepared."

"Be wise," he advised me, "Don't let this infatuation blind you. I say infatuation because you're still young and inexperienced. It could be a dangerous move for you and for Samir, since your mother would never allow it, not even anyone else in our family, you would find yourself against the entire family and sect."

I embraced my father, kissed him on his forehead, and thanked him for his love and understanding, then said, "What about you, Dad, what do you say?"

Apparently, he didn't expect my question. He fumbled for an appropriate answer, but could only come up with the same mantra of potential problems with the family and all those concerned, which led me to say, "I am hoping, when my mother realizes my love—not infatuation—to Samir is beyond retreat, she will have second thoughts for my well-being. At least, I hope so."

My father smiled, dryly, as if disagreeing on love vs. infatuation, but what I needed was more than a dry smile, I needed a miracle. The more I ignored the prince and avoided him, the harder he tried to win me over. I tried to impress upon him that he and I were opposites, and that I was not fit to be his wife—and that he would find a better-suitable girl to be his wife. However, that did not deter him, he felt certain I was the woman of his dreams. Of course, I did not mention anything to him about my conversion to Christianity—that was probably the easiest way for him to exit my life—nonetheless, I felt I had a trump card, in case the situation worsened. To top it all off, my mother was unrelenting in her pursuit of this situation, as though her advice were some kind of medicine I was required to take, three times daily. Unfortunately, this is common in our Lebanese culture, when not only mothers harangue their children about prospective spouses, but also the whole family, when everybody becomes a marriage counselor!

One evening, as I was studying for finals, my mother decided to take me to a social gathering with his 'highness', and when I refused, she became flustered because he had come especially, from London, to be with me. She then insisted I accompany him to at least one of these events, or else she would bar me from going to college the following semester—which was quite an absurd threat. I still stood my ground, but she continued to rant, rave, and threaten, she really had me worried at the prospect of her actually carrying out her threats. Not only was college a place for me to pursue higher education, but also a place where I could see Samir, and from time to time, have lunch together or go for a walk.

Consequently, I gave in to my mother's wishes to accompany the prince, to only one event, and make it clear to him; I was not the one he should pursue for a wife. That said, there was nothing wrong with the prince; he was a charming, intelligent, well-educated young man, and, who no doubt, was eyed by a huge number of eligible young women. Had he asked my hand in marriage just one year ago, I may not have hesitated. However, at this time, he had become a nuisance and a sore point of contention in my relationship with Mother. I wanted to make it clear to him, once and for all, I was in love with another man. This would probably be my best plan to get rid of him, and hence, the problems with my mother would hopefully vanish. When he came to pick me up, that evening, I was nice and kind to him, and I allowed him to take my hand, as we entered the lobby of the hotel, where the event was to take place. When we sat for dinner, I told him, "You are a very dear friend, and I am privileged to be your friend, but more importantly, I would like to keep that friendship." I then made it clear that there was no hope in developing our relationship, not because of him, but because I was emotionally attached to another man.

The prince was taken aback, by my unexpected, frank confession. He remained silent, as he seemed to ponder what he had just heard. A few moments passed, before he broke his stunned silence and thanked me for being forthcoming—and for not taking advantage of him.

He proceeded to tell me he would never forget this evening, as long as he lived, and he promised to remain friends; I then gave him a hug and an innocent kiss on his cheek, as a token of my gratefulness, for his understanding.

After the event was over, and while driving me back home, he asked, "If I may ask, Dalal, who might this lucky man be to acquire such a priceless gem?"

I did not want to reveal my relationship with Samir and further get into more trouble with my mother. I considered the matter private and ended it there. As always, he was a gentleman and did not inquire any further, but he rather surprised me when he said, "You don't have to reveal his name, but I shall attempt to test my information." I laughed and told him, that with all due respect, there is no way he could even guess who the 'lucky guy' was. He dryly smiled, as if he knew, and said, "Isn't he the man who played the guitar at your graduation and birthday party last year?"

He immediately realized he had put me on-the-spot. I did not agree or disagree, but my silence, for certain, confirmed his doubts.

As usual, whenever I spent my evenings outside of home—especially with the prince—my mother remained awake, waiting for me to return. When we arrived home that evening, she opened the door, herself, exchanged the usual formalities with the prince, and bade him good-night. Then, as expected, she followed me into my room, hoping to investigate the course of events of the evening. I told her it was an ordinary evening—and to her chagrin, there was nothing earth-shaking. I gently kissed her goodnight.

Two days later, my mother, with a grin on her face, came to show me an open magazine, "You said your evening with the prince was ordinary?" she asked. "Look at these pictures, and tell me if it was ordinary or not."

I glanced at the pictures, which showed the prince holding my hand as we were entering the hotel lobby. Another picture showed us sitting at the dinner table, and a third, giving him a peck on the cheek. This last picture made me lose my temper. How did that happen, when I did not see any photographers, nearby? My mother's grin and apparent pride on her clever schemes made it worse. I prayed Samir would somehow not get ahold of these pictures, at least not before I told him, myself. But as luck would have it, I was unable to track him down, face-to-face, or by telephone. Then I began to have second thoughts, I was telling myself just to forget about this subject, Samir is overly busy to be reading magazines; moreover, the pictures were not on the front page, and the probability of his seeing them was close to none. I then felt comfortable with this reasoning and dropped the whole idea.

That day, I went visiting the neighbor's house, and Mrs. Shaheen opened the door, smiled as usual, and told me that Amal had gone with her father to a church meeting and would be back soon. Then, she went into the kitchen to take care of something, as the twins suddenly appeared out of nowhere, and came running to throw themselves at me. I asked them if they wanted me to read them a story; without hesitation, Rima ran to get a book in one hand and something else in the other, and with her innocence, she said,

"I saw your picture here—it's so beautiful, but Mom said she didn't like the man next to you."

I was stunned. The thought of the magazine in the hands of Rima was too much to bear. I regretted my decision to keep this story away from Samir and the reason why I was afraid of doing so. I then decided, it would be best if I talked to Mrs. Shaheen about this predicament, so she, in turn, would tell Samir and explain the whole story. I entered the kitchen, sat on a chair, and told her everything from A to Z. She seemed to be very understanding, and then she said, "I had no doubt you would have an explanation about what had happened, and there must have been some sort of ulterior motive behind the publishing of these pictures. That's what I impressed upon Samir last night, as we were looking at the pictures. Quite frankly, he became quite disturbed when he saw the pictures, I could see his eyes become misty; I suggested he ask you, personally, about them."

There was a moment of silence. I felt sorry at any pain these pictures might have brought Samir. Then Mrs. Shaheen asked me if Samir had contacted me regarding the pictures, but I told her, I had not seen him for over a week.

"I guess he still must be disturbed that you have not told him," she said.

"But how did Samir get a hold of this magazine in the first place?" I asked quizzically.

Sighing, she replied, "Majdi wrote an article in the magazine under a pen name, and naturally, Samir was interested in reading it."

Speaking of Murphy's Law, this was as good as any example! What could I say or do at this point? What a coincidence. I felt badly, and my stomach began to knot, so I told Mrs. Shaheen I could not wait for Amal any longer and had to go home, but before I left, I asked her to make sure to relay to Samir exactly what I'd just told her.

The pain worsened by the time I reached the house, and it became so severe, I had to tell my mother. She did not waste any time in calling our personal doctor, because she knew I had a sensitive stomach that had to be taken care of immediately. The doctor suggested I should be taken to emergency. Lo and behold, the doctor at the hospital who was on duty was, none other than Samir. Lord, why did it have to be Samir!

The face-off that ensued between my mother and Samir was far worse than the physical pain I was experiencing.

A nurse attached the intravenous serum and medicine into my vein to ease my pain. However, before I became sedated, I was able to hear the words, "I love you" coming from what sounded like Samir's voice. I could barely open my eyes, but unmistakably, it was him. I tried to explain to him, but he shut me up. He gently stroked my forehead and wiped my tears when they began to flow down my cheeks. My mother suddenly walked in, took one look, and walked out, slamming the door behind her. As for me, I rested my head on his arm, when, by now, I realized he must have understood the story behind the pictures.

I was kept in the hospital overnight, for further tests, but the next day, another doctor came in to take care of me; I was certain my mother had something to do with it, to keep Samir away. My father was sitting next to me, so I asked him about Samir, to which he replied nervously, "He's resting, after he spent almost the whole night watching over you."

Later in that day, I asked about him again, but they told me he had been moved to another ward on a different floor. My mother knew how to wield her influence; that was her first experience after my father became the new Za'eem, but unfortunately, she directed her influence against her own daughter. Such behavior made my blood boil, at a time when I needed rest. I started to yell and demanded Samir be brought back. My request was answered, immediately, lest I suffer a relapse. Consequently, he came back, after my mother acquiesced to avoid a scandal, should something happen to me.

I was released from the hospital on Christmas Eve. However, I was unable to attend the party at the Shaheens, but was with them in-spirit. I began to imagine what they might be doing at each moment or the next, and how joyful they must be, except for my absence. My mother became more cautious with her ways with me because she feared I might relapse. She even sent Christmas presents to the Shaheens, and a special gift to Samir because he took care of her daughter.

On the last day of the year, my health had improved so much, I was back to normal. My mother gave me the option to choose where I would like to spend New Year's Eve, which made me bewildered at her recent behavior. I think my health problems must have changed her ways with me, and I wondered whether this was an answer to prayer. Regardless, since it was my choice where I would spend New Year's Eve, there was no question what I would choose, with her blessings.

I prepared myself for the party by wearing a beautiful rose-colored dress with a mink coat and a little make-up—but much less than I normally used. My mirror told me I looked fine, and that Samir deserved the best. When he arrived at the restaurant, Samir took my coat and my dress showed. He took one look at me and exclaimed, "Oh, my, this natural beauty and elegance is too much to bear. Since I first saw you at camp, I realized it was possible to combine beauty, charm, and femininity, in one single woman."

I considered my new birth and my father's salvation to be the best moments of my life, and now, I was adding another event to these. This was one of the best evenings in my whole life. Samir and I spoke endlessly about various subjects, especially about our romance and the circumstances that led to it. He said we must keep our relationship pure and honorable, at all times, and that if marriage was out of the question in the near future, we ought to be wise and cautious. I agreed, in principle, but I was ready to give him a bear hug and perhaps a kiss; however, I did not dare, because he meant what he said.

Later on, we went to join the party at his parents' house to end the evening with the rest of the family. Before I stepped down from the car, he took a simple ring from his pocket and put it around my finger. At that moment, I pictured a balance: on one scale rested this ring, and on the other scale, the rest of the world.

I made certain my parents did not see the ring; I only wore it in Samir's presence because I knew the time was not ripe, yet, to be defiantly ostentatious. It also seemed that romance was contagious—Majdi and Amal had openly expressed their love for each other. We were so happy in our relationships, I became afraid of such happiness; I was afraid I might wake up one day and realize, it was just a dream!

On the first day of spring, we all drove up to the mountains where Samir confessed his feelings for me. No one knew this secret place, so I asked Majdi to stop by the rock where, for the first time, I heard the word love from Samir, and take some pictures for us. The pictures turned out beautifully, so I gave Samir his copies and kept the rest for myself, especially the one in which he had his arm around me. I placed this one next to the red rose, which he had given me earlier, in the folds of my beloved gospel of John, which I always kept in my handbag.

The spring days were idyllic and brought welcome warmth after a cold winter. Our happiness increased, as I had imagined, but the unexpected happened. It happened more quickly than anticipated. Majdi exploded the first time bomb that shook the family like an earthquake, when he declared his conversion to Christianity. He told everyone he planned on going to seminary in the United States. Although my father, himself, surrendered his life to Christ and was aware of Majdi's conversion, his gutsy confession in public, nonetheless, shocked him. As expected, the family urgently met in an effort to sort things out and put the whole episode in perspective. No one outside the family must know about this; such matters were not to be taken lightly, but should be nipped in the bud before word got out. Lebanon is a confessional country where religious affiliations are a part of life, and conversions from one religion to another are considered taboo that they could lead to uncalled consequences. No one should cross that line. To make matters worse, while the family was discussing what measures to take next, Majdi announced his engagement to Amal in a small ceremony, and declared he would soon travel to America.

Majdi's conversion turned all eyes to me, due to my deep friendship with the Shaheens. This of course, made it difficult for me to see Samir, or even Amal, as much as I would have liked. Furthermore, my mother's relationship with me worsened, particularly when she found out I had also accepted Christ as my Savior, and consequently, it was the reason why I refused the prince. She surmised that if Majdi, with all his strong personality, intelligence and craftiness, as well as being a backbone of the Abu Suleiman family, fell in the Shaheen trap, then her poor little Dalal would no doubt have fallen much faster and harder.

Taking advantage of spring break and under the pretense of having the need to check with some doctors to run further medical tests, my mother took me to the airport and headed for London, leaving behind a dear and precious family, without me even having the chance to say good-bye to the one I love.

END OF PART I

CHRISTIAN NOVEL

WHOM MY SOUL LOVETH

Delight thyself also in the LORD:
and HE shall give thee the *desires of thine heart*.
—Psalm 37:4

PART II

Chapter 13
IN EXILE

*T*he airplane landed in London. The following day I was admitted to the Royal Hospital of London to undergo medical tests to check the underlying causes for my on-again-off-again stomachaches. There I had the best of care that London hospitals could provide; a few days later, I was given a clean bill of health. The doctors told me that some sort of anxiety, most likely, caused my stomach problems. However, I felt much better by then, hence, I was released to my mother's care.

It did not take long for me to realize the special care and kindness my mother was showering on me were nothing but a ruse to get me away from the Shaheens, and from, Samir, in particular. Her sugarcoated comments contained a clear element of blame for the "situation I created" as she said. My illness was my doing, although it was not said in such exact words. She kept on repeating the same mantra, "If you stay away and rest from all the chaos you have created, perhaps your peace of mind will be restored, and you'll be able to think, wisely, about the welfare of your family, as well as your father's political future and reputation." She figured, given some peaceful time away, I would overcome my selfishness, my Christian faith, and the ludicrous 'puppy love' I felt towards Samir—as she referred to it.

It did not occur to me, for a minute, Mother would abandon her social life and her responsibilities at the boutique to be with me in London, until I overcame the ailments she had thought I had. At first, I did not take her threats seriously, until the next day, when we went with a solicitor to the countryside, about an hour's drive from London, to rent a secluded house, where we could stay, quietly and peacefully. To me, the house looked more like a place of exile from the rest of the world. Was it possible we would live here? Yes, my mother's plan was beginning to take shape; it turned out to be a battle of wills—between her and me; she was out to prove to me that she was stronger and more defiant than I could ever be!

The house furnishings were simple, with a small television set, with rabbit ears antenna perched on top. My mother did not rearrange anything, as she usually does, but unpacked the suitcases, then hung the few clothes we brought with us, making me believe our stay was only for a short duration. Even if I accepted the status, she was not willing to abandon her social lifestyle, and living in opulence for a longer period of time. I was ill at ease, on our first night, because I had none of my comfort items with me. For example, I did not bring my phone book or my Bible, but remembered that the Gospel of John was in my handbag. When I looked for it, while still on our flight to London, it was not there—I thought it must be in a different bag—I could not wait to look for it as, I opened my other bags. I must find it; it was the only thing, other than my clothes that I owned then, besides, it was also my only connection to Samir. Our picture was in it, as well as the red rose he had given me, earlier. My Bible was not in the first bag, nor the second, or the last; I felt lost when I could not find my best friend; consequently, I became angry and began to cry. I had never felt just how badly I needed this friend. I could not live without reading the Word of God and relying on God's promises. I even looked on the bookshelf, hoping I could find a Bible among the old books that were placed there, but to no avail. I cried myself to sleep that night, and woke up early, to look for pen and paper to write some verses and psalms I had memorized, but could not find any. When Mother woke up, I asked her to give me a pen and a notebook, but she sardonically grinned and said, "I am not that stupid to give you a chance to write letters to the Shaheen family; anyway, sorry, I have neither paper nor pen!"

Had the situation reached a new low? Was this the mother I loved so much and vice-versa? What forces are driving her incredulous behavior? I never knew her to be so vindictive. It was not my intention to write letters, and even if I did, where could I obtain stamps in this god-forsaken place, or how could I get to a mailbox or a post office, even if I had stamps? The surroundings here were totally strange to me; I did not know my way around yet, but in due time, I would be able to buy pen, paper, and stamps. All of the sudden, it dawned on me; I did not have a cent to my name! What irony! I am the only heir to my father's immense wealth, yet I do not have money to buy a single stamp!

I went to look for a telephone, but that search was also futile. How could my mother live without her best friend—a telephone? I thought it would be my only connection to the outside world, whenever she was taking a bath or asleep, so I could call Samir and Amal. She, however, was not that naïve; she knew the 'dangers' of a telephone, so she had it removed! She saw me suffer and cry, but did not bat an eye. I begged her to let me phone my father, so I could ask him to intervene, but it fell on deaf ears! I was now exasperated; I felt as though I was imprisoned, forever, in a cage with no connection whatsoever to the outside world.

I then went out to the garden for a walk; I found a fallen tree trunk, I knelt down, laid my head on it, and began to cry and pray and plead with God to save me from this unbearable place of exile. I soon felt comforted and victorious; I knew with God's help, I would be the one in charge of my own destiny. I could end this agony whenever I wished by simply obeying my mother and pleasing her. Was that what I wanted to do?

Two weeks of 'exile' passed, but I had a bundle of precious memories to sustain me. I would sit all day long, in a rocking chair, review a long reel of memories with my eyes closed, and relive the not-so-distant beautiful past. My relaxed attitude was proving fruitful; my peacefulness bothered my mother a lot, for she had expected me to renounce my decisions, in the first few days, and carry out her wishes. Now, I was feeling delight in my exile, the only thing missing was my Bible, my main concern.

I did not care much to watch television, but due to my constant presence with my mother in the same room, I, unfortunately, had to watch the early film clips of the civil war in Lebanon. We were shocked at the violence we saw, to which we were not accustomed. Occasionally, we watched clashes between certain opposing factions in different parts of the country. We thought that, as usual, these clashes would be similar to previous ones, and would be squelched in no time, and Lebanon would soon return to its pleasant and peaceful state. Unfortunately, that was not the case this time. My mother, who had a better vision regarding the political scene, looked very worried. She was watching TV and listening to radio reports all day, even into late evening. I wondered how, until that moment, with every bad thing going on in Lebanon, she had not contacted anyone outside this house, and hence, knew nothing about my father. Every time I asked her about him, she would tell me he was fine. I always asked her, "But how do you know he is fine Mom, you have had no contact with the outside world? How?"

My mother was not a simple woman; she possessed an enigmatic character. She could not function without talking to my father, especially now, when the war was raging and the only news were announcement of death, maiming, and immense damage to property—on a daily basis! How could she go on living like that, when my father, who was a political leader, could be in constant danger? How about the Shaheens, who were Americans, how were they coping? This was all so scary and began to take its toll on me. I spent my nights crying, worrying, and praying—these people were the dearest to my heart.

Three months had lapsed in our self-made exile, while the war was destroying my country. As it continued to rage, so did the cold war between Mother and me. Neither of us was willing to give into the other. I spent my days between my bedroom, the living room, and taking strolls in that big yard. There was a huge willow tree at the end of the yard, just like the one we had in our garden in Lebanon; I would spend a great deal of time sitting at its base, sharing its melancholy; and, in turn, the tree shared my misery and longing for my homeland. There, I prayed, while retrieving Bible verses from memory, and pleaded with the Lord to protect my father and the Shaheens, as well as my extended family and my country. I often shouted, reproaching God, "Please, Lord, give me a pen and a piece of paper, is this so difficult? Is this too much to ask?"

I then would regret doing so and begin to sing some praise songs that I had learned, earlier. After I was done praying, reproaching, regretting, I would rest my head back on the tree trunk and daydream. In the evenings, after I retired for the day, in bed, I would daydream of Samir, as an escape from my loneliness, hoping to see him in the near future.

My nineteenth birthday was just around the corner; I had an idea what it might be like this year. I started reflecting back on some previous birthdays: beauty queen at my sweet sixteenth, Amal, Samir, the guitar, the singing, and the general glee that permeated all those present. It brought tears to my eyes. My mother had become well-aware of my developing melancholy, I heard her say with obvious sarcasm, "See what your behavior wrought upon us, as well as your Christ and

Samir? See? You want to follow them, go ahead, congratulations! Go ahead and celebrate your birthday with no concern, whatsoever, for your own mother, who sacrificed everything for you; your mother, who wanted to make you the best and happiest bride in the world!"

She cried hysterically and began to beat her head and lament me, as if I had died! Her limited human outlook on life drove her to think that, by torturing herself, she would save her daughter! She was well-aware the punishment and pain she inflicted upon me would also pain her, yet she was convinced what she was doing was the right thing, as she said,

"If it were not for your obstinacy and ignorance, you would have been now celebrating another beauty queen title on your nineteenth birthday! But alas, the prince is now engaged to be married soon, so you've lost the prince. Hope you're happy now and dreaming of your knight in shining armor. May God send a shell his way and his family and destroy all of them together, especially your Samir!"

I could not believe my mother had just uttered such ugly desires on the one I love! It was too much for me to bear, I felt a wave of anger swell up all over me; but promptly, I saw Mary Graham standing before me, as she did when I had the fight with my cousin, saying her same words, **"Do not let evil overcome you, but overcome evil with good."** The anger within me changed to boldness, so I was able to reign in my anger and decided to punish her with my silence, which often worked wonders. Consequently, I retreated to my bedroom without uttering a single word of anger in response to her ugly wish, except when I said, "Mother, you don't know what you're saying; otherwise you would not have said what you said! You are not wishing death on Samir, but on your own daughter because Samir *is* my life. If anything should happen to him, you'll regret it as long as you live, because you will have lost your daughter, as well. I am so disappointed my own mother would wish death on others!"

"Is that a threat to take your life away Miss Dalal?"

"No, Mother, killing is a sin, but there is something much worse!"

I soon went out of the house for a fresh breath of air, after being in a charged, suffocating atmosphere. As I was about to cross the threshold of the house, I turned back and said to my mother, "Mother, I do not need 'your' prince to become a princess, I am already a princess — the daughter of the King of Kings!" I smiled and continued stepping outside.

This thought gave me a new impetus on life at that moment and provided me the lift I needed to overcome my misery. I continued to take a stroll and found myself walking in a nearby wooded area, thinking how my mother could have wished the destruction of this wonderful family; I had no answers. The more I reflected about what she said, the faster I walked farther, not realizing how far into the woods I had walked. I began to feel hungry, but did not want to go back and have dinner with my mother—the pangs of hunger did not hurt as much as her hatful words did. My hesitation to go back, or not, mounted, as darkness began to fill the woods. Darkness happened to be one of my worst fears.

Amidst my fears and thoughts, a chill went down my spine, as I analyzed what my mother had said earlier, and I wondered how she was able to know the Prince was now betrothed! I also wondered how she could be up-to-date on the news of the prince, his marriage, and other news. She was always around, and I had never seen her leave the house or talk to anybody. She always listened to a small radio in the evenings, to hear the latest news on the ongoing war in Lebanon, but the radio would not carry news of the engagement of princes!

I was sure, beyond any doubt; my mother had hidden a telephone in her room, for her private use only, and did not want me to hear my father's voice. I was now upset more than before, at having come to this conclusion, a bit late. It was very late; I must have walked four hours without realizing it. I could feel a chill in the air and smell a brewing storm. To return to the house, now, would take me hours, and I would not reach it before 2 a.m., what could I do?

Rain began to wet my hair and clothes, then I froze in my tracks. "I am now alone in the woods, lost and in total darkness." Moreover, I had no idea what this country may have, of wild ferocious animals, ready to attack me! I was terrified. I looked up to heaven for rescue and shouted to God to have mercy on me and save me. As soon as I opened my eyes, I looked around and saw a glimmer of light in the distance; I began to run as fast as I could, towards that source of light, all the while, muttering under my breath, repeatedly, "Lord Jesus, Jesus, have mercy on me." I finally found myself at the entrance to an old house with a wooden gate that was ajar. I entered in and took refuge from the rain, underneath a canopy. The darkness made it difficult for me to make out the shape of the house, but I was able to see a swing in the front and some chairs; it looked like the lady of the house anticipated rain, and therefore, brought them in, under the covering. I sat on the wide swing, wringing my wet clothes and hair. The swing made some squeaky noises that caused a dog inside to bark. Soon afterwards, I saw a head peeking out, and a man's voice saying, "Who is it? Who's out there?"

I walked towards him, trembling with cold and fear; he must have been in his fifties or early sixties. I told him I was lost in the woods, and asked if I could spend the night on the porch, promising I would go back to my house early in the morning. He opened the door, and I saw a woman standing there, as well. She had a pleasant smile on her face, took me by the hand, and led me into what seemed to be the laundry room. There was a washing machine, a dryer, and a steam iron. She asked me to take my clothes off and put them in the dryer. She later brought me a dry towel and a robe, and left the room. After a while, she knocked on the door and asked me to come to the living room and sit down. She offered me a cup of steaming tea with some cookies and asked me if I was hungry.

"Thank you, but this should be sufficient." I shyly replied, although I was famished!

They sat down across from me, pondering my features and my obvious accent, then the man asked, "What's your name, young lady?"

"Dalal."

"It sounds like a beautiful name; I am sure your parents must be worried sick looking for you. Why don't you get up and give them a call?"

"I cannot remember the number, sir. We just moved into a new house." What else could I say?

The interrogation started, and they found out that I came from a respectable family in Lebanon. They also knew I am the only child to wealthy and influential parents. Of course, the questions would not stop there, but rather, went on. They asked the usual questions, "Where are you from?" and "How did you become lost?" among other normal questions. The conversation led from one question to another, and within an hour of continuous interrogation, I knew the man's name was Michael Andrews, a former university professor, and the woman was his wife, Lilly, a former registered nurse, both now retired in this quiet and secluded place. As if a floodgate opened, I told them my whole life story, including my conversion to the Christian faith. They did not appear to me to be true Christians "as I define true

Christians", since they did not seem excited at my conversion story, as I thought they would be, nor did they invoke any Christian expressions like 'thank the Lord' or "praise God"—vernacular usually associated with such situations.

The conversation continued around my conversion, and how Christ worked wonders in my life, so far; then Professor Andrews said, "You want me to believe in a god who allowed you to go through such trials, leave your country, and force you to abandon your parents and...?"

I interrupted him and said, "But you see, Professor Andrews, how much God loves you, so you could hear what He has done in my life through these trials and tribulations, including getting lost in the woods, just to have the chance to tell you about Him?"

I could not help but notice the effect my words were having on Professor Andrews. My story seemed to move him deeply, but he was not prepared yet to accept Christ that evening, as I had hoped; but deep in my heart I had prayed he would later. As for his wife, she told me how she had accepted Christ as her personal Savior when she was still a child, but had forgotten all about Him, as she grown older. My story also seemed to move Mrs. Andrews, deeply, by the impressions on her face.

I spent the rest of the night at the Andrews', and the next day, as they were preparing to take me home, I told them I had no idea where our house was. I also knew neither the name of its owner, nor the area. Professor Andrews then smiled to comfort me and said,

"Not to worry, dear, I won't get lost; I know the Oxford area like the palm of my hand."

"Oxford?" I shouted. "You mean as in Oxford University?"

"You got it!"

He told me, then, that he taught there for over a quarter of a century. Such news excited me, and I wanted to know more about this famous university. After some time, and several routes that led to nowhere, we finally reached home. In order to save the Andrews from my mother's wrath and hysteria, I asked them to drop me a little way from the house, assuring them that I would walk the rest of the way. We parted ways after we'd agreed to meet later. As I stepped out of the car, Mrs. Andrews handed me a small box; when I opened it, I saw an old Bible, some notebooks, pens, their address, telephone number, and stamps. Professor Andrews took out his wallet and gave me some money, but made me promise to pay it back. Such a jest, and love, from total strangers, deeply moved me.

I could not take the box home; I had to find a place to hide it. I then took the box and the money and walked to the base of my favorite tree, where I prayed daily, to hide my precious treasure—the Bible. There, I knelt down and gave thanks to my almighty Father in heaven. I did not forget to ask Him for forgiveness for my doubts about His leaving me in desolation the previous night, after I had thought that He had abandoned me. Then I remembered He led me to the Andrews family to keep me safe from the elements. I also remembered a beautiful verse from the book of Psalms 23, **"Yea, though I walk through the valley of the shadow of death, I will fear no evil: for thou art with me; thy rod and thy staff they comfort me."**

By the time I reached the front courtyard of the house, I was not surprised at what I saw. There were several police cars and an ambulance, flashing their lights all over the place. My mother must have been panic-stricken at my disappearance overnight, that she called the police. Naturally, this was not surprising, since, regardless how strained the situation might be between parents and children, all is forgotten; she did what any parent would do.

I approached a police officer, introduced myself, and explained my disappearance and all that followed. By then, they were all hovered around me, but seemed somewhat skeptical of my story; they kept looking at me, strangely. It turned out, the ambulance was not for me, but my mother. I hurried inside the house, only to see a number of medics attempting to revive my mother! I expected her to jump up and begin to rebuke me in front of everybody, but instead, she got up from the couch where she was lying, and to my surprise, began to smother me with hugs and kisses. The medics gave her a tranquilizer, then left, but not before giving me a long lecture and some advice against walking in the woods at night!

I did not divulge, to the police, or to my mother, my new friends, the Andrews. All I wanted to do was help her to bed, so she could get some rest. I sat in a comfortable chair, in the living room, waiting for her to fall asleep. After I was certain she was asleep, I went out and brought my friend—the Bible—which I hid in the courtyard; all the while, I had it tucked close to my heart. I took it to bed with me, opened it up, here and there, then placed it under my pillow. I immediately felt better and no longer worried about anything. Exile? I lived it. Poverty? I sustained it. Hunger? I experienced it. Fear? I went through it. Sickness? I overcame it. Death? In the Lebanon war, my loved ones were at risk. The Bible, however, now tucked under my pillow, said these comforting words in the book of Romans chapter 8 verses 35 - 37, **"Who shall separate us from the love of Christ?** *shall* **tribulation, or distress, or persecution, or famine, or nakedness, or peril, or sword? As it is written, FOR THY SAKE WE ARE KILLED THE DAY LONG: WE ARE ACCOUNTED AS SHEEP FOR THE SLAUGHTER.**

Nay, in all these things we are more than conquerors, through Him that loved us."

Chapter 14
THE SAD DEPARTURE

ᘒ

*M*y mother tried so hard to find out where and how I spent the night, after I became lost in the woods. All she knew was what I had told her and the police. I thought she would change the way she was treating me after what had happened, but she did not. To the contrary, she watched me, more closely than ever before, and did not let me out of her sight. The only change I'd observed was her feeling guilty for hiding the telephone; consequently, she placed it out in the open, near her bed, but still did not allow me to call my father. I had to live with this farcical rule, so I spent more time reading the Bible and resumed annotating it, here and there. Reading it during those trying times gave me more pleasure than ever before. It seemed when, we are at our lowest, the Word of God becomes more meaningful. Furthermore, since Mrs. Andrews gave me a supply of pens and paper, I wrote a letter to my father telling him about my life in exile and everything that had befallen me. I also wrote letters to Amal, Mary Graham, and of course a special one, to my beloved, Samir. Thank God, I had memorized their addresses; otherwise, it would have been futile. However, where would one mail his letters in this isolated and remote place, and how would I keep them away from Mother's eyes? Then, I remembered, the Andrews; they would certainly help me with this.

One day, I waited for my mother to take her bath, went into her bedroom, and called the Andrews. We agreed on a place to meet, close to our house. When they arrived, I took them to the willow tree where I prayed, and agreed that a hole at the base of the tree would act as my mailbox, so whenever I wrote letters, I would call them, and they would drive by, at night, to pick them up. At the same time, they would place any letters for me in the same hole, for I had used their own address as my return address.

To alleviate the effects of my exile, I began to write a diary, beginning the day Amal and I first met, until we left Lebanon. I was able

WHOM MY SOUL LOVETH

to remember every single event that took place; the memories were vivid, as though they had just happened, especially Samir's love and his uplifting words to me. I wrote them down as I had felt them, and read them aloud almost daily! I wrote several letters to the Andrews, telling them more about Christ and my experiences with Him. They, in turn, were prompt to reply, almost every other day, but no one else had, yet. "The war in Lebanon must be the reason for any lack of mail delivery," I thought, "but Mary is in California and must have received my letter by now; but there was no reply from her. She was the only one who could provide me with news about everyone," so I began to wonder. I still had the letter I'd written to my father, but I had to find a reliable way to mail it to him. In a few days, we discovered a solution. The Andrews would take my letter to the Lebanese Consulate in London and let them know about my predicament. The consul there agreed to hand the letter, personally, to my father, as soon as he traveled to Lebanon, since he knew who he was. In the letter, I asked Father to send the reply to the Andrews' home address instead of ours.

I checked my secret mail, daily. One day, as I went to check the mail, I found an iron box—apparently to keep out the incessant rain of England—full of letters! One of the letters said, 'I'd like you to know that you'll be the happiest girl to learn that my husband's walls have tumbled down before the love of Christ Jesus, and he has accepted Him as his personal Savior, and that I rededicated my life to Him, as well. We are both thankful to the Lord and you, our dearest Dalal, for entering our house through His plan and that you brought Jesus into our house and heart. We love you so much and will never forget you— signed, Mrs. Andrews!'

No riches of the world could evaluate such news for that day; I had *really* become a rich woman! I must have read the letter scores of times; I no longer felt in exile. Only if I could now receive news about my loved ones, I would feel totally at ease. My mother's attitude towards me no longer upset me, and I no longer felt a prisoner. The roles seemed to have reversed; she became the prisoner and I the jailer. Her behavior indicated boredom, loneliness, and confinement. She began to feel she was waging a losing battle against me; consequently, she began to think of a different strategy. One day, she mentioned the possibility of moving to a different house, closer to London, but she was first expecting my father's arrival here at any time. I quietly answered, "But I like it here, Mom; I don't want to go anywhere else, especially closer to crowded London; you know I hate London and its atmosphere."

Mother jaw promptly dropped, and her eyes widened in disbelief at what she had just heard. She must have thought I'd lost my mind, but I continued, "We cannot move before Dad arrives here to talk things over. Time for going to the university is closing in on me, and we haven't done anything, in that respect—and you know how much I want to continue my studies."

What I said must have triggered an idea in her, perhaps a new weapon with which to fight. It was my university studies. She would use the deep desire I had for obtaining an education by denying me one. However, when I mentioned my fears to Professor Andrews, he told me not to worry; he could help me in that area. A few days later, I confronted her and told her I was going to enroll in Oxford and continue where I had left of.

"OK, do whatever you wish; when I was your age, I was married. You're free to stay here, go back to Lebanon, marry a gypsy, worship your own God, or whatever, but don't consider me your mother, or you my daughter—and do not count on me for any money, either."

Mother thought I would take her threats, hands down! She would give me freedom, and throw me into the lion's den! She did not realize that once people accepted the Lord as their Savior, they became His children; and as their Father, He had a will for their lives. No one— including her—could do anything to change His will.

That was exactly what happened. After I met with Professor Andrews, concerning my university studies, he told me, "Since we have no children of our own, God sent us a daughter to fill our lives. We will be able to pay your way to Oxford. However, although your situation is rather a difficult one, and Oxford's regulations are quite stringent, in accepting transfer students, and without all the necessary paperwork to get through the red tape, I can solve this problem, with my many contacts, as well as my previous official responsibilities."

I then realized, God had answered my prayers more quickly than I'd expected. Then I thought about my poor mother, whom I love immensely, for I really did not want to stay away from her, nor hurt her feelings. I tried again to make amends with her and reach a solution, so I went to her, gave her a bear hug, kissed her on the forehead, rested my head on her bosom, and told her, "Mom, I love you so much, and I don't want you to be angry with me; let us clear things up and be like we always were."

"I have no problem with that," she said while pulling away from me, "I also wish we would restore our relationship like before, but that would be totally up to you. Go back to your mind, our faith, and I will give you the whole world—including your college expenses."

How could people who have not experienced God's grace understand, there is no going back? "But Mother, you know this is not possible; even if I were to forget about Samir, how can I forget my Lord Jesus, this loving God who loved me and died for me?"

I went on to tell her more about salvation, Christ, and *true* Christianity, and not the traditional Christianity she knew from her friends and acquaintances, but rather the Christianity of love, repentance, forgiveness, and life eternal. I consequently told her about my total conversion experience and the new joyful life I was living with Christ. Mother was listening attentively, and I thought, in my innocence, that I moved her and might win her trust. I wish I had stopped there; perhaps I made my biggest mistake by invoking my father's similar experience, for she went totally out of control, screaming and yelling.

"What am I hearing? Your FATHER? You even played mind games on your own father? You have nothing better to do than compare gods and see which one is better than the other? What about your father? I need to know right now, right now!"

She must have sensed my slip of the tongue and, hence, my unwillingness to answer. Now she went berserk! I ran away to my bedroom and locked the door; all she could do was holler in anger and hurl more threats. She even cursed at me for conspiring with my father against her, and if I'd heard her right, through the closed door, she threatened to prevent my father from seeing her and me! She said she would take me to a place where the magi, the Christian gods, or any other gods could never find us—that would be a lesson we would never forget.

After she'd exhausted the use of all threats and her screams were abated, she went to her room and began to talk loudly, over the phone, but I was not able to figure out what she was saying or to whom she was speaking. I knew my mother meant every word she said—and more, she left me very few options. I waited for her to sleep so I could execute my plan. I packed my clothes, Bible, my diary, and other items, and stealthily left the house in the still of the night. This time, I stayed on the road and avoided the woods. I knew there was a public telephone about a half hour's walk away, so I kept on walking in that direction, praying and avoiding drunkards or anyone who looked menacing. I hid behind a tree every time a car drove by. I finally reached the telephone and called the Andrews. In no time, while still in their nightclothes, they came to pick me up and drove me to their home. Nobody said anything on the way; my condition spoke volumes.

I woke up the next day, around noontime, and I told them everything that had transpired between Mother and me. I asked for their protection and assured them my father would compensate them every penny they might spend on me.

They agreed, wholeheartedly, despite some trepidation and concern about any potential problems I might cause. I allayed their fears, should the police come looking for me—because I had been an adult for over a year, and I was being kept against my will.

Despite my deep sadness over running away from my mother, I felt a sense of freedom and relief, leaving the jail she had created. My mother, the only 'jailer' willing to lay down her life for me, was also willing to drive me away, at any cost, from my own father, and from Samir whom my soul loved, and even my new faith in Christ!

Mary Graham's telephone number in California was the only one I knew by memory; but whenever I rang, a message told me the number was not in service. One day, Professor Andrews noticed my frustration and disappointment, and he told me, "I am sure God will intervene somehow and relieve you from this gloom; and incidentally, what did Mary say in her letter?"

"What letter?"

"Mary Graham's, I believe."

"Where? I mean, where the letter is?"

"I left it in your private metal box under the willow tree."

"A letter from Mary?" I asked with excitement and concern.

Interjecting, Mrs. Andrews answered, "I saw the letter, myself, but did not read the return name; the stamp was American."

"When was that?" I asked with apparent anxiety.

"The day before last."

"Oh, goodness!" I blurted. "It was the time Mother and I had our squabble, and I did not check my mailbox!"

I now began to think of a way to retrieve the letter; Mary was my only connection to my loved ones. "How could this have happened, and why is God trying me again?" I asked myself. There was no way now to retrieve the letter, as I was certain my mother's house must be surrounded by a fleet of police cars by then, and police searching for any clues for my disappearance. I felt anger at God, there was no need for this distraction now. I almost uttered a profanity, but I immediately remembered that, now there are two people to whom I was witnessing my faith, and I must watch my behavior, lest I cause them to stumble. "I must be a good example at any cost, and not a poor one." I also remembered the words of Mary Graham, Amal, and Samir, that "God makes no mistakes." These words gave me the strength to endure this adversity.

A week went by, and nothing drastic happened. The police were still looking for me, and I was again a prisoner of four walls, not daring to wander outside my forced confinement.

One day, Professor Andrews went out of the house to run some errands, one of the items he brought back was a newspaper with my picture plastered all over the front page—the caption read: MISSING. I knew my mother would spare nothing to find me; she even had a £25,000 reward for anyone who might find me or had any information on my whereabouts—Scotland Yard was now in pursuit! At one point, Professor Andrews joked by addressing his wife saying, "What do you think, Lily, if we turn Dalal in and get the reward? The amount is quite tempting!"

Mrs. Andrews did not even crack a smile, but said, "It certainly is a huge sum—and tempting, I agree, and this town is small, if Dalal goes to the university here, she will no doubt be exposed."

What I'd just heard came down on my ears like a thunderbolt! After a while, however, she smiled and said, "Eureka, I found the solution!"

What she said was quite plausible in principle, but rather difficult to execute. In two days, I had short, blonde, curly hair—my long, silky chestnut hair was gone.

"Not to worry, Dalal; I worked as a hairdresser for four years to pay for college tuition. I have ample experience in this area," Mrs. Andrews said, assuredly.

As she finished her last touch, I went out to try the experiment on Professor Andrews. He could not believe what he saw, he brought his camera and began shooting picture after picture, saying, "You said your mother thought you were beautiful? Well, she should see you now!"

Not only did my look change, but I also had to change my name, as well, to Helen Andrews, so I would be able to enroll at the university.

Now, no one could recognize my identity, even those closest to me. Every time I looked in the mirror, I laughed and asked whether the image I saw was really me!

I enrolled at Oxford, miraculously. I was required to take an entrance exam which I passed with flying colors; it allowed me to enter my second year of college. Of course, without Professor Andrews's help and influence, none of this—the name change and lack of transcripts—could have been possible; moreover, he was able to obtain a scholarship for me for that whole year. Of course, when the truth would come out, he would have some explaining!

On the other hand, my mother by now had doubled the reward to £50,000, and all indications said I was still in the vicinity of Oxford—and might even be enrolled at the university!

I guessed that many people would now be looking twice as hard for me! I had to be extremely careful, and consequently, had to take precautions. I began to wear fake prescription glasses, and I restricted talking to anyone or mixing with others. Furthermore, I commuted in either Professor Andrews' car or his wife's, who also restricted inviting others to their house. Thus, with the Lord's help, the first semester ended without any significant problems.

Chapter 15
BELATED LETTER

*I*t was the day before Christmas, and indeed, it was an unusual day which I spent with the Andrews', in celebration of the birth of our Lord Jesus. We all woke up early, only to witness the fresh, pristine snow covering the ground—a remarkable sight; it reminded me of the mountains of Lebanon, my home country! It also brought to mind what a Lebanese émigré poet said upon seeing snow in his diaspora, yearning for his mountain village Baskinta, "O snow, you stirred my emotional anguish for my homeland, O snow, you reminded me of my loved ones in Lebanon."

Although the snow did stir up feelings of homesickness for my country, it did not have to serve as a reminder, for I had not forgotten this dear place so close to my heart. An image of my father flashed in my mind. I saw sadness covering his face, and his eyes staring at me with reprimand, as if, in a way, blaming me for being so inconsiderate in asmuch as telling my mother about his decision to accept the Lord. Moreover, how could I have forgotten the Shaheens who had become occupants of my heart? I kept looking out the window at the driven snow, and found myself transported to my beautiful, yet suffering, country.

I stood there, motionless, until I felt Mrs. Andrews' gentle hands take me by the shoulders and lead me into a comfortable chair. She did so in an effort to cheer me up and drive my mood of melancholy away, by injecting some humor, "You look beautiful as a blonde, but one must be careful not to allow the brown roots to show, which may give you away!"

She knew how to amuse me, and like a lamb, that closely follows its mother; I followed her to the bathroom for another session of hair coloring. I sat in a chair, surrendering my head to her expertise without uttering a single word or looking into the mirror, as I was still in Lebanon. I began to remember when I joined the Christmas choir with Mrs. Shaheen. To add to my misery, another image passed through my memory, the Christmas presents for each other and for the needy, but now, I had no money, no presents, and none of my loved ones were around me. These images distressed me further, and made me feel so lonely and abandoned.

Despite the continued, yet unusual, snowfall, Professor Andrews donned his English hat, topcoat, and of course, grabbed his umbrella on the way out—as any Englishman usually did—without uttering a single word. It seemed my hair dyeing spread the contagion to Mrs. Andrews, who apparently had a dormant urge in her to look prettier for Christmas—she proceeded to tint her hair, also, blonde. Suddenly, the phone rang; but her latex gloves, now covered with dye, kept her from taking the call; instead, I picked up, despite strict orders from Dr. Andrews not to answer the phone, myself. But since humans tend to act reflexively, I found myself answering, "Hello?" "Yes, who is it?"

The caller asked for Dr. Andrews, I told him he was not in at that moment, but if he'd like to leave a message, I'd be glad to take it.

The voice sounded familiar; there was a 30 second or so silence on the other end, when I heard someone excitedly, "Dalal, Dalal, is that you?"

"Dad! Dad! Is that you?" I said, as I burst into tears of joy, mixed with sadness and heartache. We exchanged greetings of "How are you", repeatedly, and then hows, whens, whys. After we both settled down a bit from the shock we'd experienced, he told me he did not know anything about anybody; the war was raging and had taken a toll on all telephone lines and other means of communication. I also understood that he was still at our house in Beirut, and that he had read my letter, which upset him severely. He also said he would be flying within a week to be with us for the New Year! That was certainly the best news I'd heard in a long time. He also mentioned he had sent me a letter, earlier, telling me he had no news about the Shaheens, except that they had already left Lebanon!

I thanked God for my father's well-being and the Shaheens safe departure from the insanity of war. My mind wandered, repeating every part of the conversation I'd just had with my father. He had mentioned a letter; I did not receive any letters from him, where could that letter be now? Could it have fallen into my mother's hands, by chance?

Within a few minutes, Dr. Andrews came back plodding in the snow—his coat covered with snow—he carried a metal box, the very same one we had improvised to use as a mailbox. He had a wide smile on his face—the kind that carries good news—and his face flushed red and blue from the cold.

"I am willing to do anything for you, my sweet Dalal. When I saw you crying this morning as you looked out the window, I could no longer take it; I had to go and fetch the letter you had missed. "Go ahead and open it," he said with obvious excitement.

With tears in my eyes, I said, "Dr. Andrews, my father called me while you were out, and I spoke with him." Since our conversation was in Arabic, Mrs. Andrews, of course, did not understand anything; that's why I told both about my conversation with my father, in detail. Mrs. Andrews then asked, "What about the letter your father said he sent?"

"I don't know; time will tell."

I opened the box, hurriedly, and found several notes and letters from Mrs. Andrews, and another letter, with American stamps, addressed to the Andrews. My eyes widened when I saw that the return address was in California; I was certain it was from Mary. However, to my utter surprise, the letter was written in Arabic and signed by my father! In it, he mentioned he was sending the letter with a friend who was going to California. I was reading the letter silently, but translating it aloud. In that letter, my father stated he had been deeply troubled by my news and concerned over the wide rift between my mother and me. He assured me he had no idea of her intentions; she would call him and tell him all was well and that I was in summer school, preparing to enter college! Furthermore, he told me about the ferocious war in Lebanon and that a shell had landed in our garden, killing our gardener, Abu Wafiq; and when Samir rushed to his aid, another shell followed that wounded Samir, who, was then hospitalized. He had no other details.

Feelings of pain and guilt overcame me. I stopped reading the letter, wiping tears running down my cheeks, and I thanked God for His wisdom in all this. If I had received the letter at the time it was sent, I could not have been able to endure all the news. I cried loudly, asking Jesus to forgive me. I promised the Lord not to complain and question his wisdom ever again. That no universities, seminaries, or the greatest preachers and theologians could teach or preach, took one small belated letter to know! It simply brought this verse to life, **"Cast thy burden upon the Lord, and He shall sustain thee."**

This verse re-energized me spiritually, and somewhat dissipated my sadness over the death of our gardener whom I loved immensely. Even though I now knew my father would not be able to fulfill his promise to come and see me, due to the increasingly-raging war, which restricted his travel, furthermore, and despite the fact I still did not receive a letter from Mary, peace, nonetheless, encompassed me. This could not be but the peace of God which passes all understanding.

With such a renewed spirit, I was able to finish my second year in college on the dean's list. It qualified me for an extended scholarship for the rest of my college career. I was working hard and taking summer courses, in an attempt to finish my undergraduate degree early.

My birthday came, and Mrs. Andrews prepared a cake on which she neatly placed twenty candles in a circle. As I was about to blow out the candles, the phone rang; it was my father, wishing me a happy birthday. I asked him from where he was calling. He said he had just arrived in Paris for important meetings, and that he would certainly come by to see me within two weeks. From then on, we spoke often, by phone, and, at times, for long stretches. I never told him about my new hair color or that my new name was now Helen Andrews; I thought it was too sensitive of an issue to discuss over the phone, and it could wait until we met. I also wanted to see his reaction to my new hair-do.

Two weeks passed that felt like an eternity, but Dad made good on his promise and arrived at the appointed time. I had been impatiently standing by my window waiting for the taxi. The Andrews opened the door and greetings were underway, when he said, "Dalal must be at college, I take it?"

Neither of them answered, but took him to the living room where the Andrews asked him to rest from his trip and insisted he feel at home. Mrs. Andrews then called, "Helen, Helen, come and say hello to Dalal's father."

I came down with some apprehension; I could hear my heart thumping in my ears and my hands trembling. "How will he react to my new image?" I wondered. As I appeared; he stood up, extended his hand to shake mine, and in a fake British accent, I welcomed him among us. We spoke for a few minutes, then I left the room, saying, "I am honored to have met Dalal's father!" The trick worked. I stood behind the door and heard him, "If Dalal had not been the most attractive girl in the whole wide world, I would have said Ms. Helen was!"

I could no longer hold myself; I had to give him a hug. I ran back, threw myself at him, hugging, smothering him with kisses, and shouting, "Dad, I am Dalal, Dalal; don't you recognize me?" I soon found Mrs. Andrews bending over Dad's face in an effort to revive him, as he was overcome with emotion. It was obvious the game we played was much harder than he could handle. When he came to, I told him the reasons for the changes, but he was initially dismayed and hesitant to accept my explanations, especially my new name. However, after some thought, he agreed that, sometimes, certain situations in life demanded radical actions.

When dinnertime came, we all held hands, a la Shaheens, and gave a prayer of thanks for God's faithfulness and sovereignty in making this reunion possible, against all odds. I personally praised God and lifted a special prayer to continue his work in us and reunite us again with our loved ones, especially my mother who had suffered a nervous breakdown and was in treatment.

This sad news about my mother broke my heart, especially when I heard she adamantly refused to see or talk to my father, or hear anything about him. Although my grandmother and my aunts were now by her bedside in London, she still did not talk to anyone or leave her room. My father said, all day long, she perused my picture albums, which she'd requested from Lebanon.

Her behavior, in general, and her attitude concerning my father, disturbed me so much that I told my father about my strong desire to visit her, despite what she may say or do; she was, after all, the mother I had always loved and would continue to love, but my father advised me against doing so at that time. The visit would have to wait.

My father and I spoke about college, and I showed him my high marks. Whenever I went to classes, I would leave with him my journal so he would read it and not be bored. All through that time, we did not have the chance to bring up the issue of his spiritual life. I felt in my heart, he was still not ready to declare his new faith in public. His political and confessional standing as a leader prevented him from doing so, but I was determined to have a talk with him about it, when the opportunity permitted. However, reading certain words and expressions in my journal about what I had to endure for the sake of Christ, must have left a burning mark within his heart. Before I even said a word, he told me he had promised the Lord he would return to Lebanon, liquidate his assets, and move to America, where we could live in peace! This sincere admission shocked me; I was at a loss for words. Yet, I knew he would not do so, which meant he would relinquish the family's responsibility in that region.

My father proceeded to invoke Samir's relationship with me, for he realized he was the man I loved, and that any love that could endure such hardships and separation must be pure and genuine. He also promised me to check on the Shaheens as soon as he returned to Lebanon, and find out where they might be; furthermore, he had no knowledge about my cousin Majdi, except that his mother always said that his faith was so strong, such faith must be quite genuine.

I did not hide my fears from my father about my concerns for not hearing from Mary Graham, although I had written her a few letters. He suggested, perhaps, I might have sent them to a wrong address. I quickly asked him for the address that he had, to compare it with mine. Sure enough, there was an error in the street number, so a whole year's worth of letters filled with tears, agony, and desperation went to waste. The letters were never returned to me since I did not leave my return address, lest my whereabouts were discovered—I did not want to take any chances, therefore, I wrote the return address inside the letter and instructed Mary about it. My father then suggested I write a letter to her, explaining everything, and he would hand it to a friend who was going to Los Angeles.

My father stayed with us for nearly two months and, seemingly, his mood changed for the better, being away from the onslaught of the war back home; he was ever-grateful for the Andrews' hospitality. He offered them monetary compensation for all they'd provided me, but the Andrews declined to take it. He then opened a special bank account in my name, which was not much, but promised to supplement it when he returned to Lebanon, because the existing London bank accounts were all in my mother's name.

In mid-September, we bid my father farewell, and he promised he would come again for the Christmas and New Year's holidays. One November evening, as Dr. Andrews and I were driving back from the university, Mrs. Andrews was standing by the front door with a big smile. We knew she must have some great news. Mary Graham, who finally received my letter, called and left a number where I could reach her at a friend's house in half an hour.

Twenty months lapsed since I'd been away from my loved ones, yet they seemed shorter than the half-hour that I had to wait to call Mary and get all the news from her. I paced the floor, looking at my watch, in frustration, over the ever-slowing clock. In precisely half an

255

hour, I dialed the number and could hear Mary's voice on the other end. I shouted, "Is that you, Mary? Where are you?"

"My sweetheart, Dalal," came the reply," Our hearts are broken and our tears are dry; whatever happened to you; where are you?"

"Did you not read my letter, Mary?"

"Yes, of course, how do you think I got the number to call you, but I want to hear it from you; I want to hear your sweet voice. You have no idea how much I miss you and how many sleepless nights I spent praying for you. My sweetheart, Dalal, thank you Lord"

The strong Mary could not hold her tears any longer as she began sobbing like a little girl. I tried to calm her down with some humor, "Mary, I am calling overseas, you're wasting my money on your tears? I am quite poor now!"

I could imagine her smiling; her voice gave her away. The first thing I did was to ask her for her phone number; she gave me my aunt's new number. Now, I had the end of the string in my hand. We spoke for nearly an hour, in which she told me all she knew about everybody and everything. We agreed on another time for another call, as now she had to leave her friend's.

Mary did not know anything about the Shaheens, except they were now living in Cyprus, where Dr. Shaheen worked. Moreover, she knew nothing about Majdi except that his family disowned him after his conversion to Christianity. As a result, Mona had some problems with her father and brother, Suheil, for the same reason. She felt it was best to leave California with her mother's approval, but Mary did not know her whereabouts or phone number. As for Samir, he was in Cyprus for some time with his family, but had to return to America where he came to my aunt's to ask if they knew anything about me. Mary told me he looked frail and seemed to be suffering from our separation, especially since he had not heard about me since I'd left Lebanon! The only information my aunt gave him was that I disappeared in London — even my family knew nothing about me! After four or five calls from Samir to Mary, inquiring repeatedly about me, he apparently gave up and she'd lost track of him. After I told all this to the Andrews, I burst into tears, saying, "I'm back to square one. Mary did not give me any more news than my father did. What good does it do if the Shaheens were in Cyprus and their address or phone number is unknown — or Samir in America, and I still cannot talk to him?"

I excused myself and went into my bedroom, lay on my bed, and as usual, began to think about what Mary told me. Perhaps I could find another string to hold onto. Poor Samir, I was not surprised to learn he'd traveled all the way to California to ask about me, or that he was frail and unhappy. The love we had vowed to each other was stronger than The Rock of Gibraltar. I thought so much about him and even wished that if I could not see him in person, that God, somehow, would send someone his way to let him know I was OK, and that my love was still as strong as ever. I had missed him badly.

As I was recalling all Mary had told me, I paused at a small, yet important, point—regarding my aunt who, apparently, was more understanding than the other members of the family, because she approved Mona's departure from California, in order to not face further negativity due to her conversion. I saw in this a dim, yet flickering, light: Perhaps she, too, loved the same Jesus her daughter loved, as well as her niece Dalal and Majdi, who must have suffered and sacrificed much for the sake of Jesus, who had become their Lord.

My father did not make it back as planned, nor did he transfer any money into my account as promised; but as I saw the ravaging war worsen in Lebanon, I understood. I was afraid my mother might have sent word to a warlord or a family member, telling him that my father had converted his religion, perhaps to get back at him, and might now be pursuing him. These thoughts must have been the result of my wrecked nerves. My emotions were affecting all aspects of life—my health, my studies, and my disposition. Only, and only, with God's help, was I able to finish my school year and enter summer vacation.

Chapter 16
A MAN IN MY LIFE

❧

I had wished I would not touch a book, a paper, or a pen, all summer long; I was tired of studying, but how else would I spend my time, except studying? I had set a goal for myself, and it was crucial I continue my school-year activities well into summer. I accepted a post at the university, working during the summer months, earning a modest salary, in addition to taking some classes. That arrangement helped me make some badly needed money and continue studying, in the hope of finishing my degree soon.

As I was sitting in the garden one day, enjoying the flowers and the well-trimmed-and-set shrubbery, I could not help but remember our garden in Lebanon, the weeping willow, our gardener Abu Wafiq and the red rose he used to give me daily. Tears welled up in my eyes as I pictured that savage hand lob shells on our garden to kill our beloved gardener, in the arms of Samir. "Is Uncle Abu Wafiq in heaven with Jesus right now?" I wondered. "Did he really accept Christ as his Savior prior to his death?"

The thought of someone dying without Christ is an awful and scary end to a human life. The merc idea made me think of my mother who had not accepted Christ, and if she died, she would not make it to be with the Lord. Did not the gospel speak clearly in the book of John, **"He that hath the Son hath life, and that hath not the Son hath not life, but the wrath of God is upon him"**

As far as I knew, my mother did not know Jesus, the Son, and therefore, did not have eternal life or the hope of one. I feared for her, the wrath of God, and felt I had not done enough to talk or witness to her about Christ Jesus; moreover, I felt I'd ignored her so much lately and my responsibility was to let her know I had forgiven her. Who else could tell her about Christ except me? If I kept on ignoring her, who could teach her and direct her towards the path of salvation?

These questions prompted me to rethink my attitude towards her, even though she had wronged me profoundly. I wanted so badly to get back into her life, perhaps now, with the passage of time, she would be more willing to accept me. In a month's time, precisely on June 25, I would turn twenty-one. This would be a good occasion for me to see her again, but where would I find her? I did not know where she was or whether she was even alive. All I knew was she kept the house she had rented on our arrival in the United Kingdom, but I did not know if she still lived there, or if she was still in London. My musings became an incessant preoccupation. I became fixated on finding my mother. I must think of a way or someone to help me, but whom? My father? I had not heard from him in a while. How could he have left me alone and with no money? I quickly arrived to a conclusion that something terrible must have happened. I promptly sought Dr. Andrews and told him of a daring plan I'd just thought of. He was incredulous, and asked me repeatedly if I were serious. I told him, "I must see my mother."

Reluctantly, he drove me to the old rented house in the hope she still lived there. I walked among the trees, leading to the house until I reached the old willow tree where Dr. Andrews and I used for our post office, and rested there a few moments. I saw a woman carrying what looked like garbage bags, but she did not look like the maid we had.

"Good morning." I said.

"Good morning, what can I do for you?"

"I am looking for a Mrs. Abu Suleiman, isn't this where she lives?"

"Yes."

"Can I see her? Is she here?"

"She went out with her daughter-in-law and her children, since morning, don't know when they'll be back."

I knew then, she was not talking about my mother but rather about my aunt, Majdi's mother, for she was married to her cousin who also carries the same last name, Abu Suleiman, and apparently had been living here since the outbreak of the civil war in Lebanon. I continued my questioning, "But where can I find Mrs. Huda Abu Suleiman, I thought she lived here?"

"She does, from time to time, but she is not here right now."

"Where is she, how can I find her, do you have her address?" I asked, my voice becoming sharper and matching the increasing beats of my heart.

"Sorry, I have no idea where she lives in London, all I know is she owns a house there."

"Do you happen to have her phone number?"

"I do, but you have not told me who you are or how you know the family."

"I am a friend of the family."

"OK, wait here; I'll go fetch the number."

Before she went in, I asked if I could use the powder room first. When I entered the house, I noticed everything looked the same, with the exception of children's toys scattered here and there. I also noticed my picture, wearing the beautiful gown at the beauty contest, was hanging on the wall; I stood there, a moment, contemplating the picture, and I wondered why my mother had chosen that picture. The housekeeper returned while I was still staring and asked me, "Did you know the young lady in the picture?"

"Yes. I had seen her before"

"Poor girl, she was killed in a car accident!"

"What did you just say?" I asked in disbelief.

I was surprised that my death had become an explanation for the mystery of my disappearance. The news stunned me. A little later, I left the house carrying so many odd and conflicting stories that only my mother could concoct!

The summary was, Mrs. Huda Abu Suleiman bought her daughter an automobile, and one day, as the daughter was driving in the rain, she had an accident, and as a result, was burned beyond recognition. Her mother first believed she was kidnapped because of her wealth, and the kidnappers had demanded a ransom; after weeks, the vehicle was found, and some of her daughter's remains retrieved, including a gold ring by which she was able to recognize her. Consequently, she had a nervous breakdown and moved to London with her family, the father had cancer. Of course, she later flew back to be with her husband, despite the ravages of the civil war in Lebanon.

What a story! Of course, none of it was true. I told Dr. Andrews all I'd heard while driving back to the house, sometimes shaking my head with laughter, and at times, with evident sorrow at the fabricated stories my mother had spread. It was true my father told me about my mother's nervous breakdown, but the word 'cancer' made me uneasy. Was it a genuine cancer or a genuine fabrication? Dr. and Mrs. Andrews tried to calm me down and alleviate my anxiety in different ways, but nothing worked!

That evening, as I attempted to catch some sleep, I was awakened by a series of nightmares that left me with insomnia. For sure, the

Shaheen family must have heard about the rumor of my death—including Samir—and maybe they believed it, but Mary Graham had never heard of it. Did other members of my family know the real truth, or was my mother able to convince everyone I was killed in an accident? With this newly acquired-news about my "death", I began my first day of work at the university, working with a team of three: a doctorate student, Eric Garrard, a chemistry professor, and myself, of course.

Eric, intelligent and a ruggedly handsome young man, slightly older than Samir, were always considerate and courteous. Soon enough, I noticed, every now and then, he would steal looks in my direction. Although we both worked in close proximity, Eric and I exchanged no serious conversation beyond work, but at times, I would see him in the break room or sitting outside under a tree reading a book. I had no idea what kind of book he was reading, but I wished it had been the Bible. With such high ethical and moral codes that he exercised, he reminded me of Samir' and his Christian behavior and traits.

I had been feeling lonely and sad at the time, despite the kindness the Andrews' showed me; I, however, needed to befriend someone close to my age. I needed this kind of companionship during this stage of my life. One evening, we had to work late; Dr. Andrews called me, repeatedly, to ask when he should pick me up to take me home. I finally gave him the exact time, within an earshot of Eric, only to call him later and tell him we were going to be delayed, again. Upon hearing this, Eric said to me, "Miss Andrews, there is no need to bother your dad any further; I will drive you home, if that's OK with you."

I then called Dr. Andrews and told him a colleague would be driving me home as soon as we finished our work, but when he expressed some concern, I assured him he should not worry.

I had not been with a young man close to my age in a long time; as we drove along, we almost ran down a shirtless man staggering along the road. Eric then commented, "Poor man, if only he knew Christ, he would not be in this miserable condition." Before I could ask him if he were a Christian believer, he continued his speaking on the need of this world for Christ, "There is no hope or salvation without Jesus, neither is there freedom from bondage from drunkenness, drugs, or gambling. Our young people are running straight to hell, without Christ, and our universities are nothing but knowledge feeders," he said with fervent passion. He was trying to impress on me, the need to believe in Christ. Smiling, I looked at Eric and told him I agreed 100%

since, I, also, at some point in my life, surrendered my life to our Lord Jesus, but without divulging any other information, lest I accidentally gave myself away.

His words were so similar to what I'd heard earlier from Samir, at camp. I felt so comfortable with this newly-found Christian friend and, therefore, did not need to test the level of his Christianity because I knew, based on the Word of God, **"Wherefore by their fruits ye shall know them."** I was quite happy to be around Eric, I did not need Dr. Andrews to drive me around any longer. Although he expressed some regrets, I am sure he must have been relieved from being my chauffeur for so long, yet he never complained. Even my birthday that year had a special flavor, as Mrs. Andrews baked me a special cake and invited Eric, to what turned out to be a beautiful party. I put out twenty-one candles.

My work lasted all summer long; the days seemed shorter and the workload lighter. I took on other responsibilities in addition to my work at the university; I began to go with Eric after work to his church, where I volunteered for a few church activities. It was some summer I spent! I learned so much and experienced life outside home and school, and for the first time, I'd earned my own hard-worked for money. Furthermore, I learned the joy of giving my own money without having to rely on my father's deep pockets. I also experienced the joy of serving Christ by providing the scriptural 'cup of cold water' in His name.

These positive aspects notwithstanding, I had an ominous feeling a storm may be brewing. It was not an intuition, but more a sense of hidden guilt, as I carried on my friendliness with Eric, without telling him, or even giving him the sense, I might be in love with someone else. I could sense his feelings towards me were moving away from those of friendship to a bit more. I avoided facing that, and did not want to jeopardize the deep platonic friendship I was enjoying. Samir was still the one who occupied that part of my heart, and the kindle of love we had was still as strong as ever, despite our lengthy separation. "Lord, I need your help in this," I thought.

I knew I was in big trouble, because Eric had become deeply enamored with me. By keeping my secret from him, I felt I had led him on, by using his friendship to fill the vacuum Samir had left in my life; hence, I felt intensely guilty. I spoke with the Andrews about this dilemma, only to have them confirm my fear that I was really in trouble. As it were, I began to become somewhat attached to Eric; I was happy around him, and had it not been for Samir, I might have fallen in-love with him.

I prayed to God to help me and give me the courage to tell Eric the truth, but with each passing day, I procrastinated and kept coming up with excuses not to tell him. One day, unexpectedly, and to my utter shock, yet satisfaction, he asked me if I were engaged or attached to anyone else. Rather than take advantage of the situation and tell him the truth, I evaded his question—I just left him suspended in mid-air. I tried to reverse things to an earlier level, where we were enjoying each other's company without the romantic issue, and I started to come up with excuses, ranging from schoolwork to family and home obligations, in order to prepare Eric for the hour of truth, and therefore, close a dear chapter in my life

In the meantime, nothing had changed as far as my family and loved ones were concerned. I thought no news was good news. I missed Mary Graham and decided to call her at my aunt's house. My heart jumped when my aunt answered. I yelled, "Auntie! This is Dalal!"

"Dalal? Dalal who?" She inquired!

"What do you mean Dalal who? Your niece, Dalal!"

"You must have the wrong number," the voice came from the other end. Has senility come so early to her?

"Auntie, please hear me, you only have one brother Salah who is married to Huda, and I am their only daughter Dalal, remember?"

I heard her sobbing at the other end as she yelled back, "Oh, sweetheart! Where are you, are you all right? We have not heard anything from you for so long!" she repeated repeatedly.

I gave her a summary of my news, then asked her, "Auntie, do you know anything about my father? I made several attempts to find him but did not succeed."

She did not reply at first, but later said, "He's not feeling well; he was sick all last year."

Before I asked her my next question, I asked God to help me, here, to endure the reply I strangely expected. "Auntie, does my dad have cancer?"

"He does," came the dreaded reply.

I could not control myself as I began to cry, my aunt unsuccessfully tried to calm me down by telling me he was feeling much better, and there was a good chance he might be coming over to Johns Hopkins for further treatment, as soon as the opportunity arose. Then I asked her about my mother. My aunt told me my mother had gone back to Lebanon to be with him, despite their separation. She added that she was always in contact with her sisters, and all reports that came from home indicated my father was feeling much better. I also asked her about Mary, she said she returned from Texas after her sister's death, but not in the house right then. Then, I asked about Mona, but she did not answer. I asked if she knew anything about her, because I wanted to hear her voice; then she began to cry and said, "I don't have her number nor her address; she occasionally calls, so do not worry about her; I believe she now lives in Washington D.C."

"Auntie, do you happen to know a Samir Shaheen?"

"Of course I do," she said.

"Do you know where he lives?" I asked, my heart, thumping.

"A short while ago, he was here in L.A; he came here and asked about Mary and seemed so desperate to see or talk to her. I felt sorry for him, and I gave him her phone number and address in Texas, so he immediately flew there. That's all I know about him."

"Auntie, do you remember Danny Roper?"

"Yes, of course."

"Do you happen to know his phone number or address?"

"I do not; he moved from his apartment and do not know his new phone."

"Auntie, if you speak with Mona, could you please tell her I love and miss her; let her call me; here's my phone number."

But alas, before I was able to give her the number, she hung up; it sounded as if someone had just walked in on her. I began to cry, out of frustration, while recounting to the Andrews the details of my conversation with my aunt Sue.

Regardless of the news about my father's cancer, God gave me the peace I sought. I realized my father's silence and "neglect" were not an act of abandonment. Furthermore, his reconciliation with my mother did not mean he had to compromise his new faith in Christ, but rather, it was a paternal attempt to shield me from further anxiety and worry. I expected Mary to call me, but that did not happen. She must have given Samir my number, I thought, when he went to visit, and surely, he would call me, I reasoned, but he had not, either. 'What was going on?' I wondered. Every time I called my aunt, someone else would pick up the phone. I would hang up, as not to cause problems for my aunt with anyone else in her family. Why Mary was not picking up, I did wonder.

As for my dad, I prayed very hard for his health. I had a recurring dream, where he was lying in bed, reaching for my hand to save him, as a drowning man would. I reached for him with both hands, pulling him, while crying for Jesus to help, until he was able to stand on his feet. Those disturbing dreams kept on recurring, until one day, I dreamt he stood up, wore a new suit, and placed a white carnation in his lapel. I was wearing a purple evening gown, my arm in his, walking by the seashore in the Pigeon Rock area in West Beirut. I woke up the next morning, feeling comfortable and optimistic. I shared my dream with the Andrews', but Dr. Andrews did not comment. He was holding some papers in his hands, looking at them carefully, and then asked, "How much money did your father leave for you in your account, if I may ask?"

"I think no less than two thousand pounds, but now, there must be half that amount or less. Why, is there anything wrong? I really never bothered to look at bank statements?" He then told me my bank account had twenty thousand pounds in it. I was shocked. How did my father manage to find someone he trusted and arrange for that much money to be deposited in my account, despite all of the difficulties and interruptions of normal banking transactions during the war. "Oh, how much I love you dad," I thought. "You're the best dad in the world; forgive me for thinking you'd abandoned me!"

This large sum of money did not make me any happier. Money had become meaningless to me, unless I used it on those dearest to me. I hadn't bought an expensive dress since my arrival in London, nor did I uselessly squander money as I used to. However, I did spend a large amount when Christmas came, and with Eric's help, bought clothes and medicine for the poor and needy. As Majdi and the Shaheen family did on a previous occasion, we dressed up as Santa Claus and went from house to house, distributing what happiness; we could, to those in need. Eric tried, in vain, to find out the source of the money spent, but I did not tell him; instead, I told him to ask every recipient to pray for the healing of someone dear to my heart. Eric noticed tears well up in my eyes and asked for the cause, but I remained quiet; he respected my silence and did not insist.

That was my third Christmas without Samir and his family; the memories of the first Christmas lingered in my mind and heart—including the choir, the Christmas tree, the twins, the presents, the homemade sweets that Mrs. Shaheen baked, and the ring Samir presented me as a token of his love. These fond memories tugged at my heart and brought tears to my eyes. Eric saw me wipe my tears away, as we rode back; he then stopped by the side of the road, took my hand, gave me a comforting hug, and said, "I wished I could know the cause of these tears! I wish I could wipe away every drop. I love you, Helen, I love you!" I do not know what happened, but I did not resist nor protest, but kept my head resting on his shoulder and wept. His shoulder was Samir's shoulder, and his words of love were Samir's words when he told me, "I love you, Dalal!" This took me back to those scenic Lebanese hills where Samir told me of his love. In a few moments, I snapped back to reality when Eric suddenly moved his head back and said, "If you can return a fraction of the love I have for you, I'd be the happiest man in the world!"

At that point, I finally mustered enough courage to tell him the truth about me, but before I could open my mouth, he continued, "I'd like to introduce you to my family; I've already told them so much about you; and they're eager to meet you."

"Eric, I have something to tell you, but I don't know where to star." Before I could finish, he cut me off, laughing, and saying, "If you have something good and positive to say, say it; otherwise, I don't want to hear it!"

Since what I was about to tell him was neither good nor positive, but rather disastrous, I held back. I was in an unenviable predicament and had no idea how to deal with it. Why did I not tell him about Samir earlier; why was I cowardly? Why was I selfish and cruel?

Eric had invited me to his parents' house for Christmas, where extended family and their friends had assembled. Christmas was a special event this year, as Eric's brother and his wife had their first baby—a boy. He also told me that other friends and relatives would be coming from the United States—all eager to meet Helen—especially his mother who was counting the days to see the girl who was able to charm her son and win his heart. "Again, God help me!" I prayed as Eric continued. "I cannot wait for Christmas Eve when I would be able to hold your hand and shout, 'this is the girl I love.'"

I was not able to turn down his invitation; his fervor overwhelmed me, and any excuses I had, did abandon me; once more, I surrendered. Although I knew, down deep in my heart, our relationship was fruitless, and that I would tell him about Samir after the party. I, nonetheless, wanted to make sure I looked my best. Mrs. Andrews arranged my blond hair quite nicely in a royal fashion; I wore an elegant evening gown—the first expensive item I bought after the discovery of the new fortune I had—and took my time applying appropriate make-up over my face. I wanted to be nice and caring with Eric that evening, making sure not to ruin his Christmas. It became difficult for me to see Eric so happy; the happier he felt, the guiltier I felt.

During our ride to his parents' house, he attempted to hold my hand, and I would slip it away gently, only to tell him, laughingly, "Aren't we getting ahead of ourselves?" He would reply, "Sorry, Helen, if you only knew how much I loved you, you would not blame me, at all!"

"Eric, do you believe that nothing can happen without God's permission?"

"Of course, I do, but what are you trying to say?"

"And would you accept God's will for your life?" I continued ignoring his response.

"These are profound theological issues, Helen, why are you bringing them up now when we're only a few yards away from the house, going to a Christmas party?"

I replied coyly, "I just want to know where you stand when your will does not agree with God's will."

"That's a good question that needs a lot of consideration, and frankly, right now, I am not ready to go into this. I can firmly say, that the motto I have been guided by is, **'But God, is faithful, who will not suffer you to be tempted above that ye are able; but will, with the temptation, also makes a way to escape, that ye may be able to bear it."**

Eric was repeating these words as he was parking in front of the house that glittered with all sorts of lights. As we entered, more lights were glowing here and there, as well as lit candles. The house was bustling; I was scared—and bewildered; I was not used to being around so many people after my seclusion with the Andrews. Despite all this, I tried to convince myself I was still Dalal—and not Helen. Dalal was always capable of handling crowds and entering their hearts. Eric then held my hand and said, "Feel at home, Helen. I want you to be yourself, enjoy the evening, and feel comfortable."

He held my wrist tightly, as he led me inside; a very elegant, handsome woman—who looked a little like Mrs. Roper (Danny's mom)—hurried to greet me at the door; she gave me a hug and said, "My Lord! My son did not do you justice when he said you were very pretty," as she hugged me repeatedly, all the while, I was feeling guilty, as I was torturing her son. Then, she introduced me to her guests.

"I present to you my son's girlfriend, Helen Andrews."

I began to move around, shaking hands with everyone. They greeted me very warmly, even as if I were family, already. Eric, on the other hand, made exaggerated statements about me, as someone trying to pinch himself to make sure it was true, I was present in his parent's house. For a so-called stiff English family, they displayed an exaggerated sense of welcome, and I, an exaggerated display of a conservative British woman. Within a few minutes, I felt Eric's hand wrap around my waist, as he introduced me to his brother, his sister-in-law, her brother, as well as another guest that had accompanied them. I was shaking Lillian's hand—Eric's sister-in-law; and her husband's; the wife's brother turned out to be none other than Danny, and the guest, of all people, was none other than Samir himself! Yes, it was Samir Shaheen, in flesh and blood. How could such coincidence be? I felt it must be God, directing my destiny, that such incredulous matters were simply to happen! I nearly fainted. Perhaps my experience of getting lost in the forest was by far much easier for me than the odd situation in which I found myself.

I was not sure whether any of them recognized me with my newly acquired British accent, and posing as a short-haired, blonde woman named Helen Andrews. My heart was beating so hard, I felt it was going to jump right out of my chest, as if drawn by a team of wild horses. What a predicament, and a bittersweet moment. To meet Samir after such a long separation was certainly not anything I would have as well dreamed would happen. What were the odds, of all places, to meet him there—one in a million? I was afraid my eyes would give me away to Samir, so I put on my sunglasses, pretending the lights were hurting my eyes. I then began to wonder about what might have brought Samir and Danny there.

As usual, Danny, in his playful ways, whispered something into Eric's ear, turned towards me, kissed my hand, then excused himself and left the room. Later, I was told it had to do with his new nephew whose name he had chosen. To make some talk, I asked his sister about her baby's name. She replied, "Samir," as she pointed to my Samir who was standing curiously looking at me. I said, "Samir?" The way he reacted at hearing his name coming from my lips made me feel he had recognized my voice; I looked at him, and simultaneously, our eyes met. I shivered at the thought he may have recognized me, so I looked away and sat next to Eric, who flashed a huge grin.

From my secure vantage point, I could look intently at Samir without being seen by him. Although the food was plentiful and smelled so good, Samir had not touched it, nor was he talking to other people; he seemed sad. He also looked thinner than before, and his hair had a few grey hairs, despite his young age of twenty-seven! I began to wonder, even more, what had brought Danny and Samir to Eric's family Christmas party. When did he arrive? When would they be leaving? And what were the chances Samir might be looking for me? What were their plans? Did they come looking for me somewhere in London? Didn't my aunt Sue tell me Samir had met Mary in Texas, and she'd told him everything she knew about me? Did she not give him my address and phone number? Eric told me his guests had been there for over two weeks. Samir was staring at me, again, as he walked towards me. I got up, went to the powder room, and tried to regain my composure. I took one look in the mirror and was alarmed at my ashen face. I applied more blush and more lipstick before I went out again. Eric was waiting by the door, worried about my delay. He said everybody was waiting, now, to begin singing and praying; the American guest would deliver a short devotion! I sat beside Eric's mother, and unexpectedly, Samir, holding the Bible, sat beside me, after asking permission. I remained quiet, and said nothing. I was feeling flushed and despondent not knowing what to. I began to pray for this Christmas Eve to end peacefully and promised, by tomorrow, I would explain everything to Samir. However, how and what could I explain to the shy, Eric when he was behaving as though we were engaged and madly in love with each other. I glanced at Samir and saw him staring at me, likely trying to figure out my real identity; after all, there were so many tips and signs imprinted on his face—one might be able to change a few outward appearances, but it would be much harder to change his features, his bodily movements, or the tone of his voice. Then, abruptly, he excused himself from delivering the devotional and left the room. "He must have recognized me!" I thought. "He must have noticed the ring he gave me three years ago; how was I to know he would be at the party?" What would he say now? He simply would think I had forgotten him and fallen in love with another man. I could not blame him; but come tomorrow, I would explain all that had happened, and he would believe me, hug me, kiss me, and in his love, make me forget the pain of separation I had endured. That night was going to be the longest ever.

I thought about all these things, sitting again in the powder room. I looked for a piece of paper in my purse, and hurriedly wrote a note with a shaky hand, "Sorry we had to meet under such conditions after such a long time. I hope you're not angry with me, for what you may have noticed this evening is far from the truth. The false identity I took was a matter of life and death; please try to understand. I'll clarify everything later."

When I finished writing the note, I went back to rejoin this strange party. In a few more minutes, everyone, except me, closed their eyes, as Eric's father concluded the evening with a word of prayer. I looked around to see if Samir was still there. I saw him nearby, looking at me, pondering. After I bid all farewell, I approached Samir, shook his hand, slipping the note in his pocket; I then took Eric's hand, indicating it was time for us to leave.

After we drove a few miles, I mustered some courage to let Eric know the whole truth—I felt it was time to do it and not a moment too late. He seemed alarmed as I changed my tone and began to recount the tale of my relationship with another person without revealing any names. He remained silent until we reached the house, but he looked heart-broken, pursing his lips the whole time. I would not let him drive away before he had said something, or reacted, one way or another, whether in anger or reprimand; anything would be better than his deafening silence. I was crying and pleading with him to say something. He remained speechless, neither laughing nor crying, just like another Sphinx! After what seemed to be an eternity of silence, he finally said, "Why have you waited so long to tell me about the other man in your life? Why did you reveal this truth tonight?

"Because I felt your behavior tonight was exaggerated, and everyone thought we were more than just friends, and that your family was expecting you to announce our engagement; so I was afraid of false expectations."

Eric shook his head, sadly, and asked forgiveness if he had, in any way, imposed on me anything I might have deemed annoying. He stepped out of the car, opened the door for me, and walked me to the door. Before I opened the door, he said, "I have one question," but I cut him off before he could ask, "No, I will not reveal his name."

"No, that's not what I was going to ask; all I want to ask is, if you did not have this person in your life, would you have accepted me as a husband?"

I looked at his sad face in the darkness of the night and saw the glistening of tears welling up, and I wanted to slightly mend his broken heart by saying, "Be assured, Eric, you would have been the first man to crown my heart!"

Apparently, feeling slightly better, he took one final look at me, got into his car, and drove off. I could hear the engine rev so violently, it sounded like an aircraft engine; I prayed for God to protect him so he would make it home, safely. I entered the house, but the house was so quiet, everyone was in deep sleep, it was well past midnight. I picked up the phone to call Mary, and to spill all my anger and blame on her for all that went wrong. Her soft voice came over the wire, "Hello, Dalal, did you see them, did they find you?" she asked with apparent joy and innocence!

"Who are you talking about, Mary?" I asked, pretending ignorance of her question.

"Mona, Samir, and Danny, of course!"

"My cousin Mona is here?" I asked with real surprise. I had no idea, nor did I expect to hear about Mona, in particular.

"They're all there, haven't you met, yet?" She asked, perplexed. "It's my fault, Dalal!"

Mary must have realized, by now, I had not seen any of them, yet, from my questions and answers, but I kept up my charade of ignorance.

She told me how sorry she was, then she went on to tell me everything that had happened, beginning with when Samir went to see her in Texas, in his efforts to find me. Her story cleared much ambiguity regarding what I thought I knew. Before I began to undress and go to sleep, the phone rang, and Dr. Andrews answered—it was near 5:00 a m. I heard him say, "Hello, yes. When? Where? Yes, yes," and he hung up.

He wanted to tell me something, but before he could, I said, "Eric had an accident, didn't he?"

"Apparently, he was driving at great speed and ran into a truck, overturning his car, and was transported to a hospital."

"How's he doing?"

He told me that Eric's father called, and asked him to inform me, to get ready to go with him to the hospital, because his son keeps repeating my name. I hurriedly changed my evening clothes to something more comfortable, removed all make-up, and waited outside. Dr. Andrews wanted to accompany me, but I told him I preferred being alone.

I wished I could cry then, but I felt like a moving statue. Eric's father and Steve, picked me up, and we headed to the hospital. I looked away when I saw people I knew in the hallways, even when I saw Samir. I kept walking at a fast pace, next to Steve, who led me into Eric's room; Eric looked worse than I thought! Tubes, instruments, machines, bandages, were all over the room. I stood by Eric and began to cry out in a loud voice,

"Eric, do you hear me? It's Helen." Then I whispered in his ear, "Forgive me, please; it's my fault, entirely."

Everyone present felt they should leave us; they must have thought we had a lovers' spat. How far the truth was from what they were thinking!

I knew that, without any shadow of a doubt, Samir must have recognized me. The paper I'd slipped into his pocket the previous night, was sufficient. He also must have known that circumstances dictated my behavior, which was beyond my control: the changes of name, the fake identify, as well as the hair color. At that moment, in the hospital, I appeared to be a heart-broken fiancée. My overwhelming guilt masqueraded as profound sadness; my sentiments, all bundled up, in a spectrum of emotion, were wrapped in a deep sense of heartbreak. I was happy I had finally found my long-lost love, yet I was consumed with worry that, based on appearances, Samir must have believed I was a worried fiancée. My behavior stood in stark contradiction to what I had explained in my brief scribble of a note that I had tucked carefully in my beloved's pocket, the night before.

The separation had lasted over three years, and we had known each other for only a short while. Our vows might have been fleeting; he might have been thinking I was a child who rushed to express adolescent emotions. He had no way of knowing how seriously I took those vows, how many sleepless nights I'd spent, praying and hoping, against hope, that I would see him again. Now, here I was, crying at the bedside of someone who, essentially, seemed to be the one I loved! Who could have not believed that Eric and I had some sort of romantic relationship after witnessing my distressed condition and apparent anguish? I was so distraught, I was not able to eat, drink, or speak, to anyone. Since I'd arrived at the hospital, I kept on holding Eric's hand and tenderly whispering in his ear, I left his side only when doctors or nurses came in to check and tend to his serious wounds. His brother, Steve, was supposed to take me back to the house that evening, when Samir offered to accompany him. I had not spoken with Samir yet; but it so happened, Steve had to pass by the house, first, to fetch something, so he asked us to come in, since it could take a while.

Samir was quick to decline by telling Steve we would be all right in the car, even when the temperature was dropping. I took this to be an excuse for Samir to wanting to talk with me alone. I was glad for this opportunity; here was my chance to make some clarifications. Samir was sitting in the back seat and I was in the passenger seat; for a moment, I felt he was going to jump out of his seat and come sit next to me to hold me in his arms; but, of course, he did not, and he could not, since there was no room in the front. It took over one minute before he began to talk to me. I could see anger and disappointment in his eyes, "And, now, Miss Andrews," he facetiously said, "What is your next plan, after you nearly destroyed your friend or your fiancé—or?"

His remarks stunned me; how could he, out of all people, be so insensitive and callous? How could he be so judgmental when he had no idea of the facts? Was he the man I loved, the man who meant the world to me? Did he not read what I wrote him yesterday? How could he not try to get the facts first and ask, with genuine concern, about what had transpired through these years? He spoke no further, neither did I, but after a while, he turned to me again and said, "I see you're keeping silent; have you nothing to say, Miss Andrews?"

It hurt me to hear him use this name with such sarcasm indeed; but understand he was not one to talk in this manner unless he was utterly devastated. This new Helen must have hit a raw nerve. I finally broke down and replied, "Samir, please, do not be angry with me, try to understand what I am about to tell you. The new name and look were a matter of life and death for me; I was in dire straits, and—" he cut me off, "What dire straits? What life and what death, made you step on my heart and feelings, and while I was tearing up the whole world looking for you, here I see you were well-adjusted, and have found a new love."

273

I was secretly happy to hear him say that, despite the harshness of his tone and words, it meant he did care—and still loved me. I started defensively explaining, "You are mistaken, Samir; you are my first and only love, and you know that. I am awfully sorry the circumstances brought us together again on the wrong foot, and via such misunderstanding. I want you to remember that my promise to you remains unwavering; I still love you more than anything in the world; God has chosen you to be the desire of my heart—forever. There is no love between me and Eric—there never was—at least on my side. He is a special friend, who has helped me so much in my dark hours, and I cherish his friendship—no more and no less—just as I cherish my friendship to your friend, Danny, or to Majdi, my cousin."

I drew closer to him as I reassured him, stroked his head gently, and smiled for the first time since I'd seen him. Then I asked, "Have you forgotten that I left my parents and family and my country all because of you?"

I thought these tender words might appease him, but he pushed my hand away and said, I just hope you did not accept Christ because of me!"

"Samir, what are you saying, how could you say this?" I asked with obvious annoyance. I was deeply hurt that he would even think that way; it hurt much more than his initial accusation of my finding a new love.

"I was seeking Christ before I even knew you existed; just ask your sister, Amal! You have nothing to do with my faith in Christ, even though you are the person who led me to Him; but for His sake, I'll pretend you did not make such an offensive remark. I just want you to be certain of what I am saying."

"At any rate," replied Samir coldly, "I do not blame you for doing what you did; what you had to go through was intolerable, and I am sure, at times, that you felt lonely and forsaken. I am terribly sorry for having been so crass and even rushing to judgment; there is nothing between us to make you owe me any explanation about your private life."

"I don't owe you, what do you mean exactly? There's nothing between us? You're saying this with such simplicity? How about the vows we made in the past, you call this "nothing between us?""

It is sad that you believe what suits you and disbelieve what doesn't! Since your thinking has taken you to a new level of nonsense, then you're free to think as you wish!"

"What do you expect me to believe? After years of fear, grief, pain, war, death, searching, and impatiently waiting for you to show up, I was not able to find you. Mary gave me your address, and I rushed to Oxford, looking for you! Yet, no one had ever heard of Dalal Abu Suleiman, not via the university student records, nor the employees; and in my darkest hours, you walk in like a princess holding someone else's hand? What did you expect me to do, run and give you a hug? I recognized you the moment you sauntered in, despite your new looks. You forgot that the ring I gave you still adorned your finger, but you did not care, you tried to avoid looking me in the eyes! Moreover, your overflowing tears over Eric, your extraordinary care, and every move you made, were nothing but signs of a romantic relationship! You even left the room, hand-in-hand, and stayed out until four in the morning; how was I supposed to take all of this? Think about that. What happened between the two of you that caused Eric to drive off at such a high speed and get into that horrible accident? All these things took place within a few hours, and you want me to believe you, just like that?"

"Would you like to know what I was doing with Eric until four in the morning, Dr. Shaheen? Do you really want to know? Well, listen. I was making the biggest mistake in my life; I was stupidly sacrificing a man who truly loves me for a man like you! Do you want to know something else? I am truly sorry that I broke this loving young man's heart for your sake!"

"You told him about me?"

"Not to worry, Dr. Shaheen, your distinguished name remained unscathed!"

Before any of us could speak another word, Steve rushed towards us excusing himself for being late. It was good that I was on the way home, so I could shut the door behind me, contemplate all that had just transpired and have a good cry. I did not wish to tell the Andrews what happened. It was too incredible to believe! My sad face, however, gave me away. When they insisted that I tell them, I did, but I pleaded with them not to talk to me about this subject, even when they heard that Eric took a turn for the worst. I also did not want to hear Samir's name—or talk about him—or any of this.

My stomach-aches and overall discomfort were recurring, but this time, worse than ever. I took some pain medication, entered my room, and shut the door behind me for two whole days, hardly eating or drinking. I did not return any telephone calls, remaining in seclusion. The Andrews attempted to persuade me to answer the phone, but I refused—most calls were from Steve, Lillian, and Eric's mother, as I was told. Even poor Eric tried to talk to me, but the only answer was, "She is sick." Of course, I *was* sick; Mrs. Andrews knew all along. She'd even arranged for a physician to come and check on my condition, since I was not able to go anywhere. I also knew Samir had been calling, all the time, but his request to talk to me was refused, as well—just as I had instructed. I figured he must have been suffering and wondering when this situation would be over. What Samir said was inconceivable; it would be very difficult for him to redeem himself. His words deeply hurt me, especially when he alluded to my faith in Christ. In the state of mind I was in, my emotions were oscillating like a pendulum, from one extreme to the other. On the one hand, I realized Samir was very hurt, but on the other, signs of jealousy indicated that he still cared for me. Should I blame him? Or should I consider these endearing furies of a lover scorned?

These latest episodes not only affected me physically, but also devastated me, emotionally—and weakened me, spiritually. I quit reading the Bible and ceased praying. I was afraid to speak to God in my prayers, lest He stirred my heart to forgive Samir and have me ignore what he did. My pride stood in the way; it also stood between my Lord Jesus and me. I knew my behavior would grieve the Holy Spirit, as I had read in the New Testament, yet I remained adamant.

Christmas passed, while I was still incommunicado. I had no idea how the Gerrard family spent their Christmas with their son still in the hospital, nor did I want to. I also knew nothing about Mona, despite my love for her and longing to see her. I was unhappy staying away from Samir—maybe even torturing him—but I was perhaps savoring the moment, at the same time.

Even Dr. Andrews scolded me, one day, for my irrational behavior. He said,

"I am so sorry that after all the time we spent together under the same roof, and in which your presence was a blessing to us, as well as your having been instrumental in our return to the Lord, that we now find in you a grudging heart, and the love that covers a lot of sins is now, simply, thrown away. What happened to the commandment that Christ gave us about turning the other cheek? You're coming across as a prideful, obstinate woman. Allow me to add, that the way you're acting is no different from the way your mother treated you! Although I have never met her, I see her in your behavior and attitudes—all due to a prideful heart!"

Dr. Andrews's words pierced my heart, as his wife tried so hard to calm him, but he went on—to criticize my attitude towards Samir. He also included some truths, which I was not aware of. My tears flowed down my cheeks, as I questioned if that was the real me who Dr. Andrews was describing! Was it possible that I'd reached this low in my Christian faith without realizing it? Is the flesh *that* weak? Could it be true—I might have inherited my mother's inclination of pride and vindictiveness? Was it really me who was begrudging, hateful, and vengeful? Was I following in my mother's footsteps, when dealing with such issues? I ought to be careful not to slide down such a path; my Christianity demanded it. Oh, how ashamed I felt. I was repeating, to myself, a silent prayer, "Oh, Jesus, you are the one who taught us forgiveness; I have now wronged you first, then Samir. I may have even become a stumbling block to the Andrews! Please forgive me for my ignorance, pride, and foolishness."

New Year's was just around the corner—only two days left, to be exact. While at the hospital, I overheard that Danny and Samir were going to a Middle Eastern country, right after New Year's Day, where they would work as physicians for one year—open to extension—and Steve would follow them a month later, leaving Lillian and their son with his parents. I did not have much time left to reconcile with Samir, nor did I know where to begin, so I rushed to Dr. Andrews and told him, "I am willing to do what you suggest, even if I have to walk to him on my hands and knees! I am so sorry that I acted in such a vindictive way, Dr. Andrews, I also ask your forgiveness for my unchristianlike behavior."

Dr. Andrews knew I meant every word—and told me how proud he was of me to feel such remorse and that I was willing to make up for it. Naturally, he could not forget to invoke Shakespeare's famous saying, "To err is human, to forgive, divine."

Mrs. Andrews came in after she'd had been shopping; after unloading the bags, she handed me a note from Samir, but her somber looks did not indicate good news. She said, "He does not wish to come to the house, he just asked me to give you this message."

Before she finished telling me all this, I began to cry and went into the kitchen, where Dr. Andrews was. He realized something must have taken place that caused me to cry again! He then approached his wife and began to question, further. I heard her say she saw a car following her at high speed, trying to catch up with her before she entered the house, then Samir handed her the note and told her he had to rush to the airport.

Hearing this, I felt deep pain in my stomach. I was overcome with abject feelings that I might be losing my love, forever. Time was running out, and I had no say in the matter. I did not open the letter, but went straight to a chair where I sat, held my head between my hands, and wept, bitterly. In the meantime, Dr. Andrews tried to do something; he was on the phone, pacing, talking. He finally contacted someone from the Gerrard family and wrote something down. No sooner than that, Mrs. Andrews was handing me my trench coat and my hat, and leading me to Dr. Andrews' car. As if moving in a trance-like state, I found myself in a speeding car, heading towards the airport. I felt as though I was in a different world. I was praying to God that we would make it in time, and to not allow me to drink the bitter cup of separation this way.

I had never known Dr. Andrews to drive like this, before. He was certainly intent on beating the flight time. Traffic was horrendous, yet he was weaving in and out of traffic. Our arrival in time, to see Samir, was a matter of life and death to him. Mrs. Andrews was in the backseat, hunched over the front, rubbing my shoulders with her hands, and stroking my hair with tenderness. From time to time, Dr. Andrews would grab my hand and squeeze it, reassuringly. Nobody said a single world as we drove, but I could hear Mrs. Andrews gasp from time to time. At one time, we drove through a red light, and the police stopped us for nearly fifteen minutes! My heart sank, as I was certain we would never make it! At the time, I did not feel the Lord would show up on a cloud to help perform a miracle, despite my intention to forgive; I just felt that, perhaps, He was teaching me a lesson that I'd deserved, **"Whatever a man sows, he shall also reap."** Sometimes, even when we ask forgiveness for our transgressions and God forgives us, some scars consequences remain, just to remind us. I then said to Dr. Andrews, "There is no reason to put our lives in harm's way; we will never make it on time, anyway. It is now a quarter after six; Samir must be in the air, by now. I am not sad I won't be able to see him, to ask his forgiveness; I deserve this punishment. But I am sad for Samir, as he leaves his loved ones behind, going to a strange land. Moreover, he will be spending New Year's Eve alone and broken-hearted!"

Dr. Andrews pretended not to hear me, he was adamant on making it. He stopped the car in front of the airport entrance and asked Mrs. Andrews to find a parking space, and told her where we should later meet. He grabbed my hand and walked briskly, as though he was still in his twenties, running a marathon. Despite all our efforts, we never made it. We did not see anyone from the Gerrard family, Danny or Mona. Perhaps they never came, or they had already come and left. Did not Mrs. Andrews say he was in a taxi-cab? Was Danny with Samir? Or did he travel alone?

According to Mrs. Andrews' account, Samir was alone when he handed her the note. I had a strange feeling, a mixture of anger and disappointment, and I began to put the blame on poor Eric; it was his fault this had taken place, I thought. At least, I could have called his house now and asked about Samir and his destination, and if anyone else was traveling with him; but here I was—helpless.

Mrs. Andrews suggested I should read Samir's note, perhaps there was a clue in it, but I did not, although the letter was in my handbag. Amidst all this chaos, I heard a familiar name on the loudspeaker. I was totally absorbed in my own woes, but that name I heard rang a loud bell. As if to wake me from a stupor, I remembered whose name it was I just heard. It was the name of my old friend, the prince, being called over the loudspeaker. The airplane was delayed—still waiting for his highness. It turned out to be the same airplane on which Samir was traveling, since its destination was the Middle East! Such occurrences do not ordinarily happen, except in the movies, but it seemed the delay was due to a very important reason. Nonetheless, this was irrelevant to me, so I took out a piece of paper and pen and wrote a quick note, "Samir, Please forgive me for giving you a hard time and making your life miserable; forgive me, my love; I have not changed my vows. I love you, forever, Dalal."

I ran towards the prince, who was almost running now, and I asked him if he could give this to a young physician on the same plane, by the name of Dr. Samir Shaheen. At first, he did not recognize me, so I introduced myself to him all over again. After his initial shock, he said he would gladly do it.

I was elated—as we returned home; it felt as though I was coming from a lover's meeting instead of a farewell. At least, now, Samir could be happy, knowing how I felt about him; and had been able to forget the misery of this whole episode, not forgetting the old vow was now renewed.

I could not be certain whether the prince gave Samir my note, since I was not exactly a source of happiness to him either, but I'd also left a bitter taste in his mouth when I rejected him. I wondered if, out of curiosity, he might have read the note; I had no way of knowing. Would he avenge, for my rejection of him, by not giving Samir my note? I hoped not. He'd was always been an honorable gentleman. His character gave me the assurance he would do as I'd asked of him. Then, I began to wonder if Samir would not read it, but tear it, if he knew it was from me! All thoughts, including others, crossed my mind. Nonetheless, I was feeling happy because I'd renewed my vows with my Lord and God, and now, felt as if I were a new person. Very few feelings can surpass the feeling of forgiveness. Bearing a grudge had exhausted me, and my obstinacy left me worn-out; but today, my mountains were removed by placing my burdens at the feet of the cross. This feeling was not different from the feeling I had when I first accepted Jesus, as my Savior. Four years into my new faith, I'd discovered that Christian life was not always a bed of roses; there were also trials and tribulations, good times and bad, but without Christ, life was, for sure, unbearable.

I was still feeling good when we returned home, especially knowing my Lord was pleased with my actions. Even the hot shower I took felt special, until Mrs. Andrews broke the serenity of the ritual by yelling, "Dalal, Dalal, Samir is on the phone!"

In a flash, I rushed out of the shower, put my bathrobe on, and ran to the phone with my hair dripping all over the place. The whole process must not have taken more than ten seconds! My heart was pounding so hard, he must have heard it on the other end! "My love, my love," I heard him say; I began to shout his name, as though it were the first time I'd heard him! Thank you, Lord! Our spoken words were jumping like a herd of gazelles, as if this moment erased all the bad memories of the last two weeks. He spoke the most reassuring words that I so much needed to hear, "I was saddened, Dalal, because of miscommunication or misunderstanding; I was in despair. I asked the Lord Jesus why He allowed this bitter episode to happen, but now I know. God must have known, in His foreknowledge, if I had met you in London, I may have had a hard time leaving you, and thus would not have heeded His call to be in His service this year. God does not try us beyond our capacity, but with the trial, He provides the solution."

"Samir, I have not read your letter yet, so I have no idea what you are saying; I don't know why..."

"What are you saying Dalal?" he interrupted, "Then, how, why?"

"Never mind Samir, just hear me out. God permitted this to happen to me so He could do surgery on my spiritual life; He extricated my pride, deeply-embedded within me, yet unbeknownst to me, to save me from, spiritual disaster; ready to happen. The cup was quite bitter, and restoration would not be easy until He readied me to become the bride of the most noble and honorable groom!"

On this note, we ended our conversation, which also signaled the end of a bitter period in our lives, and the beginning of a new chapter.

***

If I had to choose how to spend my New Year's Eve after my phone conversation with Samir, I would have chosen to go into my room, lie down on my bed, and recollect our dialogue word for word; but that was wishful thinking. Steve called earlier, inviting the Andrews and me to welcome the New Year. He insisted I come, since Eric still needed me. I felt obligated to Eric. It would not be appropriate for me to excuse myself, when Eric was still suffering; and furthermore, I needed to clear matters with him, as well as his family, regarding Samir. I was thankful to God that He'd given me what seemed to be a golden opportunity to explain matters to Steve, when he came to pick me up.

It was a very cold day; I wore a heavy top-coat, and the fur hat that Mrs. Andrews used to wear; it covered all my hair, only my face was visible. As I sat in the passenger seat, thinking of how to start my explanation, he glanced at me and said, "You do look like someone my wife Lillian knows; I've never met her, but I've seen many of her pictures, especially in this hat! When Lillian saw you the other day, she said you looked familiar."

"Oh, thank God, he brought it up," I thought to myself. The break in the ice made it easier for me to start talking. Therefore, as I began to explain, he spoke again, "I am really worried about Eric; his recovery will take a few months, and I feel badly that I have to leave him in a month's time, to follow Samir and Danny who left two days ago."

"Tell me Steve, why did they leave before New Year's Eve?" I asked.

"We asked Samir to leave after the holidays, but he insisted, and Danny had no choice but to leave with him."

"Why was he in such a hurry?" I asked, although I knew the reason, but I wanted to hear Steve's version, to see if he'd mentioned anything about Dalal.

Steve began to tell me about Samir and Dalal, the girl who'd captivated his mind and heart, and who'd accepted the Lord Jesus through him, but her parents forced her to abandon her new faith and the man she loved. However, she'd refused, and boldly held onto her faith in Christ, as well as the man she loved. But suddenly, she had disappeared. Samir then looked for her all over the globe, not leaving a stone unturned, to find her, until he—recently heard she was in this country and area. He promptly left America, and for a whole month, looked for her, but came up with nothing. He lost all hope, everything darkened for him, and he became despondent. He preferred to leave before New Year's Eve because, according to him, it reminded him of his girlfriend; and that same evening, he had given her a ring that was a token of his love for her. Consequently, he fled on the first available flight.

Although I knew almost all the details that Steve had shared, tears welled up in my eyes, as I said, "What a pity! If he had remained behind, I would have directed him to his love."

Steve raised his eyebrows in astonishment! "What do you mean? Do you know Dalal, or where she lives?"

"You're talking with her!" I said in a soft voice, barely audible.

"Talking with whom?" he asked, as if he'd heard something that did not make sense.

I wished I had a camera to capture the looks on his face; his jaw dropped, and his mouth was agape for a good while.

"Steve, I *am* Dalal!"

I repeated my name. He stopped in the middle of the road; that sudden halt caused traffic backups, and horns began to blare. He finally realized what he'd done and moved on, but not in the direction of the house. He parked on the side of the road to continue his questioning Dalal; still in doubt.

"I am Dalal Abu Suleiman; my father is the Za'eem—a feudal lord—in Lebanon. The Shaheens were our neighbors; my best friend is Amal, Samir's younger sister. I became acquainted with Danny in America and later—became acquainted with his sister, Lillian, and his father, Billy Roper, who was my father's old college classmate and friend. They all came to Lebanon on an invitation from my father and stayed with us awhile. I fell in love with your wife, Lillian, I gave her many clothes I hadn't worn. Mona, Danny's friend, is my aunt's daughter in California, and Majdi is another first cousin. What else would you like to know? At any rate, I have no other evidence, is this enough to convince you I am Dalal?"

Needless to say, my story stunned him like a bolt, out of the blue! He basically told me that what he just heard was more than he could absorb, and needed time to figure it all out.

"What about Dr. and Mrs. Andrews?" He asked, as if to complete the last piece of the puzzle. I told him they were not my real parents— which he already knew—and went on to tell him the rest of the story, since I'd first set foot in London, until the moment I met the prince at the airport and handed him the note to give Samir. I finally said to Steve, "I am ready to do whatever you advise, since now you know everything you need to know about Samir and me, as long as it does not jeopardize my relationship with Samir."

Steve, indeed, needed some time to ruminate on all the data I'd just spewed out; but he had not figured out how Eric could react to all of this, so I hastened to make it a little easier on him, "Eric knows I am in love with someone else. I told him so, just before the accident; I therefore blame myself and bear all responsibility." I noticed tears flow down Steve's face as he said, "I am very happy for Samir, only God knows how much he had to endure, for you were everything to him." He was silent a moment, and then continued,

"As for how you and I will break the news to Eric and the family, we will leave it to the Lord to guide us. I am not too worried how Eric will react, but more worried how he will feel when he knows that you almost lost your love because of him, after you sacrificed so much for his sake."

We were still in the car for quite a while; I was afraid the family might think we were in some other accident, so I suggested to Steve that we should move on. As expected, everybody was looking out the windows, waiting to see Steve's car pull into the driveway. Mona and Lillian rushed out to meet us; Mona recognized me right away and shouted, "Dalal, Dalal!"

I yelled back, "Mona, my dearest Mona!" We both hugged and began to cry and laugh. Steve whispered something in Lillian's ear, she stood there speechless, he then put his arm around her and led her into the house. Mona and I remained for over five minutes in the cold, talking, hugging, and kissing.

The Lord was sweeter and kinder than either of us had ever imagined. He managed matters quite smoothly, everybody accepted Dalal Abu Suleiman much more readily than I'd expected. As for Eric, I saw him in the privacy of his room; we opened our hearts to each other and made peace. In the end, we each wished each other happiness, and then turned a new leaf of friendship, as the New Year knocked on the door.

Chapter 17
WOES and BLESSINGS

*T*he New Year started well. I'd wished I had a thousand tongues to praise the Lord, who worked marvels in my life, as well as the lives of my loved ones. Hour by hour, I could sense His holy and blessed presence and the deep fellowship, which was strengthening by the day. His greatness and majesty enriched my life daily. Despite being an only child, I, nonetheless, was now enjoying deep fellowship with many sisters and brothers in Christ.

It was not very hard for me to persuade my cousin, Mona, to stay longer and spend more time with me in London—she was supposed to spend one week with the Gerrard family after Danny, her fiancé, had left. I told her, since I was making enough money, we could stay in a hotel or, if she preferred, she could stay with me at the Andrews' house. The love the Andrews had for me had spilled over to my cousin, Mona; they both insisted she become their guest.

Amal and I resumed contact, when she called me from South Carolina, after Samir had given her my phone number and address. I also spoke with my cousin, Majdi, who was about to graduate from seminary and marry Amal, the following summer. I was told Dr. and Mrs. Shaheen were still in Cyprus with their twins, and that Dr. Shaheen's contract with the Lebanese government would expire soon, and therefore, he was about to return to America by the end of summer, to work at Johns Hopkins Hospital in Maryland. Soon, afterwards, I spoke with them, and for the first time in three years, I heard the voice of the twins, Walid and Rima. How sweet it was to hear their voices again.

I still had not heard anything new about my father except what my Aunt Sue—Mona's mother—had told me, during our weekly conversations. All she'd said was he was doing very well. I was quite happy and thankful that God answered my prayers and healed my father from cancer. My aunt, however, refused to tell me anything about my mother; I was still in the dark and had no idea what was going on.

Friendship between the Gerrards and the Andrews grew stronger. Steve traveled to the Middle East where he joined Samir and Danny, but not before we overloaded him with so many items to take to both: copies of my daily journals, my gift to Samir, were on top of the list. I wanted to make him privy and share with him all the issues I had experienced during the years of our separation.

Eric's health was improving by the day, but he was still on crutches, due to the severe injuries he had sustained in that woeful accident. He went back to working on completing his dissertation. As for Mona, she'd extended her stay; eventually she volunteered to serve in the church where the Gerrards were members. She felt unspeakable joy serving her Master.

I was nearing the end of my graduate program. A couple of foreign students happened to be in one of my classes. One of them, a Lebanese graduate student from a prominent family who I had known, was sitting in an adjacent seat, near mine. He looked at me, smiled and nodded, then introduced himself. I returned the courtesy and thought nothing of it. Ever since, he would come to me at every occasion possible, and at times, make up chance meetings, attempting to flirt; but to his dismay, I ignored him. He would separate from his friend, and sidle in my direction to make small talk or just look for a way to impose a conversation. One day, and unbeknownst to them that I was Lebanese, I overheard a conversation in Arabic between them, daring each other as to who would be the first to take me out to dinner. If there was a way of "being a fly on the wall" to be in on a conversation, that was the opportunity for me. I worked hard to cover my amusement and bemusement at their lame conversation and not laugh aloud. With my thoroughly English name, and blonde hair, an accent perfected to a degree that would leave no room for doubt, it was not possible for them to have any suspicion I could be a compatriot and able to speak their language!

Hearing their conversations had a sobering effect on me. I compared the behavior of the two to the behavior of my born-again Christian friends and the way they looked at women. Those who love the Lord are bound to live a life intent on glorifying God, than those who live for the flesh, who are governed by the ways of the world. 'What a difference,' I thought. These were educated men who had the chance to attend the best schools and universities, yet their education did not change their basic human character, only God could.

At times, I could hear them, making remarks about the way I looked—most of which were rude and disrespectful. Despite my disdain for their remarks, I, nonetheless, felt sorry for them, especially Kamal, the Lebanese man, and the more attractive of the two; his friend, Khalid, who was from an Arab Gulf country, almost equally handsome and rich. It feels weird how in an instant, both would switch their tune from derogatory language, to a more polite claiming morality and high ethical standards. The two men were the embodiment of hypocrisy.

Kamal, after he gave up on beguiling me with his Lamborghini— the only such vehicle at Oxford—resorted to the weapon of envy, making certain I saw him with the most gorgeous university co-eds. He would tell his friend, Khalid, it was my loss not to have had the chance to go out with him. Such a remark filled me with more revulsion.

I thought to myself, perhaps one day, I should let him think he'd won me over, and I had fallen for his charming ways. Before long, I accepted his invitation for lunch at the local pub on the university grounds. He was the perfect gentleman, if there ever was such a category. Before we began to eat, I shut my eyes and thanked God for the food before us, even though I knew he was from a different religious background. We touched on every subject that came to mind, discussing the latest scientific findings we were studying to literary topics, and naturally, religion. I made it clear to him I was Christian, by choice and by conviction—and that my faith in Christ was the best thing that had ever happened to me.

I could see he was becoming slightly irritated and sped through the rest of our lunch, informing me he had a meeting to which he must go—and he did. The next day in class, I heard him tell his friend about his misfortune, "She turned out to be some kind of fanatic religious Christian." His friend asked, as if to make a point, "Aren't all the girls that throw themselves at you, Christian? Give her some time, some jewelry, a ride in your luxury automobile, and you'll see how she will give up her Christ and Christianity."

That statement was so revolting, I wanted to throw up upon hearing their dim-witted conversation; it stabbed in the heart. I could no longer take their abusive remarks about my Lord and my faith—my blood was boiling in a rage, not so much at Khalid's remarks, but at those so-called Christian girls who could care less about embarrassing Christ and Christianity with their un-Christian behavior. They make it easy for men, especially Arab men, to think of them as easy game in the cheapest ways. I embarked on a journey to make sure these two knew that there was a big difference between true Christians and nominal Christians, those who had made a conscious decision to follow Christ, and commit themselves to Him, and those who simply inherited the title, because, they were born into supposed Christian families, but who had no idea what Christianity entailed nor cared to know! Many think that by wearing a cross around their necks, or by attending church, gives them a transit visa to heaven! Little do they realize that Christianity is a way of life, and requires Christians, to practice it according to what the Word of God says. That was my new mission in life.

I started with Kamal. I told him about the love of the Lord Jesus Christ and the assurances of eternal life. My argument was simple. Life, no matter how long, will eventually come to an inescapable end. Mortality is at a 100% rate. I basically impressed upon him what Jesus said in Matthew 16:26, **"What good will it be for a man if he gains the whole world, yet forfeits his soul? Or what can a man give in exchange for his soul?"** One could own the jewels of the world: cars, palaces, titles, degrees, and the resultant fame, yet the ending would be a certain death, and an eternity marked with hopelessness. All the while, I spoke to him out of love for his soul; at the same time, I was praying to God to move his heart and speak to it. My remarks seemed to have hit a raw nerve within him. I could tell by the expressions on his face.

The next time I heard these two discussing me, I was astonished to hear Kamal quote certain things he'd heard from me about Jesus! He was asking his friend, "What if what she says is true? What if hell and eternal life are real and not just a figment of one's imagination, as we tend to believe? What if salvation is only through Christ, as Helen said?" He continued, "I have never heard anyone so sure of their eternal life. You know, she's not stupid; she's educated and seems intelligent, unlike some uneducated, poor little girls. She can have anything she wants; there must be some merit to what she is saying; otherwise, what would make her live her life the way she does? Right?"

His friend, Khalid, made fun of his naïveté in letting some girl mess up his mind. Then he went on to give him one piece of advice after another, one of which was never to discuss religion with me or allow me to threaten him with hell.

"Those religious nuts, especially women like Helen, pretend morality and chastity, yet are the first ones to fall from grace." A little later, he put his hand on Kamal's shoulder, signaling to move on, and he began to whisper in his ear.

My distant friendship with them remained unchanged. I continued to talk to them about the Lord Jesus, backing it with quotes from the Bible. I even bought them a couple of New Testaments as gifts. From time to time, I would spend some time with them discussing religion. Since I came from the same religious background, I knew the intent of every question they'd asked, and with the Lord's guidance, and some effective points made, which I had learned from Samir and my cousin Majdi, I was able to expound on the Word of God, convincing them the best I was able. I felt that I was winning the battle over Satan.

Winter, with its cold, and at times, snowy days, was coming to an end. Although it is generally chilly in England, winter can be unbearable, so now spring was in the air. Samir had been away for three months. My friendship with Kamal and his friend Khalid grew; both confessed that I had played a major role in dispelling their erroneous notions and stereotyping that they had about western girls, in general, and Christian girls in particular. Moreover, they could distinguish between true Christians and other Christians—meaning, western nations are not Christian, but some individuals are, In other words, nations are not religious, but people are—personal relationships are between individuals and their God, not between nations and God!

I was so happy they were finally able, to make distinction between Christians. Furthermore, they also confessed how they began to have more love, respect, and admiration for Jesus—and that whatever they had heard from me about the love of Christ, his forgiveness, salvation, and their Bible reading in the Bibles I had given them, became of interest to them. I was able to notice a drastic change in their behavior; they showed kindness, consideration, and respect. Their integrity became quite apparent; all they needed was the real love for God, and focus on their Creator, and to accept Jesus as their only Savior. They needed someone to lead them by the hand, on the right path, but before anyone could preach to them, that person must first live what he preaches. Sadly, and often-times, too many people preach what they do not practice; they do more harm than good.

Jesus said in Matthew 5:16, **"In the same way, let your light shine before men, that they may see your good deeds and praise your Father in heaven."** These two young men were no longer chasing after women, as they had done before, but focusing on their studies and success, as I was doing. There was no better way of being a good witness than by that example.

One day, after class, Kamal asked me if we could go somewhere quiet, where we could talk about an important subject. After we met, he told me, since he heard about Jesus; he was unable to shake the judgment day concept. He pictured the flames of hell, the gnashing of teeth, and eternal damnation. I felt so badly for him and proceeded explaining the love of God that is manifested in the sacrifice of Christ and His atoning death for us. I quoted, John 3:16, **"For God so loved the world that He gave His only begotten Son so that those who believe in Him may not perish but have everlasting life."** I continued explaining based on my own experience, "You misunderstood me, Kamal; Jesus is not only about judging people on Judgment Day; you must have forgotten what I told you about His love and forgiveness. He came to give you rest, carry your burdens, throw away your sins in the depths of the oceans, clothe you with the robe of righteousness, put the fatherly ring around your finger, protect you like the pupil of his eye, and give you the peace that surpasses all understanding. You no longer will live in worry and fear of Judgment Day. Salvation and eternal life are God's free gift for the taking; all you have to do is extend your hand to receive this gift. God reached out to humanity through Christ, for there was no other way by which we could pay the wages of sin, which is death. In the beginning, following creation, man was in perfect harmony with God, but after the fall, sin broke the communication and disrupted our fellowship with the creator. God's plan was to restore that relationship with him. The Bible says, **"For the wages of sin is death, but the gift of God is eternal life in Christ Jesus our Lord."** (**Romans 6:22-23**) It is true that judgment in hell is the consequence of rejecting Christ, but then God has given us the gift of life, through Christ. There are many assurances to that fact in the Bible. The choice is up to you. It is up to you Kamal; you're the only one who can decide if you'd like to accept Jesus and the gift of eternal life with Him, or not."

With a troubled voice, he said, "That's what scares me! If what you are saying is true, then I fear that after having known all these truths and still reject Christ, then I will lose my soul and eternal life in heaven. If, on the other hand, I accept Jesus, as Savior, and become his follower, then all kinds of problems and persecution for and from family and friends will overwhelm me. I don't think my family and friends would accept me, I know they would fight me and oppose me. I am afraid and don't know what to do!"

"Your soul is extremely precious, Kamal; it is the most valuable asset you possess, and if you place it in the hands of Jesus, the Savior, He will assure you eternal salvation, joy, and inner peace, and hence will dispel the fears you mention. He guaranteed a secure entrance to heaven for you by the shedding of His blood on the cross. His death on the cross means life eternal for us. The Bible tells us there is no greater love than one who gives his life for the ones he loves. There are also assurances in the Bible that Jesus has given us, He said, **"And Jesus answered and said, Verily I say unto you, There is no man that hath left house, or brethren, or sisters, or father, or mother, or wife, or children, or lands, for my sake, and the gospel's, [30]But he shall receive an hundredfold now in this time...,"** (Matthew 10:29-30)

I was on a roll and wished I could tell him that I knew exactly how he felt, but could not. I was praying for wisdom and for God to put the right words in my mouth. I continued, "Despite all these promises and assurances, the Word of God, nonetheless, tells us we will pass through trials and tribulations as long as we are on earth, but that we are to trust Him because He has conquered the world. Christian life is not an easy life; there are crosses we have to bear every day; there could be persecution by our families and friends, as well as pain and suffering." In the book of Romans 8:18 the Bible says, **"For I reckon that the sufferings of this present time are not worthy to be compared with the glory which shall be revealed in us."** The sufferings that we might face are confined to the time we live in on earth; they do not last forever. As believers, we will be in a state of security even though we are suffering. Our hope lies outside the boundaries of time, we need patience, our way could be rough and long; but the hope of the glory, we will receive, overshadows the temporary suffering. It is not worth it to sacrifice eternal life for a few years on this earth. Which is more important, to upset our families or to grieve the Holy Spirit? What is more beneficial for us, suffering with Christ or momentary happiness in the clutches of Satan? Alternatively, is it real peace that Jesus gives or temporary peace and security that our family or friends give? Think hard on these questions, Kamal, and make certain you invest in your soul in a secure plan, and contemplate what Jesus said. But let me say, despite any suffering we might face, we are always victorious, and our suffering is negligent compared to those who don't have Christ in their lives."

I was saying these words while Kamal sat opposite me, his head between his hands, apparently troubled by what he had just heard. For a while, he made no comments, at all; I felt he must have been considering my words; perhaps I might have convinced him, or at least stoked his interest. After a few moments of silence, he finally looked at me and said,

"There is a common saying in my country; *it is easier to count the lashes than to receive them.* "How easy it is for you to be talking from a position of safety."

His response did not disturb me, for that had been the very precise response I had given Samir when he told me I should please the Lord before I please my parents.

"I know what you mean, Kamal; I appreciate your concerns and fears," then he interrupted me saying, "How could you understand my fears and feelings? You have no idea about my situation, my family, or me. It is easy for you to preach to me and ask me to sacrifice everything for Jesus, and then you go home to your family; and the next day, find you another poor soul to preach for them to sacrifice all."

He rose from his chair, apparently disturbed, and left without saying anymore. I remained seated thinking about his dilemma, to which I was no stranger; yet, I did not feel any anger towards his reaction. On the contrary, I felt sorry for his situation. I prayed for him and tried to think of a solution to help him. Should I tell him the truth about me and my religious background so he can be encouraged, or would this only add to his fears, knowing what happened to me could happen to him a thousand times worse. Perhaps his family would disown him or even have him killed, without remorse. Faced with a new dilemma; what would my next step be?

I did not see Kamal for the rest of the week; I could not tell whether it was a purposeful act of avoidance, or if he'd been pulled into something that prevented him from coming to class. However, I had a similar talk and discussion with his friend Khalid, who I found out, came from the same country which Samir, Danny, and Steve had recently traveled to, for work. His father was a prominent politician. Khalid was expected to return to his country after his graduation, where a secure position was awaiting him. I then proceeded to tell him, my fiancé and his friends were practicing medicine in his country, I included the name of the hospital. To my surprise, he did not ask me about any of them. And I did not volunteer to divulge any more information, either. We left it at that, and we never had any conversation afterwards.

Few days later, my cousin, Majdi, called from America, insisting we visit my aunt, his mother, who was living in my mother's rented house in the suburbs of London. The next day, Mona and I went and parked the car, close to the house; from there we walked to the door. We expected to see my aunt alone, but instead, we saw several cars parked in front of the house, and people were walking in and out. We pondered a moment, and we decided against going in, but curiosity got the better of us, and we continued to stand behind some trees watching and trying to figure out what was happening. We noticed most people were clad in black, with long, grim faces. Something must have been dreadfully wrong. Since we were not able to figure out anything, yet, we returned home so Mona could contact her mother in California, who would certainly know, she had a knack for gathering information—good or bad! I heard Mona gasp, let out a cry, followed by a shrieking, "What?" The dialogue continued back and forth, "How, when, why. Are you sure?" When did that happen? How come no one told us about this?" After the phone call, Mona sat down in a chair and closed her eyes, shaking her head.

"What happened, Mona. Tell me?"

"My aunt's husband, he passed away."

"Majdi's father, died? When, where?" I asked, also panicking.

"By a car bomb!"

"What are you saying—car bomb? Who was with him?"

"I don't know. Mary doesn't have more information. Mother is on her way to London to see her sister and stay by her side. She will contact us when she arrives."

We both sat looking at each other, totally at a loss for words. Mona was apparently shaken over the news, while I went on a mental journey, and found myself wandering back to Lebanon. I was praying fervently for my father and asking God to keep him safe. I called Majdi at the university but did not find him. I called Amal to ask her about the car bomb and pleaded with her, to tell me the whole truth, as to whether my father was in the car or not.

"Dalal, thank God for saving your father; your prayers must have done it!" By then, I knew all I needed to know; overcome with emotion, I was not able to continue my conversation with Amal. I handed the phone over to Mona. I rushed to my room, knelt down by my bedside, and offered the Lord my heartfelt thanks for His divine intervention for my father, as tears began to flow down my cheeks.

My uncle's death helped break the log-jam between members of my family and myself. Mona and I went to my aunt's house to comfort her and offer our condolences. I paid my condolences, as Helen Andrews, Mona's friend. No one present was able to recognize me, although many stared at me, curiously, as though I reminded them of someone they knew. On the other hand, Mona's meeting with our aunt and our grandmother was somewhat reserved, but very touching. Majdi's mother cried openly as she hugged her, saying, "You have Majdi's smell on you, my sweetheart."

I was not able to control myself any longer. My own pain of separation from my loved ones also surfaced. However, biting my lower lip, and in my nearly-perfect English accent, I offered my condolences for this horrendous tragedy—and planted a tender kiss of love and longing on my aunt's cheek; she reciprocated by embracing me and kissing me back, as if the blood within both of us gave me away.

Moreover, I had no idea why my grandmother asked me to sit beside her, which I did. My heart was now pounding and felt uneasy because of my deep love for her, yet circumstances prevented me from uncovering myself. I wanted to give her the warmest hugs I could, and rest my head on her bosom. I did not know what my grandmother felt, but she took my hand, and in broken English, told me, had it not been for my blond hair, I would have been that same girl in the picture hanging on the wall, pointing in its direction. Then she took me in her arms again, kissing me, and at the same time, crying. At such an emotional moment, I could not hold myself any longer and whispered in her ear, "Teta—Teta" (the word for grandma in Arabic) I am Dalal, Teta! I love you Teta!"

In a few moments, and to everybody's shock, I made myself known to all. There were no words of blame or chastisement, but of unfathomable love, acceptance, tears, and kisses from all. To break the ice, I concluded with these words tinged with slight humor, "Do you have any Middle Eastern bread (pita), yogurt-cheese, olives and some thyme and olive oil in this house; I am hungry, and I have not had this food in ages!?"

Mona and I visited for nearly four more hours. All the while, I told everyone my story that had transpired since I'd left Lebanon, but in doing so, I relied on the wisdom that God had put in my mouth through the Holy Spirit. I also made certain to make it known that my father's miraculous escape from sure death was because of the many prayers I had raised to the Lord to keep him safe and well. My aunt was, nonetheless, visibly shaken, despite the survival of her brother; she thus asked me, while tears still flowed down her cheeks, "Don't you think Majdi was also praying for his father?"

"I have no doubt that he did, auntie; but one thing I learned throughout all this, God's ways are not our ways and his thoughts are not our thoughts. Who are we to question the Creator; a clay pot cannot question the potter, as to why he made it the way it is."

Everyone became silent in the dining room, following what I said, as my own mother suddenly entered the room and angrily said, "Are you all deaf? Where…" She stopped mid-sentence. No years of absence and short, blonde hair were enough to deceive a mother from recognizing her daughter, especially if the mother's name was Huda who had a daughter called Dalal! My mother recognized me right away. My legs gave way when I attempted to get up and embrace her. I was scared—and did not know what to expect from her. I tried to control my worry and fear; after all, she was my mother.

"Oh, God, please help me," I prayed silently. My mother stood in the middle of the room, scanned those present, turned her back, and darted towards the door. I stood up heard myself holler, "Mom, Mom," but before I could reach to embrace her, she exited the house faster than when she came in. I ran after her, but she was already in her car and on her way.

I was deeply disappointed, as was the rest of the family. For a few moments, all thought a mother's compassion would have overcome any issue, but they were wrong. A few moments, later, I bid everybody good-bye and left them broken-hearted; my joy at reuniting with them was incomplete.

The week before graduation was extremely busy; I did not have one minute to contemplate all that had happened. Despite my pain and grief over my mother's behavior and my father's inability to attend my graduation, or Samir's absence, a special kind of peace enveloped me and lessened my pains and grief. Kamal, whom I had not seen for awhile, came with Khalid. He apologized for the way he'd talked to me earlier, and that he would be honored if I were to consider him a friend and brother. Consequently, I felt the Lord had opened up the way for me to reveal my real identify to them, which I did. I told them my life history and concluded with these words, as tears welled up in my eyes,

"Remember what I told you, Kamal—that I knew how you must have felt? It was because I was still experiencing and enduring all kinds of persecution and rejection by my family and friends! But believe me, today's pain and suffering cannot be measured against the glories that await us, for the Word of God says, "**For me to live is Christ, to die is gain.**"

I handed Kamal my Bible to read the highlighted verses in the book of Romans chapter 8 beginning with verse 27, "**Therefore, there is now no condemnation for those who are in Christ Jesus, because through Christ Jesus the law of the Spirit of life set me free from the law of sin and death,**" Continuing to verse 28 (my favorite all-time verse), he continued reading, "**And we know that, in all things, God works for the good of those who love Him, who have been called according to His purpose. [29]For those God fore-knew He also predestined to be conformed to the likeness of His Son, that He might be the firstborn among many brothers. [30]And those He predestined, He also called; those He called, He also justi-fied; those He justified, He also glorified.**

[31]**What, then, shall we say in response to this? If God is for us, who can be against us? [32]He who did not spare His Own Son, but gave Him up for us all—how will He not also, along with Him, graciously give us all things? [33]Who will bring any charge against those whom God has chosen? It is God who justifies. [34]Who is He that condemns? Christ Jesus, who died—more than that, who was raised to life—is at the right hand of God and is also interceding for us. [35]Who shall separate us from the love of Christ? Shall trouble or hardship or persecution or famine or nakedness or danger or sword? [36]As it is written, "For your sake we face death all day long; we are considered as sheep to be slaughtered. [37]No, in all these things we are more than conquerors through Him who loved us. [38]For I am convinced that neither death nor life, neither angels nor demons, neither the present nor the future, nor any powers, [39]neither height nor depth, nor anything else in all creation, will be able to separate us from the love of God that is in Christ Jesus our Lord.**"

Kamal closed the Bible and handed it back to me with utmost respect without saying a single word; for when the Holy Spirit speaks, every worldly wisdom pales in comparison.

Chapter 18
A NEW PLACE, A NEW CHAPTER

*T*he weather on graduation day was a bright, sunny, and almost perfect. It was an important turning point in my life. Dr. Andrews took it upon himself to videotape the events throughout that day. Besides my small adoptive family, I expected only the Gerrards to attend. Just before we left the house, I heard a car stop in the driveway. As I looked out the window, I saw a man getting out of the car, carrying a basket of red roses. I was not able to recognize the man, as he deliberately hid his face behind the basket. I ran to open the door, only to find my father at the door! If this visit was meant to shock and surprise me, it was not surprising to the Andrews'—for they were aware of his arrival the night before, but schemed with him to surprise me. Dr. Andrews, who was hiding in a corner, had his video camera ready and began to shoot the reunion scene.

Thank God for the videotape, without which no word could ever have captured that moment. My father asked me to continue to use my pseudonym for security and political purposes, which he did not have time to explain, but told me we would be traveling to America, sometime after graduation. I was able to sense the urgency in his request and guessed there must have been a compelling reason for that decision. Despite the concerns, my father's presence made my graduation day a special day in my life that I shall never forget.

With great sorrow, I bid my university good-bye, as well as Kamal and Khalid who came, afterwards, to congratulate me and bid me farewell, and to take pictures in our graduation robes for lasting memories. I cried as I was saying my good-byes to Khalid who was returning to his homeland the next day. I did not know why I asked him to go and meet Samir when he had the chance and show him the pictures he had taken. I also gave Kamal my cousin Majdi's address and asked him to keep in contact with him. Kamal protested as he was wiping tears of farewell, "Only Khalid is leaving, I understand, but I am staying here and we'll be seeing each other, so why are you giving me directives as though we're saying good-bye?! Won't we meet again?" he asked.

"I have no idea what tomorrow holds, Kamal," I said, and extended my hand to shake his, but without telling him that I would also be leaving tomorrow. We returned home only to have another surprise awaiting us, the Andrews had prepared a little party to celebrate my graduation.

My father informed all that we must leave for America the first thing in the morning to avoid any harm. The thought of leaving the Andrews, so suddenly, shocked me; I was not emotionally prepared for such a move. For over three years, they had become more than parents to me, how could I leave them just like that? My father then felt compelled to explain the urgency. Due to some political stances he'd taken in Lebanon, during the war, some opposing groups wanted to assassinate him. The assassination of my aunt's husband was meant for him and not for his brother-in-law, and later on, he received a threat that his only daughter would be kidnapped as a means to punish him! The Andrews were alarmed at hearing this, so they began to encourage and urge us to leave England immediately.

Once more, I found myself on an airplane heading to America, leaving a piece of my heart behind: two adoptive parents in the Andrews, and a dear friend, Eric.

After having lived in England for over three years, I still found it difficult to adjust to the continuous rainy and damp cold weather. I missed my blue-sky Mediterranean weather in Lebanon. I was now about to cross the Atlantic and could hardly contain my excitement and anticipation for the future that awaited me in America. Looking back, I thought to myself, if I were to choose any place other than my country to live in, it would definitely be the United States. The only homesickness I experienced after leaving England was missing the dear adoptive families and friends I'd left behind.

My mind was racing, as I was making a list of all the dear people I was about to be with once I arrived in North Carolina: Amal, and I could not wait to see Majdi, my cousin and brother-in-Christ, and by the end of summer, the Shaheens, when they resettled. In due time, Samir and Danny would also be there.

On the way home from the airport, I sat in the back seat of Billy Roper's car, thinking about my adoptive parents and feeling sad for having left them behind. Then a thought flashed in my mind, "Why not buy them a house in North Carolina as a payback for everything they had done for me; my father could definitely afford it, and in essence, it would be a small payback. Would they accept the invitation to move here and leave their cherished country, at their age?" I wondered. As soon as we arrived home, I picked up the telephone to let them know that we'd arrived safely, and to test the waters about the possibility of having them move to the United States, since I would feel lost without them. At first, I thought, perhaps, they might not give me a definitive answer, "We'll think about it" or "We cannot leave our own birth-place" or "whatever the Lord wills," and so on. But I was surprised when Dr. Andrews' voice was clear and unhesitant when he declared, "We cannot bear to live without you either; we'll be glad to visit you the first chance we get. Good-bye dear."

The Ropers insisted we stay with them until we find a place of our own. Knowing my father, he took me by surprise when he accepted the offer! His profound love for this family must have affected his decision to accept, readily, after we all had come back from vacationing on the beach, where we'd be reunited with Majdi and Amal.

It was early June; the weather was quite delightful, many flowers were in full bloom, and lovely nature exuded serenity and tranquility. The ocean at the Outer Banks of North Carolina, seemed to be glorifying the Creator with the constant rhythmical waves that hit the shore. I was eagerly awaiting the arrival of my cousin, Majdi, and Amal.

No sooner had they arrived than I pulled Amal away from the crowd. We then sat for hours, reminiscing about our beautiful days in Lebanon, as well as the painful ones. The memories took us back to our first day in school, through the last day, when I left Lebanon. With sadness, we remembered Uncle Wafiq, our gardener, but Amal soon reminded me that he went ahead of us to heaven. Majdi was not cross with me at having neglected him by spending so much time with Amal, for he knew the depth of our love and friendship to one another. However, I gave him enough time the next evening on the massive balcony of the roomy beach house my father had rented to accommodate several guests. We spent memorable times in this beautiful place. I even confided in Amal and Mona that this place would be where I would like to spend my honeymoon with Samir, if it came to fruition.

As each of us was already madly in-love and spoken for in some way; our conversations led to talks of marriage, and who might be the first to tie the knot. We were giggling giddily, a woman's prerogative, but at the same time, I wondered at this unspeakable happiness that was engulfing me. We arrived at a definitive conclusion, Mona and Danny would be the first among us to say, "I do"—after all, they were the older couple—in February, a Valentine's Day wedding. Amal and Majdi, would follow, three months later, in May, which coincides with Majdi's birthday; then, finally, Samir and I, in August, our shared birthday month. Amal interrupted me, "But your birthday is in June, why not June?" I smiled and replied, "That's true, my first birthday is on June 25, but that's not as important as my second birthday, when I was born again."

We laughed all night long. Our joy of being together, again, was indescribable and gratifying. Those two days seemed to bridge the gap and eliminate the three years of separation I had gone through while living in England. Precious time with the people I love was winding down. As the saying goes, "Every good thing must come to an end." The Ropers returned to their home and church; Majdi and Amal went back to Bible College. As for Mona, Danny's mother insisted she go with them to give my father and me some time alone; meanwhile, the Ropers would be looking for a house for us in which to settle—close to theirs—when we returned.

My father and I stayed another two more weeks, at the beach house, to make up for lost time. We would get up early, walk hand-in-hand on the beach, barefoot, to welcome the rising sun in the horizon. We would drive around, visiting all the beautiful places close-by, return in the evening, and often prepare dinner together. We told jokes, laughed a lot, and discussed serious matters. Towards the end of the night, I would take my Bible and read several chapters aloud to him; afterwards, we would conclude our day in prayer.

Despite our apparent joy, there was a cloud of sadness hanging over us. My father missed my mother very much; he did not have to tell me that, I could read it in his eyes; and I would see an occasional tear. Similarly, he was also able to read my longing to see Samir. One day, he said to me, "There is no comparison between our situations, Dalal. It's true, the people we love are both away, but in your case, you are still young and the days and years are still ahead of you. The months of separation will soon pass, and you will see yourself, with Samir, again sharing your love and forgetting the agony of separation you've both endured. As for me, the days are behind me; I have no idea how many days or years are left in my life. Although my health seems fine now, I do not know how it will hold up tomorrow. It is during this crucial time in my life when I need your mother, most, by my side — I find myself alone." He was quick to add, "Do not misunderstand me Dalal, you fill that vacuum quite well, sweetheart, but your mom is at a different level that none can replace, not even you."

His words pierced my heart, as I attempted to ease his pain and give him some hope in the possibility of my mother's return; but he shook his head and said, "I thank God you have not inherited your mom's stubbornness and bitterness. I know how much she must be suffering and longing to see us, but her pride is keeping her away." I wanted to tell him he might be wrong in his assessment, that I did indeed inherit those particular traits, but had it not been for the Grace of God who broke these two idols at the foot of the cross, I would have been far worse than my mother in this respect. However, I said nothing, and quickly changed the subject.

My poor father, I could not have even begun to fathom the depth of his pain. I could only pray that the Lord be with him and give him the health and strength to carry on. The fact that the pain and suffering he was going through, were not exactly for the sake of the gospel, saddened me. His exile in the US was a result of his political views and not because of a stand he took for the Gospel of Christ. Even his spat with my mother was not caused by disagreeing over his acceptance of Christ, since he denied it to her, but because, for the first time in his life, he did not acquiesce to her demands concerning me. I just wished he would experience the joy, peace, and comfort that accompany suffering for Christ. How could I impress upon him these truths? How could I tell him that Jesus ought to be first in his life and the guiding light for his decisions? How could I show him that he must fully surrender to the Lord and allow Him to guide his steps in life, and not only for convenience? How could I convince him that his miraculous escape from sure death in Beirut was a clear voice from God that he ought to put his spiritual house in order by putting the world behind him? How could I tell him to forget his past glories, authority and power, and replace all by throwing them at the feet of Jesus his Lord? What must I do to succeed in presenting this message to my own father? I had no answer but to keep on praying for him, and to take it upon myself to neither tire nor yield until I would see him win the battle.

***

The house we moved into was located between the Ropers' house and the church—a perfect location—thanks to Mrs. Roper who was able to find it for us. It was a fully furnished old house, quite large, and extremely charming. The yard was immense with two massive willow trees—my favorite—almost shielding the house from view. The house, however, did not reflect a residence of a wealthy, political leader, but that was how my father wanted it, since threats on his life had increased. His only desire was to spend some peaceful and valuable time with me until the threats had subsided. I was not sure how he was going to resolve the issue of such threats, nor did I know what kind of assurances he was seeking in that respect; perhaps he sensed that the war in Lebanon would soon end, and threats on his life would disappear. However, according to the news, the warring factions continued battling, ferociously, as ever. Despite my father's seemingly fearless, carefree attitude that his façade showed, I could see these were only attempts to put my mind at ease; but one's eyes cannot hide troubled hearts. He spent much of his time reading all the newspapers and listening to the news; and to keep me from hearing his conversation, he would make phone calls behind closed doors. Such clandestine behavior only enforced my fears about the threats. He was always telling me it was sufficient for him to open up his eyes in the morning and close them at night, seeing the smile on my face. Nonetheless, I always could read the anxiety signs written all over his face and in his behavior that was caused by the rift with my mother, his loss of his political leadership and authority. My main concern, now, was, to entertain him, keep him company, and primarily, to be a blessing, and instrumental in enriching his spiritual life. I scheduled every minute of every day to keep him in an atmosphere free of any worrisome elements. We would go on long biking trips in the morning on a nearby trail, followed by some gardening that he loved to do. We ended up having the best-looking garden in the whole neighborhood. We normally ended our days in the comfort of our home, reading and studying the Bible.

One day, as I was shopping in a nearby mall, I remembered what a good and talented sketcher my father was. I promptly wanted to revive this pastime in him, so I bought him all the tools needed and made him draw sketches of me.

"You sly one, how did you remember I like to draw? That was a long time ago, but now I don't even remember how to hold a pencil." We started taking road trips with an easel, a sketchpad, pencils on board, and we would stop at scenic views for him to draw. He regained his skills, so well, that he started spending hours sketching beautiful scenery with his pencil. He once told me he was willing to put all his abilities into drawing the most beautiful woman in the world on a piece of canvas.

One day, I planned, with Rev. and Mrs. Roper, to volunteer my father to give Sunday school children drawing lessons. I encouraged him to go and do that more than once for more than one class. With time, as he became more attuned to church folk, he began to feel at ease around them. Eventually, he participated in a Bible Camp for the youth for a whole week with Rev. Roper, his son, Johnny, and the youth group from the church.

Meanwhile, Mrs. Roper, Mona, and I went to a women's retreat at a different location. I was wondering how my father was faring with these young men. Spending the nights in sleeping bags on the ground, eating and showering on campgrounds was not among my father's points of strength. I, on the other hand, was enjoying every moment of every day at the women's retreat. Several women came to accept the Lord Jesus as their Savior. One evening, I was asked to share my testimony, as we gathered around a bon-fire. The request was music to my ears; I was thrilled at the thought. With great joy, I sat before twenty-five young women and told them how my life was changed. I also made some precious new friends, one of whom was my tent-mate. She was a twenty-eight year old young woman named Lauren Milano, who had a master's degree in special education from the University of North Carolina. Apart from her education, she was beautiful, with Mediterranean features, tanned lovely skin, dark hair, and a bright contagious smile. She commanded a sweet charm and personality with a sense humor, warmth, and deep loyalty. It did not take me long to develop a deep friendship with this young woman. One evening I shared, with her, my story about Samir, and told her my real name (since I had kept that a secret from everybody else at camp).

When I told her that my real name was Dalal Abu Suleiman, she surprised me by yelling, loudly, that she was half-Lebanese on her mother's side, and her father was Italian. I, in turn, shouted back, in surprise, at her revelation; but by this time, every head had turned towards us, wondering what was happening. She told me she had a sister who was my age, Marcella. Although Lauren was born and raised in North Carolina, she, nonetheless, was fluent in Lebanese-Arabic because of her devout grandmother who lived with them all their life, and passed away two years prior. She also told me she was the only true Christian in her family, whereas her sister Marcella did not want to hear anything about religion. Additionally, her mother claimed to have been raised as a strict Christian, but because she married someone who was not a believer, not only was she unable to persuade him to surrender his life to Christ, but also she turned her back to Christ and adopted the ways of the world. Lauren then cited, **"Be ye not unequally yoked together with unbelievers: for what fellowship hath righteousness with unrighteousness? And what communion hath light with darkness?" II Corinthians 6:14.** Her mother had stopped going to church or having fellowship with other believers, as well as reading the Bible or praying. She told me, despite her father being a good husband and father, he nonethcless, was in bondage to drinking; they hardly ever saw him sober, when at home. All she could do was watch her mother suffer and watch him, help-lessly, succumb to drinking unable to do anything. Lauren looked me in the eyes and wanted to tell me more about her mother, "But my mother is a pleasant person, a good housekeeper, and a great cook. She makes the best Lebanese dishes, especially tabbouleh[1], this side of the ocean." I gasped at the mention of tabbouleh; I told Lauren I had not had it in years! She quickly said, "Inshalla [Lord willing], we will invite you all when we return home; tabbouleh would certainly be on the top of the list."

The retreat ended, and we all returned to the Ropers' towards midnight. Rev. Roper welcomed us and told us, they, too, had just returned from camp. I immediately asked him about my father and if he had managed to get through camp without any problems. His face reddened, his eyes widened, and then beamed, "Oh, not to worry about your father anymore Dalal; I assure you he spent one of the best weeks of his life. You should have seen him climb hills, play volleyball, fry eggs, wash utensils, and pitch tents; you would have been proud of

---

[1] Tabbouleh is a famous Lebanese salad made mainly from parsley, mint, tomatoes, lemon juice, olive oil and burgul.

him. More importantly, had you heard him sing in a loud voice and praise the Lord who saved him, you would not have recognized him."

As Rev. Roper was driving me home, I thought about how much joy and blessings my mother was missing by being away. I felt guilty. While we were all having a great time, together, receiving all kinds of God's blessings, joy, and peace, there she was, in London, spending her days in constant worry and going to bed in tears. I felt a sudden wave of pity and compassion for her, and I decided to call her as soon as I arrived home. Let her hang-up on me, all I needed her to hear from me were the words, "I love you Mom."

I opened the door to the house, expecting to see my father happy and beaming, as Rev. Roper had described him; but what I saw, scared me. My father's face was pale and his eyes red, as if he had just received some bad news. I ran towards him, asking what was the matter; he told me that having been in such a joyous spiritual state all week long, he decided to call my mother to tell her he loved her. Unfortunately, she reacted by accusing him of betraying his country, his people, and her; moreover, she called him a dishonest trickster who snatched her daughter away from her! She even threatened to reveal his whereabouts and seek to harm him wherever he might be hiding. Additionally, she would be able to find him, get even with him, and so on. She left him no chance to explain and hung up at the first utterance of a word from him.

What I just heard saddened me, and I tried, in vain, to ease his pain. Then I tried to tell him about the dinner invitation at Lauren's parents, perhaps that would help. Finally, my father gave a faint smile and agreed to go to dinner at the Milanos. The next day, we were driving, merrily, towards our host's house, where appetizing Lebanese dishes awaited us, most-especially tabbouleh.

When Lauren had told me about her mother, I'd expected to meet a simple, overweight woman who was kitchen-bound, cooking and eating all day long. I expected them to be living in an old, dilapidated house, where the father staggered most of the time, smelling of liquor and tobacco. However, my preconceived ideas embarrassed me when we arrived at their house. It was a huge, luxurious house, with a large yard, surrounded by a beautiful garden. Mrs. Milano, a handsome, elegant, and friendly woman, was standing outside to welcome us with world-famous Lebanese hospitality. She shook my father's hand, gave me a hug, and complimented me. I surmised Lauren must have already filled her in about me.

The house was immaculate and very tastefully decorated. The Ropers and Mona were already there. As I was still admonishing myself about my preconceived ideas, and thanking God I did not share them with anyone, Mr. Milano came and greeted everyone. He looked quite sober, maybe because I expected him not to look so, and all through the evening, he displayed deep kindness and a very witty sense of humor. For a man his age, he was quite handsome, as well— just as Lauren had described him, minus his liquor problem. I heard him talk to my father and Billy Roper, who was praising the architectural design of the house and the garden. Later, I found that Mr. Milano was a renowned architect, and that his wife, Nadia, had earned a degree in economics from the American University of Beirut.

As for Marcella, despite receiving us dressed in short shorts and disheveled hair, I, nonetheless, felt that under that façade, lay a precious soul, for whom Jesus died, in his stead. I felt deep compassion for her. I forgot everything around me and spent a good deal of time with her, talking about various subjects, including education. She was impressed I held a master's degree in Chemistry from Oxford. She told me she had hated to study, but loved singing, and she had a beautiful voice. I also learned she was interested in music and wanted to try to make it on Broadway. Later, she played the guitar and sang a beautiful song. No doubt, she was Broadway material; her voice was even more beautiful than she'd claimed, and her dancing was no-nonsense. Her Lebanese-Italian looks added to her charm. Despite her looks and talents, it was sad she loved the world and cared nothing about her spiritual life. I could see sadness in Lauren's eyes, as we prepared to leave that evening—sadness for her parents and sister, who did not know the Lord.

After knowing the joy of salvation and accepting the Lord Jesus Christ as my personal savior, I felt what Paul had expressed so freely in Romans 9:2-3, **"I have great sorrow and unceasing anguish in my heart. For I could wish that, I myself were cursed and cut off from Christ for the sake of my brothers, those of my own race."** In essence, I wanted to see everyone come to receive the heavenly blessings I was enjoying, and be rescued from the consequences that would result from their unbelief. I could neither ignore nor be insensitive to the eternal condition of my fellow men. I therefore prayed, constantly, that the Lord would open the door for me to witness and tell of His love. I also prayed that those, who I am in contact with, would indeed inquire about the reason of my hope, as we are admonished in I Peter 3:15, **"But sanctify the Lord God in your hearts: and be ready always to give an answer to every man that asks you a reason of the hope that is in you with meekness and fear."**

Mr. Milano, having almost finished drinking a bottle of wine during that evening, had a slight stagger now as he bid us good-bye. Mrs. Milano was so happy at making our acquaintance, thus making this evening one of the best she'd had in a long time. She kept repeating, in the Lebanese tradition, that her house is our house. When the time came for her to tell me good-bye, she squeezed my hand and said, "I thank God Lauren found a friend like you; I hope you could also be a friend to Marcella—she's now your mission."

I was so humbled by what I had heard. Was it a voice from God? This was more like the story in the book of Acts 16:9, **"And a vision appeared to Paul in the night; there stood a man of Macedonia, and prayed him, saying, Come over into Macedonia, and help us."** Why was I entrusted with such a mission when a pastor and his wife were present, or why was not her sister Lauren given that responsibility? "Why me, oh Lord?" I muttered.

I began to suspect what brought us to this family was not the good food, but our desire to see the Lord Jesus glorified in this family. Mrs. Roper took the opportunity to be better acquainted with Nadia Milano, strengthen their friendship, and help her get back to the joy of fellowship with believers.

It did not take long; I sat next to Marcella in her car, recounting the story of my life, including my faith in Christ, and as usual, waited for my testimony to bear fruit. I waited to see Marcella's eyes shed tears after hearing my moving testimony and, consequently, accept Christ as her Savior—precisely as what had happened with me during camp. However, my expectations, this time, did not come to fruition. Marcella seemed irritated the entire time, she was fidgety, not only did she not rush to accept Christ, but displayed such coldness towards me that left me a bit baffled and disheartened. Later, I heard she had left her parent's house, without bothering to say good-bye, and headed for New York, in her quest to fulfill her dream of stardom on Broadway.

Marcella's departure and her turning the cold shoulder were a sobering experience. I began to re-evaluate my approach. What went wrong? Where did I err in witnessing to Marcella? I felt saddened that I had disappointed Marcella's mother and sister, especially when she entrusted her to me. Mrs. Roper noticed my disappointment and, consequently, sat next to me to tell me, "I wish you to know that not every time you give your testimony it will bear fruit. I do not want you to feel sad and discouraged whenever this happens. Winning a soul for Christ is not as simple as you might think; all you have to do is sew the seed, and God will make it grow and take care of the rest. After all, His Word is sharper than a two-edged sword. The only thing you can do is pray for the person you witness to, so the Spirit of God can open up the heart. Just remember, it is not the eloquence of your testimony or your interesting style of presentation that counts, but rather your faithfulness in presenting it. Moreover, one must also first live what he preaches, and then God will take over."

Her words bore deep into my heart. Whereas I failed in winning Marcella over, my father succeeded in winning over her father, Mr. Milano. Whenever he disappeared from sight, I would find him with Mr. Milano, at his house, or vice versa. I was intrigued to find what common denominator they shared. My father did not drink or smoke — at least not after his illness — and Mr. Milano was not a bit interested in politics or politicians; so what brought these two opposites together? More often than not, after their discussions, they would drive together, and Mr. Milano found less time for drinking and watching television. I don't know in what, did my father get him preoccupied, that kept him away from indulging in his habits. I was certain my father did not invoke religion in their discussions; but he nonetheless succeeded in building a relationship.

Mrs. Milano began going to church with us, not only to Sunday Service but also to all other church meetings. I saw her raise her hand, tears streaming down her cheeks, after a sermon that moved mountains. Rev. Roper gave an invitation for rededication of one's life to the Savior. Lauren's joy at seeing her mother take this step was indescribable. She then said her joy would be completed only after seeing her whole family come to the Lord. Today was Nadia's dedication to Christ, and perhaps God had chosen my father to bring his new-found friend to the Lord and give him a taste of joy to free a sinner from the clutches of Satan. That was what came to mind when, one Sunday, I saw Mr. Milano accompany my father to church and saw them sit together in the rear row. This sermon was to be the last in a series during the revival meetings at which my cousin Majdi was preaching. It was August 31, Samir's birthday, as well as both Majdi's and my own fourth spiritual birthday.

Majdi was not about to forget this fact, it was the subject of his message that evening. He mentioned my name several times, indicated I had been present in church, and intertwined his testimony with mine. Mona, Amal, Lauren, Rev. and Mrs. Roper were praying for the salvation of souls at the invitation, especially for Mr. Milano. As for me, I was praying the Lord would give my father his first soul and put one star on his eternal crown for bringing his friend to Him—a crown he would throw at the feet of Jesus in heaven. I was unable to control myself when I saw my father, his face shining, as I had never seen before, holding Mr. Milano's arm and leading him down the altar to accept the Lord as his savior. I wept at the sight.

That evening, at the Roper' house, as planned by Amal, we all celebrated four birthdays: Samir's, Majdi's, Mr. Milano's, and mine. Heaven was rejoicing.

Chapter 19
THANKSGIVING

$\mathcal{J}$ was having a great time in North Carolina, but that did not keep me from feeling homesick for my adoptive parents in London. I constantly called and corresponded with them. Perhaps what added to my happiness was the fact they were coming for Christmas. Likewise, I was constantly in touch with the Gerrards, especially their son Eric. After having known Lauren for some time, I thought she would be the perfect mate for Eric. I kept throwing his name around whenever Lauren and I were together; moreover, I was also telling Eric about her and highlighting her qualities. I played a true matchmaker, trying to make each of them eager to meet the other.

The opportune moment finally arrived for them to meet—it was on Thanksgiving Day. We all decided to spend Thanksgiving at the Shaheens in Maryland, where they had settled. I could no longer keep my plans about Eric and Lauren a secret, but discussed them with my father, Mona, and his aunt, Mrs. Roper—just a week prior to his planned arrival. Mrs. Roper welcomed the idea of their meeting, while Mona did not feel comfortable about such a move. She then whispered to me, "I hope you have not inherited this habit from your mom."

With this sarcastic remark, we changed the subject and decided we would let events take their natural course. We were going to treat him as a guest from London who came here to spend Thanksgiving with his aunt—no more, no less.

My plan was to pick Eric up at the airport, accompanied by Mona and Mrs. Roper. However, everything seemed to take a different turn; the Ropers had to leave town unexpectedly, Mona slipped and fell just moments before getting ready to leave the house, and had to go to emergency, so I had to call on Lauren to accompany me to the airport. This brought to mind an old Lebanese saying, "Some people's calamities become other people's blessings." We arrived at the airport delayed by the events to find Eric waiting outside on the curb looking worried. I asked Lauren to stay behind, and then hurried towards

Eric and apologized for the delay. I then called Lauren and introduced them, "Lauren, this is my dear friend, Dr. Eric Gerrard; Eric, this is my friend Lauren Milano."

I had expected both to only shake hands, since Eric was the serious type and Lauren was shy, but to my surprise, I saw them hug each other, as if they had known each other for years. Nevertheless, I was elated and began to feel comfortable with my plan, since it helped clear my guilty conscience over what I had caused Eric in London.

Mona's slight accident turned out to be more serious than originally thought. Her foot sustained a fracture. The accident did not ruin the meeting between Eric and Lauren, but it ruined the rest of our plans, especially Thanksgiving. It would be difficult for Mona to travel with us to Maryland with a cast on her foot. As a result, we agreed the Shaheens would be spending Thanksgiving in North Carolina, and we would be spending Christmas and New Year's in Maryland. Everyone was quite happy with this arrangement, especially yours truly, because I wanted the Andrews' to accompany us to Maryland, as the Shaheens lived close to Washington, D.C., so we could show them around the capital.

While we were busy helping in the kitchen, we spoke a good deal about marriage, love, children, and the future in general. Nadia Milano loved Eric and hoped, if it were God's will for her daughter to marry him, they would be able to give her a grandson. Tears welled up in my eyes upon hearing what this mother wished for her daughter — unlike what my own mother would say to me. Last time I spoke to her about the one I loved, she wished him dead. Upon hearing this, Nadia gave me a comforting hug, and said, "Not to worry dear, our God is the Lord of impossibilities; He can change things when no one can, including your mother's heart."

Amal and I returned home late; everyone was asleep, except for Majdi, who was up reading a book. He seemed distressed over something. He told us that my father called my mother again, and pleaded with her, but she hung up after she threatened that time was on her side, and she would get back at him. Blood rushed to my head, and I asked Majdi, worriedly, "Has not my father learned his lesson? Why does he not ignore her as she does? For one time, he should make her feel he can live without her quite easily. Perhaps, if he breaks her pride, she will soften towards him and ask his forgiveness."

I could no longer finish what I'd wanted to say, so I went to my room, picked up my journal, and started penning my raw feelings on paper, as I lay in bed.

I did not sleep a wink that night. I remained awake, in silence, trying not to disturb Amal with my sobbing. I did not want to cast a shadow of sadness over the bright reunion we would be having with the Shaheens. Amal had not seen them for almost a year, and had not seen them since they left Lebanon over four years ago. That would be a joyful occasion, which called for a celebratory spirit.

As expected, the reunion was very emotional and beyond what words could express, especially when I hugged the twins, who were now four years older and bigger. Rima was on her way to becoming a beautiful young lady, while Walid looked more and more like Samir. The twins and I stayed awake until after midnight talking and chatting, while others went to bed. I sat on the floor in the middle of the room, with Rima on my right and Walid on my left. We reminisced about old times; the twins amazed me with how much they remembered, even the most, minute details. Samir's name came up, from time to time, during our chat, and they often reminded me of things I had completely forgotten. Suddenly, Rima surprised me with this question, "Will I be the flower girl at your wedding?"

I gave her a hug, as well as Walid, and replied, "Yes, and Walid will stand next to his brother carrying the ring."

"When will the wedding take place?"

"End of August."

"And where do you plan to live?"

"Oh, I am not sure yet. All I know is Samir and Danny will return to practice at Johns Hopkins, so my guess is the wedding will probably be somewhere in Washington, D.C."

"So, why don't you both live with us? We could all be happy!" Walid asked innocently. "When we moved here, mom pointed to a room and said this was to be Samir and Dalal's room."

I could not help bursting into laughter at this revelation; I just planted a kiss on his forehead and said, "Thank you. I have no doubt we will be spending some time with you until we find a house close-by; but we will be talking more about this when Samir returns."

Walid was satisfied with what he heard and excused himself to bed, while Rima wanted to dwell on matters a little more philosophically.

"Do you plan to have a big house like you did in Lebanon? Are you still rich like before?"

I wanted to send her to bed, diplomatically, to avoid more curious questioning, but I did not; I answered as if such questions did not come from a ten-year old child. "I am not rich; my parents are. They have the money, I don't. The only thing I have is my degrees, and through them, I plan to work and earn *my* own money. The money Samir and I will earn should be enough to build our little nest and live happily ever after. It is not important that we own a big house; but, more importantly, that Jesus becomes the Lord of the house in which Samir and Dalal will live."

I squeezed her hand and continued, "But I will not forget to have a special room for you and Walid whenever you come to spend the weekends with us." I thought she would be content with these words, excuse herself, and say goodnight, but my father, who apparently heard every word, appeared suddenly, and called me. I went to his room and sat on his bed, after I closed all doors. He began to chide me with sharp words, "Your mother was right when she said I had no word in this house, I am the last to know. Many thanks to Rima and Walid for letting me know of your future plans, your wedding date, even down to the flower girl and ring bearer, as well as your future home. Have you forgotten that no one—I repeat—no one has yet asked me—your official father—for your hand in marriage?"

I was hearing a new language from him, but not of him; he must have spoken with my mother. I closed my eyes shut and asked the Lord to help me, and then I approached my father who was now pacing the floor, and said in a very natural, gentle tone of love rather than anger, "Dad—I understand your point—and your little secret even though you've not bared it to me. You are now living in an atmosphere of love, happiness, and peace—each person here is with a companion and living in harmony, except you. You are troubled and worried you are missing so much in this life. You are not upset because I did not tell you about my wedding plans; even Samir does not know. The date I mentioned to the twins is fictitious. Moreover, you're not upset that no one asked you for my hand in marriage; even I have not seen the man I love nor held his hand for over three years. If you are upset because of what mom told you, it is because you allowed her. For once, you have to muster some courage, stand up to her, and teach her a lesson, in marital duties, she will never forget. You have to impress upon her that holding grudges can only backfire on the person holding them. She will be the one to regret that she is not living the life of love—the panacea that will squelch any grudge. Call her up and let her know that her only daughter is quite happy being away, not to learn her methods of love and mistreatment of her husband." I left my father stunned at hearing such words, wished him a good night, and went to bed.

I woke up late the next day—Thanksgiving Day—a sunny and serene calm engulfed the house. I went out of my room and saw Mona sitting down, reading. She told me Amal and Majdi went to help Nadia in preparations for the famous American Thanksgiving turkey dinner. The Shaheens and my father went out sightseeing. I did not comment, but she apparently noticed I was disturbed about something. She stared at me and said, "What's wrong, Dalal? You don't look OK."

"Have you seen my father this morning?"

She was not expecting this question from me, but an answer to her question, yet she replied, "Yes, I saw him; we also had coffee; in fact, we had a pleasant morning together chatting about different things, but am glad my morning was with him and not you; you look so grouchy today. At least your father's face seemed pleasant; he even planted a kiss on my forehead. Now tell me, what's with you?" I thought for a few moments and decided that I should look normal since what took place between my father and myself the night before was obviously a tempest in a teacup, and would not say anything further on this subject—even to Mona.

Thanksgiving Day that year met all my expectations of what a truly magnificent day would be like. Everybody gathered in our house, and by afternoon, Nadia proceeded to spread the various Middle Eastern and American dishes she prepared on the table. The centerpiece was an American tradition—a massive, browned turkey lying on its back. As we all stood around the dining table, my father welcomed all and asked Dr. Shaheen to say grace.

Oh, how I missed hearing him pray in such a simple yet expressive way. It took me back five years to our house in Beirut, specifically our dining room, where the Shaheens met the Abu Suleiman's for the first time. I fondly remembered Dr. Shaheen's prayer that shook my being and affected my life. I loved this man so much and felt extremely proud and excited that, one day, he would be a grandfather to my children, Lord willing. When Dr. Shaheen ended his prayer, a huge knife sliced through the turkey; at that moment, the phone rang. Samir and Danny were on the other end. I was certain Danny called to inquire about the condition of his fiancée's foot—Mona—and Samir to wish, "Happy Thanksgiving" to all present. The receiver went from one person to another, everyone eager to talk. Mona was the first, and I the last, after forty-five minutes of anxious waiting. Samir's voice rang in my ear, "Dalal, my sweetheart, I love you so much; you're more precious to me than my life—you *are* my life—can't wait to see you again. I miss you terribly."

We spoke for a long time, to quench our longing to hear each other's voices. My conversations with my beloved left me feeling completely satisfied and fulfilled, both emotionally and physically. I looked at my plate, filled with scrumptious food, but I could not lift a fork. My heart, mind, and stomach felt completely full and happy. After dinner, Rev. Roper suggested we spend some time before dessert to thank God for his providence. We had an impromptu fellowship session with some readings from the Bible, and a brief testimony where each of us shared praise for the blessings bestowed upon us during the past year. Reverend Roper asked my father to prepare a word as the host of this gathering, and I would conclude with a word, as well.

From my vantage point by the window, I could see the main road leading into our driveway. I saw a car drive up, then heard the car door slam. I saw a young woman walking up the driveway towards the main entrance. I opened the door and, lo and behold, it was Marcella! I gave her a big hug shouting, "Oh, thank God you came; now the gathering is complete; your family will be so happy to see you."

Marcella did not want to disturb the momentum of the devotional period, so she opted not to go into the living room until it was over. She mentioned she was hungry after having spent ten hours driving. I immediately filled a plate with food and handed it to her on a tray; one could tell how hungry she was by the way she was eating. I did not want to irritate her by asking why she waited until the last minute to decide to come. That did not matter a bit. What mattered was she was now with us. I left her alone and went to the living room to continue the devotional. Rev. Roper presented my father to share whatever he had on his heart, but at that point, he and I had not had the chance to talk over last night's entanglement; but what I heard satisfied me. My father began his little speech by thanking God for everything, as well as his very own existence, especially this year, since God saved him from certain death in the assassination attempt on his life. He attributed his escape to prayers—especially his daughter's—and her faith. He made it clear it was my faith and not his that performed the miracle, for Dalal was the greatest blessing in his life.

After hearing these words, I rose from my chair, went to sit at his feet, kissed his hand, and laid my head on his knees. I offered a silent prayer, thanking the Lord for him. The others proceeded to share their testimonies; Amal thanked God for my return after such a long time, and Majdi thanked God for the safety of his uncle Salah. The twins each thanked the Lord for bringing me back to them with presents and toys, which triggered some laughter in an, otherwise, serious session. Lauren thanked God for her newly-found and faithful friend Dalal who was heaven-sent to bring Christ and salvation into her home, as well as many blessings. To top all, she thanked God, who brought her together with a future husband. Dr. Shaheen thanked the Lord for bringing Samir and Dalal back together. Eric was thrilled as he thanked God for Lauren, a beautiful believer in Christ, more than he deserved. Finally, my turn came, and I began to share my testimony.

"As you know, I am an only child who, until the age of sixteen, lived a pampered, privileged life, until the Lord said, "It is not good that you remain alone, Dalal," He sent me a beloved sister named Amal, which means 'Hope'. She brought hope into my life when she introduced me to Christ. However, God was not done yet, being a generous Father, He also sent me three other sisters: Mona, Lillian, and Lauren. Then God saw I also needed a few brothers, as well, so my cousin Majdi became my spiritual brother in Christ, but Majdi was somewhat serious and reserved, so he sent me another brother, Danny, who is full of humor and vitality. I thank the Lord for all the sisters and brothers he gave me; they are all so precious to me, but I needed something else—a friend. The Lord said, "I will give you a friend to comfort you in your grief and trials; I will give him a big heart and a pleasant disposition to make you happy—He gave me my dear friend, Eric. Before Eric, God also blessed me with a loving, faithful friend in Mary Graham. Then He thought I also needed the kindheartedness of a mother who had been missing from my life recently, so He gave me two mothers instead—my adoptive mother, Mrs. Lily Andrews, and a mother-in-law to-be, Nancy Shaheen. God also provided me with two dear 'aunts'—Sandy Roper and Nadia Milano; and because my father is also an only child, God gave him four brothers in Billy Roper, Dr. Shaheen, Michael Andrews, and Alberto Milano. Then the Lord asked me if I were satisfied and happy with what He had given me, and I answered, "Yes," but I am a little greedy; I needed a fifth sister, so the Lord said, "OK, I'll give you this one—call her from the kitchen." To everyone's surprise, I promptly yelled, "Come on in, Marcella, my fifth sister."

Marcella walked in, wiping her tears, as everybody rushed to her with hugs and kisses; her sudden appearance was akin to the biblical story of the prodigal son's return, unfolding in our living room! That was really a big surprise to all, especially to her parents and sister. After, calm returned, following the commotion Marcella's entrance created, everybody sat down again to hear me finish my testimony despite having told them that was all I had to say. They wanted to hear more from me; to satisfy their curiosity, I told them, "OK, I have one more important thing to add—I forgot to thank God for helping me earn my degrees from Oxford University."

Everybody objected loudly, as Amal said, "What about Samir, you mentioned everybody except him?"

"Oh, Samir? Samir who?" I asked mischievously, as a few cushions from all directions hit me.

After a short period of merriment, I regained my poise and continued, "The Lord put my father, my newly found uncles, sisters, brothers, mothers, aunts, and friends in one scale and asked me if there was anyone else for Him to put in the other scale. I said, "Yes, there is— Samir who will be my brother, friend, and mate for the rest of my life." I am so grateful and thankful to the Lord for such a blessing and pray the balance of both scales will always remain the same." And with a wink, I concluded, "But do not ever forget, all of you are in one scale and Samir is in the other scale—for he is the one whom my soul loveth.

Chapter 20
SAD HOLIDAYS

❦

*T*hanksgiving was our first holiday in North Carolina; I recorded it in my journal as another day among the best days in my life. Soon enough, it was over and everybody started heading home, to rest, and prepare for tomorrow's work. Eric was ready to fly back to England, so the day after Thanksgiving, Lauren and I drove him to the airport. The farewell between him and Lauren was touching; she cried as she hugged him and bid him farewell; she continued crying, intermittently, as we drove back home. She also complained about the pains of separation, despite having met her dream husband-to-be for only a few days. It seemed to me, her sadness was a bit of an overreaction and the whole episode somewhat irked me; I told her, "Please Lauren, get a hold of yourself; you just saw the man you love a few minutes ago; I have not seen mine for several years." She apologized, and we changed the subject.

The departure of the people I loved and cared for did not sadden me that much, because I knew we would be meeting again at Christmas and the New Year's holidays at the Shaheens in the Washington, D.C. area. Dr. Shaheen invited everyone for Thanksgiving on the upcoming holidays, including the Andrews', who planned to be in the United States within the coming two weeks.

I could not believe my eyes as I saw Mr. and Mrs. Andrews come from behind a wall at the airport into full view. Our reunion was exactly as I had envisioned—highly emotional, filled with tears, and laughter. Mona was also there to meet them, but still on crutches. Three days later, my father took advantage of their presence at our house and arranged to go, early, to Washington, for some medical tests at Johns Hopkins Hospital. He simplified the reason for his trip with an old adage, "An ounce of prevention is worth a pound of cure." I, however, wondered why he was going to Washington, accompanied by Mr. Milano. What an unusual friendship has developed between the two? I was curious, and wished I could figure it out. However, the

Andrews' presence with us soon necessitated I play the perfect hostess and attend to the needs of my guests.

Only a few days left until Christmas; the media never ceases to remind you! We eagerly waited for Majdi and Amal to come by, so we could drive together to Washington. One evening, we met with Nadia Milano and arranged to travel in three cars. However, Mrs. Andrews, who always has good ideas, suggested we rent a van instead of using three cars; this way, we would all travel together. We rented a van and loaded it with whatever space allowed for Christmas presents, in addition to the snacks, coffee, and soft drinks that Mrs. Milano had prepared for the road trip. We drove for nearly five hours, but time flew as Rev. Roper entertained us with his guitar and singing, apart from our constant chatter on various topics, especially coming marriages. A great deal of time was spent discussing preparations for Mona and Danny's wedding the following month, and a little later, Lauren and Eric's engagement party, but most important to me, was Samir's expected arrival in mid-January. Everything around us suggested joy and peace, as we looked forward to blissful holiday reunions, especially what the New Year might hold for us. I then lay down on the back seat and stretched my legs to relax and daydream, but soon enough, I was in a deep slumber.

Our plans went as scheduled, and after an arduous and exhausting trip, albeit enjoyable, we finally arrived at the Shaheen house in Baltimore. Everyone came out to welcome us, but my father and Mr. Milano were clearly absent. We were told they'd gone out for a walk. It was December 23; the weather was unusually warm—as we were told—and could not be any better or more beautiful. While the Shaheens were becoming better acquainted with the Andrews, Walid and Rima were each holding my hands, in an effort to show me around their new house and their Christmas tree. They told me they had finished setting it up the day before, so it would be ready for my presents. I chuckled at this and thought of the innocence of children and their small worries.

The house was as I envisioned it to be, simple, yet tasteful. The aroma of Christmas sweets prepared by Mrs. Shaheen filled the house. I particularly spent more time in the room that Walid and Rima referred to as Samir and Dalal's room. It looked different from the other rooms, decorated differently. Somehow, Mrs. Shaheen made the room look more like a bridal suite than a simple guest room. To my astonishment, a huge picture of Samir and me adorned the wall. It was our picture taken on that beautiful rock in Lebanon. I stood there a long time, reminiscing on our young love the picture displayed, while wiping tears away. I did not heed the call for refreshments, but sat on the bed thinking about Samir. I relived those moments when he surrounded me with his arms and I heard him utter softly, "I love you, I love you."

I did not notice the others viewing the room, but none said a single word except Mrs. Shaheen, who must have noticed my teary eyes. She put her arm around my shoulder, caressed my hair, and began to encourage me by saying that, soon enough, Samir will be here and just to think about the good times to come when he arrived. She also apologized for hanging the picture, and said if she had known it would distress me, she would not have hung it. I quickly dismissed her notion and told her the picture held a special meaning to me, and that one, in particular, because it stirs my emotions. Then I began to cry and said, "Our long separation has taken a toll on my emotions; it has become unbearable to be without him; the weeks feel like years. Please pray for me, Auntie Nancy, that, the days will pass quickly for our reunion." I held her hand, tightly, and did not want to let go, until I heard my father's voice, when he returned from his stroll with Mr. Milano. I got up, went to the powder room, washed my face, and used some make-up to conceal the teary eyes. I put on an artificial smile and ran down the stairs, pretending to chide him for leaving me alone, and asked him if Washington made him forget his only daughter. We sat down alone for some time, and I began to ask him about the results of the tests he had taken, but he was quick to put my mind at ease and tell me everything was fine. Despite his apparent carefree attitude and gladness to see me, something I saw in his eyes bothered me; he looked as though he was concealing something as I watched him throughout the evening. He was easily distracted and projected a certain, uneasy somber look whenever he was finished talking. I wondered if my mother were to blame for this again; I, therefore, did not want to delve into it, for tomorrow would be Christmas Day, the holiday of God's love, the Prince of Peace, so let peace prevail, including my father's and mine.

None of us stayed late that evening, due to exhaustion from the long trip. I wanted to get a good night's sleep, but since Rima turned out to be my roommate, it was not to be. She kept on talking and asking me questions until she fell asleep in the wee hours of the morning. Naturally, we both slept until noon the next day. When we woke up, the whole house was abuzz with commotion and laughter. We took advantage of the balmy, sunny day and took the Andrews to Washington for some sightseeing. When we returned, Marcella had already arrived; everybody was happy to see her. The evening that followed was quite enjoyable and eventful; everybody was waiting for the phone to ring at any moment now to hear Samir's voice, Steve's, and Danny's, but we were disappointed that none called—not even on Christmas Day, New Year's, or any other time. We tried to call them, but to no avail; nobody picked up the phone. No matter what time of day we attempted, all our attempts were futile. Everybody was worried because, not all three could be away, simultaneously. We began to pray for their safety and asked the Lord to put our minds at ease.

The last couple of minutes before the arrival of the New Year, the phone rang; I was the first to pick it up, as I felt it must be Samir calling. I was disappointed when it turned out to be Eric's voice from England, but was alarmed when I heard Lillian cry in the background. She was worried about her husband Steve because she had not heard from him in over two weeks, which was quite unusual. What made the situation even more alarming, it was the holiday season, and people who normally do not call, take the time to call. She asked us whether we had heard from either Samir or Danny, but we tried to assuage her fears in traditional clichés when we told her that we have not. We spent New Year's Day attempting to reach them in the Middle East. Feeling sad and worried, we boarded the van back to North Carolina while my father, Marcella, and her father went to the airport to catch a flight back.

The trip back felt much longer and more draining than before because we were all worried and heartbroken despite Billy Roper's attempt to remind us to trust in the Lord who was in control.

"As believers," he admonished, "We must not fall prey to fear and worry. Was it not the Lord, who told us, **'be careful for nothing; but in everything by prayer and supplication...'** and why do you think of bad things instead of good things?" He went on to admonish us further by citing more passages from the Word of God, **'Whatsoever things are pure, whatsoever things are lovely, and whatsoever things are of good report think on these things.'** I was totally convinced of what Billy was saying, but could not put it into practice; my gut feeling was telling me something was terribly wrong. Was God testing my faith? I do not know, time would tell.

My father was already in the house when we arrived; he looked troubled and worried, but said nothing concerning Samir. The rest of our party went home after we all agreed to remain in contact if we heard anything. The Andrews' slipped quietly into their bedroom, and so did Majdi and my father. Amal, Mona, and I remained awake until the early morning hours despite our exhaustion and sleepiness in an attempt to reach Samir, Danny, or Steve, but there was no answer. Majdi and Amal stayed with us for the next three days, then left to return to their college.

Two long weeks went by without any word from the threesome. We were all uptight, worried, and in constant communication with the Shaheens in Maryland and the Gerrards in England. Lillian was going through a period of depression, and her family thought it was best to send her to North Carolina with 'little Samir' to be around us. At any rate, her whole family was planning to come the following month for Danny and Mona's wedding.

On January 16—the day Samir and his friends were supposed to have arrived—Lillian arrived to be followed by her husband, Eric, and her aunt once the wedding date was confirmed, if it were to be held, as Mona remarked. She was constantly crying, not knowing if she should prepare for her upcoming wedding or travel to the Middle East looking for her fiancé. She was truly in an awful mental and emotional condition, as well as in a dire state of confusion. To make matters worse, we received a call from Samir's father telling us he had contacted the hospital where they were working and learned their work visas had expired and they were now out of the country. This bit of news only added to our worry. If they were neither at the hospital nor in the country, or their apartment, then, where in the world were they?

I remembered Khalid. His name suddenly popped in my mind. I ran to my room to fetch Kamal's telephone number in London; he was the only one who could give me Khalid's phone number. When Khalid finished school, he went back to his country. I remembered giving him Samir's information and the hospital where he was practicing medicine. Samir did recount to me, in his letters, he had met Khalid and, from time to time, he visited them at their apartment; and they, in turn, had dinner at his house more than once. Khalid must surely know something about them, so while dialing Kamal's number in London, I was, at the same time, praying God would come through in this critical situation, or that Kamal had not moved or changed his number. Oh, thank God—unmistakably, Kamal's voice rang in my ear! He became troubled when, from my tone of voice he sensed something must be amiss. He did not ask too many questions, but he immediately gave me Khalid's phone number, and to my surprise, he cited a biblical verse that comforted me, **"For I reckon that the sufferings of this present time are not worthy to be compared with the glory which shall be revealed in us...Nay, in all these things we are more than conquerors through him that loved us."**

I told my father about my plans to call Khalid; furthermore, I told him who Khalid's father was, and that he would be the one who could solve this mystery. He promptly agreed. I then did not waste anytime calling Khalid, who answered the phone and asked if he could do anything for me.

"Hi Khalid, I am Helen Andrews, remember me?" I said, expecting him to be thrilled at hearing my voice. Instead, his voice was quite solemn when he replied, "I don't have time to discuss this now, why don't you leave your phone number, and I'll contact you at the proper time."

I immediately responded that I would be waiting for his call as soon as he could—day or night. I hung up after he assured me, but not before I made certain he wrote down my phone number. Lauren and her mother came by to check on our news and brought with them some sandwiches, because we had not eaten all day. However, before I was able to eat a bite, the phone rang. Everybody became quiet, waiting and hoping. It was Khalid. He apologized for being short in his conversation with me earlier because he was in an important meeting with some officials. He told me how glad he was to hear my voice. Then he asked, "So, what's the big surprise? What's going on?"

I sensed Khalid was hiding something; some of what he said was contradictory. If he were really in a meeting, he did not have to address me in using Arabic masculine forms in his pronouns, as if I was a man. I felt he wanted to hear from me, first, the reason for my call. When I told him that, he laughed and said, "I forgot you are an Oxford graduate and quite smart." I was in no mood for jokes, so I asked a direct question, "Do you know anything about Samir's whereabouts?"

He went silent for a couple of moments, and then said, "Samir, Danny, and Steve—" then went silent again. I screamed at him, "Please, tell me, do you know anything about them? When was the last time you saw them?"

"The last time I saw Samir was the 18th of December when we had dinner together, and, and—"

"And then what? Please do not go silent on me again."

"Samir is fine, and so are Danny and Steve; the two will be traveling to America soon."

"What do you mean the two of them? What about Samir?" I asked with my heart sinking.

Khalid hesitated, and then answered in a weak voice, "Samir was kidnapped for a time, but I know where he is now and shall help in his release soon enough. Do not worry; he'll also be traveling soon."

What I just heard did not comfort me at all; on the contrary, it made me worry more. I felt dizzy and must have passed out. It seemed like a dark cloud covered my eyes and fire burned in my bosom. When I came to, I found myself lying on a couch in the living room and everyone standing around me, except my father. I was too weak to ask about him, but Mona read my mind and told me he was in his office on the phone. Within a couple of minutes, I heard sirens, and in no time, I was in the emergency room at a nearby hospital for some tests. Test results showed I was suffering from exhaustion, so I was taken back home. Consequently, everyone avoided mentioning anything about Samir lest I pass out again. I waited until everybody left the room and called Khalid, again, to inquire in details about Samir. I could not believe some things he told me; I was scared. He asked me not to divulge anything to my father about this, per dad's strict request not to tell me. That said, Khalid dispelled my fears and assured me Samir was OK, and that within a few days, he would have better news for me. He concluded his conversation with these words,

"I am certain that the God you worship and pray to, is able to protect Samir and bring him back to you safe and sound."

I did not tell anyone about my conversation with Khalid, and despite my promise not to let my father know, I, however, could not hide such a dangerous and serious matter from him. The same men, who had attempted to assassinate my father earlier, kidnapped Samir, Danny, and Steve. I wondered how they knew my father and Samir knew each other, or that he was practicing medicine in the area they controlled. I went on analyzing the events, trying to remember everything that had happened, in the hope of finding the missing link that would lead me to those who knew of the connection. I finally concluded that the note I gave the Prince to hand-deliver to Samir was the beginning of the thread. Was it possible such a nice person as the Prince would reveal such harmful information? Did not Samir, in one of his letters, tell me the prince was such a great friend? No. I did not think he was capable of such malice, for he had nothing to gain. But then, if not him, then who? The more I thought about the possibilities, the more I was convinced Samir was not the target. The picture became clearer the next morning, when I rushed into my father's bedroom and told him my deductions.

My father sat on his bed, alarmed at what I thought, and rubbed his sleepy eyes to absorb the gist of what he had just heard. "What are you saying, you figured out what?"

I noticed him rub his stomach as he spoke, as though there were pain in that area, but I did not focus on it because I was still troubled. When he asked me to elaborate, I said,

"Can't you see they're trying to get back at you? When they failed in finding your own daughter to use as hostage, they resorted to kidnapping Samir, when they knew he would be their next best hostage, and consequently, would get back at you. It is very clear, Dad. Samir is the means, and you're the end." My father looked at me, puzzled; his face whitened, and he replied in a low, sad tone, "That woman is a criminal. I cannot believe the grudge she holds against her husband and daughter could lead her to stoop this low and endanger the lives of these young men." I yelled, not believing what I'd just heard,

"Mother? My mother? "

My father did not reply, but stood up, pressing his stomach, walked into the bathroom, and remained there for over half an hour. All the while, I sat on the edge of the bed, thinking about what he had just revealed about my mother. I later understood he had recently sent her harsh communication to tell her he was through with her forever, and that he only had room in his heart and life for me and Samir, his future son-in law. Moreover, he told her he would pull the curtains down on this dark stage of his life with her; consequently, she threatened him with revenge, even if it meant her life. Now, she was making good on her threat.

On the last day of January, despite my pleading, as well as the others', Dr. Shaheen arrived, from Washington D.C., to convince my father not to expose his life to danger. Disregarding all, my father stood up, and with an authoritative voice of the leader he was, said, "It is time I come out of my seclusion, take responsibility, and save Samir's life the only way I know how. All I need from you is to remember me in your prayers in my effort to do what I have to do. The Word of God says, **"With men it is impossible, but not with God; for with God all things are possible."** I promise you, Dalal, that in the name of Jesus, I will bring back Samir to you safely and soundly so that joy returns to your saddened eyes. You too, my second daughter, Mona, I also promise you the return of Danny in time to celebrate your wedding, as planned; you will enter the church holding onto my right arm, and I personally will give you away to Danny."

We said good-bye to my father, as he and Dr. Shaheen headed to the airport. In the evening, the whole family gathered into prayer groups to remember my father throughout his journey. Rev. Roper asked his church to join us in prayer, and Mona called her mother and Mary Graham to also pray with us. My aunt Sue and Mary arrived on February 3. On the fourth, my father called to tell us Steve and Danny would be with us in the next few hours, as he accompanied them to the aircraft that would fly them home to be with us. As for Samir, he was in good health and negotiations for his release were under way.

Although the release was still on paper, everybody was nonetheless overjoyed when Steve and Danny arrived. The next day, my father called me, again, to inform me he'd met Samir, face to face, and that everything was going smoothly for his release, according to God's will; moreover, he applauded Khalid's courage and his love for Samir. He again reiterated that plans for the wedding would remain unchanged; this prompted all to prepare for the wedding around the clock.

On February 11, the Shaheens arrived; on the following day, Majdi, Amal, and Marcella arrived. While we all gathered in our house, the phone rang; I ran to take the call. It was my father, but instead I heard Khalid laugh, as he spoke, "Are you OK and strong, Dalal, and will you not pass out if I were to tell you something?" With a renewed sense of hope, I replied, "Try me."

Then I heard these words, "My sweetheart, Dalal; it's me Samir."

I felt lightheaded, as the usual dark cloud passed over my eyes again, which made me pass out. This time, I did not need to go to emergency, as two doctors and a nurse were standing next to me. When I opened my eyes, I heard Mrs. Shaheen say, on the phone, with a smile, "She's fine—trust me, she's fine. She must be overwhelmed by hearing your voice. You are fortunate my son," she continued, as she turned her head towards me and smiled, "because you found the woman that loves you so much," and hung up. After I felt better, everybody was teasing me as Danny asked Mona, "Howcome you never fainted when I spoke to you?"

While all were happy and having a good time, I took Steve aside and expressed my concern about the fainting spells I was experiencing, lately. Moreover, I expressed fear that I may faint again upon seeing Samir. My eyes became misty as I said, "I do not want to appear weak, and certainly do not want anyone to treat me with caution for fear of how I might react. Furthermore, I do not want Samir to worry about me." Steve was quick to put my mind at ease by telling me this was nothing more than a temporary condition due to the difficulties I had experienced, lately, and that would soon disappear when Samir returned, and tomorrow, for certain is another happy day.

***

My father and Samir were supposed to arrive on Thursday, February 14, just two days before the anticipated wedding of Danny and Mona. Khalid called to inform met he'd just returned from the airport after having driven my dad and Samir to catch their flight, but I was told they would spend some time in London. He wished me the best, and he proceeded to tell me I knew who to choose, and Samir was the noblest and most truthful man he had ever met. I then proceeded to ask him about his relationship with the Lord, to which he told me to ask Samir when I saw him, "He knows a lot, and will tell you all the good news."

I began a countdown for Samir's arrival by making myself busy so time would fly by; I prepared a special room for him, and placed a basket of red roses in it. I also bought various gifts, clothes, and things I thought he might need. Moreover, I hung a huge poster for my father on which I wrote, "Welcome back, our hero, Salah Abu Suleiman." I was so happy, I decorated the house with all kinds of flowers and balloons and felt like an adolescent again, waiting for her first date with the boy she loved.

Two hours before the flight landed, I went in the powder room, washed my hair, and called Lilly to give me the best hairdo possible. I wore a beautiful dress and made certain I looked flawless. I stood before the mirror, primping, and applying perfume on my neck, took one last look, and smiled, approvingly. Amal walked in, took one look, and sighed without saying a single word. As I walked out and entered the living room, all eyes moved to look at me, but none smiled or spoke. Their reaction surprised me; but before I could ask anyone if there was anything wrong, Danny whistled in admiration and said, "Samir is fortunate not to see you like this today!"

I had no idea what Danny meant; but as we joked, I gave no further thought to what he'd said; Mrs. Shaheen thought there was a need to clarify Danny's comment.

"Dalal, while you were in the powder room, Samir called and told me that, due to unforeseen circumstances, neither he nor your father will be flying in today, as planned; they will arrive tomorrow morning. They are both well, not to worry." What she just told me simply did not sit well with me. I wanted to know why; but while everybody expected me to break down and cry, I nonetheless, kept my cool and asked, "Didn't Samir give you a reason for this delay? Was there no explanation?"

She replied that she personally did not talk to him, but with Majdi. I looked at Majdi; he shrugged his shoulders and said, "That's all he told me, then he asked to talk with Steve." I then turned towards Steve, wondering what was going on, then he said, "There is nothing to worry about; rather than arriving today, they'll arrive Saturday; one day won't make much difference. At least they're in London, safe and sound."

Anger swelled within me, but I kept it under control, so as not to hurt anyone's feelings. My eyes probably did not conceal it. It was not easy for me to wait another day; I'd waited long enough. I then promptly returned to my room without looking at anybody, changed my clothes, and left the house without explanation. All eyes were gazing at me, wondering where I was going, I headed towards my car. However, before I could turn on the ignition, Marcella suddenly appeared, opened the passenger side door, and insisted she accompany me. If it were anyone else, I would have turned down his or her wish, but I did not want to upset Marcella. Then I wondered why was it only Marcella who followed me and no one else. Why would God want her to be by my side at this inopportune time, when I really wanted to be alone?

I was thinking of an answer, as we drove aimlessly. Ten minutes had passed without either of us saying as much as a word, but from her body language and sighs, I could feel she wanted to tell me something. I then broke the wall of silence and said, "Thank you, Marcella for your love; no doubt you must be worrying about me while driving the car in such a situation, and perhaps you think I will lose control and have an accident. In fact, I am fine and not as stressed as everybody thinks. I am certain the Lord permitted this to happen for some good reason, for as He said, **"All things work together for good to them that love the Lord..."** Your presence with me, at this moment, means a lot." I then held her hand and squeezed it, saying, "I love you very much, Marcella; you are a sister and a friend."

I did not expect my words to warrant any tears from her, but to my surprise, she sobbed like a little child and finally said, "Believe me; I don't know where to begin. Every time you call me sister, it feels like a knife piercing my heart. Since the moment you mentioned God's blessings in your life at Thanksgiving and named me as one of those blessings, I felt pain deep down in my heart, and still do."

"But why, Marcella?" I shouted. "Why are you living in pain and suffering? I truly love you like a sister and a friend."

"Because I do not deserve your love: not from you or my mother, Mona, Lauren, or anyone in my family, especially you, Dalal. I deceived you all."

I tried to convince her otherwise, but she asked if she could be frank and explain. She went on to tell me she saw in me what she wished for her, then added how my behavior with her embarrassed her and pricked her dormant conscience that began to make her feel guilty. When she sensed the effect our presence had on her family, especially her father, it made her envious that I took her place in her family as the pampered girl, and hence, she wanted to get back at me. Moreover, she mentioned her mother never stopped talking about me, that she began to hate coming home. She, furthermore, said from that Thanksgiving up until that moment, she suffered even more upon hearing about the pain and suffering I had to go through for the sake of Christ.

"Here," she said, "I was born in a Christian home, but brought nothing but shame to the name of Jesus. I envy you, Dalal, for the joy and happiness you have in your life, as well as the innocence and the purity you possess."

As we approached a school, I pulled in, parked, and turned off the engine. I held Marcella's hand and said, "You more than exaggerated in your depiction of me, Marcella; I really do not deserve all this praise you just heaped upon me; had it not been for the saving Grace of God, I would have turned out to be the worst of sinners. But God looked down upon mankind and saw that **"All have sinned, and come short** of the glory of God...There is none righteous, no, not one." God's love is marvelous and beyond description; it is higher than the heavens above and deeper than the deepest oceans. **"For God so loved the world that he gave his only begotten Son, that whosoever believeth in him should not perish, but have everlasting life."** God offers this love, unconditionally, and without exception to anyone willing to take it. The Lord has offered it to me, and now He's offering it to you..."

She interrupted me, and said, "You are different from me; you are a good, pure girl."

"But I was a sinner, and very far away from God."

"You were never like me, I live in sin."

"But Jesus did not come to save the righteous; He came to save sinners like you and me."

"Dalal, you know nothing about me or my life; no one does. I have been living in sin since I was fourteen."

"But as the Word of God says, the blood of Jesus cleanses us from all unrighteousness; there are no big sins or small sins that Christ cannot cleanse and forgive."

"So, what must I do to atone for my sins?"

"You cannot do anything on your own; Jesus did it all on the cross; he paid the price for your sin by taking your place on the cross, the only thing you have to do is just accept Him as your Lord and Savior so you can receive His forgiveness, peace, and holiness."

"How do I do that? I am tired of living my life this way; I yearn to live a holy life. I am a sinner and want that forgiveness, for I am suffering and need peace in my life; I am weary."

"Jesus said, **"come unto me, all ye that labor and are heavy laden, and I will give you rest."**

"I want to come to Jesus, I want Jesus—I want—" She said and began to cry on my shoulder while I repeated the passages I heard from Samir in a similar situation, and in turn, told them to my father. "Jesus can see your genuine tears of regret and repentance."

I asked her to repeat after me, as we began to pray these simple words, "Have mercy on me, Lord, come and live in my heart, cleanse me from my sins with Your Precious Blood and make me a new creature. The old Marcella is passed away; all things have become new. I surrender my life to you."

I looked at Marcella's face, which seemed to be shining; her eyes were glimmering with the light and the peace that came upon her from the Lord Jesus. She now looked even more beautiful than a few minutes ago! Whoever said that grace is a free gift to someone who does not deserve it, was absolutely right.

On the way home, Marcella said, "I want to confess this to you; I did not follow you out of the house because I feared for you, but because my heart had been on fire for the last two weeks, and wanted to talk with you alone. I wanted to open my heart up to you, but the grim situation you were in, kept me from doing so. When I heard Samir and your father were going to arrive late, I decided to follow you and talk in seclusion. What I did was, in fact, not for you, but for me."

"I also want to confess something to you. When I left the house, I was reproachful of how God permitted the delay, but now, I find myself incapable of thanking God for his devices and the way He manipulates situations for His glory. He turns bad situations into good situations whenever a precious soul surrenders to Him." I said with a wink and a smile.

Marcella stood in our living room and boldly confessed her salvation to all present. Hallelujahs and Amens were shouted throughout the house, as Rima in her innocence, said, "On February 14 next year, we will place one candle on your birthday cake." Everybody left and went home but not before I heard a knock on the door. I ran to get it and heard Steve say, "Sorry, Dalal, for telling you that one day's delay in Samir's arrival won't make any difference. I was wrong; it has made a big difference when a young lady by the name of Marcella moved from the kingdom of darkness into the kingdom of light."

Chapter 21
A MAGNIFICIENT DAWN

⁓

*A*t last—Samir arrived. Both he and my father arrived just two hours prior to Mona's wedding, so we did not have time to meet them at the airport. They had to take a taxicab, to first drop Samir at the church to be with the groom.

Dad looked tired from the long travel he'd endured. He had obviously lost weight, but the hero's welcome he received made him forget all the dreadful days he had to go through. He was so happy to see his sister, welcomed Mary Graham into the house, and met the Gerrards. He was in good spirits, as he was talking and joking with everyone, but he refused to discuss his trip abroad until after the wedding, and had time to catch his breath and get some much-needed rest. Everybody respected his wish and asked him no further questions. After awhile, I went into his bedroom and found him asleep; he slept for one hour, after which, I helped him dress in his formal wear, and placed a white carnation in his lapel. I stood next to him in my purplish dress that Nadia chose for me, to wear, as the maid of honor.

Mona looked beautiful in her gown. I controlled my emotions and, for a change, my tears. I did not want to ruin my make-up or the joy of the day. Mona looked like an angel in her wedding dress. My aunt was so happy, despite her incomplete joy when no one from her family came to attend the wedding. Nadia was acting as though she was the mother of the bride, as she was running here and there in an effort to arrange things. Mary's eyes focused on her precious Mona, whom she raised, and was now able to see her as a bride—her face shone with joy and happiness. As for Mrs. Andrews, whom we called our other mother; she was also beaming with joy, as if it had been one of her adopted *daughters* getting married.

We reached the church and waited in a special room until all the invitees took their seats, but I wanted to peek and try to see Samir, even for a second, before he entered the church. I was fearful I might get emotional if I did. Everything, however, went smoothly, as Mona and I watched from a concealed place what's going-on. There was Mona's mother, aunt Sue, led in by Majdi; and Danny's mother, led in by her son, Johnny; and behind them, Leila and Suheil, my cousins from California. That was a real surprise. When did they arrive? I heard Mona cry, but she was able to control herself. As the music played, the bridesmaids, Lillian, Amal, and Lauren, marched slowly down the aisle, and then came my turn. I felt uptight as I approached the sanctuary door and saw the crowd, most of which were members of the church, but I was happy to see those who knew our story were there to share our joy. I lifted my eyes to where the groom was standing, and I saw Samir, who was looking at me with misty eyes. I pretended I was the bride walking down the aisle to meet her groom. Inadvertently, I walked towards the groom's side, but Amal was quick to pull me in the other direction to remind me I was only the maid of honor. The processional music struck, and everyone stood up to watch the bride walk in; she looked astounding and walked like royalty. After the vows were made and a short sermon in which the bride and groom were admonished to live a godly life, it ended with, **"Except the Lord builds the house, they labor in vain that build it."** At the end, Rev. Roper presented "Dr. and Mrs. Danny Roper" to the applause of the crowd, which resonated throughout the building. Danny took Mona's hand, kissed it, and they both walked out, arm-in-arm, amidst more thunderous applause. Samir and I were next to walk out; he took me by the arm, but this time, it was not me who was trembling; my role was trying to calm him down.

The reception and dinner lasted for over three hours; amid shouts and dispersed applause, I stood by Samir, as he readied himself to make a little speech to honor his friend, Danny.

First, he thanked the Lord for His Providence, and then, my father, who was instrumental in saving his life. He called him to his side, and my father stood between us, holding Samir in one hand and me with the other, then raised his hands in a victory sign. Dad, in turn, proceeded to utter a profound word—fit for a revival meeting—reminding everyone of God's mercies and goodness. He gave his testimony and told of how Jesus showed him his mercy in his miraculous escape from certain death, after an assassination attempt. He surprised me and everyone else for bringing this up on such an occasion in which he opened up the fortified gates of his heart and declared his faith, so openly, as well as mentioning his name and political position back home. It sounded as if he were closing the chapter on his past life forever, only to begin a new chapter with his Lord and Savior, Jesus Christ.

It was ten o'clock, when Mona and Danny cut the cake. Then she threw the traditional bouquet of flowers to all the single ladies who gathered, enthusiastically, to catch it. After a couple make-believe attempts, Mona finally let go of it and threw it up in the air. All held their hands high and open, to catch the bouquet, and to her delight, Amal caught it. Afterwards, Mona and Danny left the hall, and Samir, dad and I, followed for a surprise we'd planned earlier.

Samir opened my car door and sat beside me; my father sat in the back. I then took off like a rocket, to which Samir commented, "Where are we going? Is this another kidnap operation?"

As we drove farther, we were away from the town and on into a flat stretch, and his questioning took on a more serious tone. I stopped the car and asked Samir to drive.

Mischievously, I quipped, "Please, drive carefully, Samir; my life is precious to me, for I have many plans for the future."

My father laid his head on the backseat and fell asleep. Then I laid my head on Samir's shoulder and whispered, "Do you remember the letter I sent you in which I mentioned how I wished to welcome the early morning sun on the beaches of North Carolina? Well, we are going there. "

"What?" Samir asked, startled, and to my surprise, he hit the brakes. When I realized he was taken aback, and did not comment, I pulled away from him and said, "I am sorry. I did not mean to put you on the spot; all I wanted was to spend some time alone with you. I am in need of peace and quiet, and thought this was our chance for the three of us to wind down and relax."

I took his hand lightly, kissed it, and said, "Are you mad at me?"

He took a deep sigh and answered, "I—mad at you, why? You are my life, my love; my love to you is too deep for any mind to understand. You have no idea how much I love you; every heartbeat says, *I love you.*"

I did not let him continue when I interjected, "No matter how much you love me, it cannot measure in comparison to my love for you, for we both are in the same boat..."

"No, Dalal, I am responsible for you, before God first, and before me, second. The horrific days of our separation were stronger and harder than my nerves could handle; I do not trust myself with you; what I told you four years ago, still stands. We cannot grieve the Holy Spirit; we must be careful with our emotions and keep ourselves pure and without blame. The way I felt about you, then, cannot be compared to how I feel today; I therefore, do not want to give Satan the time of day."

Suddenly, and thinking he was still asleep, my father's voice surprised us when he said, "Well-said, young man. I congratulate, you from the bottom of my heart, on your noble character; in fact, I am proud of you, may God bless your faith, son."

It was twelve, midnight, when we arrived at the hotel. We were all tired and needing plenty of rest after a hectic day; so each one of us carried their bag and went to their room. I was not able to sleep all night, as I paced the floor, tossed about my bed, read some, and tried to watch television. The thought that Samir was in reality, present with me, three years later, was unbelievable, that the turbulent days of our life were now behind us. Here he was, sleeping only a few steps away from me, in an adjoining room, it was too much to soak; when, for the last few years, we were thousands of miles away. However, we were savoring the moment, reclaiming our love, and watching how God's plan for our future life together was unfolding. I decided to tell Samir, first thing in the morning, that we could get married sooner rather than later, it did not matter to me, anymore, whether we had a big wedding or a small one. What was important to me was being together and living happily ever after. I turned on the lights in my room; it was four in the morning. I went to the window and pulled the curtain away; it was a beautiful dawn, with the ocean's wave breaking along the shore, and Samir sitting on the sand, which made me remember the beautiful dream I had, to welcome the dawn, alongside Samir. I put on my clothes, walked stealthily towards Samir, put my arms around him, and gave him a kiss on his head. I must have startled him, as he leaned over to my side; at this point, I saw his clear blue eyes, strongly gleaming. Perhaps this beautiful dawn and the sound of breaking waves made us forget who and what we are supposed to be, including what Samir had preached a few hours ago, that he felt a strong urge to take me tightly in his arms. Suddenly, he let go, as if a he was snake-bit, ran away, and sat alone with his head between his hands. After a couple of minutes, he came back, took me by the hand, and walked back to the hotel. I entered my room, and he went to his room, without uttering a single word.

I thought I would spend a sleepless night blaming myself for what had happened, but to the contrary, I slept like a baby. I did not wake up until mid-morning, when I heard some hard knocks at my door. When I opened the door, there was the bellhop carrying a basket of red roses, which he placed on the table. I took one look at the card between the roses, and read the card, "Good morning, sweetheart, the most beautiful among all roses; your father and I went for a stroll on the beach and won't be late; we'll be back to have breakfast together. I promise you, we will soon welcome the dawn on the beach in North Carolina as newlyweds, but not now—not now."

I put on my clothes and wore a coat and hat. I then walked towards the beach, to meet my father and Samir. I waved to let them know I was ready for breakfast. Samir walked towards me, leaving my father behind, and then we walked back to the hotel hand-in-hand. Soon, my father caught up with us, and we sat in our suite to have our breakfast. My father said a prayer that brought tears to our eyes. I had never heard him pray like this before; his words were like music to the ears, as he lifted his heart to the Lord Jesus as a sacrifice of gratefulness for his salvation, forgiveness of sins, and eternal life. He also thanked the Lord for the extra days He had given him after his bout with cancer, and for the son-to-be, that he never had.

As we finished breakfast, my father, a cup of coffee in-hand, went and sat in a rocking chair by a raging fireplace, he was looking at us with love and happiness. He suddenly said, "Dalal, this is one of the happiest days in my life; I thank you for this opportunity that you provided for us and congratulate you on this wonderful idea that brought us here. I feel we all needed to get away from the crowds and be alone by this secluded place on the beach. I know that you always loved the sea and the sound of waves; your choice of place could not have been better."

I looked at Samir with a smile and said playfully, "Thank God there is a person who appreciates my taste and choice, and that I am able to make a sound decision." Samir said nothing, nor smiled or commented, but still waited for my father to continue his seemingly unfinished thoughts. He took another sip of coffee and continued, "This morning, Samir officially asked for your hand in marriage, with my blessings."

I was thrilled to hear these words, not for me, but in honor of my father, his pride, and feelings. Moreover, I was surprised why Samir had chosen that morning, to officially ask for my hand, and then Father turned towards me and asked, "Don't you want to know what my reply was, Dalal?"

"Father, you love Samir a lot, like your son, and therefore, I know what you must have replied, but of course, I'd like to hear it from you."

"I told him...I told..." but he could not continue, as tears welled up in his eyes and began to stream down his cheeks. I then felt the air was emotionally over-charged and needed some humor to break the deep emotions my father was experiencing. I walked over to him, sat on his knee, began to wipe away his tears, and said, "What did you tell him, Dad? I hope you did not agree because I can't stand this guy."

My father did not laugh, or even crack a smile, but instead, he gently nudged me away from him and directed me to go and sit next to Samir again. He sat up straight and continued where he had left off, "I told him that Dalal is my only child and the most precious person in my life; there is no one on earth I can entrust her to except Samir Shaheen." Again, he began to sob. Neither Samir nor I were able to quiet him down. I noticed him clutch his stomach from time to time, as if in pain. Samir became a little alarmed and decided to take him up to his room and check him out, while I remained in the lounge. It was ten minutes before they came out. I did not run after Samir to check out what was wrong, as I took it to be a bout of emotional stress, as fathers find it hard to give a daughter away.

After Dad came out of the room, he looked quite normal and went back to resume what he did not finish in the same emotional expression, "I am entrusting Dalal over to you; so be to her the father, the brother, the husband, the friend, and the lover; you're the only one who can fill the emptiness in her life." My father continued, "What I mean to say is, if I should die now, I shall die happily, because I know she is in your care." He went on like that, longer than I'd expected; his talk sounded more like a person on his deathbed. I had to interrupt by saying, "Strange, you have been talking for nearly a whole hour, Dad; don't you think your daughter has an opinion in all of this? It could be different from yours."

Smiling, he replied, "That's true, do you agree?" Playing my game, I continued,

"As you may well know, Dad, marriage is a colossal responsibility; we ought not to take it lightly. I, therefore, need some time before I can give you an answer; moreover, I would like to be better acquainted with the groom-to-be, before I commit my life to him. Perhaps a walk on the beach, or an evening dinner, together, will help me know him better, will you accept?"

My father laughed heartily, as did Samir, who stood behind me, donned his coat, and helped me with my coat, as we both walked out, together, for we were now officially engaged, and could go out, alone, according to Lebanese traditions, even when in America!

We walked arm-in-arm for over two hours, along the fine sands of the beach, chatting about a variety of topics. Samir did not directly bring up what happened the night before; but, instead, impressed upon me the fact that obeying and glorifying God in his life had priority over anything else. He continued, "First and foremost, I am a servant of the Lord, then a physician; and, soon, a husband. My service and calling are to serve amongst young people. If I did not practice what I preached, then I would have no right to preach it from pulpits or tell others to abide by it."

I did not object to what he said, nor questioned it because I was quite convinced with what he said. I considered myself fortunate to be marrying such a man; furthermore, I began to imagine the kind of life we would live—a life without doubts or fears of infidelity that prevailed in our society. We stayed for three full days at this beautiful place before we headed back home. I wished we could have stayed much longer, but we had to think of the Shaheens. It was not fair to keep Samir for myself when his family was equally eager to see him after a long separation. We spent a splendid and enjoyable time on our way home. My father sat in the back and was soon sound-asleep. I told Samir about Marcella surrendering her life to Christ, while he told me about Khalid's experience that reminded me of my father's. He wanted to have it both ways—Christ and authority over his clan. He also mentioned that Khalid knew a lot about the Lord, but had not yet taken the step to surrender his life to Him. Furthermore, he promised he would be the first to accept our wedding invitation, which brought to mind something that surprised Samir. "Speaking of weddings, do you know that until now, you have not asked me if I would marry you, as Americans usually do—as I was told?"

"And what do Americans do, pray tell?" he asked, puzzled.

"They say...the suitor takes his future fiancée to a nice, elegant restaurant, or anywhere similar..."

"And...?"

"He brings flowers to his darling, kneels down on one knee, then proposes."

"Then?"

"The girl says either *yes* or *no*.

"And?"

"If she says *yes*, he proceeds to put a ring around her finger, if she says *no*, then he pouts and takes her home."

"Then?"

"Then she shouts, he gave me a ring, he gave me a ring."

"Then what?"

"Then it's done with."

"That's all. He kneels down, proposes, puts a ring around her finger, and it's over?"

"If the suitor was of Samir Shaheen's mold, the story ends there; but for others, he kisses his bride-to-be without lecturing her."

Samir chuckled at the way I put it, but did not comment, so we continued driving and chatting, mostly about marriage, but we were unable to set a date. I told him Majdi and Amal's wedding was set for June 25, so I suggested April to him—April 21, to be precise, which was my father's birthday. Samir said that two months was a long time and he could not wait that long. Then I laughingly suggested August 30, his birthday, at which he reacted, "What? Six more months? This is crazy."

My father must have heard the last few sentences, and he said, "After what I saw on the beach the night we arrived, I suggest you both get married as soon as possible—say first Saturday of March."

Samir's face took the color of a ripe beet, for that incident on the beach was the last thing he wanted others to know about, but nonetheless, he pretended not to have heard it, and agreed on the date. After I protested this very early date so as to give myself more time to prepare, we agreed on March 21—the beginning of spring—the season of love—as our wedding day.

Chapter 22
I FOUND MY FATHER

☙

*O*ur families received the news of our wedding day with joy and relief, and waited for the newlyweds, Danny and Mona, to return from their honeymoon to celebrate the occasion; hence, we became busy in the preparations for the anticipated wedding. Samir stayed at our house until March 10, leaving me with the last touches and details for our wedding, including the list of the invited guests. What a chore that was in sifting through who should and should not be invited. He then flew to Washington, D.C. to take care of business at Johns Hopkins, where he planned to return to work after our honeymoon. Dad, accompanied by Nadia and Mr. Milano, also flew to Washington, to have a look at the house Dr. Shaheen had selected for my father to purchase. I personally would have rather selected it myself, but due to the immense undertakings I had on my hands, I put all my trust in my father and Nadia's taste, but not before I gave them certain specifications and guidelines for the design. Primarily, I wanted the house to be within a reasonable distance from the Shaheens' house and Samir's work. Second, I wanted it to be large enough for my extended family, guests, and visitors.

Unfortunately, things do not always go as smoothly as we would like. Only two days before my wedding, I had to fly to Johns Hopkins, accompanied by Danny and Mona. Samir told us my father had been admitted, due to severe bleeding in the stomach, but as soon as we arrived and saw Dr. and Mrs. Shaheen's gloomy faces, I knew it was something much more serious than a bleeding stomach. When I saw Samir, the look on his face confirmed my worst fears. What was even worse, I was not allowed to see or talk to my father, as he was in a coma in intensive care unit.

The following day, March 21, our planned wedding day, my father was battling death and my husband-to-be was caring for him. Billy Roper had arrived with the rest of the family. After surgery, Samir came out and told us they had done everything they could, and the rest was up to the Lord. My father remained in critical care for over twelve days, before the doctors allowed me to see him. Samir took me into the room where my father lay, feeble in his bed. When he opened his eyes and saw me, he began to cry and said, "Sorry, sweetheart; I ruined your wedding." As soon as he said that, his condition worsened; they had to take him back to ICU, and they would not allow anyone to see him, including me. I prayed, pleaded, fasted, and reminded the Lord of his promises, but my father's condition kept getting worse. I followed Samir and other doctors to hear, perhaps, a word of encouragement, but to no avail. When I saw him again, he looked better, but did not mention anything about our wedding, which, of course, was put on hold, but he asked to see my mother. He asked me that I talk to her, personally, and let her know of his desire to see her. This was a tough request, but anything for my father became easy. I dialed her number, but she hung up the moment she heard my voice; I tried again the next day and pleaded with her to hear me. The deep sadness in my voice must have softened her heart to finally listen, "Mother," I said in a serious tone, "Father is gravely ill and is in critical condition; he is now at Johns Hopkins Hospital, and he wants to see you."

She replied with harshness, "Ask your Jesus to heal him; there is no need for my presence." Then she hung up.

My aunt and Mona also tried to talk to her, but they were also unsuccessful. Upon my father's insistence, Samir flew to London to see her, hoping she would concede. He spent a couple of days there and returned empty-handed. After picking him up from the airport, we did not go directly to the hospital, but went home where I picked the telephone and dialed my mother's number. When she picked up my call, I shouted, "Don't you dare hang up before hearing what I have to say, or else I am coming to London in person to crack the phone over your hard, obstinate head. I have no idea why Father still cares for you after the way you have been treating him. If I were him, I would never ask about you, and would prefer, a thousand times, to die before seeing you. It is true that he is on his death-bed, but this is much better for him to leave a world with people like you in it, for if he lives, he will live among people who love and respect him, and if he dies, he will go to heaven where Jesus will be waiting for him. You, on the other hand, will be the loser, living a life of hate and bitterness; you really do not deserve his love or him. Now, you can hang up."

Samir was within earshot of what I'd just told my mother, and again, I saw a dark cloud pass over my eyes and felt like passing out for a few seconds, but I quickly regained myself. I saw Samir looking worried, as he was trying to make me sip water from a glass and wipe the perspiration off my forehead with a wet towel. I wanted to appease him, but could not look him straight in the eyes from embarrassment at the way I spoke to my mother. I was afraid that my behavior and words would only bring him fears at seeing this side of me that he'd never expected; I even surprised myself at such behavior. I began to feel badly at having spoken to her the way I had; after all, she was still my mother, and I had no right to talk to her in such an impertinent manner. I began to cry, but was comforted when Samir said, "Apart from some harsh words you uttered, I believe you did the right thing; some people do not come around with gentle words, but require some toughness, and such is the case with your mother. I expect that your method might not only be of benefit to her husband, but also to her."

I was glad my behavior did not seem to upset Samir, as I had thought it would, yet his words comforted me, and I did not feel as badly as before. Nonetheless, I was still feeling miserable at my mother's vengeful attitude. My throat became a little sore; it soon developed into a fever, cough, sneezing, and a severe cold that lasted for almost a whole week. My father knew about my condition and called several times to check on me. His voice sounded strong and full of hope and joy, as he wished me to get well soon. Strange, was this the voice of a dying man? I always asked Samir about him, and he would say, "What is not possible with men is possible with God." These words seemed to inject new hope for me, regardless of how slight, and I began to think God may answer my prayers and heal his frail body, enabling him to walk me down the aisle.

I woke up feeling better in the morning, having thought on such a possibility. I took a shower and slightly primped myself, afterwards. I splashed some good perfume here and there and planned to go pay him a surprise visit at the hospital, reminding him it was April 21 — his birthday. Samir was surprised when he saw me, with his lips quivering because he thought I was still sick in bed. I approached him and jokingly asked if he liked my perfume, perhaps even give me a peck on the cheek. However, he apparently did not care for this kind of joke, as he went back into the living room and waited for me. In a few minutes, we were in the car, with Dr. and Mrs. Andrews in the back seat, headed for the hospital. Samir seemed fidgety as he tried to say something, but never finished it. I thought he was readying himself to lecture me again on prudence. Soon, we entered the hospital and stopped by the florist to get some carnations, my father's favorite. Samir carried the flower bouquet, but still looked agitated. At this point, I had to ask, "What's wrong, Samir? I was only joking; you're overly serious, and at times, your serious behavior bothers me. What did I do *this* time, eh? OK, OK, I won't joke with you again on this subject."

He took me to the side and said, "Your mother is here."

"What? What are you saying?"

"Your mother is here."

"When did she arrive?" I asked in a trembling voice.

"Last Saturday—the day you fell ill."

"What are you saying? I telephoned her on that same day."

"I guess she left London that very day."

"Why didn't you tell me then?"

"Well, you were sick, and I did not want to agitate you, but I'd planned to tell you in the morning."

Afterwards, he reminded me kindly on showing my mother how to be a Christian woman, and to act it, so she could see what Christ and his love could do in her life. I agreed with him, in principle, then went straight to the flower shop where I bought flowers, then proceeded into my father's room to wish him a happy birthday. I placed a white carnation in his pajama lapel, and with all courtesy, I shook my Mother's hand—who remained seated—and gave her a kiss on the cheek. I sat by my father's bed, squeezed his hand, and jokingly said, "You look much better, Dad; had I known you'd get better with my absence for a week, I would have gone back to North Carolina."

Dad smiled and took it to be a compliment for my mother's sake, since, in fact, his health and disposition improved since she'd arrived; Samir always said one's disposition is very conducive to his healing. When, on the next day, I visited him again, my father was not in his room—nobody was able to tell me where he was. I could not understand this sudden disappearance. Half an hour later, of anxious waiting, I saw my father in his regular attire, being wheeled into the hospital by Mr. Milano, my mother behind them, laughing and chatting—apparently having returned from a little walk outside. I could not be happier. None noticed me, and I felt it would be best if I just quietly left and returned later. I exited from a side door and suddenly ran into Samir, walking in. He told me he was home, trying to get some sleep, after having spent the whole night at my father's bedside.

I did not tell Samir about my father's latest excursion. I went back inside with him and saw my father smiling and looking well, and back in his bed wearing his hospital gown. To my surprise, my mother was held his hand and smiled, as if nothing had ever happened. Nadia Milano was also sitting with them, but her husband was out of sight. What was going on between my father and Alberto Milano? Where did they wheel him? There were many questions going through my mind, but I waited until Samir asked him how his morning was—and whether he got up and walked a little. My father told him he felt a little tired; however, that admittance, as well as the way Dad concealed his short trip out of the hospital, bothered me. I began to feel they were keeping me in the dark about certain things, such as my mother's arrival seven days ago, and my father's sudden travel to Washington with Alberto Milano, just before Thanksgiving, for some tests. Everybody knew the bad news the tests had shown, and my father's cancer had returned; where I thought he had beaten cancer, for good. Now it made sense why Samir and my father were held up in London—he must have become ill and had to check in the hospital. Today's incident made me wonder if the same thing was not repeating itself. I sat in a chair, thinking about my doubts, but because I was so distracted, I did not even hear my dad until he had to call out my name for the third time. There was no one left in the room except my father and me, so he asked me to sit near him and began to plead, "Dalal, I really feel sorry for your mother; she hides behind power and authority, yet she has a good heart. I therefore beg you to forgive her and be nice to her, as a Christian should. She acquires love from a wicked world, but you acquire it from the source of love and forgiveness—Jesus Christ. Let her see Jesus in you."

My father was obviously emotional as he was saying these words; he began to shed a tear. I did not wish to make him more sorrowful, so I said, "Father, what would you like me to do? I am willing to do anything you ask me to, because I love you and want to please you. I'll do anything to make you happy." He took my hand, kissed it, and continued, "OK, when your mom returns here, I want you to apologize to her because of what you told her in your last call; it so happened she told me all about the harsh words you used with her. Perhaps your motive was good, but respecting your mother is a requirement. You surely remember that the Word of God says we must honor our parents—right? I am sure you did that for my sake, and I appreciate it, but that is now history. Today is a different story—everything has changed. She is here, by my side, and loves me more than ever, and I am so happy she came. Moreover, I need to see both of you have a good relationship, so my joy will be complete."

Despite my affirmative promise to my father to do what he'd asked, he, nonetheless, was skeptical. He wanted me to do it, not just to please him, or because it is required, but because of inner sincerity. That said, I could not lie to Father and tell him everything would be fine, as though nothing had happened. It was only yesterday I'd discovered she had been there for a whole week. I, however, made certain he understood my love for her never ebbed and never entertained any grudge towards her, despite all the ugliness and embarrassment she cast upon me in England. I had forgiven her, and it sufficed me that she had brought joy into my father's heart again.

To prove my point to my father and reassure him, I waited for her to return. When she entered the room a little later, I arose from my chair, opened my arms, gave her a hug, and kissed her with much emotion, then said, "I am terribly sorry, Mom, I was harsh and unkind to you—it was out of character for me to do that. I promise not to ever behave in such a manner again. Please, forgive me with your big heart."

I felt her arms embrace me, but felt it was more of a dutiful gesture, rather than done out of real love. Neither of us exuded that old love in our relationship; with time, something was amiss—yet, I believed the old love would, undoubtedly, return, even stronger. However, despite how each felt towards the other, now, what was more important was the happiness and the smiles that enveloped my father's face, and his feelings. He seemed to be in high spirits over this reunion of family. When it was time for me to go home, my mother remained by my father's side and never left, except for very short periods. She also slept in a chair by his bed, ever since her arrival from London, as Samir had told me.

Samir took me home. Along the way, I told him what ensued at the hospital between the three of us. He promptly smiled, as he heard this wonderful news and expressed pride in me for having done so

The next day—April 24—Father called and asked me to come with Samir to the hospital, in the same formal attire, we'd worn at Mona's wedding. When I told Samir about this request, he was surprised, but nonetheless, he took me back to the hospital at the requested time. As

345

we entered into my father's room, I saw a huge white carnation on his lapel; he soon began to compliment the way Samir and I looked together and said we made the perfect couple. He turned towards my mother and asked her, "Have you ever seen any couple look better than this?" Mother did not say anything, but nodded in agreement; she barely cracked a smile, accompanied by a little welling-up of her eyes. Father kept on laughing and cracking jokes until 9 p.m. He then asked Samir and me to sit at the foot of his bed, me on the right, and Samir on the left. He took each of us by hand and squeezed, strongly—something I did not expect from an ailing man—then he asked Mother to place the wedding bands on our right fingers, first Samir, and then me—the Lebanese way. After this ritual, he asked her to place her hands over his, where his were over ours, and began to pray God would bless our marriage, and he ended it, "In Jesus' name, Amen."

As we opened our eyes, we were able to see his face shine, as never before, and he laughed and said, "According to the authority vested in me as a father, I now declare you both to be officially engaged. Good night."

Every time I wanted to leave, I came back, one more time, to give him a hug and a kiss, on his forehead, not forgetting to thank him for the nice, yet surprising gesture. In the end, I gave Mother a big hug and a kiss to show her my sincere love, and not only to please my father. Meanwhile, Samir remained silent, throughout; I had to ask, "What's wrong, aren't you happy with what my father did?"

I kept speaking in a positive tone while Samir drove me home, but still, Samir did not respond. He apologized that it was too late to come in the house to continue our talk; after which, he drove off—tires squealing. I thought his behavior was due to this emotional engagement; perhaps he considered this event a call for some romantic actions, and as usual, was afraid and ran away. I smiled.

Before I went to bed, I took off my engagement ring and took a good look at it: there was a fine inscription on it, and hence, I put it under the light to enable me to read it. Engraved were these letters— "SSD" on the inner part of the ring. I figured they must be the first letter of these names: Salah, Samir, and Dalal. There was also a date engraved, "3/21," our original wedding date.

I did not understand why my father chose that day in particular; nor did I know when he thought about the rings, to have them engraved. However, I was too tired to analyze this any further—tomorrow was another day when I would ask him, rather than guess my way through it. I slept like a baby.

Although I thought tomorrow would bring more good news, it was just the opposite—my father died. His death hit me in the core; I could not reconcile with this fact; if it had happened a few weeks earlier, I would have accepted it more readily, and more easily, but today, after his health seemed to have improved, the news shocked me. All the while, Samir had been telling me, my father's condition was worsening, and that my father would either have an internal hemorrhage that would end his life, or he would slowly slip into a coma—but none of this happened.

Everybody expected me to pass out at the news, because I normally passed out, for the slightest reasons, but to the surprise of many—including myself—I did not. Not only that, but I was not able to shed a single tear, nor cry out, "Why, why, why?"

Samir, Danny, and Steve did not see this as a healthy reaction to my father's death, so they began to worry about my condition. I sat in a chair Samir brought to me, my eyes glassy, unfocused, and my face as pale as a ghost, as Amal told me later. Samir, still worried, kept shaking me and pleading with me to cry, shout, say anything, but I must have been in a different world.

On the fourth day after my father's passing, and despite my unchanging condition, Samir had to remain by my mother's side in her support, as she decided to take my father's body back to his homeland, for burial, despite the ongoing war. Samir and my aunt accompanied her on the trip back.

I was aware of everything around me. I was able to remember when Samir came to say good-bye before departure, to justify his need to travel with my mother. He told me how sorry he was for having to leave me behind in such a time of need, but there were many people who loved me and would take care of me, whereas, my mother was all alone and needed support. Besides, he told me, my father would have wanted him to do it. Samir's face was pale, and his eyes, gaping from exhaustion and sleeplessness. He took my hand, kissed it, and waited for me to utter a single word, but no word came out. I was stone-faced.

All those who were present thought it might be a good idea if they took me back to North Carolina; perhaps, getting away from the mournful scene would minimize my shock. Consequently, that is what happened. The moment I stepped out of the car and saw our house—the house my father had purchased, just prior to Thanksgiving, and designated it for family and friends—in which I lived some of the best days of my life—I snapped back into reality. All the flowers we'd planted were now in full profusion of color. I walked towards the weeping willow and began to shake its drooping branches that had been weeping for my father. I, uncontrollably, cried, "My father is dead, my father is dead." At this point, I shed my first tear, which opened up the floodgates. By now, I wept as if in agreement with the willow. I heard the twins, Rima and Walid, shouting, "She's crying; she's crying," as if weeping were a strange phenomenon, or the balm I needed, at the time, to soothe my aching soul. They must have concluded, and were satisfied, that I'd returned back to life.

Samir returned after a two-week stay in Lebanon, only to be surprised that my condition had not improved, except my tears were flowing freely. At this time, however, I had some questions to take up with the Lord, "Why Lord, why? Why not right after surgery? Why did my father improve to give me hope, but then all hope was dashed so quickly?"

Samir, patiently and logically, tried to explain to me about the will of God, and tried to convince me that God's ways are *not* our ways...and that He does not make mistakes. If we question Him, it is akin to telling Him—He is incapable of handling the situation. He repeated the mantra from Romans 8:28, **"All things work together for good to them that love God,"** and that heaven was a much better place to be, among other things, which did not make much sense to me at that moment of grief; perhaps I could not, or did not, want to accept such rationale.

I did not know how I was able to make it to church, to my father's memorial service. Every family member and friend got up to say a few words about him; either how he had influenced their lives or the love he'd exuded as a friend, especially Alberto Milano. They all expressed their deep sorrow, and then comforted each other at the loss of a great friend and brother. Towards the end of the service, everyone sang and praised the Lord for His unquestionable wisdom and grace, and turned over this sad page in their lives. Before I retired to my room, Samir took me in his arms, to comfort me, and attempted to kiss me goodnight, but I was too numb to react.

I knew Amal and Majdi had set their wedding date for June 25. I also knew they did not want to delay their marriage any further, because they both had planned to serve in Billy Ropers' church, where Majdi would serve as youth pastor. They were still working on their wedding preparations, even when Dad was in his worst days. I had promised to offer Amal my wedding dress, since my wedding was to come before hers. The dress was expensive and elaborately tailored; however, I was somewhat sad they had to move up the date of their wedding out of respect to the passing of my father. After all, Majdi was his nephew, and as was customary in Lebanon, weddings are postponed in a reverential gesture when a close family member dies. Poor Amal, I knew how she must have felt; but having been born and raised in America, she apparently was not aware of such customs, as she one day barged into my room to tell me I did not have to lend her my wedding dress since I have not used it yet.

"I can start to look for another dress, immediately, since our wedding is just around the corner," she said.

Of course, I could not believe what she'd just said, for she knew how much I loved my father, and that I was still in mourning. However, Amal was not to blame, since she was ignorant of our customs, but I blamed my aunt and Majdi because they both knew. All Majdi had to do was let Amal know. Amal waited for my reply, but I was still dazed and in another world. Perhaps, by then, she had figured out the answer through my silence, so she said, "I don't blame you Dalal; you promised to offer your dress *after* using it…and not before; so I guess I'll just have to go and look for another. Sorry I asked, but you are right."

I sat down after she'd left and thought about what had just transpired. If Amal got married on the scheduled day, this meant I was supposed to be the maid of honor, but I was in no shape or mood to play that role, so I went to her room, closed the door behind me, and quietly told her, "Amal, we must talk."

"Oh, I do not want the dress; you have not used it, yet."

"The dress is not the subject I have in mind. You can have it; it is yours, and I do not think I'll need it anytime soon, but sorry, I am unable to be your maid of honor."

"What? What are you saying? You won't be my maid of honor? You must be joking, right? This is my dream, Dalal; we both had planned this since we first met."

"No, Amal; I am very serious."

"But why Dalal? What's going on?"

"Why? Are you not aware the cement over my father's grave hasn't dried yet? How can I be a maid of honor, let alone attend a wedding while I am still in mourning? "

"But your dad passed away two months ago and is with the Lord Jesus Christ; so why all this mourning?"

"But the one who died was *my* father, and not a pet dog to forget him so easily." The clash of two cultures was taking shape now, as she replied defensively and with an attempt at reasoning.

"Whoever suggested you should forget him? Nobody forgets their loved ones who die. This is a matter unrelated to a wedding. Majdi is not only your spiritual brother, but also your cousin, way before I met you."

"So, why can't he remember my father is also his uncle—and that there are certain courtesies in this life that one has to observe, especially respect for the dead?"

"I really do not understand what you're implying, Dalal; there are no dead people in my dictionary, but people sleeping until the return of our Lord. Wasn't it Jesus who said, **"He that believeth in me, though he were dead, yet shall he live"**? If you consider your father dead and finished, then I can't blame you for not wanting to share my joy. I am really sorry you still think this way."

Amal soon left the room, and I did not see her for the rest of the day. Apparently, she must have shared our conversation with the rest of the family, since to my surprise, none stood by my side. Samir remained silent about this matter; he obviously ignored it altogether; meanwhile, Amal asked Mona to be her maid of honor in my stead. Everybody, in his own way, tried to talk me out of my old country stance, including my aunt, Majdi's mother, who came all the way from overseas to attend her son's wedding. She attempted to carry on in an exemplary manner by telling me how she'd lost her husband and brother at the same time, but I remained unmoved. Consequently, I cried as I told her, "Isn't it sufficient I attend the wedding without taking part?"

Samir was very careful not to upset me, as he was quite patient and compassionate with me. He often said he yearned to see the old Dalal who was full of vitality and spunk and not the gloomy Dalal, but I remained unmoved, like the Sphinx. I had obviously lost the verve for life, when I lost the dearest person to me in this whole universe.

Just two days before Amal's wedding, when everybody was outside the house putting the last touches on the preparations, I was still inside the house, sitting near Mary Graham, with my head in my hand and crying, Samir suddenly entered the room. When he saw me in this miserable condition, he stood before me, pale-faced, unsmiling, eyes wide open, and seemingly having lost all patience with me; Mary sensed trouble and promptly excused herself. He then let it out.

"OK, young lady, enough is enough, my patience has run thin. Why can't you understand your father is in heaven, enjoying his Master's company, and I am down here suffering? Who in your opinion deserves all these tears and attention?" He went on to accuse me of selfishness and only thinking about myself, with disregard for other people's feelings, who'd gone out of their way to give me support in my darkest hours. He chided me for putting Amal in an unenviable position when I backed out of her wedding. It also made her feel guilty, and hence, pondered postponing her wedding, had he not intervened. He kept it up as he paced the floor; all the while, I just sat there, bewildered, and said nothing. I did not expect him to chide me in such a manner, because I thought he was the only one who'd understood my situation. I was not able to reply to his accusations, except with more tears. The tears, however, did not deter him a bit, as he went on with his barrage of reproach.

"Life must go on; if death was a tool to paralyze the living, the world would have ended a long time ago. We, as true Christian believers, look at death differently than others. It is true that we grieve the loss of our loved ones, but we do not grieve like those without hope; for we know, the moment a believer dies, he also begins to live with the Lord. We have the hope that someday we will meet our loved ones in heaven; this is our source of comfort and joy, instead of grief and mourning."

He was silent a few moments, when he angrily sent his sister, Rima, outside to play in the yard, and then continued, "Do you realize it is insulting to our Lord and the glory of heaven when we behave in such a manner, especially when we know He promised us a place which no eye has seen nor ears heard what He has prepared for those who love Him? And here you are, doing the opposite, when the Lord has given your father this amazing privilege to be in His presence?"

What Samir said made a lot of sense, but it did not alleviate the anguish I experienced at the death of my father. An Arabic saying came to mind, which I said it loudly and irritably, "A glowing ember only burns the one holding it," then added, "It is not your father who died, Samir, but mine. You can sympathize but not empathize with my situation. You cannot feel what I feel."

Samir looked sideways at me, with apparent reproach that tore my guts apart; I immediately realized I must have touched a raw nerve. I wanted to apologize, but he did not give me the chance. With tears in his eyes, he responded, "You're right, it was not my father who died, but you forgot a very important fact; I was the one who spent nearly two months near your dad, caring for him, shaving him, washing his face, feeding him, and at times, entertaining him. Moreover, I was with him in surgery, feeling the pain of every cut the attending surgeon made. You must have forgotten that, in his last moments, your father kissed my hand and said, *May God bless you, my son.* You're right; it was not my father who died, but yours." Then he left.

I ran after him, as he stumbled, and almost fell over a ball his brother, Walid, was playing with. He kicked the ball so hard, it struck my face. He obviously did not realize what had happened, because he got into his car and drove off.

The ball hit me with such impact, it made me dizzy; so I sat on the stairs holding my face between my head to regain my balance. Rima, who was watching, ran towards me to inquire on what happened, and she asked, "Why did Samir kick the ball in your face?"

"It was not deliberate; the ball happened to hit me."

"But he seemed angry; does he still love you?" she asked, concerned.

"Of course he does, and I love him."

"But I heard him say he has had enough of you, as he was leaving."

"He was feeling miserable because of the condition I am in."

"Really? Why are you always crying? You look better when you're laughing and playing with us. What happened?"

"Have you forgotten? I lost my father, Rima, and I loved him, a lot?"

"But your father is now in heaven, Dalal; is he not?"

"Yes, he is. I lost him two months ago, and he's now in heaven, with Jesus."

"I don't understand. You say you lost him, and then you say he's in heaven; how do you lose somebody when you know where he is? It is like saying, *I lost the ball that is under the tree.*" Then she began to laugh as she was loudly chanting, "I lost my father; he's in heaven."

When neither adults nor wise godly women could convince me, including pastors, a little child of ten was able to do it. Mary looked horrified, as I entered in with my lips now looking like balloons, my face red, and a blue-black bruise under my left eye. I cried, profusely, over her shoulder, and told her everything that had happened. Mary knew, this time, my tears were not tears of grief, but of joy, because they were tears based on what the word of God says, **"Because I live, ye shall live, also."**

Just one day before Amal's wedding, I got up from my bed, knowing, full-well what I must do. I gave it ample thought, and all I had to do was execute it. I entered the powder room, took one look in the mirror, and I was horrified This horrific view took me back four years ago, when the same thing happened at Samir's birthday party, when I was hit by a ball. I recalled when Samir came the next day to say good-bye to our gardener, Uncle Abu Wafiq, and I suddenly came in, smiling, despite the pain and the blue-black face I had, then how Samir told me, later, that he could not erase that picture from his memory. He thought I was the most beautiful girl he'd ever seen; I now wondered whether he would say the same thing, today, after the problems I'd caused him and Amal.

It was only a few moments before Mary came to check on my condition. I asked her to call Amal so we could talk in private. Amal came in quickly and saw me sitting on my bed, my head between my hands, and the curtains drawn that made it very dark. Before she said anything, she went straight to the curtains, pulled them open, and turned on the lights. I did not waste any time telling her, "I am terribly sorry, Amal, that I was a pain to you in the last few days, just before your wedding. I know I've behaved inappropriately, so, do you think you can forgive me?" I asked.

"What are you saying, Dalal? I am not angry with you; you are my sister and a piece of my heart. I am only sad because my dream will not be fulfilled in its entirety."

"Amal, I want you to be frank with me; is your original request to be your maid-of-honor still valid? Do I still have a part in your wedding?"

"What are you saying, Dalal? You want to be my maid-of-honor? Is that what you're saying, or did I hear you wrong?"

Before I could answer, she was all over me, hugging and kissing me; but she retracted, horrified, when she noticed my face. She began to inquire about the incident, so I laughed as I told her exactly what had happened, but she did not seem to believe my story, until her parents and the Andrews came in and heard Mary Graham recount the details.

Everyone was so happy to learn of my change of heart, despite the way I looked. Rima, who did not realize she had a big part of my decision, was startled when everybody patted her on the shoulder for a job well-done. After all, she told them, all she did was laugh and chant, "I lost my father, and he's in heaven."

Because of the continued pain, I was not able to attend Friday evening's rehearsal. That said, I had no idea what they might have told Samir about my absence, but I knew I had to apologize to him for my behavior, and give him back the old Dalal he'd known. Saturday morning—the day of the wedding—I stealthily disappeared for three whole hours, and returned to shock everybody. I got rid of the old Helen Andrews forever; there was no more need to hide my identity to anyone; for I was in safe hands, and so was my father. I had my hair tinted back to its original color, after it had grown back to its original length, and combed it so it fell in cascades over my shoulders. I was certain Samir would love it this way, since he always asked me to return to the old Dalal. When I arrived, at church, with Amal and her father, I could not ignore Samir much longer; I saw him, standing, with Majdi, and looking grim. In an instant, I wrote him a note, "Samir, my reason for not being the maid of honor for my best friend is no longer valid, even as my face looks horrible. See, it was not my fault, but instead of being a physician, you should have become a professional soccer player, who is able to find his target with ease. Despite that, I still love you."

I handed the note to Walid to deliver it to his brother, but as the procession began, there was not enough time to see the look on Samir's face after reading the note.

Amal and Majdi's wedding was one of the most emotional weddings I had ever attended. Its memory would linger with me for a long, long time. As expected, and despite his profuse apology, Samir was so content and ecstatic to see his old Dalal back.

Chapter 23
THE BLUE DREAM

❧

*P*reparations for my wedding were well underway. Everyone had to travel again to the Washington area to help, with whichever task required, for this monumental wedding. The whole family considered my wedding to be one of its most important joyful events in recent memory. However, due to my father's illness and his recent death, all were praying everything would go smoothly, this time, and that they would see me in a wedding dress, at the altar, and Samir by my side. It had been a long haul on a roller coaster for both of us.

Samir and I felt like we were suddenly transported to *seventh heaven*, enjoying each other's company, and were content that He—the Lord, who began a good work in us, would complete it. Moreover, we were certain nothing was going to stand in the way this time; for God—who does not try us beyond that we can endure—knew I could not bear another mishap to ruin my wedding.

I did not know why Samir chose the last Saturday of July as our wedding day, when he had been in such a hurry for us to get married, *as soon as possible*. Moreover, I could not understand why he chose an enormous cathedral in Washington as the venue, when he was always against extravagance. What was even stranger were the numerous travel projects and medical conferences that befell him at that time; but since I trusted his judgment and decisions, I knew he would not take any task beyond his means, so I did not tire him with any questions.

I was missing my mother so much, as well as feeling her pain at my father's death. The day we decided on the wedding day, I tried to reach her in London, at her rural house, but was not able to find her. In fact, I tried several times, Samir by my side, and even sent her a wedding invitation, in which I pleaded with her to come, but I never heard from her. I felt sad; her presence was essential to me, as well as to my father's wishes.

The wedding was approaching quickly. Khalid, who'd received an invitation from Samir, arrived, accompanied by Kamal, who'd became *another* Majdi in his faith, as Majdi relayed to me. This news made me so happy, I snapped out of the sadness created by my mother's absence, and therefore, had to make some last-minute changes to the wedding arrangements to accommodate him. I asked him to walk Marcella, one of my bridesmaids, down the aisle, in lieu of Majdi. Friday evening, the entire wedding party was there for the rehearsal. It did not last over half an hour; everything went quite smoothly; afterwards, we went to the rehearsal dinner.

I was quite hungry by then, famished. I was also very jittery and felt a bundle of nerves. Being surrounded by physicians, and about to marry one, I went and sought help. Steve gave me a mild sedative that calmed me, and I became very drowsy; when I tried to walk out, I walked like a drunkard, but Samir quickly came to help me make it to the car. All the while, everybody was telling me to stop this charade of pretending, so I could get Samir to hold me up! Of course, I was not pretending, whatever Steve had given me must have knocked me out and caused my muscles to become rubbery! Then, as if to disappoint their thinking, they had to carry me into the car; Samir drove me home and carried me into my bedroom. Before he left, he brought me another tablet and made me drink it. The minute I swallowed the tablet, my system shut down completely, and I slept like a log.

By the time I awoke, I had slept through the day, but remained listless. It was 4 p.m., just a couple of hours before the wedding, which caused anxiety for all. It was probably the first time ever where a bride-to-be woke up that late for her wedding! It was also probably a first when the groom walked into his bride's room to wake her for her wedding. However, there was a reason; to prevent me from a recurring history of passing-out during the day of my wedding, or even, during the wedding. Thus, Steve and Samir both agreed to give me a relaxant. However, each of them gave me a relaxant without knowing the other had already done so, and the result was that I became over-relaxed and slept that long!

The hairdresser's job was easier than usual, as I did not fuss over anything he did, and left it up to his creativity. It worked quite well, and all who saw me commented on my nice hair. Within a few minutes, Amal came into my room, carrying a huge box, with all members of the family behind her. "It's for you, Dalal." Amal said. However, I told her that time was short and we could open it later; but everyone insisted I open it then. I complied and opened it. To my surprise, there was a brand-new wedding dress. I screamed, "Mom, Mom," and ran out looking for her. My aunt told me my mother was not there, but a chauffeur delivered the box in the morning while I was still asleep.

It was the dress my mother had designed a long time ago, and had said it was fit for a princess. The wedding gown was quite exquisite; every bride would have loved to wear it—everyone who saw it, said so. Mother must have finally realized I was her princess who would wed a prince.

I was twenty minutes late to church, which is acceptable for a bride. What caught my attention at the church were the excessive decorations which filled the place. There were hundreds of colored balloons at the entrance, and flower arrangements everywhere—especially an arch of flowers right at the church door, under which I passed. To my surprise, Walid and Rima stood on each side of the church door, passing presents to all attendees. This was not in the program, because the plan was, at the reception, I would pass by each table and hand every lady a rose and some sugarcoated almonds, a Lebanese tradition. I was trying to guess, what kind of presents were handed out, so I asked Amal, who shrugged her shoulders and showed me what was inside the boxes. I was astonished that the present was a silver plate with Samir's name and mine, our wedding date, and my favorite verse from John 3:16 engraved on it. **"For God so love the world."** What a surprise and a wonderful idea. How did Samir think about this and agree to spend so much money on such a matter. Anyhow, what happened, happened; I was sure to find the answer to this mystery after the wedding.

I stood with Amal and Dr. Andrews, watching the procession. The music emanating from the organ filled the whole cathedral and sounded as if it were coming out of the walls; it gave it an enchanting soothing effect, adding joy and happiness to the occasion. Suddenly, the organ music stopped; and suddenly, it erupted from several guitars as the wedding procession began. No one told me about this change, but nonetheless, it was a good change, as guitar music added a special twist to the program. My bridal party began marching down the aisle, with Eric and Lauren up front, then Mona and Khalid, and Marcella and Kamal. When the turn came for Amal, my maid of honor, to march down, accompanied by Majdi, the music changed again—a saxophone, one of my favorite instruments, began to emit its lovely tones. The procession was winding down as Walid, the ring bearer, and Rima, the flower girl walked down. Finally, my turn came. I took

Dr. Andrews' arm and started on my new journey. Dr. Andrews, with misty eyes, looked at me and whispered, as a father would on such occasions, "I must be the happiest man alive today; it is a great honor for me to walk you down the aisle and give you away in marriage. What I missed in my life, you compensated for today; thank you, my precious daughter."

His words were full of emotion, I almost cried and ruined my make-up, but I took control of myself and held back my tears. When Steve, our designated organist, began to play the processional, everybody stood up, as usual, with clamoring women extending their necks trying to get a good peek at the bride. As I entered, I noticed the cathedral was bursting at the seams with invited guests; I had no idea where they all came from. Anyway, the music stopped, and silence prevailed; at that point, Samir grabbed a guitar that he placed near him and began to play a melody that enthralled the hearts. Within moments, in a clear voice that came from the heart, he proceeded to sing soft lyrics that sounded like water flowing over pebbles in a stream.

At one time, Samir told me to wait until our wedding day to show me the kind of love he had for me; perhaps this was only a taste of what was to come. I had not anticipated anything like that, or even imagined he would serenade me on our wedding. He sang to me one of the most beautiful songs I had ever heard—every word came from the heart:

"The days of separation have made me weary, and I longed to see you, my dove.
You are flesh of my flesh and bone of my bones.
Your countenance is like the rising sun, and as pure,
As the moon, in its fullness, and as captivating in its charm.
You are my beautiful bride, a gift from heaven above.
Our happy days are ahead as we walk the road of life,
Nothing can separate us except death, my sweet love."

When my beloved Samir ended the song, sighs, ooohs, and ahhhs were audibly echoing throughout the cavernous cathedral. Putting his guitar away, he stood up to watch me walk down the aisle, waiting for my arrival at his side. I thought his song was the last surprise, but I was wrong. Dr. Andrews left my side and went to sit by his wife, leaving me to walk the rest of the way, all by myself. I continued taking the short steps on the longest route I ever had to cross. My mind was wondering what to expect next. I exerted all efforts to control myself. I wanted to make sure I did not fall, faint, or collapse. I lifted my heart towards heaven, seeking help from above, and wishing, perhaps, my father might be peeking at his daughter on her wedding day. I imagined his face gleaming, extending me his hand to hold me and keep me from falling. Suddenly, I felt strength going through my body, as I regained my balance and walked towards my groom alongside the music, head held high. I was not sure whether the plan was for Samir to meet me half-way and take me down the aisle, all the way to the altar, or my wobbly steps signaled the need for intervention. It mattered not; all I knew was that, now, I was in the safety of his arms. We walked together until we reached the altar, which was bursting with flowers: roses, lilies and carnations. Samir had requested from Rev. Roper for us to stand facing each other instead of turning our backs to the congregation when it was time for us to exchange vows, but we did so from the beginning of the ceremony.

Majdi opened the ceremony with a prayer, seeking the Lord's presence and His blessings upon the wedding. Then I expected a song from Amal, but more surprises came. Chanters now surrounded Samir and me in a circle, as Marcella began to sing and Kamal echoed the lyrics. I was surprised at Kamal's beautiful and powerful baritone voice; something he told me about while we were at the university. I just wondered when he had the time to practice. All throughout, I was giving Samir playful looks of displeasure and reprimand at what was happening, but then Rev. Roper came forward and stood in the middle, Bible in hand, and asked the first traditional question, "Who gives this bride away to this young man?"

As rehearsed, I was expecting Dr. Andrews—my adoptive father— to give me away, but I heard another's voice, "Her father Salah Abu Suleiman and her mother."

I turned towards the direction of the voice and fainted when I saw my mother. In a few minutes, I was sitting in a chair, Samir kneeling down, holding my hand, and Rev. Roper rapidly asking the last questions, "Do you take this woman, Dalal, to be your wedded wife?"

"I do."

"Do you take this man, Samir, to be your wedded husband?"

"I do."

"According to the authority vested in me, I now pronounce you husband and wife. Ladies and gentlemen, I present to you, Dr. and

Mrs. Shaheen." Rev. Roper said amidst the loudest applause I had ever witnessed at a wedding.

Samir carried me out of the church, running. I was quite exhausted by then, as the double relaxant I was given the day before had lost its effect. While I was beginning to enter into my comfort zone and free myself of the initial wedding ceremony jitters, everything changed when I saw my mother. Seeing her, unexpectedly, in such a manner, was too much for me to handle. I felt badly that Dr. Shaheen's sermon was cancelled due to my fainting, among other portions of the ceremony. What was worse, we were not able to have family pictures taken together or with friends. Equally unfortunate, I would not be able to attend the reception. We both lay down on the bed to get some rest, but within a very short time, my mother arrived with Majdi and wanted to see me, alone. After clearing up the air over what had happened, I laid down my head on my mother's chest, as she washed my face with her true tears. Again, I imagined my father's face looking down, smiling, as if to tell us how pleased he was.

My mother did not stay long, as we said our good-byes, and at the door, she gave Samir a big hug and kiss to show her genuine love for him, and referred to him as the *son*. Samir shut the door and hung the "Do not disturb" sign on the outside door latch.

"I will love you and obey you as Sarah obeyed Abraham when she called him, *Master*. I will care for you as I would care for the apple of my eye, and will make up the days that we were away from each other. I will always be your faithful wife and make you hold up your head high, proud of me. I will also be your helpmate as God intended for Adam when he said, **"It is not good that man should be alone; I will make him a helpmate..."** and be the source of your happiness and joy, for better or for worse, in sickness and in health, for richer or poorer, and what the preacher might say, "What God has joined together, let no man put asunder."

I wanted to take these vows before all, but I am saying them to you now, from the bottom of my heart, because I believe that, by the Grace of God, I am certain, I can fulfill these vows."

As I was speaking these vows, I could see Samir's face radiate with happiness, as he lay beside me, his left hand underneath my head, his right stroking my hair, for I have truly found *the desire of my heart. The one, whom my soul loveth.*

We fulfilled God's will for our lives on a remote island, St. Thomas, we'd chosen for our honeymoon. Amid all the love and happiness, Samir never forgot his relationship with the Lord, but rather the Word of God took on a new meaning when it described the relationship that Christ had for His church, as the relationship of a man to his bride. Samir always repeated to me the text in the book of Ephesians 5:21-33. **"Submit to one another out of reverence for Christ. Wives, submit to your husbands as to the Lord. For the husband, is the head of the wife, as Christ is the head of the church, his body, of which he is the Savior. Now as the church submits to Christ, so also wives should submit to their husbands in everything. Husbands, love your wives, just as Christ loved the church and gave himself up for her to make her holy, cleansing her by the washing with water through the word, and to present her to himself as a radiant church, without stain or wrinkle or any other blemish, but holy and blameless. In this same way, husbands ought to love their wives as their own bodies. He who loves his wife loves himself. After all, no one ever hated his own body, but he feeds and cares for it, just as Christ does the church—for we are members of his body. For this reason a man will leave his father and mother and be united to his wife, and the two will become one flesh. This is a profound mystery—but I am talking about Christ and the church. However, each one of you also must love his wife as he loves himself, and the wife must respect her husband."**

Moreover, and from time to time, he would repeat to me that only after marriage he knew the real meaning of the words, **"Flesh of my flesh and bone of my bones..."** It was why God chose the love of man to his wife to describe the love of Christ to his church, rather than the love of a mother to her child or the love of a father to his son. It is a holy relationship which God created and established its laws, rules and regulations. Similarly, the depth of the love of God for us when He said that husbands ought to love their wives as Christ loved the church. The word "as" was the greatest measure that God set for us to follow in our love for each other. "If I, the speck of dust and ashes, and the wretched man, could have such a great love for you, how much more is the love of Christ for his church?" Samir asked.

He went on to unravel all the secrets of his heart since the first time he'd seen the picture Amal sent him of me with his twin brother and sister playing in our backyard, until the time he first saw me at camp.

He also mentioned the day he came by our garden to give me a red rose and bid me farewell when he traveled to America, as well as the day I stood with him on a massive rock in the mountains in Lebanon. He went on to divulge his strong feelings for me at those times, and the way he hid them from me, waiting to see the will of God. He also told me, how he wanted us to get married much sooner, had it not been for certain preparations, my mother had requested from him, for the wedding.

"When the time came, "he said," and I saw you standing at the entrance to the sanctuary, in your beautiful, white wedding gown, at that moment, I saw you a symbol of purity without blemish, with unparalleled beauty. It was not planned for me to leave my place at the altar to meet you halfway, but the immeasurable love I had for you pushed me to do so and, from that moment on, to walk life's highway together, forever."

Samir proceeded to describe his love for me as the love of Christ for his church, when he continued, "No doubt that Jesus felt sadly when he had to leave us behind on earth, while He ascended into heaven, but only did so to go to prepare for us a place, so that when He comes back, He will take us up unto Him in preparation for the big wedding day with his church. That day will be the day when His longing for his church overpowers Him, and hence, He will return on the clouds, to meet us halfway and take us home to glory. That's what I precisely did."

Although I knew of Samir's immense love for Christ and his living for Him in order to please Him, I, nonetheless, never saw him manifest such love with such fervor as I did that day. I figured he would some- how bring up the relationship of Christ to His church for as long as we lived and would be a topic for many sermons in the future. If he should make our marriage an analogy in his sermons, it meant I would have a great responsibility to ensure him the proper home atmosphere, such as submitting to him as the Lord commanded, so that we could glorify Him in our life and be usable vessels in His service.

I had no idea why the period that follows the wedding is called "honeymoon" since moon inferred a whole month. It was supposed to last for as long as he still loved me, just as Christ loved his church and laid his life for it. My basis for submission to my husband emanated from my heartfelt biblical conviction, unlike many officiating pastors who try to be politically correct by opting to skip this vow! As it stood, the Bible, in its infinite wisdom, did not give us this as a suggestion, but in direct exhortation, given us as a command that would be the glue in keeping families together. If the church was to submit to her groom—the Christ—it, likewise, becomes also incumbent upon us women to submit to our husbands.

Our family life was supposed to offer a glimpse of the Garden of Eden that God had prepared for Adam and Eve. Regardless, and as happened in paradise, Satan could enter the picture and destroy what God had planned. For this reason, we must resist any "apples" Satan might throw our way.

Our honeymoon, as scheduled, was over; we were now packing our bags to return home as husband and wife, for the first time. Before we left, and with a tear in my eye, I took one last look at this little enchanting island that was a witness to our love for each other. Samir walked towards me and asked, "Why are you crying; we could always come back one day, but duty calls for me to return to my practice that I've neglected for the last eight months. For man cannot live by love alone." He said with a smile, then took me in his arms and continued, "I bet I know why you seem so sad; I promise you I will not allow anything to keep me away from you, but will always be by your side, as the Good Book says, *For this cause shall a man leave his father and mother, and cleave to his wife.* I shall cleave to you until you're bored to tears, and then you'll just have to plead with me to go away."

We were supposed to arrive in Washington on August 29, to celebrate Samir's birthday with the family. However, before the plane landed, Samir reminded me that we'd promised not to hide anything from each other, so he must tell me that he had called his parents to let them know we were all fine and let them know the date of our return. But they told him that my mother had already planned an elaborate affair with wedding set-up, from flowers to a full-blown reception. She'd also arranged for photographers to be there and wanted everyone to wear what they had worn to the wedding, including me in my wedding gown. Samir told me this in one breath, thinking I would be upset. However, I was excited at the thought, that at least we could have pictures to remember the occasion in the future, as well as for our progeny, should the Lord bless us with some. I told him that since my original plan was to get married on his birthday; my wish would be fulfilled, now, to hit five birds with one stone: our wedding, Samir's birthday, the spiritual birthdays of Mr. Milano, Majdi, and mine, the day we all surrendered out lives to Christ.

This reception was not the only surprise that awaited us as we landed. The whole family was at the airport to welcome us. My grandmother was leading the parade, carrying a bunch of multi-colored balloons, and waving them at me while tears streamed down her cheeks. Next to her, were my mother and my aunts carrying a sign that said, "Welcome, Newlyweds." Frankly, I had not thought about any member of my family during our honeymoon; but my heart melted when I saw them again, and I hugged each of them warmly. Within minutes, I learned that Lauren and Eric had set their wedding date on the next Thanksgiving Day. Marcella and Kamal established a partnership to begin a studio for recording Christian music, and more importantly, my mother was quite happy and content. Dr. Shaheen—from now on, my-father-in-law—later informed me, my mother got along real well with the Andrews and fell in love with them, and that Nadia Milano became her best friend, including Alberto Milano, Auntie Nancy, and Mrs. Roper. Mary Graham became her primary adviser, while Danny became her 'court jester' relieving tension and alleviating the drama.

The party began with picture taking, as planned, but it seems it ended with a complete wedding ceremony. All songs, music, procession, vows, and exchange of rings were repeated. Dr. Shaheen finally had the chance to deliver his sermon that he missed at the wedding. After the rituals, we all went to the reception my mother had prepared.

It was so dark, we had no idea where we were headed; all I could remember was that dinner took place in a garden, with dinner tables decorated with flower arrangements, balloons, and candles. My mother spared no expense for this elaborate affair. Before eating dinner, Samir stood up to thank everyone who took part in this event, followed by his father who prayed over the food. Towards the end, Samir and I cut a huge cake that had, written on it, "Happy Birthday, Samir, Majdi, Dalal, and Alberto."

Before we said "Good Night" and went to stay with my in-laws for a few days, I heard Amal suggest we open some presents, but I whispered in her ear to postpone this, as I was too tired. There were too many presents to open, and it might take hours to open all. However, Amal and Mrs. Milano insisted and handed me the first package. I reluctantly opened it, and hence, I understood the kind of presents I would be receiving that night.

The first present was my picture my father had painted and signed in his last days, which he gave to Nadia to put in an elaborate frame and present it to me as his wedding gift. I took the picture in my shaking hands and wept openly, but Danny was quick to crack a few jokes to get me back on track. He took a wad of cotton and placed it on my nose as a charade simulating a fainting gesture. It worked—I laughed as everyone else did, then I proceeded to open other gifts. The next one was from my new in-laws; it was a blown-up picture of Samir and me standing on that massive rock in Lebanon. The third gift, from Mona, was also precious to me, in that it was a picture at her wedding: she in the middle, flanked by Samir and me, with my father between us, embracing both.

Finally, it was the turn for my mother's gift; it did not seem to be a picture, as its size indicated, but I did not think it was any kind of jewelry, although I was certain it would be similar to the others gifts— of sentimental value. Complete silence by everyone, I attempted to open it gingerly; and then, I ripped open the gift paper, I screamed and rushed towards my mother to give her a big hug and many kisses, all the while repeating, "The Gospel of John? My red rose? Amal's book? Thank you, Mom; thank you, Mom."

A few minutes passed before I could catch my breath and contain myself before this lovely family to thank them for their wonderful, priceless gifts that I will have for keeps. However, before I tried to escape and retire to bed, Mr. Milano shouted, "Wait a minute, not so fast. We're not done yet; there's still your father's gift!"

I remembered the clandestine meetings between Mr. Milano and my father that had me a little worried for a long time, but now it all came back to me. Why would Mr. Milano present me with my father's gift? Danny raised the wad of cotton, again, signaling he was ready in case I fainted, so I smiled in response and gave him the thumbs up. As I opened it, there was a picture of a house—or perhaps a villa. There must be a mystery behind this picture. Mr. Milano did not wait long enough for my imaginations to wander off before he gave me a letter in my father's handwriting, dated just two days before he went to be with the Lord, in which he explained the mystery. I was not able to read it, so I gave it to Samir to read, "My beloved daughter, Dalal, and beloved son, Samir," Samir's voice cracked and his face contorted a bit, after reading this first sentence, but he composed himself and continued, "If you're able to read this note, it means I've traveled to Glory, and you are now both husband and wife. Congratulations my dearly beloved; this is my gift to you—the house you see in the picture."

I was not able to remain standing, so Samir went to bring me a chair lest I faint, and he put his arm around me to make sure I did not fall. My father-in-law then proceeded to continue reading the letter. In summary, my father instructed Mr. Milano to build, the most beautiful house for the newlyweds. Moreover, he asked Samir for forgiveness, "I realize your faith and Christian principles will perhaps keep you from living in such a luxurious dwelling, my son; and I can hear you, now, say, "How can I live in such a house, when my Master did not have a place to lay his head?" Nevertheless, this is my gift, and the gift cannot be refused, bought, or sold. This is my gift to you, to live in and a place large enough to accommodate family and friends, alike. In this beautiful house, which the Lord; permitted me to see nearly-finished. That's the place where I'd like my grandchildren to grow. My dear and beloved friend, Najeeb, will be the executor of this will." He ended the letter with the Lebanese word *"Mabrouk"*, which means congratulations.

Dr. Shaheen stopped reading here to wipe away some tears he could not contain so he could continue reading. He asked Nadia Milano, the decorator with fine taste, to decorate the house, and then he spoke directly to me, saying, "Dalal, my sweetheart, I know Samir has captured your heart in its entirety, but I beg you to leave a small corner for your mother. Furthermore, I know you will have a special room for her in your house whenever she comes to be with you, and I'd like to have it painted purple, the same color as our bedroom, back in Beirut."

Amid the silence that prevailed, Mother lost control over hearing my father's wish. She let out an audible cry, but quickly recovered when the lights came on to reveal a beautiful house and a garden full of shrubs, ornamental trees, and flowers everywhere. Samir and I stood at the entrance to cut the ribbon, in an inauguration posture and enter into *the loveliest nest for the most beautiful lovebirds*, as Dad put it.

Everything in this house was ready for our use, not only that night, but also for as long as we lived. What caught my attention was a framed verse, written in beautiful, arabesque-like calligraphy, which hung on the wall, "Except the Lord builds the House, they labor in vain that build it."

It seemed the family took advantage of our absence, for a whole month, while on our honeymoon, to prepare, decorate, and put the final touches on this house, as well as moving our personal items. Tonight would be our first night in this house, and many, many more days and years to come, Lord willing. After few minutes, everybody left, and we were all alone, then, to get some rest from a very hectic day. We proceeded to make a quick tour of the house. What we saw left us in awe; Mrs. Milano seemed to have put all her heart in decorating the house, while I was able to notice some of my mother's touches here and there, especially in our bedroom, and my closet in particular. In it, were several dresses she'd bought from downtown Washington, as well as an array of house robes and nightgowns. Nobody can do it like Mother. I wanted to wear a fancy nightgown to surprise Samir, but retracted when I saw him sitting on the bed looking grim. I immediately realized what was bothering him, so I ran towards him, knelt down, and took his hands to tell him, "Samir, my love, I am ready to leave this house today, before tomorrow, and live in a hut, if that's what you prefer. We don't have to live in this luxurious house; it was a good gesture from my father, but we are not bound to it. You can do whatever you think is best, without having to kowtow to anyone else's wishes. All I want is for us to be happy, for what is a house, if it feels like a cage?"

For a few moments, Samir did not reply, but looked me straight in the eyes, and said, "Do you really mean that? Would you be willing to relinquish opulence if I asked you, and live in a humble apartment? Would you be willing to go against your father's wishes? Will you be willing to upset your mother, and you've just reconciled? Do you really mean that, Dalal?"

These words took me back a few years to recollect Mary Graham's words when she told me, "Samir fears Dalal, the epitome of the pampered girl, who comes from an extremely wealthy, influential family; for he can see the difference in the unequal social level between your family and his, let alone the material level." I felt Samir was going through this crisis, so to placate him, I continued, "If you doubt my words, try me."

Samir pulled me by the hand, stood me up, and embraced me. He did not say anything, nor did he comment on what I'd said, but felt my sincerity satisfied him. To augment his confidence, I added, "And who said that wealth is a curse? It could be a curse if it came through diabolic schemes, but the wealth the Lord provides—such as Job's wealth—is goodness and a blessing."

Samir listened to me, unbelieving that such words would emanate from my mouth; it seemed what I said was to his satisfaction, because he changed the subject and asked,

"But what will we do with such a cavernous house? It has more than six bedrooms, when we're only two."

I wanted to humor him, so I replied, "If you plan to keep on loving me this much, in no time, this house will be full of children running all over."

"Six children, just, to fill the bedrooms?" We both laughed.

Soon we became more serious, knelt down by the bed, and vowed to dedicate this house and all its contents, as well as the residents thereof, to God's glory. However, although I was exhausted, sleep was elusive and I remained awake until the morning, reflecting on all that transpired the day before. Mr. Milano's and my father's little secret came to mind. If I had followed them one day to where they used to go, I would have discovered the secret of the house earlier. A relevant verse came to mind right away, **"If ye then, being evil, know how to give good gifts unto your children, how much more shall your Father which is in heaven give good things to them that ask him?"** As I reached for a pen to underline this verse, I thought that this house, which my father gave us, is a drop in the ocean compared to the gifts our heavenly father gives us. My movement to reach my Bible caused Samir to turn over, so I asked him, thinking he was now awake, "Love, how did Mother know my favorite book was the Gospel of John?"

With a sleepy voice, he replied, "I gave her your journal."

"Gave her my journal? When?"

"When we were in, Lebanon, for your father's burial."

"What?" I protested, "You gave her the only copy?"

"I have the original; I did not need a copy." He said, as he hugged me and went back to sleep.

We were not able to see the whole house the night before, especially the outside; so before the family came to bring us breakfast, we went out early enough, at dawn, to view the outside of the house. We first went out in the garden that backs up to the woods, and walked along its myriad walkways. There was a swimming pool, swings, and patio chairs everywhere. I particularly took special notice of the pool, and said, "Oh, father, how much I love him; he knew how much I loved the sight of water and sea."

Samir turned around to see if I wanted to take my first swim, but I surprised him when I said, **"See, here is water; what doth hinder me to be baptized?"**

"If thou believest with all thine heart, thou mayest..." he replied.

In no time, nine people were standing by the pool to obey the Lord in baptism. Majdi was baptized earlier when he first arrived in America, so he went into the pool with Rev. Roper to assist him in baptism. The first to be baptized was Majdi's mother, followed by Dr. Andrews, his wife, Lilly, Nadia Milano, Marcella, Kamal and Alberto Milano. He thanked the Lord for this great opportunity to testify in obedience, as well as to his friend Salah who was a blessing to him.

I was the last to step down in the pool, accompanied by my husband Samir, as I had requested. He stood beside me, holding my hand, while tears streamed down my cheeks, and a smile on my face, answering the questions Rev. Roper asked, with great joy and confidence.

"Dalal, do you believe that Jesus Christ died for you on the cross?"

"Yes, I do."

"Have you accepted Him as your personal Savior?"

"Yes, I did."

"According to your faith and confession, I baptize you in the name of the Father, Son, and Holy Spirit," he said as he immersed me under water. I was buried and rose to a new life in obedience; then I lifted my eyes towards heaven where my father was with our Lord, and said, "Thank you, Lord; thank you, Dad."

Chapter 24
THE DESIRE OF THE RIGHTEOUS SHALL BE GRANTED

❦

our years lapsed in our marriage. The huge house I'd promised Samir would fill, did not come to fruition—we had no children. Perhaps some people might have said I must have been like my mother, who had a hard time bearing children. At any rate, we didn't make the same mistake Mother did, and we didn't waste our time running from one doctor to another, on the contrary Samir and I, unencumbered by children, used all this free time serve the Lord, soul-winning, traveling to various locations, and holding revival meetings.

Even my mother, despite her difficulties, and the agonies she'd gone through in bearing, did not bring up this subject or bother me with any suggestion. She often spent the best times of her life, traveling with us and marveling, with pride, at Samir's faith, loving him like the son she never had, and at times, favored him over me.

Praise God, my mother accepted Jesus as her Lord and Savior, because of one statement Samir had said to her, "If you love us so much and cannot live for one minute without us, you therefore should be with us in heaven. The way to heaven is well-known, as Christ said, *I am the way, the truth, and the life; no one comes to the Father except by me,* so...why not join us?"

Immediately, the walls my mother built around herself came tumbling. She became a new creature, having the assurance that, should she die, today, she would be with Jesus and her husband in heaven. Should the Lord give her a long life, she would be with us, investing her money in the service of the Lord Jesus Christ, whom she loved with all her heart and mind.

When my cousin, Mona, and Danny, had their second child, whom they named Samir, Mother and I were so happy. And prior to our fifth wedding anniversary, when I took Amal and Majdi's daughter, Dalal, in my arms—their second after their son, Billy, my eyes welled up with tears, as I prayed a silent prayer, asking God not to deprive me of the joy of motherhood. On our fifth anniversary, Samir surprised me with a trip to our honeymoon island, where we spent ten great days. On August 30—Samir's birthday, as well as the other spiritual birthdays—I stood up to give the family, in general, and Samir, in particular, the best gift I could ever give, an announcement that shook the whole place; I was pregnant. A few weeks later, I updated them that I was carrying twins.

Who would have thought that, for the last five years, I was barren, and today, after much prayer and supplication, the Lord would honor me with twins---a first in my family?

Amal's dream and mine were to marry, and if we had daughters, we were to name them Amal and Dalal, respectively. I, however, called the twin Salah and Huda to please Mother; they both became the apple of her eye.

Before a year had lapsed since the twins were born, I found myself in a hospital having our unplanned third child. At the same hospital, my dear adoptive father, Dr. Andrews, was in another wing, battling death. I prayed to God to touch him and heal him, even for awhile, so he could see our newborn. At this point, Samir insisted we call our son Michael rather than Najeeb, as was planned, in honor of what Dr. Michael Andrews did for me while in England. Before I left the hospital, I took little Mike and placed him in Dr. Andrews' arms; God answered my prayers and honored our faith in giving him a few more months to live and enjoy his 'grandchild'.

Surprisingly, on our tenth wedding anniversary, I had twin boys whom we called Najeeb and Eric. Members of our extended family began to joke, as they told us they were praying for us that we have children, maybe it is time now to pray in reverse, but I always countered that I would not stop until I have added Amal to the family.

The days passed when we found ourselves packing for a visit to my beloved Lebanon after the lengthy, horrific civil hostilities ended. I was so excited to see family and friends that I had not seen in years, as well as to introduce the country to our children. My mother was returning there, especially, to inaugurate "The House of Salah" that she had built in memory of my father. The house would care, physically and spiritually, for the war orphans and children who became homeless due to the warfare.

The old memories flashed in my mind, as Samir and I sat beneath the old willow tree in our garden in Beirut, which had shed its mourning garment and put on a joyful one, signaling an end to the misery that beset my beloved country. Suddenly, a light breeze blew and the weeping willow danced with joy at the return of Dalal to her old playground—a playground only she had played in, but now, it was full of children— seventeen to be exact—five of ours, and the rest, Amal's, Lillian's, Mona's, and Lauren's. My mother, who was then in her late sixties, looked much younger, took off her high-heels, wore her denim jeans, tied her grayish hair in a ponytail, and played with them on a daily basis.

With one hand, I wiped a tear and with the other, I stroked my tummy in a playful jest for our expected daughter Amal, my eyes focused on my beloved husband Samir. At that point, I thought of the verse in the book of Proverbs 10:24, **"What the wicked dreads will overtake him; what the righteous desire will be granted."** This took on a new meaning, and truly, I was able to say, I had found, "Whom my soul loveth" (Song of Solomon 3:1).

***

Acknowledgements

I would like to thank my husband, B. Hatem, for taking the arduous task, of translating my first novel I wrote in Arabic. It probably took him as much time as it took me to write the novel, yet he persevered.

It is never an easy task to translate from one language into another, especially, when the translator, attempts to find the right and closest word equivalents in keeping the spirit of the intended thoughts intact. I hope that he has done so; he usually does.

I would also like to thank my dear friends, Dr. George Hanna and Margaret Saliba, among other family and friends, in assisting in different ways to bring this novel to life.

Finally, I would like to thank, my Lord and Savior, for providing me the desire and the means to write such a novel, which I am certain, will glorify His name. I hope this story will be a blessing to all who take the time to read it.

Summary

*D*alal Abu Suleiman, the only child, heiress to one of the wealthiest and the most influential families in Lebanon, comes to know Christ as her personal savior through the influence of her Christian classmate and next-door neighbor.

The new Christian faith, adopted by this pampered teen-age girl—as her name suggests—causes her to lose everything at one point. She is torn from her own home and country, forsaken by her own mother and family, loses her identity and goes through the shadow of the valley of death for the sake of Christ.

God, in his mercy and grace, is faithful to the girl that loves Him so much, sacrifices her life for Him, and endures persecution for his Holy Name, by giving her the desire of her heart, the man *"whom her soul loveth"*.